THE LAKE
OF
LOST GIRLS

Also available by Katherine Greene

The Woods Are Waiting

THE LAKE
OF
LOST GIRLS

A NOVEL

KATHERINE GREENE

NEW YORK

Published in the United States by Crooked Lane Books, an imprint of The Quick Brown Fox & Company LLC.

Crooked Lane Books and its logo are trademarks of The Quick Brown Fox & Company LLC.

Library of Congress Catalog-in-Publication data available upon request.

ISBN (hardcover): 978-1-63910-908-1
ISBN (ebook): 978-1-63910-909-8

Cover design by Heather VenHuizen

Photographs courtesy of Cottonbro Studio, Pexels (p. 14, 184, 278); Yuvabadiger, Pixaby (p. 29); Andrea Piacquadio, Pexels (p. 81); Picjumbo.com, Pexels (p. 81); Ronni Kurtz, Unsplash (p. 94); Monica Turlui, Pexels (p. 127); Pixaby (p. 127, 243); RDNE Stock Project (p. 243)

Printed in the United States.

www.crookedlanebooks.com

Crooked Lane Books
34 West 27th St., 10th Floor
New York, NY 10001

First Edition: November 2024

10 9 8 7 6 5 4 3 2 1

To following dreams and chasing ambitions.

Ten Seconds to Vanish: The Unsolved Disappearance of Jessica Fadley

Episode 1

Stella: Hi, True Crime babes, I'm your host, Stella, recording from the United Kingdom—

Rachel: And I'm Rachel, recording from the good ol' US of A.

Stella: And this is *Ten Seconds to Vanish: The Unsolved Disappearance of Jessica Fadley.*

Insert theme music

Rachel: So, get your wine and your favorite gal pal and settle in for one hell of a ride.

Stella: Can I say I love that we're doing this together?

Rachel: I know, right? Guys, Stella and I met on a true crime subreddit, and we hit it off right away. We have so much in common. How did I ever function without you, bestie?

Stella: Awww. We bonded over tales of Jack the Ripper and the Golden State Killer. How sweet are we?

Rachel: Well, like our morbid beginning, this story is the beginning of a dark and twisted journey into the disappearance, and possible murder, of a girl at uni in the late 90s and its likely link to the disappearances of three other young women, all students at Southern State University in Mt. Randall, North Carolina.

Rachel: Oh, I've seen pictures of Mt. Randall. It's so quaint. Stereotypical small town America.

Stella: Pretty much. And it seems like a weird place. You have this small, quintessential southern town, then you have this gorgeous college that sits up on a hill, overlooking everything below.

Rachel: Like two totally different worlds all squashed up together.

Stella: Exactly. And the murder rate in Mt. Randall is like one murder every twenty years and the crime rate on the Southern State campus is nonexistent. Yet, that one school year in 1998 saw the mysterious disappearances of not only local girl Jessica Fadley but three other coeds.

Rachel: And twenty-four years later it looked like we were no closer to knowing what happened, so that puts it up there with some of the most baffling cases of all time. So, let's set the stage. It's the late 1990s in this small town in North Carolina. Our probable victim, Jessica Fadley, is home for the weekend to visit her little sister, whose birthday is that Saturday.

Stella: Jessica is your typical uni freshman in the late 90s. I can picture her dressed in flared jeans or a baby doll dress with a choker. Very Drew Barrymore. Just like me in the 90s. Though clearly the British version. So maybe I was more of a Baby Spice than a Drew.

Rachel: And from what everyone says about Jessica, she was smart. She was a pledge at Pi Gamma Delta and was going to be inducted in the spring. I know you don't really understand sororities or American Greek culture, Stel, but it would have been a fun time. Plus, she had a hot boyfriend.

Stella: So, Jessica, the ever doting big sis, is home to see her family for the weekend as a surprise for her little sister.

Rachel: Everyone is thrilled to see her. Jessica then remembers she left something in her car.

Rachel: It was the cake, right?

Stella: Yep, she went out to get the birthday cake. It's evening, though there's still some light—it's late spring after all. The sister watches from a window as Jessica opens the trunk.

Rachel: And then . . .

Stella: And that's it. She's gone in a matter of moments.

Rachel: Ten seconds to be precise, which is how we came up with the name for our podcast.

Stella: That's right. There's this creepy recording that was leaked to the press where you could hear a little kid's voice wailing that she only looked away for ten seconds. We won't link it because it's a kid on that tape and we're not complete ghouls, but if you go digging for it, you'll easily find it.

Rachel: One minute she's there and the next she isn't. The little sister got distracted and when she turned back to look outside, Jessica was gone. But the trunk of her car was still open. And no one has seen her since. No clues. No signs. Nada!

Stella: Nothing but speculation and unsubstantiated rumors. Nothing until . . .

Rachel: Dun-dun-dunnnn!

Stella: There's been a discovery, almost out of nowhere. Human remains found by a couple of kids fishing at a lake the police had searched already back in the day.

Rachel: Hmm, that all sounds a little strange.

Stella: That's because it *is* strange, Rach. It looks like the recent heavy rain brought the bones to the surface, where they'd been buried for the past two decades. Of course, people are saying it's Jessica because it was a place known to be special to her. Her family, particularly her mother, were convinced that's where authorities would find her. The remains have been sent off for testing and the results are being kept firmly under wraps for now. But . . . it finally opens the door again on a case that has been relegated to the freezer for far too long.

Rachel: Not only that, but the word on the street is that other missing person cases are being linked together now, too. Everyone knows about the other missing girls, and for years, if you can believe it, authorities never connected them. People always said that these disappearances were connected. Some of the families openly criticized the police department for not doing enough and for refusing to see what seemed so obvious to everyone else. Which smells like good old-fashioned police incompetence to me, Stella.

Stella: Oh, absolutely. If these girls are officially connected, like it's always seemed they were, then this is about to seriously blow up, and the police have a lot to answer for. And just saying, selfishly, the timing is good for us with the start of this podcast, because it looks like we're going to get some new information two decades after it all went down. Can't get better PR than that!

Rachel: And maybe with your help, listeners, we'll finally figure out what happened to the missing women of Southern State University.

Stella: I have a feeling we're on the cusp of getting some answers. And Rach, I *am* here for it.

CHAPTER

1

LINDSEY

Two weeks ago

MY STOMACH DROPPED to the floor as my eyes took in the image on my phone screen. My mouth went dry and my palms began to sweat as the blurry words came into focus. Mom and Dad noticed the shift in me right away.

"What is it? You look like you're going to be sick," Dad asked, glancing up distractedly, his attention mostly on the latest edition of Car and Driver magazine he'd been reading.

"Lindsey-Bug, what's wrong? You're scaring me. Are you coming down with something? I can make you a doctor's appointment." Mom put the back of her hand against my forehead to check for a temperature.

She peered over my shoulder at my phone, seeing what had caused my reaction. The picture was of woods being cordoned off, the glistening water of a large lake in the background. People in white coveralls all the way up over their heads lugging bags from vans, masks obscuring their faces.

"Is that where I think it is?" she whispered, bracing herself on the back of my chair.

I glanced back at her and nodded.

"What is it, Cara?" my father asked, finally closing his magazine and giving us his full attention for the first time. He took in our horrified faces before taking the phone from my shaking hands. "What is this? Is this right now?" he demanded, his expression morphing from polite disinterest to terrified.

I took a calming breath, feeling my stomach knot up. I gently took my phone back and scrolled down to the text. "It says they found human remains yesterday morning. They appear to have been there awhile, though they won't know for sure until they're tested."

"At Doll's Eye Lake?" Mom's voice was tiny.

"At Doll's Eye Lake," I confirmed.

"Is it her?" Her words quavered and I knew she was holding in twenty-four years worth of tears.

"I don't know, Mom." I sounded hollow.

"What the goddamn hell?" my dad suddenly roared. "Why weren't we told this was happening? Why didn't they call us?" His anger was justified and completely understandable. Why hadn't we been prepared for the news? Had no one thought that the family should have been notified before the press got ahold of it?

"They don't know who it is." I continued to read, my eyes skimming the article quickly. "But they do mention Jess. The police haven't released a statement yet."

Dad had his phone pressed to his ear and I heard him demanding to speak to someone.

"Put me through to whoever's in charge of the shit show happening at Doll's Eye Lake!" My father yelled into the phone.

Mom gripped my shoulder so tightly I winced. "Is it her?" she repeated, sounding like a little girl, lost and terrified. "Is it my baby?" Her eyes brimmed with tears as she stared down at the image on my phone.

I put my hand over hers. "I don't know, Mom," I repeated. I tried to swallow around the lump in my throat.

"I don't know."

* * *

Present Day

The Bronze Monarch Hotel lobby was busy. It usually was on Monday mornings with guests checking in and out after the weekend, with the constant turnstile of visitors revolving endlessly.

I left Pete and Marnie, my two front desk clerks, to it. They were more than capable of handling the rush. I headed to my office, closing the door behind me.

I felt muted today. Like my head was underwater and the world was muffled. Just the soft echo of voices and my steady heartbeat to fill my head. But I preferred the absence of feeling to the barrage of emotion I had been overwhelmed with since *that moment* two weeks ago. I knew I needed to pull myself together; Mom and Dad needed me. But some days were harder than others.

My parents and I had been waiting for twenty-four long years to find out what happened to my sister. After so much time, I was hoping my parents could finally come to terms with the loss. That we could close that ugly chapter instead of constantly waiting for her to walk back through the door as if nothing had happened.

Perhaps now, I would have a chance to relinquish some of the guilt I felt for being the last person to see her.

I leaned against my desk, gripping the edge, as I stared down at the floor. It was hard to concentrate on anything but *Jess.* Or Jessie, as I used to call her. My beautiful, smart, impossible-to-live-up-to sister. A stranger I loved and longed for more than I could sometimes bear.

We had been called down to the police station not long after my father laid into the new lead detective, Lieutenant Jane Higgins. But once Dad's anger had run its course, he was back to being calm and charming, jovial even. Dad in control made me feel a lot better.

The lieutenant was full of apologies. She explained they normally wouldn't speak to a victim's family until they had confirmation of who the remains belonged to, but that the press had gotten a hold of the story and things had spiraled before she could put the brakes on. She sounded angry about it too, which went a long way toward settling both my parents down. There was nothing, at the moment, that indicated it was Jess and that the media were simply jumping to conclusions.

Mom had asked to see the body, but she'd been denied this request immediately. Dad had been up in arms, once more, about how badly the case had been originally handled and how, this time, we needed to be kept in the loop about what was happening. We'd been promised we'd be the first to know once they got the tests back, though it wouldn't be for a few weeks. They were still searching the area and had called a dive team in from a nearby city to search Doll's Eye Lake again.

Doll's Eye Lake. Just hearing the name unsettled me.

Officially, it was called Baneberry Lake, but over the years, the kids began to call it Dolls' Eye Lake for the nickname given to the pretty, yet creepy flowers that bloomed around the large body of water. They definitely looked like tiny eyes growing on bright green stalks. So, of course, generations of children used them as a way to scare each other.

It was a favorite spot for those that lived in Mt. Randall. During the summer, local kids flocked to its cold depths, even though their parents warned them not to swim there. Doll's Eye Lake was a man-made reservoir and no one really knew how deep it was. It had been created over a hundred years ago as a secondary water supply for the county to use during a drought.

But, eventually, it simply became a place to hang out. A place to make out. A place you went to when you wanted to be alone. There were decades old rumors that an old town had been flooded when it was made. Families displaced, memories forgotten. And townsfolk say that on a clear day, you can see the rooftops of houses far below the surface. Proof of that old, lost town lingering at the bottom.

Twenty-four years ago Mom had been convinced that's where they would find Jess. My sister spent so much time there over the years, that Mom swore that's where she was.

Dad tried to reason with her, arguing that it didn't make any sense.

She claimed it was a mother's intuition and against his wishes, she had demanded police search the area. Clearly investigators had been appeasing a hysterical mother when they gave the lake a barely cursory look. Because now, decades later, a body had been found and police were searching for more. If they had done their job properly in the first place, perhaps we would have had answers years ago.

We were told that attempts to identify the body through dental records were inconclusive, so they would have to submit DNA to compare to the remains and it was agreed I'd provide the sample, which I was more than happy to give.

It was a nightmare, but one that I desperately hoped would have an ending soon.

My office door creaked open, the noise viciously loud in the enveloping quiet.

"Sorry to bother you, but we have an issue with a booking." Marnie winced apologetically. She, like everyone else, knew why I wasn't in the best mood. How could I be when it was possible my sister's bones were lying on a cold table in a forensic lab waiting to be tested? I had caught a couple of my employees talking about it last week. I recognized the quick hush that descended when I walked into the break room. I had been the focus of enough gossip over the years to know the signs.

I wasn't mad though. The story had been dominating the news for weeks. Everyone was talking about it. I barely remembered what it had been like before, in 1999. Back then, I had been too young to grasp the severity of the situation. Even being the last person to technically see my sister, it didn't register that she was gone. Not until months went by and I started asking when Jess was coming back and my mom, overwrought, screamed 'never.'

Childhood trauma, table for one, please.

But the news was different today. With social media, fact and fiction became tangled up and the stories being floated around were somewhere between sort of accurate and absolutely ridiculous. Pair that with the new podcast—a podcast using my own words from a police interview as its title—and people were going nuts dissecting a case that had grown cold a long time ago.

I listened to the first episode. I couldn't help myself. When it came to Jess, and what happened to her, I became as obsessed as any amateur internet sleuth lurking in the dark corners of the internet.

I hated it. It was exploitative and downright disrespectful. It was two women, with no connection to my sister, glugging wine and giggling over hottie boyfriends and nineties fashion. It made me sick to my stomach. Yet, I had listened to it three more times, digesting the details.

Some of it was new, even to me. I had no idea that my sister had been a pledge at a sorority. It was something my parents never mentioned. I knew Jess was close to her roommate, but I didn't know the girl's name was Daisy Molina. It was strange, learning facts about my sister from people who never actually knew her.

My parents rarely spoke about Jess and if they did, it was by accident. I knew they grieved for her, that they missed her, and I also knew talking about her was off limits. So as a result, I had grown up never really knowing anything about Jess except for my own hazy childish memories and whatever I happened to discover along the way.

The hosts of the podcast talked a little about the remains and whether they were Jess's. They couldn't be sure, as the authorities hadn't yet made an official statement, but they believed that it was most likely my sister. They had done their research and dug up old newspaper articles about the original investigation at the lake. And like me, they expressed disgusted disbelief at how shoddy it had been. But now, according to the podcast, this was much bigger than Jessica Fadley. And it wasn't only one missing girl's story anymore.

I had always wondered about the other missing women, but had been too consumed with my sister's case to pay them much attention. But these two random podcasters, with their laughter and off color comments, were connecting dots I— and apparently the police—had never thought of.

"Sorry," Marnie apologized again as I walked with her out of my office.

"It's fine," I assured her, my voice calmer than I actually felt. I smiled to put her at ease.

Marnie was a worrier. She was younger than me by a handful of years, and was sensible, considerate and a great employee. Plus, being annoyed with her felt a lot like kicking a puppy.

At the front desk, the line was now snaked around to the bar. Never a good sign, but easily managed once I knew what was going on. Bellhops pulled luggage carts through the lobby towards the bank of elevators, dodging a pair of kids running around unchecked by their exasperated parents.

Yet it wasn't chaotic. The Bronze Monarch Hotel didn't do chaos. It was luxury and refined taste. It catered to the rich and those looking to impress. I loved every overpriced inch of the place and, despite it not having been a part of my life plan, I was glad I was there. As the newly promoted front desk manager, I knew that the inner workings of a hotel, especially a hotel of the Bronze Monarch's size and reputation, were like cogs in a clock. Every part had to work perfectly to ensure it chimed on the hour.

The Bronze Monarch was comprised of tall windows with a dramatic arched entrance. It had marbled floors and a lobby filled with red leather furniture. The front desk was made of ornate, hand carved wood imported all the way from somewhere in Europe. We had been renovating for the past year and a half and the front desk had been the most recent, and most ostentatious, addition.

"Hello, I'm the front desk manager. How can I help you?" I greeted the man waiting by the computer. He was good looking in an easy going way and was clearly quite a bit older than me, probably in his late thirties or early forties. He had dark hair swept across his forehead, but he had a baby-faced appeal about him. I didn't typically notice attractive men, I saw enough of them at the hotel, but there was something about this guy that drew my attention.

He wore a generic, impersonal smile meant to charm. That was, until he looked at me. Then it faltered before failing entirely. He blinked; his frown deepening. When he hadn't said anything after several long moments, I became irritated, good looks be damned.

"Sir, can I help you?" I repeated with a hint of impatience.

The man seemed to force a neutral expression. He met my eyes and the earlier awkwardness vanished. "Yes. I have a reservation, it was booked on the company credit card, but this young lady," he paused to smile politely at Marnie, "says I need the actual card to check in. The problem being, I don't have it with me. In my rush to get into town, I left it back home in Chicago."

I turned my attention to the computer. "Let me have a look at your reservation. What name is it booked under?"

"Ryan McKay."

I pulled up the reservation. "Ah, all right. It actually looks like you've already paid for the room, so it's not a problem that you don't have the card. It's normally our policy that the card used to book the reservation be shown at check in, but as long as you have another form of payment for incidentals, we'll make a note in the system."

He breathed a sigh of relief. "Perfect, thank you." He retrieved his wallet and handed me his personal card.

Marnie was now checking in the family with the two out of control kids running around the lobby. They were getting dirty looks from the other guests. I pulled a couple packs of crayons and a coloring book from beneath the counter and handed them to the flustered parents. "Here, these are for the kids. They can sit over by the fireplace and I'll have someone bring them some cookies and lemonade."

The parents took them with visible relief. "Thank you," the mom said, waving the kids over who took the crayons and coloring book excitedly. They hurried off to have a seat, out of the way.

I turned back to Ryan McKay who grinned at me. "Nicely handled."

For some reason I felt myself blushing at the compliment. I smiled dismissively. "Um, Okay, um," I stumbled.

What was wrong with me? I coughed to cover my awkwardness. "You're all checked in Mr. McKay."

"It's Ryan. Mr. McKay is my father," he laughed.

"Here's your keycard, Mr. McKay. You're on the fifth floor. The elevator is across the lobby," I said pointedly.

"Ouch, okay, I can take a hint." He winced with a chuckle while taking the keycard from me. He picked up his satchel and slung it over his shoulder. Before leaving he looked at me again, narrowing his eyes slightly. "This is going to sound strange, but do I know you?" He peered at the name tag on my shirt. "Lindsey . . . Lindsey what?"

I had to stop myself from rolling my eyes. Realizing how his question sounded, Ryan held up a hand. "No really. I know that sounds like a line, but you look so familiar."

My smile was now decidedly frostier than it had been before. It wasn't the first pickup line I'd heard and unfortunately it wouldn't be the last. You couldn't be a female in the service industry and not be inundated with unwanted advances. I had learned the best way to handle it was to shoot it down . . . hard and fast. The worst thing was giving them any sort of opening.

"Unless you've stayed with us before, I doubt our paths would have crossed." I handed him his printed receipt, never giving him my last name. "We hope you have a nice stay at the Bronze Monarch." I turned away from him and let Marnie know I was heading back to my office.

As I walked across the lobby, I couldn't help but feel eyes on me, watching me leave, and I knew that if I turned to look, it would be Ryan McKay.

Ten Seconds to Vanish Podcast
@TenSecondPod

The first episode is up! We can't wait for you guys to dig in and start trying to unravel this case with us! There are so many twists and turns and suspects you won't see coming!
#tensecondstovanish #newpodcast #truecrime

4:17 PM Jan 5, 2023

⟲11   💬 23   ♡ 820

2

LINDSEY

Present day

"LINDS, YOUR MOM and I are going out for dinner. You're on your own to get yourself something to eat" My dad said, poking his head around my bedroom door.

I pulled my Airpod out of my ear and gave him a nervous smile. He had no idea he had caught me listening to the first episode of the Ten Seconds to Vanish podcast for the fifth time since its release. The new episode was due to drop over the weekend and I could barely contain my impatience.

"I'll be fine, Dad. I'll have some of Mom's leftover lasagna."

"Your mom told me to tell you that she made a casserole if you wanted it." He peered hesitantly into my room. "And you know what she'd say about excessive screen time. Do us both a favor and read a book or something, otherwise I have to hear about it," he laughed absently, indicating my phone with its lit up screen and the podcast graphic in plain view. Dad wasn't one to lecture, or be too involved with my life in any way, which was in stark contrast to my mother's hovering. Ultimately, they seemed to balance each other out.

I quickly flipped it over before he could see it. "I'm listening to a podcast, no eyes necessary." I wanted to smack myself as soon as the truth left my mouth.

Dad raised his eyebrows. "A podcast? Which one? Maybe I've heard of it. I'm down, I hear stuff," he joked.

"Oh it's nothing exciting. Just a podcast on fancy hotels," I lied, feeling awful at how effortless it was for me to do so. Lying to my parents wasn't natural for me. We had an open and honest relationship, which made me feel ten times worse.

Dad made a face. "Sounds like a pass." Dad and I didn't share interests, so it wasn't hard to put him off the scent.

"Not a sports car in sight, I'm afraid," I teased. My dad loved muscle cars, particularly the bright yellow 1965 Mustang Boss 429 he kept parked in the garage and I had never seen him drive.

Mom and I didn't understand why he kept it out there. The garage's roof often leaked when it rained, and it was freezing in the winter and boiling hot in the summer. And for a brief time, when I was younger, it seemed to be where every animal in the neighborhood went to die.

I remembered as a kid, that to combat the stink of a raccoon that had crawled up into the eaves and began to rot, Dad had filled glass bowls with white vinegar and left them lined along the floor and on the shelves. He had also taken to dousing everything in peppermint oil. Apparently, it was a problem with the way the houses on the street were built. Our neighbor, Mrs. Lewis, complained of a similar issue.

Eventually the smell subsided after Dad told us he boarded up the hole on the side of the house. Regardless, Mom and I steered clear of the garage. It wasn't exactly a place you wanted to spend much time in.

"Definitely not for me then." His eyes crinkled at the edges as he smiled.

My dad was incredibly handsome. He had aged well and it was impossible to go anywhere without women noticing him. He was the epitome of masculinity; tall, broad shouldered, dark haired, chiseled jaw line and an easy-going smile. He had charisma and was very likable. But he only had eyes for his car magazines and his phone that seemed permanently attached to his hand.

His job as a real estate agent demanded a lot of his time. He was a broker and had started his own agency when I was a little kid. He had worked hard to become one of the 'best goddamn realtors in the county.' As a result I rarely saw him growing up, though Mom always told me it was all in the name of keeping a roof over our heads.

"Okay then, we'll be back in a while." Dad paused, as if deciding whether to come into my room. I couldn't remember the last time he had stepped inside. He didn't make a habit of venturing to this part of the house. The proximity to the permanently closed door across the hall acted as a barrier, keeping him out most of the time.

Eventually he took a step back, away from my room. Away from me. With a quick glance around and a slight wave, he headed downstairs.

My parents and I existed easily together for the most part. Dad gave me all the space I could have ever wanted, my mother all the nurturing I had ever needed. I loved them both. They had always been the most important people in my life, which is why, at thirty years old, I still lived at home. Some adults may find it suffocating, and if I was being honest with myself, some days I did as well, but mostly I appreciated that I could depend on them for anything.

Most people couldn't understand how the thought of leaving my parents alone with their unending grief, left me with a sinking feeling of guilt that was much worse than letting my mom continue to do my laundry and my dad to dutifully pay my car insurance.

When I went away to college, Mom struggled. She would call constantly to check that I was okay and ask what I was up to. She wanted to know who my friends were and if I was dating. It had been unnecessarily hard on all of us, considering I could have lived at home and gone to the great school that was less than fifteen minutes away.

But going to Southern State University had never been an option. Even though my parents were both alumni and it was where they had met, it would always be *Jessie's* college. That had been *her* life. And it would never be mine. Any other prior claim was forgotten once she had gone missing. The college would forever belong to a girl who would never be going back.

So, together, my mom and I decided I'd go to North Carolina East College, knowing it was only four years. And the moment I graduated, I came back home. We had never discussed it, but we came to a silent, mutual agreement.

I was a grown woman stuck in limbo between my old life and the prospect of a new one. But I wasn't in a hurry to rectify the situation. Because moving on had proven incredibly hard for me, too.

I turned the podcast back on as soon as I heard the front door shut. The high-pitched voices of the two hosts, one clearly from the South, the other with an indescribable British accent, filled my ears as they laughed and joked about something that wasn't remotely funny.

"What do we know about Jessica Fadley?" one of them asked, her question taking on the dramatic cadence of someone putting on a show.

"We know she was super smart."

"I read she graduated top of her class in high school, which is pretty damn impressive," Rachel, the first host, laughed.

"Yeah, not everyone is like you, Rach, drinking their way to a solid D average during their teenage years," Stella teased.

"Well, it's not like she was Miss Perfect. Sure, Jessica was smart, but once she was off to school, like most of us, she had a good time. People who knew her said she partied and stayed out late— she was getting the full college experience," Rachel interjected.

"She sounds like my kinda gal," Stella cooed.

Okay, I'd had enough. I turned it back off, shutting down the streaming app before I was tempted to turn it back on. Listening to people making light of my sister's life and disappearance was the worst kind of masochism.

This was *their* entertainment, but it was *my* life. *Her* life.

"Ugh," I groaned, leaning back in my chair and pressing the heels of my hands into my eyes. "What is wrong with me?"

I knew I was torturing myself, and I knew it wasn't healthy.

A loud thump caught my attention and I froze. My ears strained in the throbbing silence.

Was that a rustling? A sign of movement?

It was coming from the direction of my open doorway. I dropped my hands and glanced toward the closed door across the hall. I stared, imagining it gradually creaking open.

There was a barely audible sigh. A release of pent-up air. And it came from *her* room.

There was an uncomfortable buzzing in my ears, and my palms started to sweat. This wasn't the first time I had experienced unexplained noises, yet I never grew accustomed to them. Each and every time, I became paralyzed with an irrational fear that felt rooted in the grief that permeated the house.

I got to my feet and slowly, quietly, made my way to the door of the room that hadn't been occupied in twenty-four years.

I put my hand on the knob, willing myself to turn it. It felt warm, as if it had been held only moments before.

There was an echo of a presence. As if I had only missed *her* by a few seconds. I could almost feel her on the other side. Waiting for me.

I hurriedly backed away.

After that, I decided that staying home was a bad idea. I needed to get out of that house and the remnants of ghosts that sometimes, on days like today, made themselves known.

As I sped away from home, I glanced in my rearview mirror, seeing Southern State at the top of the hill, all lit up. I wondered, not for the first time, about Jess's life there.

Would I ever find out?

Instead of driving toward downtown, I found myself making a detour. I followed the main road out of town, only about five miles, until I reached a familiar turnoff. Police tape cordoned off the area, so I couldn't drive down the narrow gravel path that cut between the trees, leading to Doll's Eye Lake.

I pulled off to the side of the road and let my car idle. I watched groups of people walking through the thick growth of trees. A nondescript white van was parked at the edge of the woods. A woman wearing white coveralls leaned against the side of the van talking on her phone.

The normally quiet, secluded place was bustling with activity. Teams were combing through every square inch of dirt and rock, looking for something—*anything*—that would explain how a body had come to be buried in the ground there. In a place familiar to every person that lived in Mt. Randall.

Is this where Jess had been the whole time? I wondered to myself. *Only a couple of miles away?*

Feeling cold from the inside out, I put my car in drive and did a U-turn in the middle of the road, heading back to town.

Mt Randall wasn't always a place people wanted to visit. The Chamber of Commerce had worked tirelessly over the past ten years to put it on the map. They'd wanted to create a town that still clung to its small town roots while also embracing innovation and progress. As a result of their efforts, Mt. Randall was slowly becoming a tourist hot spot known for its shops and restaurants.

The chamber had a fight convincing some of the older townsfolk—those stuck in their old ways and how things had "always been done." But ultimately the chamber got their way, and now the town was starting to thrive.

Ten minutes later, I parked my car in my designated spot in the Bronze Monarch's lot and headed into the luxurious restaurant. The staff weren't surprised to see me because I did this often. The food at the Bronze Monarch's restaurant, The Golden Butterfly, was incredible. It had an esteemed reputation and won numerous awards, mostly thanks to our Michelin-starred chef, Pierre Rochefort.

When she saw me, Evelyn, the hostess, waved me over to my usual table near the windows. I sat down and smiled sheepishly at her.

"I've been dreaming about the clam chowder since Pierre sent me the week's menu," I laughed.

"He's outdone himself this time," she agreed, tucking a stray red curl behind her ear. "He said he's put a secret ingredient in it, and I don't know what it is, but it works. I had a bowl for lunch and I'm taking some home for Reg and the kids," she chuckled.

My stomach growled in anticipation.

"I'll tell him you want a large bowl." Evelyn gave me a wink.

"Make it *extra* large, with a basket of bread, and a large red wine, too, please," I requested eagerly.

"Coming right up," she assured me and then headed back to the kitchen.

The Golden Butterfly wasn't particularly busy tonight, so I knew I wouldn't be waiting long for my food, not that I wasn't happy to wait. These people, this hotel, were my second family. My second home. I didn't go out very often, so this was the extent of my socialization.

It may have seemed strange to some—your place of employment being your sole social outlet—but it was. I had never cared much about having tons of friends or going out every night of the week. Even as a teen, I tended to stick to myself, and was happy to do so. I never felt I was missing anything. I had always been content with my life. I had to be. Being the sister of a missing girl didn't make me Miss Popular.

"Would I be feeding you another line if I were to ask to join you?"

I looked up to see Ryan McKay, the guest I had helped earlier in the week, standing in front of me, a half drunk cocktail in his hand.

I debated whether to let him. Despite my better judgment, I found myself inclining my head in invitation. Perhaps it wasn't Ryan, but the promise of a diversion from my dark, obsessive thoughts that had me thinking that letting him sit with me was a good idea.

I surreptitiously looked him over. He was the kind of man you stopped to appreciate. I also couldn't help but notice the lack of a ring on his left hand.

"That seems to be your MO, Mr. McKay," I deadpanned as he sat down.

His cheeks flushed as he grinned. "I can tell I haven't made the best first impression. I feel like I need to rectify that immediately. I can't have you thinking I spend my time traveling around the country hitting on beautiful hotel staff."

It was my turn to blush. I wasn't usually one to be swayed by compliments, I was too guarded to let throwaway comments affect me, but something about his delivery seemed to get to me.

In that moment, he reminded me of my dad. The sort of man who was used to getting what he wanted. He saw my dismissal as a challenge and I knew it wouldn't stop him. I also knew I'd probably give in eventually. It felt like an inevitability.

I let the tension sit between us for several seconds before I took pity on him.

"You can join me as long as you drop the tired pickup lines." I couldn't help but smile secretly. "I don't make it a habit of socializing with guests, though. No matter how handsome they are."

Oh god, had I really said that?

Of course Ryan jumped on it. "You think I'm handsome," he stated with a flirty smile. "If we're going to share a meal and a drink, can we finally stop with the Mr. McKay stuff? We're old friends by this point, right?"

"Sure, Ryan," I snorted, earning me another one of his charming grins. He dished them out like candy, and it was hard not to feel all warm and giggly when he bestowed it. Diane, one of the full-time servers, appeared with my order.

Diane placed the food and wine down, looking at Ryan in barely concealed surprise. I never ate with anyone, so I knew the sight came as a shock.

"Do you want to order anything?" Diane asked Ryan.

"I'll have what Lindsey's having. Minus the wine. I'll have another whiskey sour instead," Ryan told her, his eyes never leaving my face.

I stared at Ryan in exaggerated annoyance, but the scent of my chowder demanded my attention, so I picked up my spoon and started to eat.

"One drink, that's it," I warned, in between mouthfuls.

"We'll see," he teased.

One thing was for certain, Ryan McKay was going to be trouble.

*   *   *

"That was the best clam chowder I think I've ever had," Ryan moaned as he sat back in his chair after finishing.

I agreed with a nod, my mouth still full.

Ryan was watching me closely, and despite the intensity of his gaze, I didn't feel uncomfortable. There was something about this good-looking stranger that put me at ease.

"So," I said, letting my guard down a little bit, "when you checked in, you said work paid for your stay. What is it you do?"

"I'm glad you asked, because I think it's something we need to talk about," he replied, going suddenly serious.

"What do you mean?" I took another sip of wine, my earlier ease now being replaced with conditioned wariness. I sat up a little straighter in my chair.

Ryan reached down to a leather bag by his feet and pulled out some papers. I was suddenly on high alert.

"Listen," he began, a hint of pleading in his voice. "I want to be honest with you, right off the bat." He handed the papers to me. I looked through them, and the chowder began to curdle in my stomach.

They were old articles about my sister. About the other missing girls of Southern State University. There were pictures of my house. Of the college. Of Doll's Eye Lake. My hands trembled as I came to a photograph of my parents and me at a vigil. I looked about six, so it must have been right after Jess went missing. We obviously didn't know our picture was being taken. My parents held on to each other, their faces an agonized portrait of grief and despair. I clung to my mother's skirt, my cheek pressed against her thigh. I looked distressed, though most likely because of my parents' sobs and not because I understood what was going on.

The violation hit me like a fist to the stomach.

"Who are you?" I hissed angrily.

"I promise I didn't know who you were when I checked in, but," Ryan looked around us as if to make sure we weren't overheard before continuing, "I'm a journalist."

"A journalist." It was an admission that filled me with bitterness and apprehension. The papers in my hand fell to the table, scattering as they landed.

"Have you heard of the new podcast, *Ten Seconds to Vanish?*" he asked, a hunger in his eyes that I recognized. One I had seen in the eyes of every reporter who had invaded my privacy and hounded me for interviews for the past twenty-four years.

I opened my mouth to speak, but he was already continuing, rushing ahead in his hurry to explain, to convince.

"I'd been pitching a story on the missing girls of Southern State University for years. My editor at the *Chicago Courier* never entertained the idea until the podcast's first episode went viral. Now everyone is talking about these cases I've been passionate about for so long. Then when the remains were found in a place heavily associated with Jess's cold case, my editor finally gave me the green light to come down here and start on what I plan to be a series of in-depth articles about the investigation." He paused to take a breath, his eyes drilling into mine. I felt pinned in place. Like an insect tacked to a piece of wood.

"Wait—" I began, but he cut me off again.

"As I said, I didn't know who you were at first. That wasn't why I checked in to this hotel. Call it dumb luck. Or maybe serendipity. Whatever it was, it felt like a sign. There was something about you, I just didn't know what. Now I know. You're her." He pointed to the little girl in the picture, clinging to her devastated mother. "You're Lindsey Fadley, Jess Fadley's little sister. It was only ten seconds, right?"

I had heard enough. More than enough.

I stood up, grabbing my purse. In my haste, I knocked over my glass of wine, soaking Ryan's papers. In a daze, I fumbled for a napkin, dabbing the quickly spreading stain as Ryan went to grab the documents.

Our hands brushed and I recoiled as if he had burned me. I dropped the napkin on the table and turned to leave.

"Please, hear me out," Ryan implored, but he wouldn't sway me.

I spun back around to face him, my expression thunderous. "*Hear you out?* You're all the same; a bunch of vultures. Leave me alone. Leave my family alone. *This is my life.* Don't you get that? It's not just a story."

"It's my life, too!" He snapped unexpectedly, confusing me.

"What?" I snarled.

He seemed to get ahold of himself, looking contrite. "I'm sorry, it's only . . . I've been looking into this case, *all of the cases*, for as long as I've been a journalist. I've put everything into it, wanting them to be solved. I know it must sound ridiculous to you, but this case—Jess's case—it's important to me, Lindsey."

I flinched at the sound of my name on his lips. "But that's the problem. To me, it's my missing sister, my heartbroken mom, my devastated dad. To you, it's only a story—a case. But this is *our* life that you're investigating, and for what? A fancy byline and an award or two? You'll dig up your dirt, then go back to your old world, not caring about any devastation you leave behind, just like all the others."

Feeling emotionally depleted, I quickly left, not daring to look at Ryan again. I already knew that Evelyn would put my meal on my hotel account, as that was our usual routine.

Outside, the air had turned colder, and I realized that in my temper, I'd left without my jacket. The anger evaporated as I tried to get my bearings. I had been ambushed. Or at least that's what it felt like. I felt vulnerable and exposed.

"You left this inside." Ryan appeared beside me, my coat in his hands. He held it out to me and I took it without a thank-you.

I put it on and fished my keys out of my purse. I didn't want him following me to my car. I didn't trust him.

"Lindsey, I didn't know who you were when I checked in. I just thought you were this gorgeous woman who I really wanted to talk to. But yes, you seemed familiar. And like any good journalist—"

"Or creepy stalker," I interjected coldly.

Ryan ignored the barb. "I looked you up. It wasn't hard to make the connection." Ryan turned back to the hotel entrance. "Please, let's go back inside."

"Are you joking?" I scoffed.

"Let me buy you a drink. There's more I want to talk to you about."

"Why?" I demanded, glaring at him. "So you can dig up some dirt on Jess? Pick my brain for any scrap of memory I have of her? I'll make it easy for you, Ryan, I barely remember her. All I know is that she was my sister and I loved her, everything else is . . ." I waved a hand around, unable to find the words. My anger was turning to grief like it always did whenever I talked about her. "This is all so you can gnaw at her bones for your story, but I won't let you."

"That's not how it is," he gasped.

"So, why should I talk to you? Particularly when you don't appear very trustworthy."

Ryan took a moment before replying, clearly trying to change his tactic since the old one wasn't working. He ran his hand through his hair, his cheeks reddening. "I know how this looks. But, I've been researching this case for years, Lindsey . . ."

"Stop saying my name like you know me!" I screeched, my fingers curling into claws ready to gouge his eyes out.

"But I feel like I do." He lifted his hand as if to touch me, then thought better of it. "I want justice for Jess." I had an intense reaction to him saying her name. My entire body seized up, as if to defend myself. "For the other girls too, of course, but especially Jess. I want to know where she is. What happened to her. I want her family—"

"Me," I interjected dryly.

"Yes, you—I want you to get some form of closure, if that's at all possible." His tone was carefully neutral. "But Lindsey, I also need to know what happened to her . . ." His words died off, but they hung in the air like a portent.

"Why do you care so much?" I asked quietly, daring to look at him, and then wishing I hadn't. He looked mournful. It was hard to hold on to your anger when you could understand that need for answers, no matter what.

"Because Jess was a person. A woman with a life. With dreams. With a future." He took my hand and this time I let him. "She had people who loved her—*deeply*—and we all deserve to know what happened to her. But especially you, Lindsey. Maybe you more than anyone."

I pulled my hand away, refusing to admit how much his words moved me. How much I longed for someone to see Jess as the living, breathing person she had been.

"What will talking to me accomplish?" I pressed.

"I don't know. But I think we can help each other." Ryan took a scrap of paper and pen from his satchel and hastily wrote his phone number down, before handing it to me.

"Call me, anytime. I'm here for a while and I'd like to share what I know with you. Perhaps there are things you remember—"

"I was six. I told you—I don't remember anything," I countered, taking the paper and shoving it in my pocket.

"You'd be surprised how much gets suppressed with time and sometimes a little poking and prodding frees stuff up. I've seen it happen a time or two."

If he'd been investigating for as long as he said, then perhaps he knew things about Jess's life that I didn't. My sister was my Achilles' heel, she always had been. Ryan was dangling a carrot in front of me that I couldn't resist. He probably knew it, too.

"Fine, Friday then," I suggested, finally relenting.

Ryan's eyes lit up. "Friday sounds perfect. Should I meet you in the bar—?"

"No. Not here." Talking about my sister's case at work was the last thing I wanted to do.

"Okay. Text me a time and place and I'll be there." Ryan was trying to rein in his excitement, but failing.

I started to walk toward the parking lot, but stopped, looking back one last time.

"Just so you know, I'm only agreeing to this because I want to hear what *you* know about my sister. Don't hold anything back. No secrets."

"I'll tell you what I know, Lindsey," he promised. I still didn't trust him, but I needed to see where this went. For Jess's sake.

Ryan's eyes met mine. "I'll see you Friday." He started to walk backward toward the hotel entrance. I couldn't help but laugh at how silly he looked. I half hoped he'd trip and fall on his ass.

"Goodnight, Lindsey," he called. "Sleep tight, don't let the bedbugs bite," he sang playfully and this time I did smile.

He had charmed me. I hoped I wouldn't regret letting him.

A Campus Remembers

7:00
on the quad

**A moment of silence for the missing girls
of Southern State University
#neverforget**

**for more information contact
the Health Services Office**

CHAPTER

3

JESSICA

Fall 1998

"CAN YOU TURN off your stupid alarm?"

The pillow hit me square in the face with a soft, yet violent, thud.

My roommate, Daisy, was *not* a morning person.

I knew she was most likely nursing a major hangover after spending most of last night at a frat party, getting drunk on jungle juice. I wasn't sure what time she came back, as I had put in my earplugs and fallen asleep around midnight. Daisy had spent the past six weeks trying to coerce me into joining in her drunken adventures. So far, I had resisted, insisting I needed to focus on my classes. But seeing her have such a good time was wearing down my staunch resolve to avoid anything that would get in the way of my education.

I was a girl who toed the line. I did what was expected of me. But that skin was starting to chafe. Tentative freedom was beginning to erase silent obedience. After all, Mom wasn't here to look over my shoulder.

Rebellion was incredibly tempting.

I fumbled around for the hundred-decibel alarm clock my dad got me before I moved into the dorms and sat up in my extra-long twin-sized bed, rubbing the grit from my eyes. Daisy was a lump beneath her covers—and she wasn't alone.

I couldn't tell who was sharing her bed, and most likely I wouldn't recognize him. We hadn't been enrolled at Southern State University long, so I barely knew anyone, let alone some random guy my wild roomie picked up at a party.

The first time she brought a guy back to the room, I had been weirded out, so we had established rules that involved a scrunchie on the doorknob to indicate she was "entertaining." Daisy never meant to make me feel uncomfortable, so I knew she must have been pretty wasted to not have given me a heads-up.

I quickly slithered out from under my green-and-blue plaid blanket and grabbed a dirty pair of jeans from the floor, putting them on as fast as I could. It was hard to see, and I didn't dare open the curtains, so I stumbled around, trying to find my toiletry caddy.

Slipping on the flip-flops I wore in the shower, I hurried out of the room and to the communal bathroom at the end of the hall. It was early, only seven in the morning, but the bathroom was already busy.

I had to wait a few minutes before one of the shower stalls was available. I made sure to wash quickly, knowing there would be a line of impatient women timing me down to the second if I took too long. After I quickly got dressed, I headed back to my room.

The door opened as I got there, a tall, red-headed guy shuffled out into the hallway, bumping into me with a mumbled apology before continuing his walk of shame toward the stairwell.

Daisy was brushing her teeth in the sink in the corner, her long, golden-brown hair tied up in a bun on top of her head.

"I am so sorry 'bout that. I know I should have called the room and let you know I was bringing someone back, but the night got away from me, and before I knew it, we were here," she apologized.

"Good thing I wear heavy-duty earplugs to bed, huh?" I teased. I grabbed a notebook and some pens and threw them in my book bag. My first class was in less than an hour, and I needed to grab breakfast first.

Daisy snorted. "It's not like you would have heard anything. The asshole passed out as soon as we got here. So, not only was I left unsatisfied, but I had zero room to sleep." She rolled her eyes and got back in bed, turning on the TV that sat propped on a pile of JCPenney catalogs atop a built-in shelf in the corner. Jerry Springer's nasally voice blared through the speakers.

"How can you watch that crap?" I asked, indicating the two women tearing each other's hair out on the screen.

"It's social commentary, my judgy friend," Daisy explained.

"Social commentary?" I laughed.

"Absolutely. Take these two." She pointed at the women. "That piece of shit sitting on the side loves all of this because they're choosing to attack each other instead of the cheating scum they were both sleeping with. It reeks of internalized misogyny."

I snorted. "Sounds like you're reaching, Daisy. I don't think Jerry Springer is that deep."

"I just think it's shitty that when a guy cheats, the first thing we all do is blame the other woman. But do you ever stop and wonder why that is?" Daisy sat up straighter. "Because a male-dominated society has conditioned us to view *each other* as the enemy."

I had discovered over the past few weeks that my flighty roommate definitely harbored a major feminist streak. When she got on a rant, there was nothing I—or anyone else—could do to stop her. At times, it seemed so at odds with her personality, but she would be the first to tell you a woman can be *all* things, whether they were contradictory or not.

I shrugged, neither agreeing or disagreeing. "Have you seen my ID?" I asked, looking around for the small piece of plastic that I needed to get breakfast.

"You lost yours *again*?" Daisy teased. "Take mine. It's on my desk." She pointed to the mess of papers and books on her side of the room.

Stepping over heaps of clothes and text books in the cramped space, I grabbed Daisy's school ID and tucked it into my pocket.

The dorm room was tiny by most standards, only nine feet by sixteen feet. Two twin beds and two desks had been squeezed in along with a mini fridge and microwave Daisy had brought from home. Our closet, which was filled mostly with Daisy's clothes, was covered by a shower curtain, and the walls were papered with dozens of posters of movies and bands, which was my contribution to our living area.

Daisy was a total slob, and I had taken to cleaning up after her if I wanted to be able to walk across the floor. But we had become close friends in a short time. We had bonded over the similarities between my helicopter mother and her conservative Catholic family. Even though we were opposites in many ways, we empathized with each other's need for freedom.

"Want to come with me and grab a donut?"

Daisy made a face. "I don't know how you can eat that fried fat. I think I've taken on your freshman fifteen."

I mussed her hair. "You're gorgeous, Daisy, and you know it. Mr. Redhead definitely knew it too."

Daisy swatted my hand away. "Whatever, you're biased," she muttered, though she smiled, enjoying the compliment.

I checked the time on my watch. "Crap, I've got to go."

"Wait," Daisy called out as I was about to leave. "You're still going to the Pi Gamma Delta pledge mixer with me tonight, right?"

"Sure, is this for more social commentary?" I joked to cover my nerves.

"Whatever. We can't be women warriors all the time. Sometimes we want to get drunk and flirt with the hottest guys on campus," Daisy exclaimed with enthusiasm.

I never pictured myself as the sorority type. That was more my mom's thing. I had heard stories about her time in the Pi Gamma sorority my entire life. It was expected I'd be a sister, because *she* was a sister.

"You're a legacy!" she had cried before I left for school in August, as if the choice had already been made for me. She had also attended Southern State, and it felt as though she was setting a path for me that she had already traveled.

There was a twinge of defiance when Daisy suggested we go to the rush event that was brought on by a need to separate myself from my mother's history. But I had to admit I was drawn to the pretty girls laughing together in tight-knit groups, looking like they were having the time of their lives. "I'll be there. But I have to meet you at the Pi Gamma house because my class isn't done until 6:00 and I want to grab dinner first."

There was a knock at the door, and I barely had time to move before it swung open and Tammy Estep, our Resident Advisor, walked in.

"What the hell?" Daisy complained. She disliked Tammy and made no attempt to hide it.

"Hi, Tammy," I greeted, even though she didn't bother to look at me. As usual, her focus—and annoyance—was reserved entirely for my roommate.

"What'd I do this time?" Daisy sighed.

Daisy had been on Tammy's bad side since the beginning. I wasn't sure why. The RA was meant to be someone you could talk to, someone who was there to help. Not "Tight-ass Tammy" as she was known by the residents of Westwood Hall. If she smelled fun, she was there to shut it down. None of the girls on the hall could stand her. Yet, I knew there was more to Tammy than that. A side she staunchly hid in her day-to-day life.

I had overheard her talking to her parents on the phone one of the first nights at school. I could hear someone yelling at her on the other end, and from her look of broken anguish, it clearly wasn't the first time. We had locked eyes and I was immediately sheepish at having been caught eavesdropping. I could have told her I understood having a complicated relationship with your parents. But I didn't.

Tammy slammed the door in my face with an angry huff. From that moment on I knew that underneath that rigid exterior was a vulnerable little girl. That didn't make her any less of a pain. If anything, her refusal to connect with the girls she was tasked with watching over made her easier to dislike.

"I saw that guy coming out of your room this morning looking like he slept over," Tammy accused, hands on her ample hips.

"I didn't realize you were so invested in my sex life," Daisy goaded.

Tammy's cheeks flushed red. She was much shorter than me, only coming up to my chin, but she seemed to be trying to make up for her lack of height with unearned authority. Her hair was permed into tight curls and stuck out all over head like a deranged Shirley Temple.

"You are not permitted to have overnight guests of the opposite sex, Daisy. This is a female-only dorm. You signed the resident contract. I'll have to write you up, and if you get two more infractions, you'll be taken before the campus disciplinary committee," Tammy warned.

"Oh no, Jess," Daisy looked at me, "not the campus disciplinary committee." Daisy yawned again. "Now if you don't mind, Jerry needs my attention." She turned back at the TV, clearly finished with Tammy.

The RA finally looked at me. "You need to get it through to her that this is serious. We're only ten weeks into the first semester. I've seen a lot of girls come through this place who think partying and sleeping around is more important than getting an education. I'm your RA, I'm supposed to keep you on the right track, but it's up to you if you want to be here. You flunk out, it's no skin off my nose."

"Oh, I want to be here, Tammy," Daisy said, interrupting her lecture, "I've never gotten so much action." Daisy winked. Before I could respond, Tammy turned on her heel and left. Once she was gone, Daisy let out an exasperated groan. "That bitch has some nerve. What a hypocrite."

"What do you mean?"

"I'm guessing you haven't seen her sneaking that old dude into her room late at night? I caught her last week. He looked married too if the ring on his left hand is any indication."

I felt sick. "Tammy's screwing around with a married man?"

"Sure seemed like it. They weren't playing cards, that's for damn sure." She tapped her chin. "Hmm, I wonder what the campus disciplinary committee would think about *that*?"

I took a deep breath. "I need to go. I swear to God, if Tammy makes me miss out on Krispy Kreme Donut Day, I will murder her."

Daisy giggled as I left our room.

I headed out to the quad, enjoying the crisp autumn air. I loved the walk across campus to the Commons that housed the cafeteria, student bookshop, and a snack bar and pool room called The Grotto.

I ruminated over what Daisy had told me about Tammy being involved with a married man. The idea of it made me feel horrible in ways I couldn't explain. I tried to put the ugliness out of my mind, even if it wanted to stick there like glue.

Southern State University lay on the north side of my hometown of Mt. Randall, North Carolina. It sat perched at the top of a steep slope. All the streets leading from town crawled upward toward its imposing entrance. I had grown up mesmerized by the college's stately columns and redbrick buildings. It felt like another planet.

I had graduated high school at the top of my class and scored a 1510 on my SATs. I took four AP classes and, in addition to those advanced placement courses, had participated in a large number of impressive extracurricular classes. I had been accepted to several prestigious schools, but it felt like a foregone conclusion that I'd attend the same small college in my hometown that both of my parents had attended. And if there was one thing I was good at, it was living up to expectations.

Daisy had seemed shocked when I admitted to growing up only three miles away. She was from Dallas, Texas. Going from a city to a tiny town like Mt. Randall must have been a culture shock.

"Didn't you want to get away?" she had asked me as she tried to understand. I couldn't explain that packing up my things and driving up the hill *had been* getting away. She couldn't see the invisible boundary that existed between

Mt. Randall and Southern State. Not yet. But the college students quickly learned that there was the town—and there was the school. The two coexisted but never interacted. The locals held a begrudging tolerance toward the staff and students of Southern State. Yet that tolerance easily morphed into disgust and annoyance at the smallest provocation.

* * *

"It's so pretty," I exclaimed, holding tightly to my dad's hand as he led me along the brick-lined pathways that wove through the trees on campus. "When I grow up, I want to live here just like you used to."

At six years old, "pretty" was the most important requirement when thinking of somewhere I wanted to spend time. I knew the school well. Dad would often drive me up to the college where he had met my mom. She never came. It was always just Dad and me.

Dad laughed and squeezed my hand. "Then you will, sweetheart. All you have to do is work hard and you can do anything you put your mind to." He swung me around, making me squeal. "You are super-Jess!"

When he put me back down on my feet I held my arms out wide, twirling. "I love it, Daddy! I love it so much!"

Dad leaned down and kissed the tip of my nose and rustled my hair. "Then it will be yours."

"Promise?" I asked, gazing up at the person I loved most in the entire world.

Dad's smile lit up the sky. "Promise." He looked down at me for a long moment. "You make me so proud, Jess."

* * *

I passed by the row of identical colonial-style buildings that housed the English and Foreign Languages departments. The windows sparkled in the morning light and a group of landscapers were raking up piles of leaves.

The college was just waking up, stretching and ready to start its day, and I was happy with this new life I had only now started to live. But I knew that if I made my way to the crest of the hill beyond the Commons, I could see down into the town I had grown up in. I'd see the quiet streets and dated facade of my old high school. If I turned to the west, there'd be the winding, tree-lined avenue where my parents and little sister lived.

My old life was right there. So close . . . too close. They threatened to collide, yet, for now, remained thankfully separate.

I slowed down, taking my time, even though I was dangerously close to being late for my early-morning English 101 class. The college never felt busy. For such a small school, the campus was sprawling and meticulously maintained.

I was glad I had insisted on living in the dorms. It was one of the very few times in my life that I put my foot down about anything.

My parents—particularly my mother—had wanted me to live at home.

"Why pay for room and board when we live fifteen minutes away?" she had argued. My dad had agreed with her—at first. Though, eventually, I made him see my side of things. Dad usually backed me up. We were a team and always had been.

As I passed Roosevelt Hall, which housed the Math Department, an older man around my dad's age hurried down the steps. He was looking at a piece of paper in his hand and I moved quickly, and narrowly avoided colliding with him.

"Excuse me," he muttered, only then glancing up.

"It was totally my fault. I should have been more careful," I apologized. I noticed the staff badge around his neck, indicating that he was a teacher at the school.

I felt my body flush as the much older, very good-looking man's lovely hazel eyes met mine. The ferocity of his gaze left me feeling shaken and oddly vulnerable.

"It's my fault entirely. That's what happens when you're in a rush." His voice was like warm honey.

I cleared my throat, feeling strangely breathless. "I'm sorry," I replied lamely.

"You have absolutely nothing to be sorry for." He smiled, the lines around his eyes deepening. "I'll have to be more careful next time."

"Hi, Dr. Daniels," a student called out and the professor raised his hand in a wave before giving me a quick smile and heading down the path.

I watched him leave, feeling an inexplicable anxiety in my gut. I twirled the thin silver band on my right hand, something I did when I was worried or upset. I looked down at the simple ring my father had given me for my sixteenth birthday. I had been ecstatic when I had unwrapped the light blue Tiffany's box finding a delicate silver band inside. It was a lot like the wedding ring my mother wore, but this one had swirls engraved in the metal reminiscent of the design on my favorite children's book and had my initials on the inside. I had worn it every day since my dad had given it to me.

Inside the Commons, there was a long line. When it was my turn, I grabbed a donut and a coffee, then gave the student manning the register Daisy's ID, which they swiped and handed back to me. I tucked the card in my bag and then headed to class.

For the first time in my life I felt like I was doing something for *me*. The realization that I only had myself to look after and depend on filled me with excitement.

But also dread.

This is the first part of my new Missing Women Series focusing on unsolved crimes otherwise forgotten by police—the young women abandoned by an incompetent police force and relegated to the whispered musings of a gossip-ridden town. I hope you join me for a truly devastating story of unanswered questions and frustrating half-truths that I will try hard to unravel.

This story takes place during the school year of 1998 and 1999 at a tiny college in an even tinier town in North Carolina. There are places you go to experience life—this wasn't one of them. This was a place you went to disappear.

And that's exactly what happened to these women.

All were roughly the same age. All in the prime of their lives.

But they shared more than just their age and location. All of them were connected by a complicated web of relationships that were kept a secret from their loved ones.

Yet not one person of interest has ever been named in any of their disappearances. When asked, the lead detective, a proud man named Sergeant Liam O'Neil, claimed that they ran away. Every. Single. One.

It wasn't until the parents of the second missing girl demanded action that action was in fact taken.

Time was lost. Leads were buried. Suspects were too quickly dismissed.

This is the worst story of law enforcement ineptitude I've ever encountered, and I've been deep into true crime for many, many years.

Let's start at the beginning. One by one I will pick their lives apart, looking for something the police overlooked.

It probably won't be that hard because they weren't looking for dead girls—but I am.

4

LINDSEY

Present day

"Y OU'RE HERE EARLY." Ryan slid into the booth opposite me and gave me his charming smile.

"Honestly, I wasn't sure I was going to come at all," I told him flatly.

He held my gaze. "I'm glad you did."

I looked away first, my eyes lowering to my almost-empty coffee mug. I'd arrived at Perk and Pastries, a place I usually visited on my way home from the late shift at work, early, to give myself time to back out and leave if I needed to. The thing was, the longer I sat there, the more I knew I had to stay. Ryan had made it clear that he knew things about Jess and that made him incredibly appealing to me, whether I liked it or not.

Rhonda Taylor, a girl I'd gone to high school with and who worked at the café, came over to take Ryan's order and I asked for another coffee.

Growing up, Rhonda had always been nice to me. People in Mt. Randall treated me in one of two ways—like the main event at a freak show or like someone fresh out of the leper colony. Jess's disappearance either garnered fascination or fear, and people's behavior toward me reflected that. Rhonda was one of the rare few who was neither. She was nice, but not a friend. She had no idea how much I appreciated her polite disinterest.

My phone rang loudly from somewhere at the bottom of my purse as Ryan ordered himself a coffee. I pulled it out and glanced at the screen, seeing that it was an unknown number. I turned off the ringer and shoved it back in my purse.

"You can take that," he offered as Rhonda left to get our drinks.

"It's probably another journalist. They've been hounding my parents and me ever since those remains were found. My dad thinks we should get new numbers."

Ryan winced. "Well, I can see how easy it is to lump me in with all of them."

"Yeah, I hope you bring more to the table than half-baked questions and no sense of privacy." I raised my eyebrows and gave him a pointed look.

"No half-baked questions, I promise." He crossed his heart with a finger. "So, tell me a bit about yourself, Lindsey."

"This isn't a date, Ryan. You don't need to loosen me up with small talk. And this will be off the record." I wouldn't budge on that. I knew how much damage a sound bite could cause and I didn't want to read my words in his newspaper months, or even years, from now.

"Absolutely. We'll keep this between us."

"I mean it, Ryan. I'm not a source for your article." I watched the way he picked at the skin around his thumb. It must have been a nervous habit.

"I promise." He was so emphatic that it was hard not to believe him—to trust him.

Rhonda came back and placed two coffees in front of us, before giving me a knowing smile. "Enjoy," she cooed and left.

Clearly, she thought this was some sort of date, and I hated that she thought that, but she was gone before I could correct her.

Ryan took a sip of his flat black coffee. "A sweet tooth, I see," Ryan commented as I took a long drink of my mocha latte. I didn't respond to his overt friendliness.

This whole thing had the feel of opening Pandora's box. Once we started, there was no unknowing. But I was here now, and there was no going back.

"So, you got me here, now tell me what you know, Ryan." I dove straight in, getting right to the point. My heart hammered in my chest as I waited, hating that he held all the cards.

"It's not as easy as that," he began. "It's more about—" He stopped abruptly then turned the conversation in a direction I hadn't expected. "First, tell me what you remember about Jess."

Her name had a visible effect on both of us. I sucked in a breath, he let one out.

Jess.

A thousand images flitted through my brain, but nothing concrete. They were hazy, half-real, maybe half-imagined things. Things I had read. Things I had heard. It was hard to determine what I had made up and what were legitimate memories.

I scowled, irritated by the direction of our conversation. "That's not what I agreed to."

Ryan's expression was full of uncertainty. "I know, but . . ."

"No, Ryan, there is no *but* here," I interjected abruptly. It felt like he was playing games with me, and I was not in the mood. "You said you had information. You said that if I met you, that if I gave you a chance, then you would tell me what you knew. Was that just lip service? Because if so . . ."

"No, no, not lip service at all!" It was his turn to interrupt me this time. I scowled as I crossed my arms. "She hated Thin Mints Girl Scout cookies," he said, looking at me through dark lashes. I scoffed, but he grinned. "I know, I know, everyone loves those things, but not Jess. At least, that's what I was told," he added quickly.

"I hate them, too," I said, my voice cracking. I felt an adrenaline surge at the thought that Jess and I shared something so inane and silly. Yet it felt so important all at the same time. "What else?" I asked, trying to keep the pleading out of my voice.

Ryan looked apologetic, yet firm. "Your turn."

My scowl returned. "Again with the games."

"It's not a game, Lindsey. You give a little, I'll give a little. It can be that easy." He picked up his coffee and took another sip while I thought over his proposal.

Part of me didn't want to share my sister with him. She belonged to me. I had held on to her so hard for so long, I didn't know how to begin relinquishing my grip on her.

"It's okay . . . start small. Even the tiniest details matter." Ryan's voice was hushed. I could barely hear him. We were practically alone in the tiny coffee shop. Just him and me.

And Jess.

"That's not our deal," I reminded him. "You're supposed to be telling *me* what *you* know about her. About her case."

"And I will, Lindsey. I promise." He promised but when I looked unconvinced, he caved. "Okay, listen, she liked peanut butter cookies and sweet coffee. She had a thing for Dave Matthews, she was obsessed with everything he sang. She hated the feel of her hair on the back of her neck and so she tied it up a lot. Does that satisfy you?"

My skin itched with the need to get up and go, yet something kept me glued to the seat. I felt a mixture of emotions well up inside of me. "I don't know . . . I'm not sure . . ."

"It's okay, try sharing a memory of her with me. Something tells me you need to." Ryan put his hand over mine and squeezed. "As much as this is about you getting information, I think it will feel good to share it, too."

"So you can put it in your article?" I challenged.

Ryan lifted his hands in surrender. "Off the record, remember."

I stared down into my coffee. "What if I tell you I don't remember her. Not really."

"So tell me what you *do* remember," he repeated, without an ounce of judgment in his tone.

His words were like a form of hypnosis. And for some reason I found myself starting on the worst day. The most important day.

"Everything changed in *that* moment," I admitted, staring down into my drink.

"Like what?"

"It was my sixth birthday when she vanished. There were no more birthday parties for me ever again, that's for sure." I snorted out my annoyance, but there was no conviction behind it. I had already done my grieving for birthday parties.

"That couldn't have been easy."

"It wasn't." I looked up, my eyes meeting his. "It *isn't*."

My childhood had ended the day Jess went missing.

"How do you live up to the memory of a missing person . . . you can't." I shrugged halfheartedly. Tears burned my eyes with barely contained bitterness. "I get it now, I do, but growing up with the ghost of her everywhere, despite my parents barely talking about her . . ." I stopped, not sure I could go on.

Ryan looked at me. "It's like being haunted." I drew back, startled at hearing my thoughts echoed back to me from his lips. His smile was grim. "It's hard to escape the memory of someone who has become perfect through the very act of remembering them." It was both the best and the worst thing he could say. Ryan briefly touched my hand. His fingers were warm and he withdrew them before I could react. "You're more than the sister of a ghost, Lindsey, that I'm sure of."

His words, so seemingly genuine, so heartfelt, were exactly what I needed to hear. It felt like someone was finally seeing me for the first time in my life. Seeing me as more than Jess's little sister. As more than the last person to see a missing woman. And as I gradually thawed, I felt empowered to say the things I had, up until this moment, kept locked up tight. To say the guilty truth I'd always thought, but never said aloud.

"I wish they'd find her body and get it over with." I lowered my eyes as the words escaped, the vicious conviction of that statement burning through me.

"You don't wish she was out there somewhere?" Ryan asked, his expression darkening slightly. "That maybe she'll come home one day?"

I glanced up sharply. "Of course I do. But after all these years, we have to be realistic. If Jess was out there, she'd let us know. I can't imagine she'd let us think she was . . . dead . . . if she wasn't." My voice became shaky but I kept going. "But having confirmation that she's not coming back, that we'll never see her again, is exactly what my parents need. If we knew that she was really gone instead of clinging to some misguided hope, then we could move on with our lives instead of being stuck in place indefinitely."

Ryan acted as if he got it. I was relieved that he didn't seem to be judging me. Because for years I had been judging myself. Feeling guilty for wanting to know my sister was dead. And wondering what sort of person that made me.

Despite my wariness because he was a journalist, and our less than truthful beginning, I found myself opening up to him. A voice of warning yelled in the back of my mind, telling me that this was what reporters did. They lured you in with shared confidences and empathy. But I prided myself on being able to read people. It had served me well so far, and I didn't feel like Ryan was putting on an act. He seemed sincere, and his concern felt honest.

Of course, that could be what he wanted me to think.

Because of this, I knew I needed to carry on. I realized this wasn't all about Jess, but about me, too. About getting the things out that I had never given a voice to before.

I had never really processed what happened. The impact on *me*. I had never been able to talk about my memories, what few I had. Partly because my parents made it clear they couldn't listen and partly because by sharing them, I had to acknowledge all the ways it had ruined my life. I had tried therapy a few times, but had never stuck with it. I knew it had to do with my fear of opening up and exposing all these ugly thoughts that I kept staunchly hidden away.

But Ryan, with his good-natured smile and compassion made the walls around me crumble, ever so slightly. I wanted to tell him the little things that I thought *might* be real. The memories that *might* be mine. And I wanted to tell him for Jess.

And for *me*.

"I remember her smell," I started—a little hesitant at first. Was I really doing this? Was I going to hand my memories over to this stranger? But I found once the floodgates had opened, I couldn't stop myself. That was the danger in sharing. One recollection led to another, then another. And before I knew it I'd be slicing myself open and letting Ryan see all of me. I hoped I wasn't making a huge mistake. But how could it be, when this was the closest I had felt to Jess since I was six years old? I hadn't realized how much I missed that sisterly love, the bond that hadn't quite disappeared the day she had. I had simply pushed it away to save myself the pain of feeling it.

Ryan's smile was soft. Wistful even. But I wasn't focused on him. I was back there . . . with my big sister.

"I remember sneaking into her room and spraying her jasmine perfume after she went to college so I could pretend she was still around." I smiled. "Coffee, too. She always smelled like coffee."

"She drank it practically nonstop," he chuckled. "That's what her friends said anyway."

"That makes two of us." I lifted my mug, feeling a thrill at discovering another connection.

"What else?" he urged gently, like he was reminiscing with me. Though, by now, I didn't need the prompting. Once I had started, there was no going back. I wanted to unearth everything in my mind that belonged to *her*.

"Her laugh. I can hear it even now. I can't quite see her face, though. I lost that as I grew up, but I *can* hear her." I closed my eyes briefly, transporting myself back to my earliest childhood and the memory of her laughter filling my ears and making me smile.

"This is great, Lindsey," Ryan encouraged. "What do your parents say about her? What are their memories?"

The warmth I had been feeling dissipated almost instantly and a lonely darkness took its place.

"My parents rarely talk about her, at least not on purpose. Her name is only ever an accident these days."

"Why? They're her parents. Shouldn't a father want to talk about his child?" He glowered, his voice hard. "A mother, too," he added after a beat.

"Of course my parents love her. But it's tough for them—particularly my dad." I felt defensive of my parents. I didn't want anyone, especially a stranger, to question their feelings toward Jess. They had been the subject of enough judgment and conjecture over the years. They were told they weren't doing enough to find Jess. Or their grief was too over the top. That my dad was too angry—or, in some cases, not angry enough. There was no winning in the realm of public opinion, and as such, I had grown to be incredibly protective of them.

Who was Ryan McKay to question their devotion? Their anguish?

"I don't get it." Ryan's expression had softened, but there was still an edge of tension.

"Losing Jess destroyed them. It destroyed *him,* my father. And honestly, Ryan, it's none of your business."

Ryan immediately looked contrite and if he had other thoughts on the issue, he kept them to himself, and I was glad. I shouldn't have to explain how learning to live without Jess had changed our family. Or why my parents acted the way they did. Everyone dealt with grief differently—there was no right or wrong way.

In our house, there was only one photo of Jess left on display—on my mom's bedside table. It had been taken on the day of her high school graduation. Sometimes it sat upright so she could see it, but more often than not, it was facedown, or put away in a drawer. Eventually, it would come out again, but never for long. Jess's smile played an endless game of hide and seek, and I had long given up looking for it.

Over the years, her photos had disappeared, just as she had. Gone without a trace. Her awards and trophies that had once been proudly displayed in our living room were packed away. Her life became relegated to boxes hidden in closets.

Her bedroom, however, was different. Mom had put her foot down. When Dad wanted to pack it up and turn it into a home office, she refused. It was one of the worst fights I'd ever heard them have.

Mom had gotten her way in the end. Jessica's room became a shrine—untouched. Inside, it felt as though you were transported back to 1999. A time capsule to when my family had been whole.

Ryan cleared his throat, picking at his thumb again.

"So, are you and your parents close?" he asked.

"Very. Maybe more than most thirty-year-olds and their parents. That's why I haven't been able to leave home." I flushed, feeling a little embarrassed at having admitted to this very good-looking man that I still lived at home with my parents. I knew how people viewed my decision—that to some, I looked pathetic. Maybe even a loser. But, again, with Ryan, I saw no judgment. "I know how it must look, a grown woman still sleeping in her childhood bedroom, but they're scared of losing me, too. And I think I'm scared of leaving them on their own with *two* empty bedrooms. I know it sounds messed up, and I can't expect you to understand what it's like having to live in the shadow of a missing person." I hesitated, ready to share my darkest secret for the first time. "We all loved her . . . we still do, but a part of me hates her as well."

I felt guilty saying it, but it felt good, too. There was a rush of relief that made me feel rejuvenated. And I couldn't help but feel a sense of gratitude to Ryan McKay for pushing me to this point.

Who knew all it would take for me to start releasing some of this pent-up darkness was for someone I didn't know, with no connection to me or my trauma, to provide a listening ear and to make me feel seen and heard for the first time?

"You hate Jess?" Ryan sounded confused. "Why?"

"Because I was a kid—only six years old. I didn't just lose my older sister that day, I lost what my life could have been. I was no longer simply Lindsey Fadley—crappy at math, but a hell of a softball player. I was now Lindsey Fadley—sister of a missing woman. I would never have my *own* life, my *own* identity, because it was wrapped up in this horrific event that came to define everything. It came to define *me*." My eyes burned with unshed tears, but I refused to let them fall. This wasn't about self-pity, this was anger.

"Growing up haunted by her ghost has ruined my life." Repeating Ryan's words from earlier seemed to resonate with both of us. There was a flash of understanding in his steady brown eyes. He got it. I didn't know why, but he did.

And what I said was the truth. My truth. And it was irrevocably linked with my shame. But it was about time I owned it instead of suppressing it.

Ryan looked thoughtful. "I don't think Jess would want you to feel that way."

"What do you know about how my sister would feel? Why, because you've researched her life, you think you know her thoughts?" I snapped defensively. Old habits die hard. Vulnerability clearly made me punchy. "This faux sympathy is worse than your pickup lines."

Ryan wasn't put off by my combativeness. "What do you remember about that day?"

I still couldn't help but see his questions about my sister as invasive. That as much as I liked having the chance to talk about Jess, the ingrained instinct to flee was hard to ignore. But I had to push through it. This could be my first step toward closure. Something I realized, I desperately needed. "I'm sure you've listened to my police interview."

"Yeah, but I want to hear it from you." He sat forward, his expression intense.

"Well, you'll get more from that interview than what I can tell you now. I've told you many times now, I don't remember much. All I know is that Jess came home for my birthday party. She went out to her car to get something for me. I learned much later it was a cake. I think I remember her telling me it was a surprise. I watched her from the living room window. I looked away—"

"For ten seconds," Ryan filled in and I wanted to snarl. Those words—*my* words—followed me everywhere.

"Right. Well one second she was there, and ten seconds later, she wasn't." I ignored the obvious disappointment on Ryan's face. "That's it. That's all I can give you. There's nothing else but the memory of being confused, sad, and lonely after that."

We sat in complete silence for a few minutes as we each digested what I had revealed. For me, it felt monumental. For Ryan, maybe not so much. After all, there wasn't a whole lot I could share that would matter to him. My fuzzy recollections were all I had and he had no idea how hard it was for me to relinquish them. I squirmed in my seat, needing to fill the silence. "Okay, my share time is over. It's your turn now. What does pestering me about what I remember have to do with where Jess is or what happened to her?"

Ryan looked thoughtful. "Honestly, I'm not sure. But sometimes memories come to us that can have a major impact. You were so young, but you probably saw more than you realized. People tend to drop their guards around children because they think they're not paying attention," Ryan explained. "So, there can be a lot buried that simply needs some prodding to bring to the surface."

"That's all fine and dandy, but I'm more interested in hearing the things *you've* learned. What *you* think happened to her," I pressed.

"There are a lot of dangling threads in this case. In all the cases, actually. There has to be a link. After all, each of the girls went to Southern State University at the same time. It's not a big school. I've never been able to figure out why the authorities didn't think the four missing women were connected. In such a small community, to have not one, not two, but four young women disappear, points to a predator. To think otherwise is not only ignorant, but stupid."

"But then they'd have to admit there might have been a serial killer. One that they turned a blind eye to," I speculated.

"Maybe. There's nothing worse for a police department's reputation than a killer on the loose that you can't catch." He smirked, but it faded quickly. "But I've been working for years to find all the ways these stories intersect. And it goes back to the first missing girl, Tammy Estep. Did you know she was Jess's RA?" Ryan asked.

I couldn't contain my gasp. "Jess knew Tammy? I had no idea!"

"She sure did." Ryan's expression became curious. "Did you ever visit Jess at college? Perhaps you met Tammy."

"Turning it back on me again I see. You really meant it when you said you give a little, I give a little, huh?" I remarked dryly.

Ryan chuckled. "My train of thought will make sense eventually. I promise. But remember what I said about kids picking up on things. I was wondering if you ever visited campus and maybe we can poke around a bit to see what you remember."

I gave him a bland look. "Or maybe you're still hoping to find a hook for your article."

Ryan's eyes widened slightly. "I really hope, once you get to know me better, that you realize my intentions are pure. I'm not some vulture. I'm not here to manipulate you . . ." He let out a sigh. "But I can be pushy. So, I understand if you don't want to tell me—"

"I think I remember Jess's move-in day," I interrupted, jumping straight into the deep end without a life jacket. I'd come this far after all.

He leaned forward eagerly. "And Tammy?" He got out his phone and pulled up a picture of a cross looking young woman with tight curls all over her head. She was pretty, but with a pinched, unpleasant expression. "This is Tammy Estep. Do you remember her at all? She would have been there."

I scrambled to gather my thoughts. I didn't recognize the image of the attractive, missing coed. I couldn't recall ever seeing her before. But I realized that I *did have* memories of going to the Southern State campus. Not many, but they were there, just below the surface. If I prodded hard enough, perhaps I could set them free.

Sometimes memories come to us that have a major impact.

Ryan tapped at his phone and pulled up another picture. This one took my breath away. It was Jess. Only a picture I had never seen before, though, in truth, I hadn't seen many. She was standing in the doorway of what looked like a cramped dorm room. She was wearing patchwork jean shorts and a striped t-shirt. Her dark hair was pulled back in a ponytail. I could see a messy bed behind her with a plaid blanket draped across it. There was a glimpse of a poster of Monet's *Bridge Over Water Lily Lake* on the wall. I knew the space smelled like jasmine perfume and chocolate.

Where had that come from?

"This photo was taken in Westwood Hall, the freshman dorm where she lived." Ryan's voice seemed to come from far away. I should have asked him how he got the picture, but all I could do was brace myself as a tidal wave of images crashed through my brain.

"I don't remember Tammy," I began weakly, closing my eyes, "but I think I remember something . . ."

I felt the earth drop out beneath my feet and a black awning of long-forgotten memory laid out in front of me. The day she moved into her dorm slipped into my mind and I *remembered*.

* * *

"No running in the hall, Lindsey," Dad called out as I ran as fast as I could down the hall. I skidded into Jess's room, a knitted throw in my arms.

"Easy there, Lindsey-Bug," Mom laughed, taking the blanket from me.

I had interrupted them arguing about where to hang a poster of some pretty flowers and a bridge. Jess wanted it above her desk, Mom thought it looked better near her bed.

Mom and Jess looked a lot alike. Both of them had long dark hair and blue eyes, and every time I saw them together, I wished I looked like them, too. I felt like the odd one out with my short brown hair and brown eyes. And I didn't think I was nearly as pretty as my mom and sister.

"Sorry," I shouted, jumping onto the second bed.

"Not that one, Linds," Jess said playfully, picking me up and swinging me around before dropping me onto the other bed. "This one's mine. You can jump on it all you want."

Mom shooed me off and began straightening out the green-and-blue plaid wool blanket I had brought in from the car. She draped it over the end like she did on Jess's bed at home before moving the poster above the bed. Jess sighed but didn't say anything.

"No she cannot," she scolded Jess "I didn't just spend a good hour setting all this up for Lindsey-Bug to make a mess." Her words were stern, but Mom gave me a smile letting me know she wasn't really angry with me.

"Well, whose bed is that, then?" I asked, pointing to the one I wasn't allowed to jump on. "Is that for when I sleep over?" I laughed as Jess tickled me.

"Sorry, kiddo. That's my roommate's." Jess fluffed my hair and I smacked her hand away like I always did.

"Oh, can I have one of those?" I started to reach for a chocolate on the desk by her roommate's bed.

Jess gently moved me away from the tempting treat. "Those aren't yours to eat, Linds."

I pouted when Jess took her bottle of perfume from my hands after I sprayed the front of my shirt with her jasmine scent.

"You're going to have the best time, Jessica," Mom said, putting her arms around my sister. "But remember we're not paying for you to just have fun. This school is expensive, so, do the work and get a good education. That's what you're here for." She pulled away, holding my sister by the upper arms, her expression serious. "I remember my college days, I know how easy it is to lose sight of your goals."

"I know, Mom, don't worry," Jess muttered. She looked at me and rolled her eyes, sticking out her tongue. I giggled but covered it with my hand.

Mom kissed her cheek. "I will always worry about you, Jessica. You have so much potential, you don't even know how much yet. You've worked hard to get this far, don't blow it now."

"Mom," Jess groaned. "I won't. I know our plan and I intend to stick to it. I'm going to be fine."

"Hmm." Mom sounded like she didn't really believe her. She looked to the open doorway. "Where did your dad get to?"

I hurried out to the hallway before either of them could stop me. "I'll go find him."

I ran down to the car, dodging people carrying boxes and suitcases. I didn't see Dad, so I sprinted all the way back up to the dorm room, finding Jess alone. She seemed sad and angry, even though she tried to hide it when she saw me.

"Are you going to cry, Jessie?" I asked, thinking how I would cry if I had to leave home.

Jess shook her head, but still looked like she might, so I threw my arms around her. I hugged her as hard as I could and she hugged me back, laughing about how I was growing so strong.

"Jess . . ." my dad's voice sounded loud in the doorway. When I turned around he looked upset, too.

"Lindsey-Bug, there you are!" Mom called out, coming from the other end of the hallway. "Please stop running around, you're going to get hurt. Come on, it's time to get going."

"Meet you at the car!" I yelled as I ducked under Mom's arm and started to run again. I glanced back and waved to Jess before I left.

* * *

"She looked sad, but a lot of kids do when they go away to college," I concluded, feeling suddenly very tired after the onslaught from the unexpected trip down memory lane.

"See, Lindsey, this is what I was talking about. There's probably all kinds of stuff up in that head of yours that we can pry loose." Ryan seemed invigorated, while I was completely depleted.

I had finished my coffee and he started to motion Rhonda over to order more drinks, but I shook my head. The memory had unnerved me. I had so few of my own recollections, but that day, dropping her off at college, that memory had been all mine.

While Ryan seemed to only be getting started, I was ready to put on the brakes.

"Are you okay?" Ryan asked, finally sensing the change in my mood.

Was I okay? I had no idea. I wasn't entirely sure how I felt. But one thing was certain, I had to get away from Ryan

McKay before I shared anything else that I wasn't ready to hand over. He made it too easy to part with things that felt like they should belong solely to me.

"I think I've had enough for tonight." I hadn't gleaned much from Ryan, barring Jess's cookie preference, and that should have bothered me, but it actually felt like he had helped me unearth a lot with the new memory. Now I needed to go home and process it.

"Sure, that's fine," Ryan said, trying to hide his dismay. He paid for our coffees and then walked with me outside.

"I'm parked across the street." I indicated my red Toyota beneath the streetlight. Dad insisted the Japanese brand was the safest, which is why I drove one. "Thanks for the coffee. And, you know, the Jess stuff. It was nice to be able to talk about her for a while."

"I'm glad. And if I came across as too eager, then I'm sorry. But I really feel like together we can figure out what happened to your sister." He gave me a wide-toothed smile, as if he could barely contain himself.

His enthusiasm, which before had chafed me, now felt a little contagious. I started to feel a twinge of his belief that perhaps we *could* make a good team. All in the name of finding out about Jess, of course. Feeling emboldened, I added, "I enjoyed the company, too."

God, had I really said that?

I wasn't typically forward with men I didn't know. I was reserved. I kept to myself. It had been a means of survival in the years since Jess had gone missing. It's hard to know who wants you for *you* and not because of your connection to a tragedy. It's disturbing how many people were drawn to trauma. It had left me skeptical and cautious.

A part of me hoped Ryan wouldn't acknowledge my strange bout of flirting. But of course he acknowledged it. That seemed to be the kind of man he was. He saw it as an invitation I wasn't sure I was offering. He took a step, closing the space between us, his eyes dropping to my mouth.

"I really enjoyed spending time with you too, Lindsey."

I had the feeling he wanted to kiss me. Did I want to kiss him, too? Yes, he was attractive. Yes, he had helped me unbury a memory of Jess. But . . .

We stood awkwardly for a moment, neither sure what to do. I got the impression Ryan was used to getting what he wanted and he made no effort to hide he wanted *me*. But I wasn't the kind of woman to hand over control to anyone. Even if he had nice eyes, a knee-trembling-inducing smile and potentially life-changing information about my missing sister.

"I should go," I finally said. Things had been drawn out long enough. Wanting to keep my pride intact, I waved good-bye and crossed the street.

"Wait," he called out. When I turned back, he hesitated. I felt myself tense up. With concern he would act on his attraction? Or anticipation because I wanted him to? "Can I see you again?" Ryan asked after a beat, remaining on the sidewalk. I nodded, smiling through the nervous buzzing in my stomach. His face lit up. "Tomorrow night?"

"I'm working the late shift at the hotel. How about during the day?"

"I'm on a deadline to get the first draft of my article to my editor, so I'll be slammed all day." He sighed in frustration, then he brightened. "Well, I have to eat sometime, so maybe I can time my dinner with your break?"

"Okay. I usually grab dinner around six thirty. Then maybe you can tell me more about Jess." It was important to remind him, and myself, what the stakes were in this. What our arrangement was hinged on.

For a split second his smile seemed to falter before he quickly corrected himself. "Okay then."

On the way home I thought about what was happening with Ryan. He was older than me, more Jess's age than mine—but, as much as I wanted to deny it, I felt a connection to him that was both new and unexpected.

Maybe that meant something, maybe it didn't, but, for the first time in my life, I thought I might be willing to see where it went.

**Ten Seconds to Vanish: The Unsolved
Disappearance of Jessica Fadley**

Episode 4

Stella: Welcome back true-crime lovers. I'm your
host Stella—

Rachel: And I'm Rachel.

Stella: And this is *Ten Seconds to Vanish: The Unsolved
Disappearance of Jessica Fadley*.

Theme music plays

Stella: Okay, wow, these past few weeks have been
nuts, Rach. Were you expecting this cold case to
get as popular as it has?

Rachel: Not at all. I'm glad Jessica is finally getting
the attention she deserves. Did you see Jimmy
Kimmel talking about it on his show?

Stella: And it's all thanks to you guys. You are what's
keeping the lights on.

Rachel: And we hope you keep listening, because
the twists are going to come fast and hard with
this one. So, without further ado, let's dive in.

Stella: Today, we take a left turn and focus on
another woman who has never been found.

Rachel: And how it potentially ties in with Jessica's case. Okay, I've got my bag of chips and my favorite salsa. I'm ready, Stel, bring it on.

Stella: Let's get in our time machine and head back to November 1998 in America, way down south—

Rachel: Ah, the fall of '98. I can almost hear Shania Twain and Savage Garden blasting from the speakers of my '87 Buick LeSabre.

Stella: Not a chance. Give me some Oasis or Blur anytime. Though, our next missing coed, Tammy Estep, wouldn't have been listening to any of that. She was a jam-band girl all the way. According to friends, she spent the summer after high school going to every Phish show on the East Coast. I'll be honest, I had no idea who Phish were, but from all accounts, this sounds a bit like the festival scene we have in the UK.

Rachel: I know literally nothing about festivals in England, but you can't have a nineties college girl without a good touring jam band thrown in there. And she also loved the band Widespread Panic and told a bunch of her friends she was thinking about following them around during the summer.

Stella: Which is why the police dismissed her disappearance at first, right?

Rachel: You got it, Stel. They wrote her off as another disaffected youth who had run off. Which, in reality, was so not Tammy. She may like her jam bands and to let her hair down now and then by going to some shows, but she was as straight edge as they came.

Stella: She was straight edge *and* super reliable. She had a 3.9 GPA and was the Resident Advisor in the Westwood dormitory—

Rachel: Which was Jessica's dorm. Shit, Stel, the lines are already crossing.

Stella: Exactly. So Tammy and Jess knew each other. and apparently she had a real scandalous streak. I spoke with Tammy's best friend, Brenda, who said Tammy was involved with an older man. She also says she told the police, but, of course, they did absolutely *nothing* with the information.

Rachel: We should rename this podcast "Five Hundred Ways the Police Suck."

Stella: You're not wrong, my friend.

Rachel: So, this older man—are we talking about a senior maybe?

Stella: Oh no, Rach. This guy was a professor at Southern State . . . and married, too.

Rachel: Oh, that *is* scandalous! Tsk, tsk, Tammy.

Stella: But does this married, older man have anything to do with her disappearance? Some say yes, but what about the other missing girls? Let's dig a little deeper . . .

5

JESSICA

November 1998

*T*HE PHONE RANG *and rang. I hung up and sat on my bed, my shoulders slumped, my heart heavy. I couldn't call him at home. I didn't want to talk to Mom. I didn't want her to hear the pain in my voice.*

I needed my dad.

I called his office again, knowing he'd be there. He would have snuck out after Mom went to bed. She was a sound sleeper.

Finally he picked up. He sounded out of breath.

"Dad."

It was all I said before the tears came and then I couldn't say anything at all.

"I'm here for you, Jess," he promised.

I felt silly, turning to my father. I was an adult now. I was living on my own. But sometimes a girl still needed her father, no matter how hard it was to admit.

We were close. This separation was difficult. . . .for both of us.

* * *

The hall was unusually crowded as Daisy and I headed out for dinner. I pulled the door shut behind me. Daisy wrote a note on the wipe board letting our friends know we were headed to the Commons, seemingly oblivious to the under-current of excited apprehension that vibrated around us.

"Hey guys, did you hear about Tammy?"

We turned to acknowledge the tall girl with bleached-blonde hair and thin, penciled eyebrows who was standing eagerly in her doorway, as if waiting for us to appear.

Daisy gave her a look of annoyance. "What about her?" she asked.

Kara followed us to the stairwell at the end of the hall. "She's missing."

That caught my roommate's attention. Daisy's mouth popped open in shock. "What do you mean *she's missing?*"

Kara's eyes widened dramatically. "As in, no one has seen or heard from her in like four days."

"I *thought* things were less oppressive around here," Daisy joked and I laughed along half-heartedly.

"Maybe she went home," I suggested uneasily.

"No way. Thanksgiving break is in like two weeks, why would she go home now?" Kara argued. She followed us down the stairs and through the lounge. Once outside, the three of us stopped, the other two clearly wanting to continue playing investigator.

"Midterms ended last week, maybe she's partying somewhere." I shrugged attempting to mimic Daisy's nonchalance.

"Come on, this is Tammy we're talking about. She's allergic to partying," Daisy quipped and Kara laughed. "We can come up with a better theory than that one, Jess."

"I'm sure it's nothing—" I started to protest, but Kara and Daisy were already knee deep in speculation.

"Ooh, maybe she ran off with that older guy she's been screwing."

"What older guy?"

"The married professor. I think he teaches intro to statistics."

"Oh my god, Tammy was boinking a teacher? Was it Dr. Daniels? Everyone knows he's *really* into his students, if you know what I mean."

Dr. Daniels.

An image of the handsome man with the kind smile I had almost run into came to mind.

"Maybe, I don't know his name."

"Guys, I think you're making a big deal out of nothing," I interjected, raising my voice to be heard over their excited discussion. "I overheard her telling her friend Brenda that she had tickets to the Phish show in DC last weekend. That's probably where she went. She made a big deal out of how she spent three months following them last summer, I bet that's what she's doing."

Daisy and Kara both deflated at the very realistic possibility of our missing RA's whereabouts. "Yeah, she was always going on and on about that. It was the one semi-interesting thing about her," Daisy grumbled.

"Well, whatever, she's definitely gone. So all the girls are planning a massive hall party tonight. You in?" Kara asked us, having already lost interest in *why* Tammy was missing. Who cared as long as she wasn't back before the party.

"Sure. I'll invite some of the Phi Lam guys and Jess will put together a playlist," Daisy offered and Kara practically jumped up and down.

"Yeah, sounds like fun," I agreed, looking forward to a night of carefree frivolity. "I hope everyone likes the Dave Matthews Band."

Daisy groaned good-naturedly. "She plays *Before These Crowded Streets* nonstop. I have been forced to learn all the lyrics against my will," she explained to Kara. My roommate was a classic-rock junkie. She didn't seem to have much taste for music post 1985. She and my dad would get along really well.

"It's either that or Backstreet Boys," I warned, causing Daisy to cringe dramatically.

"Dave it is," she agreed. We grinned at each other, warm with camaraderie.

"This is going to be sick!" Kara squealed before running back into the dorm.

"Well, she's something else." Daisy looped her arm with mine as we made our way to the cafeteria. "So, do you really think our irritating RA has run off to follow some band around?"

I forced myself to smile. The topic made my stomach hurt and my chest tight.

"Who knows. What I *do* know is that she's not worth the energy thinking about."

"You're totally right. Which means we really need to live it up while we can. Though twenty bucks says she's tucked away having naked time with her grandpa boyfriend." Daisy released my arm as we walked along the outer path that overlooked Mt. Randall.

She pulled us to a stop, looking down the hill at the buildings and streets below. "I still can't believe you grew up here." It was the same sentiment she uttered every time we ventured into town. It felt strange going down the hill to visit familiar shops and restaurants after enveloping myself in Southern State's cocoon. I was both embarrassed and defensive of the tiny place I had always called home.

"Why?" I asked.

"Because you don't seem like a small town girl, Jess," she commented, throwing her arm around me.

I felt warm all over. Daisy was right. I was changing. I felt it. I had thought I'd only ever be a girl from a small town. But that wasn't true. I was more than that.

We moved on, heading to the Commons. Once in the cafeteria, she waved at a group of girls sitting at a circular table in the middle of the room. "Grab me a cranberry juice, will ya?"

"Can I use your ID again? I left mine in the room." I made a face and Daisy laughed, rolling her eyes.

"I'm going to staple it to your hand at this rate." She fished the card out of her back pocket and handed it to me before walking away.

I watched her join our fellow Pi Gamma Delta pledges. Eight of us had received bids in October.

I hadn't been sure I even wanted to rush a sorority but was now glad I had. It felt good having a built-in group of friends and plans every night of the week. I was busy—maybe too busy—but I finally felt like I was having the college experience I was meant to have. Even if my new social life was starting to come at the expense of doing my homework.

But being studious and hardworking was exhausting. Letting loose and getting drunk with my new friends was a lot easier than writing a five-hundred-word essay on the misogynistic themes of *The Odyssey*.

Mom was excited about me being in "her" sorority. Though, I suspected her enthusiasm would have been dampened by my decrease in academic focus. My mom claimed she wanted what was best for me. I, however, knew that what she wanted was to see me live the life she had. She always wanted details. Play-by-play accounts. Keeping her happy was exhausting.

Which is why my father had always been the easy one. Our relationship had been effortless. We used to share knowing looks when Mom gave me one of her well-trodden speeches, barely able to hide our laughter.

After sitting through Mom's lectures, Dad would take me downtown to Carina's Custard and we'd share a hot fudge brownie sundae. It became another thing that was *ours*.

* * *

"She only wants what's best for you," he told me one evening when I was fourteen. I was trying to hold back tears of frustration after being told by Mom I wasn't applying myself enough after receiving a B on my American History test.

"By yelling at me?" I stirred the ice cream until it became a puddle of brown sludge.

Dad put his hand on top of mine. "She loves you. And I do, too. More than anything. Remember that when it seems like she's riding you too hard. No one wants better for you than your mom and me." He squeezed my hand. "Especially me."

He pushed his half-eaten sundae toward me. "Finish mine. You've turned yours into soup," he laughed.

My dad was great at making me feel better. He understood me in a way no one else did. Not Mom. Not my friends.

No one.

* * *

I loaded my tray with french fries, mac 'n' cheese, and a slice
of Boston cream pie, an extra large cup of coffee—I lived off
the stuff—and I made sure to grab a bottle of juice for Daisy.
My roommate was holding court at the table, telling the
other girls all about our missing-in-action RA.

The sisters of Pi Gamma stood out. They claimed the
biggest table and spoke loud enough for the whole room to
hear what a great time they were having. Sitting at the Pi
Gam table was akin to being in a fishbowl. But for most of
my pledge sisters, this was exactly what they had signed up
for. I was learning to throw myself into this new existence,
though I instinctively wanted to retreat to the shadows.

Southern State University boasted three sororities and
three fraternities. Each came with a well-earned reputation.
And the men and women in each organization more or less fit
into the stereotypes. But every once in a while there was one
or two that didn't quite fit. I wondered—and worried—
whether I was one of them.

"That's so scary," Phoebe Baker said softly after I sat
down. I gave the diminutive girl with long, bright red hair
what I hoped was a reassuring smile. She gave me a hesitant
smile in return. I didn't know much about Phoebe. I knew
she had grown up in a town close by. She was quiet and
unassuming. I got the sense she lacked confidence, a lot
like I did. The other girls were more outgoing, yet Phoebe
couldn't seem to break out of her shell. Even though I felt
connected to her because of our similar dispositions, I
was more determined than she was to be someone different. She seemed eager to please, and it was this eagerness,
so like my own, that at times had me distancing myself
from her even as we were meant to be bonding as pledge
sisters. She was a reminder of the characteristics I wanted
to get rid of.

"I don't think it's anything to be scared of, Pheebs." Daisy's reassurance seemed hesitant, as if she didn't quite believe
what she was saying. "Tammy's a pain. I'm sure she's out
there somewhere spreading her particular brand of misery on
someone else."

Phoebe chewed on her bottom lip. "But what if something happened to her? Is anyone even wondering about it? I was watching a show about Ted Bundy the other night. He preyed on college age girls, too." Phoebe looked around the table, her Bambi eyes wide with barely contained fright.

"Bundy's been dead for years, Phoebe," Daisy countered.

"I'm not saying it's Ted Bundy. Maybe someone *like* Ted Bundy." Phoebe was practically wringing her hands.

Everyone shared a look. It would be easy to dismiss Phoebe's concerns as paranoia, yet no one did. Because as a woman, simply existing made you vulnerable. The papers were full of stories of missing women—*murdered* women— the possibility was very, very real.

Daisy met my eyes. "Could that be what happened to her?" she asked me, wanting reassurance.

"I think we should look a little closer to home and maybe go ask Dr. Daniels." Erica Stead, a classic mean girl with a cutting tongue, wiggled her eyebrows suggestively, making the rest of the table, except for Phoebe, break into laughter tinged with relief. It was better to imagine a sordid scandal than a murderous stranger in our midst.

"So it *is* Dr. Daniels she's been seeing!" Daisy shrieked, loving that she had been right.

Erica looked smug. "Yep. Have you checked him out? He's seriously hot for an older guy. And if you're in one of his stat courses, you know how . . . um . . . hands on he is with his students."

"Do you think he had something to do with her disappearance?" Daisy asked.

I didn't want to focus on this. I wanted to forget about it and move on. But I couldn't. Because it held my morbid, self-destructive interest.

"There's no way Dr. Daniels was involved with her. He's not that kind of man," Phoebe argued primly, her voice trembling slightly with the effort it must have taken for her to speak up.

"And how do you know what kind of man he is, Pheebs?" Erica asked luridly.

Phoebe drew herself upright. "I have him for Intro to Probability and he's a wonderful teacher. He has ethics and morals and—"

"Until he sees a girl in a short skirt," Daisy muttered.

Blair Atkins, a sweet, pretty sophomore, leaned forward, her skin flushed. "My roommate is in his 8:00 class and the TA taught this morning. Dr. Daniels never showed up. She heard from a couple of girls who seemed to know the professor *really* well—" Daisy and Erica shared a conspiratorial look, "that Tammy had shown up at his office last Friday making a scene. She was crying and begging to talk to him." Everyone was listening in fascination.

"What could that have been about? Did he dump her?" Daisy pondered. While she wouldn't outright say it, I knew she was enjoying the thought of our RA being kicked to the curb.

"Maybe she's pregnant," Erica added.

"Stop it," Phoebe said, but her voice was too quiet to be heard by anyone else but me.

"Oh my god, can you even imagine? After all the crap she gives us about sleeping around and being careful. What a hypocrite," Daisy said in disgust.

"Ooh, or what if she was threatening to tell his wife?" Tina Spencer, another pledge who also lived in Westwood, added.

"And he decided to shut her up," Erica crowed.

"This isn't a TV movie, guys. This is someone's actual life. You can't go around making baseless claims against Dr. Daniels. It's bordering on slander," Phoebe said in obvious disdain.

The other girls rolled their eyes. Phoebe's moral aversion wouldn't derail them from dissecting the gossip.

"Like I said, Phoebe, I'm sure this will all get figured out," I said placatingly. The other girls' delight was making me uncomfortable. And Phoebe's obvious distress didn't help. She looked like she was going to puke.

"So, who's going to the mixer at the Sigma Kappa Phi house on Saturday?" I asked, talking over their giddy chatter in an attempt to change the subject.

"Abso-freaking-lutely!" Erica exclaimed as she and Daisy pumped their fists. "They have the cutest pledges on campus."

As predicted, the conversation turned completely around, and the whereabouts of Tammy Estep were forgotten.

*   *   *

I stared down at the red "F" on the front of my essay on *The Odyssey*. I knew I deserved it. I had written it less than two hours before class. That wasn't usually how I operated. In high school I'd spend hours upon hours researching and fine-tuning my work before submitting it. It's how I graduated at the top of my class.

Yet I was finding I was more focused on the things I *wanted* to do, like going to mixers and staying up late watching all the John Hughes movies with my pledge sisters, and less focused on things I *should* be doing, like writing my Odyssey essay for Intro to English.

But being this new Jess, the one with friends and an endless social calendar, was a lot more fun than the Jess who sat in her room every weekend planning out her future.

I enjoyed these new impulses, even if they threatened to drown me. And I would try not to feel guilty for laughing and drinking with my hallmates until the early hours, enjoying the momentary freedom until another uptight upperclassman moved in to replace MIA Tammy as our new resident advisor.

I shoved the essay into my bag, refusing to look at it any longer. I'd turn things around. I always did.

A bright pink tennis ball bounced off my shoe, landing with a thud at my feet. I looked up in annoyance, ready to give the jerk a piece of my mind.

I was surprised to find a little girl who looked about Lindsey's age, running toward me, her white-blonde hair in a messy braid down her back.

"I'm sorry," her high-pitched voice called out.

I leaned down and picked up the ball, holding it out for her.

"It's okay. Here you go." The little girl took it with a shy smile.

"I'm not supposed to throw it so hard. My dad says I might hit someone." She cradled the ball close to her chest, looking over her shoulder toward Roosevelt Hall and a man standing with a pretty woman holding a baby.

"Well, your dad's right, but it's okay. You didn't even hit me," I assured her.

"Good, because I really don't want to get in trouble," she said, her lower lip jutting out.

"It'll be our secret." I gave her a wink and she giggled before running back to her parents.

I watched her for a moment before recognition hit me.

Dr. Daniels lifted the little girl into the air and swung her around. I could hear her laughter. It sounded like innocence and joy. It made my heart clench painfully.

He kissed her on the cheek and I could see the girl clinging to his neck. It reminded me so much of my dad and me. Down to the way Dr. Daniels hefted his daughter onto his shoulders as she squealed in terrified delight, gripping his hands so she wouldn't fall.

Dr. Daniels kissed his wife tenderly before turning his affections to the baby, no more than a year old, in her arms.

They were the picture of a perfect, happy family.

They could be *my* family.

It made me want to cry.

* * *

The music was blaring from the three massive speakers someone had stacked in the corner of the Sigma Kap house. The theme was deserted island so I was surrounded by a sea of grass skirts and coconut bras—even on some of the guys.

The room erupted into cheers as four of my sisters arrived. They had gone all out for the theme, making a cardboard replica of the *S.S. Minnow* from the TV show *Gilligan's Island*. The four of them walked in a single file, holding the massive boat up with string over their shoulders, as the fraternity brothers hooted and hollered.

I pulled at the white button-down shirt I had tied at my navel. It hung open, revealing my Hawaiian print bikini top. The cutoff jean shorts I had borrowed from Daisy were a size too small and barely covered my ass. I tried not to feel self-conscious as I danced awkwardly while downing the awful beer as quickly as I could. I plastered a smile on my face that felt as fake as the bright flowers draped around my neck.

Everyone around me was wasted and I was trying to get to the same state. But it was tough when the beer tasted awful.

I had lost track of my pledge sisters about five minutes after arriving. I caught a glimpse of Daisy now and then, but she was hanging on a different guy every time. I needed to interject myself with some of that wild abandon.

I had never been a party girl like Daisy; I never had the time to be. Not with all the extra classes Mom had insisted on, and the extracurricular activities I had participated in. My life before now had been filled with winning and achieving, not partying. Not having a life. I had missed out on so much that I was determined to make up for lost time. I wanted friends. I wanted to go to parties. I wanted to be the kind of girl that was always having a great time.

I closed my eyes and swayed to the music. I probably looked ridiculous, but at that moment I didn't care. My mind was pleasantly fuzzy, which I craved. Being stuck in my own head was the last place I wanted to be.

I felt an uncontrollable shiver. A feeling of being observed made it impossible to lose myself in the moment.

I opened my eyes, looking around, wondering what sleazeball was playing voyeur.

A figure on the opposite side of the room caught my attention for no other reason than she seemed completely out of place. Not dancing. Not moving. Just standing there, her frizzy, overly permed brown hair stuck to the side of her head as if it were wet.

The strobe lights made it hard to see her properly. Her features were jarring in the flashing glare.

Tammy?

My breath caught in my throat. My palms went clammy. I blinked and she disappeared.

I knew it wasn't real. An alcohol-induced figment of my overwrought imagination. I was letting the conversation with my pledge sisters earlier in the week get to me. Their paranoia seemed to be contagious.

I scrunched my eyes closed again, terrified to leave them open.

A few minutes later I felt the warmth of someone pressing close to me. I opened my eyes to find a cute guy with an attractive toothy grin dancing beside me. He leaned in close, his lips brushing my ear lobe. "This is probably going to sound like a line, but can I join you?"

I couldn't tell him how much I welcomed his distraction. Even if he was over the top with his forwardness. The hair was still raised on my arms. The ever-present tingle on the back of my neck hadn't gone away.

The old Jess wanted to leave. To go back to the dorm and bury herself under the covers. Instead, *new Jess* gave him a coy smile and turned her back, glancing at the hot boy over her shoulder as I wiggled and shook the parts of me I knew he was staring at.

In my experience good-looking guys, young or old, were only ever after one thing. And they used their looks and easy smiles to make the rest of us go along with just about anything. My insides buzzed with bitter-tinged excitement.

"You can tell me to get lost if you want. But I really hope you don't," he shouted to be heard over the music.

I turned around, moving against him. His eyes widened, his grin broadening. He put his hands on my waist, his fingers digging into the sensitive flesh, making me shiver.

He was ridiculously attractive in a way that should make me suspicious. He was shirtless with a cheap Hawaiian lei around his neck and Bermuda shorts that hung low on his narrow hips. His longish hair was brown with blonde streaks that definitely weren't natural. It kept falling in his eyes, which gave him an adorable boy-next-door appeal.

I took another sip of beer, trying not to shudder at the taste.

Mr. Cutie stopped dancing and peered into my cup, blanching. "Who gave you the piss water to drink? Hot girls are supposed to be given the good stuff."

"Maybe the person who gave this to me didn't think I was hot."

The guy looked at me as if I had grown a second head, his hands still warm on the skin at my waist. "I may be slightly drunk, but my eyes still work." He took the cup from me, left it on the table pushed against the wall and took my hand. "Come on, I've got the good shit upstairs."

I tugged out of his grip, my feigned confidence melting away as nerves set in. "Um, maybe we should stay down here."

"I promise to be a perfect gentleman. *The* perfect gentleman." He crossed his heart with his finger. "It's just a crime for a girl that looks like you to be drinking the swill we reserve for the rest of the masses."

I laughed, allowing myself to be flattered. "So you're a brother at Sigma Kap?" I asked him.

"Not yet. I'm only a lowly pledge," he answered.

"Me too." And then I gave him a smile. A real one this time. He was cute and more than a little charismatic. There was something about him that made me want to be around him. Some people you meet, you feel that instant spark. This guy was one of those people.

"Figured you were one of the Pi Gamma girls." He seemed proud of his deduction work.

"We'll just call you Sherlock," I joked, shoving his arm.

He held out his hand again. "So can we go get something better to drink?"

I hesitated, but only for a moment. He seemed like the perfect distraction right now. I put my hand in his and let him lead me toward the stairs, taking one last look around at the drunken party before we left.

Upstairs, we headed down a long, barely lit hallway. He pushed open the last door on the right to reveal a messy dorm room that stank of stale beer and body odor. Dirty clothes littered the floor and empty beer cans lined the window sill. The room was bigger than mine, with two wooden beds lofted to allow for the desks to fit underneath.

The guy cringed as he watched me take in my surroundings. "It's not my room. I don't live like a total pig." I noted that he purposefully kept the door open, which I appreciated.

"Whose room is it then?"

"One of the brothers said the pledges could store their booze in here. I live over at Frankfurt Hall," he explained, referring to one of the other freshman dormitories. "Just give me a second to get us a decent drink."

I watched him pull out a see-through bottle of clear liquid with gold flecks on the bottom.

"Goldschläger, huh? Someone's feelin' fancy," I chuckled.

The guy laughed. "I got this on bid day. I've been saving it to share with the right person."

I rolled my eyes. "Man, you're smooth. Do these lines ever work?"

His grin grew wider and my stomach fluttered. "All the time." Then he winked at me and my knees threatened to buckle.

While he prepared our drinks, I made my way over to the two-seater sofa beneath the window. I wasn't sure I wanted to sit on it, but I didn't want to stand around either. I hesitated, not sure what to do.

"I think it's safe to sit. There's nothing toxic on the cushions that I'm aware of," he joked, handing me my drink then pushing the piles of paper and empty chip bags onto the floor with the rest of the trash.

"I'm not sure I believe you," I muttered, though I sat down beside him anyway.

The music made the floor shake and I felt the vibrations throughout my body. I took a drink of the cinnamon schnapps. It was better than the warm beer, but still kind of gross. I forced myself to drink most of it in one gulp.

"Whoa, slow down," he chuckled, filling my cup again.

I sheepishly took a tiny sip. "Sorry. It's nice drinking something that doesn't taste like it was left in the sun for four days, ya know."

"I get it. By all means, drink up, then." He took a long drink himself. "So, are you having fun?" he asked me, angling his body a little closer. Our knees brushed together as I moved toward him. My eyes lingered on his toned torso, my skin heating.

"Tonight, or at college?"

"Tonight is what matters." His voice dropped seductively. He was really laying it on thick. I raised an eyebrow and he grimaced. "Sorry, the lines keep coming. It's like an affliction. Call it *badflirtingitis.*"

I laughed. I couldn't help it. He was ridiculous, but sweet, and I found myself relaxing in his presence. He seemed pleased with himself, his expression delighted.

"The party's okay, I guess," I answered noncommittally.

It was his turn to raise an eyebrow. "That's a lie."

I took another drink. "Okay, this whole scene is definitely not my thing. But I promised myself I was going to let loose more now that I'm in college. And if I'm going to be a Pi Gam, I need to embrace my inner party girl."

He was watching me intently as if he could see directly inside me. It was disconcerting, but also strangely comforting. I felt like maybe I could be open with this guy I didn't know. This stranger with brown eyes and bleach-streaked hair like some kind of NSYNC reject.

"The Pi Gamma Delta ladies definitely like to get their party on," he observed.

"Yes, they do," I muttered.

He raised an eyebrow. "Am I sensing you're less than thrilled with your new sisters?" he asked.

"Not at all, I love being a Pi Gam," I objected.

The cute guy gave me an I-don't-believe-you look.

"Okay, so maybe it's hard keeping up with all the partying. My grades clearly don't like sharing the spotlight with my social life," I found myself admitting.

He leaned in closer. So close I could feel the heat of him. "Then why do it at all?"

"Because what else is a girl like me supposed to do?" I asked with a hint of sarcasm, thinking about my mom and all of her expectations.

"Well, if you don't want to do it, then don't. You can't live your whole life worrying about what everyone else wants you to do. You'll make yourself miserable." He pushed a strand of hair out of my eyes, but made no move to touch me further.

I wanted him to touch me, though. To make me forget. To make me stop thinking about *everything*.

Just for a little while.

"Sage advice, Mr. Frat Guy." I smirked and his eyes sparkled with amusement.

"I may be a frat guy, but I'm a smart frat guy. Just ask my mom," he quipped. He leaned back on the couch and slung an arm over my shoulder. "I say, rather than brave more bad music and crappy beer, we stay up here with this nice bottle of Goldschläger. I think the new episode of *South Park* is on."

"Sounds perfect," I agreed, leaning into him and enjoying the feel of his arm pressed against me.

We spent the next couple of hours watching TV and drinking. I was definitely on my way to being drunk by the time I suggested it was time to call it a night.

"Sure. I have a feeling Brad is going to want his room back before too long anyway," he said, grabbing his almost-empty bottle of liquor and pulling me to my feet. "I'll walk you home if that's cool."

I nodded, appreciating the offer, especially with the echo of ever-watchful eyes still dancing over my skin.

I made a cursory effort to look for Daisy as we left the frat house, but she was nowhere to be found. Figuring I'd see her back at our room, I followed the guy I had spent several enjoyable hours with out onto the street. He took my hand, as though we were walking home from a date.

It felt nice. I walked with him, hand in hand, pretending, perhaps hoping, this is how my life was meant to be.

The guy called out greetings to people as we passed. It seemed he knew a lot of people. I also knew that walking together would be a topic of conversation. I had moved from one small community to another and the basics were the same. My business was *everyone's* business.

We headed down the path that led to Westwood Hall. I noticed a car parked beneath a burned-out streetlight. It sat in shadow, the two people inside barely discernible, but I recognized the girl's bright red hair. I watched her head dip down out of sight and I stopped abruptly, wondering what was going on.

"What is it?" the guy beside me asked, following my gaze.

"I think that's one of my pledge sisters, Phoebe Baker." There was a man in the driver's seat. I couldn't quite make him out, but could tell he was much older. Was it her dad? "What's she doing?"

If I hadn't glanced at Mr. Cute at that moment, I would have missed the imperceptible change in his expression. Shock and something like anger flashed across his face.

"Do you know her?" I asked pointedly.

"I did." He sounded cryptic. He laughed, though less naturally than before. "We went to high school together." I knew there was more to the story, but I didn't know him and it felt rude to pry, even if I *really* wanted to. He cleared his throat and looked back at me. "The Phoebe I knew wasn't the kind of girl to do what is definitely happening in that car."

Just then the man turned and I could finally make him out through the fogged glass. It was Dr. Daniels.

I watched as he pulled Phoebe toward him, kissing her deeply.

"She's obviously changed a lot since high school." His eyes darkened. "But, let's not stand here and watch them like a couple of perverts." He took my arm and steered me back toward my dorm.

"I can't believe that's Phoebe. She hates parties and drinking. She didn't even want to come out tonight. There's no way she's . . ." I let my words die off, because clearly she was doing exactly what I thought she'd never do. Just like Tammy.

He shrugged, though his jaw tightened. "Everyone has their secrets."

We stopped as we reached the door. I was still trying to look back at the car and my pledge sister, hoping like hell we were wrong about what was going on. Dr. Daniels was a teacher. And he was married. He was a father.

Not Phoebe. Doesn't she know better?

I felt *betrayed*. Because the woman I was getting to know, whom I thought I had a clear read on, was the total opposite of who I thought she was.

Or perhaps, it made an uncomfortable sense that the person with so little confidence, who had trouble voicing her opinions, was exactly the kind of girl that would take up with her married professor.

I thought of that adorable little girl I had seen earlier with her bright pink tennis ball and sweet laugh. I remembered the adoration in her eyes as she looked up at her dad, the same man now making out with his student in front of the freshmen dorms.

The devastation of it made me want to sob.

For a moment I saw myself in that little girl and I despaired at the thought of her family falling apart.

"You'd better go inside. It's getting late and there are a lot of weirdos roaming around." He leaned over and pressed a kiss to my cheek, his lips lingering against my skin. Feeling unfettered and slightly out of control, I turned my face and his mouth met mine.

At the feel of his lips, I forgot about Phoebe. I forgot about everything. My mind became a blank page and I was lost in *feeling*.

It was incredible.

His hands made their way to the back of my head as his fingers tangled in my hair. Our kiss deepened, and I knew that if I were Daisy, or any other wild and free freshman girl, I would have invited him up to my room. I would let whatever this was to progress to a place neither of us could stop.

But I wasn't Daisy.

And as much as I was forcing a new Jess into existence, the old Jess was still there, whispering judgments in my ear.

So, I let myself get lost in the kiss for only a few moments longer, not letting it go any further.

"You should go," I told him after finally pulling away.

"Are you sure?" His eyes were slightly unfocused, his nose brushing mine. I nodded and he stepped back.

"Sleep tight," he said playfully, running his thumb along my bottom lip. "Don't let the bedbugs bite."

I laughed. "You're such a dork."

"I may be a dork, but you're going to see me again," he predicted, walking backward down the path, away from my dorm.

He was right, I would see him again. I *wanted* to see him again.

But it was only after he left that I realized he never told me his name.

BrendaGivens
Charlotte, NC

30 likes

BrendaGivens This feels like yesterday. I miss you, Tammy! If you're out there, know that I love you! #spreadheads #missing

View all 3 comments

6 DAYS AGO

6

LINDSEY

Present day

WORK THAT DAY was steady. Marnie and Pete had to, once again, escort a group of people off the premises who were making true crime videos. One woman claimed to be a "big time" YouTuber who wanted to interview people about my sister's case. She had also demanded to speak to me. I was happy to tell her that if she wasn't a paying guest she was trespassing.

The fervor around my sister's case was reaching a fevered pitch. I couldn't escape it. Coverage and speculation were everywhere. Every time I logged on to one of my social media accounts, I saw people I knew talking about it. I even saw shared posts from the other missing girls' families. Seeing those was particularly distressing.

People were picking through every unsolved disappearance and murder that had occurred in North Carolina in the nineties. Some of the more interesting theories revolved around an as-yet-unnamed serial killer—someone who had operated in the area and had avoided apprehension. Considering how ineffectual the police had been, it wasn't the most outlandish possibility out there.

The problem was that in the excitement to hash out every detail, everyone seemed to forget that there were real people impacted by it. These people were far removed from the events they were obsessing over. For them, it was like an online game of Clue. It was easy to lose sight of the humanity of those involved in an effort to feel part of a community that seemed, on the surface, to have good intentions—to solve a decades-old unsolved case.

I was even having to field emails to the Monarch's business account. Thankfully, the owners were understanding, but it made me incredibly uncomfortable.

On top of that, I worried that all of the attention would muddy the waters and complicate things for the investigators.

So, I was thankful to be buried in paperwork. It felt good to get lost in it and forget about the case, and everything surrounding it, for a few hours.

However, I was brought back to reality later that night when Ryan came to the front desk and I realized how quickly the day had gone.

Marnie appeared in the doorway, knocking lightly, her smile, as always, apologetic.

"There's a guest out front for you. It's the man from last week. He says he'll wait for you outside." Marnie looked as if she wanted to ask me a dozen questions, but she was far too polite to do so.

I looked at the clock on my desk—it was six thirty on the dot. I found it endearing that he was right on time.

I closed my laptop and stood up, grabbing my purse and phone as I headed to the door. I took my jacket off the hook and slipped it on.

Outside I found Ryan waiting. Once he caught sight of me, his smile widened appreciatively. "You look amazing," he commented. I was only wearing my work clothes—a black pencil skirt, white blouse, and flats—but he made me feel like a beauty queen. Receiving his compliments was starting to become addictive.

"Thanks," I said a little awkwardly.

"Hungry?" he asked.

"Starving," I replied as we started down the sidewalk.

Ryan fell in step beside me. "Me too. This hotel is great, but it's still hard being cooped up inside all day."

"We can take a walk through the park, it's really pretty at night, and there should be some food stalls still open."

"Sounds perfect," Ryan readily agreed.

We crossed the street to the large park and I guided him down a winding path toward a grove of trees. It was a chilly evening, so I zipped up my coat and shoved my hands deep in my pockets.

"I've been working on my article since first thing this morning," Ryan told me as he rubbed his hands together to stay warm, "I hadn't realized how cold it had gotten."

"Yeah, but the fresh air is nice." My stomach flipped with nervousness at being near him again, and I knew I needed to keep myself in check. But for once I pushed away my misgivings and had to trust what my instincts were telling me. That Ryan was a decent guy and I could trust him.

"Are we really talking about the weather?" he asked playfully. "If so, this isn't going well for me." He fake-winced and I found myself laughing.

I had thought of little else but Ryan since meeting with him at the coffee shop. I still wondered if I was being foolish in how quickly I was coming to enjoy his company—and to tentatively trust him. But I couldn't deny how good it felt being around him. How he gave me permission to just be *me*. And that was a feeling I hadn't realized I was missing so badly.

Yes, I wanted to learn more about my sister, but I was also figuring out a little bit about myself, too, which I hadn't expected.

"You're doing fine. More than fine," I told him. My cheeks heated, despite the cold. I kept my eyes in front of us, too embarrassed to look directly at him. I had never been this bold before, particularly with a man I barely knew.

"That's good to know," Ryan replied. "So, food . . ."

"You're going to want one of Stan's Burgers. They're the best around," I suggested, seeing the food stall on the path ahead.

We made our way over and placed our orders.

"Don't wait for me," Ryan said, seeing my eagerness and, not needing any encouragement, I took a huge bite of my burger.

"I was hungrier than I thought," I chuckled sheepishly, wiping my mouth with a napkin.

I was already halfway finished when Ryan handed me a coffee. "One mocha latte for the sweet tooth."

I smiled. I couldn't help it. I liked how he cataloged details away, making note of things that to others wouldn't have mattered. He was observant. And empathic. He was good at making me feel special. A nasty voice in the back of my mind warned that it was all an act, but I hoped that my common sense was right and that he was as honest as he came across.

We walked slowly down a cobbled path, eating in silence. It felt comfortable and not at all awkward.

"It's nice here," Ryan observed.

Even at night the park was pretty, with neat planters and clean flower beds. Old-fashioned bulb-shaped lights were strung between the streetlamps and wrapped around the wooden bandstand in the middle of a clearing of trees.

"Starting in June, the hotel puts on a summer concert series. We hire local up-and-coming bands to perform every Friday evening." I indicated the gazebo-like structure. "It's become a huge tourist attraction. People come from all over. We've had some bands that have gone on to become pretty big names."

"That sounds like fun," Ryan said.

"It is. It's a nice change from how things used to be. At one time, this town was a tourist's dead end. It's taken a lot of work to claw back from that and to turn this into a place people want to go." I finished my burger and balled up the wrapper, throwing it into the nearest trash can.

As I sipped on my coffee, my phone rang. I fished it out of my purse and saw my mom's name. For the first time I felt annoyed at her checking up on me. She called at least once during my shifts. I knew it was something born out of uncontrollable anxiety. I never blamed her for it and it had never bothered me.

Until now.

I switched the phone to silent. I only had twenty minutes before I needed to get back. I would call her then. I was already anticipating the earful I'd receive for not answering, but right now, I didn't care.

"Another reporter?" Ryan questioned.

We sat down on the nearest bench, sitting close enough that our arms pressed against each other.

"Not this time. It was my mom. She always calls to check I'm at work. Or at home. Or wherever I'm supposed to be." I cringed at how that sounded.

"She worries. It's understandable." Again there was no judgment.

He was right, it *was* understandable. It made me feel like a bad daughter for being irritated by her.

"So, listen," Ryan began, thankfully not prying any further into my relationship with my mother. "I was typing some of my notes today, and something came up that I wanted to ask you about."

"Off the record?" I asked.

Ryan looked at me uncertainly. "Does it have to be?"

"Depends on what you ask."

He paused for only a second before answering. "I guess that's fair. I want you to trust me, Lindsey." He sounded so sincere.

"Okay then, what is it?"

"Have you ever heard the name Dr. Clement Daniels?"

I shook my head. "No. I don't think so. Who is he?"

"He was a professor at Southern State University at the time Jess went there. He's retired now," Ryan explained.

"Okay . . ." My stomach twisted into knots in anticipation.

"It was common knowledge that he had multiple affairs with students. Including Tammy Estep." Ryan looked at me closely. "Remember, she was the RA in Jess's dorm."

"Right, I remember," I said.

Ryan's eyes narrowed. "He was questioned about Tammy's disappearance. By the time the local police department became involved, weeks had passed since she was last seen. And the lead investigator was useless. They dismissed Dr. Daniels as a potential suspect almost as quickly as his name entered the conversation, but everyone knows the college had a huge hand in that. They work hard to protect their reputation, and that includes the reputations of their faculty. I have sources at the school who said the president back then, Dr. Hamilton, made sure the police met nothing but dead ends."

He sounded frustrated and I could see why. If the police had been more proactive, things probably wouldn't have been overlooked. One only had to look at the recent discovery of the remains at Doll's Eye Lake. Police ineptitude was everywhere you turned. I knew the department claimed their hands had been tied because an official report wasn't made about Tammy until she was gone for weeks, yet no one can deny that it was their sloppy investigative work that was the greatest failure in these cases.

"What does this have to do with Jess?" I asked. I had never heard of Dr. Daniels. Mom and Dad had never mentioned her taking a class with him.

Ryan picked at his thumb nail. "I know for a fact that Dr. Daniels was also seeing Phoebe."

"How are you so sure?"

"A journalist never reveals their sources, remember?" He flashed his oh-so-appealing smile before becoming serious again. "Did you know she was a friend of Jess's?"

My entire body froze. "Jess knew Phoebe, too?" It came out as a broken whisper.

"They were both pledging the Pi Gamma Delta sorority. From all accounts, they got along."

"That's got to mean something right? That Jess was connected to not only Tammy, but Phoebe as well?"

"It may mean something or it may mean nothing at all. It's a small college after all. People's paths overlap constantly. But aside from that, we can't overlook the fact that all these women went missing around the same time and no one did anything about it. One disappearance would have been awful. Four is a damn tragedy."

Ryan was watching me closely.

I didn't want to ask my next question, but knew I had to. "Was Jess seeing Dr. Daniels, too?"

"Jess audited one of his statistics classes during that spring semester. And yes, there were questions about what else was going on between the two of them," Ryan said almost angrily.

"I find that difficult to believe. I can't imagine Jess getting involved with her teacher—"

Ryan's expression hardened. "People have secrets, Lindsey. We don't always know everything that's going on with them."

I was taken aback by his harsh tone, but wondered if I'd misinterpreted it. "Sure. I get that. But from everything I know about my sister she wasn't that kind of person."

Ryan looked away. "That you know of." He was quiet for a beat before continuing. "But maybe you're right. I hope so, anyway."

I instinctively disagreed with Ryan's assessment of Jess and her potential relationship with her professor. Everything I'd ever learned about her was that she was studious, hard-working and had a lot of friends. Thinking of her with an older man—one of her teachers no less—didn't fit the image I had of her. But what did I really know of her?

"So the police never made Dr. Daniels a person of interest?" I asked, trying to shake the strangeness I was feeling.

Ryan shook his head. "There was nothing tying him to any of the girls but rumor and speculation. He was a respected member of the faculty. He was close to being tenured. No one could believe he would prey on his students. People are willfully blind if it's something they don't want to believe. Because of that, the police barely questioned him. And no one wanted to think he could be a killer."

There he said it.

This wasn't a case of missing women.

This was a case of *murdered* women.

"But I've been working on getting someone on the inside to talk to me. Okay, maybe I've been hounding them, but I think they're about ready to spill. And I think they have the information I've—*we've*—been looking for."

"That's good. Hopefully we can get some concrete answers." I felt impatient. I wanted to knock the door down and blow this thing open *now*.

"And get this, apparently Dr. Daniels left his previous teaching job pretty quickly. He taught at a small community college in Tennessee before coming to Southern State. He was only there for a year before he uprooted his family and came to Mt. Randall. I dug into it, but on paper, there's nothing I could find that says why he left. But, I drove there, had a poke around, talked to a couple of people who are still around from the nineties, and it seems there were rumors at that school as well."

"About him with his students?"

Ryan nodded curtly. "Yep. But it seemed that the administration was less inclined to turn a blind eye than Southern State." He picked at his thumbnail, clearly agitated. "One man said it was thought that Dr. Daniels was asked to resign to avoid charges being filed against him. One day he came into work, spoke briefly with the college president, then packed up his stuff and left without talking to anyone. That same week he left the community college, sold his house to a family friend, and got out of Dodge. He resurfaced a few months later when he was hired at Southern State University. It was clear he moved his wife and kids two hundred miles to get away from something." His eyes met mine.

My head was buzzing. "It's not enough though, is it?" I asked. Ryan shook his head.

"It's only hearsay. It doesn't actually prove anything."

"But it at least shows that this guy should be looked at a little more closely" I argued.

"That's true, but it's not enough to press charges. It's not even enough to get a warrant to search his house, that's for sure," Ryan reasoned.

I balled my hands into fists. "But it can't be a coincidence. Anyone with half a brain can see that." The burger I'd eaten churned in my gut.

"It doesn't matter how it looks. It only matters what can be proved," Ryan countered. "After all these years the police are going to be careful in how they handle this. And right now, there doesn't appear to be any evidence to tie anyone to those missing women. Someone knows what they did and they got away with it."

"But the body that was found may be the key. Maybe they've uncovered something that will finally bring that scum to justice." I sounded desperate, probably because I was.

Ryan looked away from me, staring at some point off in the distance. "My sources say there's nothing. Not a scrap of suspect DNA. Only an old blanket, and even that doesn't appear to hold any clues."

I briefly closed my eyes in anguish and frustration. Eventually, I opened them, feeling the sting of angry tears. "So we're back to where we started. With nothing."

Ryan's face was expressionless. "I need to get my inside source to talk." He threw his coffee cup into the trash can next to us. "I'm hoping that by hearing more about the case and the evidence, then perhaps I can find something that points to Dr. Daniels hurting Jess—hurting all of them." He sounded slightly frantic.

"So, that's what you think happened? That he hurt her? Hurt all those women?" I asked.

Ryan seemed sure of himself. "Yes, Lindsey, that's exactly what I think happened. I think Dr. Daniels wanted Jess. She was this beautiful, intelligent girl and he couldn't help himself. And I'm going to prove it if it's the last thing I do."

"What about the idea that it's an anonymous killer who decided to make Mt. Randall his hunting ground?" I asked.

Ryan appeared to not hear me. He was too lost in his theories and conjecture. He seemed to have a one-track mind when it came to who he thought was responsible for Jess's disappearance.

Then a thought came to me. "We have a couple of boxes of her college stuff at home. I'll have a look through it, see if there's anything of importance. I'm sure the police have combed through it already, but if they weren't looking for something that ties her to the other girls or to this professor, they likely would have missed it."

Ryan's eyes lit up. "That would be great, Lindsey. Maybe you could bring them to me and we'll look through it together. They say two sets of eyes are better than one." He seemed to barely be able to contain his excitement. But then his face darkened into something dangerous. "It's not fair. He's still happily going about his life and living in his big, beautiful house with his sweet, unsuspecting wife. If he's responsible, he's gotten away with it for decades. Hell, he could still be preying on young girls. And all because the police couldn't put A, B, and C together."

I wasn't sure why this case affected him so much, but it was obvious it did. It was his passion for finding the truth that made me believe if anyone could discover what happened to Jess, it was Ryan McKay.

"Maybe we can go and get those boxes now," he suggested eagerly. I was about to answer when his phone rang. He looked at the screen. "Sorry, I need to take this." He stood up and walked a few feet away, putting the phone to his ear.

At the same time, I felt my phone vibrating in my purse. I pulled it out, seeing Mom's name. I needed to answer it or she would really start to panic. Guilt bloomed in my chest.

"Hey, Mom."

"Lindsey, where are you? I've been trying to call you." She sounded upset, but that was to be expected.

"I'm sorry. My phone was on silent and—"

"Your dad and I got a call from Lieutenant Higgins, the lead detective on your sister's case." She sounded winded, barely able to get the words out quick enough.

I stood up, needing to move.

This was it.

"I wish they'd find her body and get it over with."

"She got the results of the DNA test." I could hear her short, uneven breaths. Her voice whispery soft as she gulped back tears.

"Is it Jess?"

I braced myself for the affirmative. I waited. Soon, after all this time, I'd be able to say the words that everyone else dreaded, yet in some twisted way, I welcomed.

Jess would no longer be missing. She would be dead.

The air felt thick and I became dizzy.

I looked over at Ryan who was pacing back and forth. Then he stopped. He glanced at me, our eyes locking. He spoke words I couldn't hear from this distance. His face was a mixture of emotions I couldn't quite place.

What was going on?

"Lindsey," Mom cried, and I sucked in a breath, "it's not her. It's not my baby girl."

I didn't know what she said next. The phone fell from my hand and I squeezed my eyes closed.

It wasn't Jess.

There was relief. But also so much anguish.

It wasn't Jess.

I felt Ryan beside me. He cupped my face between his hands, his eyes bright. Was he holding back tears, too?

"It's not Jess," I choked out.

"I know. I just heard," Ryan said softly, pressing his forehead to mine.

I stood there for a few minutes, needing his presence, then I realized what he'd said. I took a step away from him and he dropped his hands.

"What do you mean you just heard? How do you know?"

"I have sources, remember. It comes with being a reporter for the past decade." He was unapologetic. "That was my guy in the police department. He could lose his job telling me this stuff, but we go way back. He and I were in the same fraternity in college. You know, brotherhood and all that." He gave me a wry smile. "He told me that the DNA report came in and it said with 100% certainty that the remains at Doll's Eye Lake aren't Jess's." He seemed relieved.

"Do they know who it is?" I asked.

Ryan narrowed his eyes. "It's Tammy."

We stared at each other, taking in the news.

"They found Tammy Estep."

ATLANTIC COAST GAZETTE

Wednesday, December 9, 1998   Mt. Randall's Place for News $1.50

Another Girl Missing at Local College

By: Regina Stanley

Southern State University Admission Guide

It has been almost six weeks since Tammy Estep, 20, went missing. Her disppearance, at the time, was not treated as suspicious. Her friends told authorities that she had planned to follow the popular touring band, Widespread Panic, as they traveled the east coast. As a result, no one questioned her disappearance until last week, when Phoebe Baker, 18, also went missing.

Both girls have been described as reliable and academically minded. Yet, rumors have been circulating among students at Southern State University in Mt. Randall, North Carolina, about the girls' relationship with a reputable member of staff.

However, the administration at the small, yet elite university, have been quick to quash these stories. "There's no proof of these outlandish allegations," Dr. Hamilton, president of Southern State, told reporters on Friday. "Our staff have spotless reputations. The professor at the heart of these unfounded allegations, is a highly respected teacher. He's well regarded by his colleagues and students. We, at Southern State University, are committed to providing a safe environment for our students and are working closely with local authorities to locate the missing girls."

7

JESSICA

December 1998

THE CAMPUS WAS in chaos.

For most, it had to do with the impending Christmas break.

For others, for the terrified and the gossips, it had everything to do with the fact that another girl had gone missing. And it was harder to say this one was a runaway.

Whispered rumors were everywhere. A very real fear had taken hold and no one could shake free from it.

People were beginning to suspect that something dangerous was lurking out there.

I didn't feel this same level of panic, but a paranoia *had* gripped me. I looked over my shoulder. I checked every deep shadow. I felt eyes on me, even when I was careful. I couldn't escape the feeling I was being watched.

My life careened recklessly and I couldn't stop myself from driving head first toward the very obvious brick wall.

I was having the time of my life, and this thread of darkness was bleeding into everything. I hated it.

People realized something might be wrong when Phoebe missed our weekly pledge meeting.

"Someone call her room," Erica suggested with irritation. We had been waiting twenty minutes for her to show up.

"Why are we waiting on Phoebe anyway? We can start without her," I proposed, looking at the other girls.

"Because we're supposed to hold pledge elections, that's why. We need all of us here," Erica snapped.

We were meeting in the lounge of Westwood, since several of us lived there and it had the most comfortable couches. Phoebe lived in Marion, another women-only dorm on the other side of campus.

"I'll call," Daisy offered, picking up the receiver of the phone on the wall. She waited a few minutes before hanging up. "She's not answering."

"Where the hell could she be?" Erica demanded. "It's not like she has a life."

"I wouldn't say *that* . . ." Blair piped up, clearly wanting to share something she knew.

Tina was the first one to bite. "What do you mean?"

"So, a couple of weeks ago, I had to pick up some notes from a class I missed. Phoebe said I could copy hers. I didn't tell her when I'd be by, but thought I'd pop over after hitting the gym," Blair began. Everyone listened in rapt attention.

I felt bile churn in my stomach, wishing I could think of something to say to stop her. I didn't want to hear what she was going to say.

"Guys, I don't think we should be talking about her—" I tried to tell them, but Blair cut me off.

"I knocked on the door. It took forever for her to answer and when she did, she had clearly thrown her clothes on in a hurry. She was all flustered and practically shoved the notes in my hand. But before she could close the door I saw a man in her room." Blair looked around at all of us, her eyes wide with excitement at sharing a juicy story.

"Who was it?" Daisy asked.

"I swear it was Dr. Daniels," Blair announced. All the girls gasped in salacious glee and obvious shock at the revelation.

"No way." Erica snorted.

"That's pretty ballsy if it was him—to get a booty call in a freshman dorm in the middle of the day," Tina piped up doubtfully.

"Maybe he gets off on the thrill of almost getting caught. Wouldn't be the first dirtbag to think that way," Blair argued.

Melissa Voss, another pledge, smirked. "Are you seriously saying that Phoebe was knocking boots with a professor? Have you *met* our pledge sister?"

"If this was a couple of weeks ago. Why didn't you say something before?" Tina raised an eyebrow skeptically.

Blair drew herself upright with indignation. "Because, unlike the rest of you, I'm not a gossip. I don't spread stuff around that could get someone in trouble."

"Yet you're telling us now," Erica deadpanned.

"Because . . . because we don't know where she is and she might be with him," Blair sputtered.

Daisy rolled her eyes. "I call bullshit. There's no way our little Phoebes would screw a married professor. That was more Tammy's MO. That's the same professor she was banging." There was a murmur of agreement.

"Girls like Phoebe and Tammy like the attention," I found myself saying, with a hint of distaste, annoyed by the whole situation. I shouldn't have said anything. It was best to keep my mouth shut and my opinions to myself, but I couldn't stop the words once they started tumbling out.

"Sure, who doesn't?" Daisy giggled, and a few others laughed with her. She threw her arm around me and gave me a sideways hug.

I shrugged her off after a moment with a pained smile. "Yeah, I guess so." There was more I wanted to say, but I didn't dare. Some thoughts were best kept locked up tight.

Nothing else was said about Phoebe and after a few more minutes we voted without her.

* * *

Sometimes I called just to hear him tell me I can do this. That mistakes happen and, together, we would fix them.

We had always been a team. Stronger together.

He was my loudest cheerleader. My best friend.

I needed his reassurance that it would all be okay.

I clung to his assertions like they were a life raft. I waited for the day I no longer needed them.

I was growing up. Forging my own path. Eventually, our roads would diverge. I knew he dreaded it as much as I did.

So, for now I called him. And he was always there, as he promised.

It was a pact made with love and tears.

* * *

Five days later, Phoebe was officially pronounced a missing person.

Unlike with Tammy, her parents immediately demanded action from the local police department. This was treated as a potential crime from the moment her family was made aware of her disappearance.

I didn't know who called them, but I assumed it was her roommate. All of the Pi Gamma pledges were interviewed by the police in the weeks leading up to Christmas break, but none of us really knew anything, only gossip.

I was currently nursing a major hangover from a party at the Kappa Epsilon house last night. It had started with some serious pregaming before the Southern State men's basketball game against Central Carolina and ended with me doing my first keg stand.

* * *

"Chug! Chug! Chug! Chug!" The mob around me chanted. They sounded crazed, and I should have been frightened by the intensity of their cheering and screaming, but I wasn't. I relished it.

I swallowed the last of my beer and tipped the red cup upside down on my head. I felt a couple of drips of warm beer trail down the side of my face as I licked my lips and pumped my fists victoriously.

I grinned as someone took a picture, the flash momentarily blinding me. "I want a copy of that," I slurred to the girl holding the camera.

The Phi Lam guy I had been having the contest with threw his cup down in annoyance and stormed away, pushing his way through the crowd in frustration. The crowd cheered louder.

I grinned and tossed my cup into the air, not caring where it landed, and then a pair of large, strong arms snaked around my waist, holding me tightly before picking me up and spinning me around. The world blurred as I squealed happily. When I was put back down, I swayed from side to side, unsure if I was going to puke or not. I had never been that drunk before. Everything felt vaguely off kilter. Like I was watching a movie of my life rather than living it.

"Ever done a keg stand?" someone asked. I shook my head, my sweaty hair sticking to my forehead.

"Alright, come on then." A guy grabbed my hand and dragged me to the other side of the fraternity house's basement, where the kegs were. The guy, who wasn't nearly as cute as the boy from Sigma Kap that I met a few weeks ago, leaned in close. "I never knew you were such a party animal. It looks good on you." His eyes were heated and I felt a stirring low in my gut. It felt a lot like power.

I wasn't sure if I imagined him kissing my neck, but I shuddered all the same. I knew that this wasn't me, not really. And somewhere, deep down, the old Jess was shouting at me to stop. That I was ruining everything.

It was time for her to shut up for good.

"Lift me up," I murmured, giving the guy a seductive smile.

He let out a whoop and then he and one of his brothers hoisted me upside down over the keg nozzle.

Afterward everyone wanted to talk to me—to hang out with me. I was the life of the party. And it felt amazing.

* * *

It was the first time I stayed out later than Daisy, who was already asleep by the time I came home. Too drunk to get undressed, I fell asleep on top of my covers. I slept through my alarm, missing my first two classes.

Daisy seemed shocked when she found me still in bed after returning from class at lunchtime. She forced me to go with her to get something to eat, though the thought of food made me want to throw up.

"I told them she was sleeping with Dr. Daniels," Daisy announced, sipping on her cranberry juice. The Commons was busy and we were sitting together in our usual spot in the middle of the cafeteria. Only this time, one of the chairs was empty.

The silence of Phoebe's absence was ten times louder than her presence ever had been.

"I did, too," Blair said. Erica and the others all nodded.

"They needed to know. Because that's two missing girls who were screwing Dr. Handsy and he should be held accountable," Daisy stated and I was glad she'd told them.

"They're probably dead," Tina announced without an ounce of sensitivity.

Erica glared at our pledge sister. "You can't go around saying something like that, Tina. If the police thought they were dead, there would be a full-blown investigation or something."

Tina looked contrite. "Well, I know they took him in for questioning."

"They questioned us, too, stupid," Erica scoffed. Now fully chastised, Tina shut her mouth.

"It's scary, though, right?" Daisy put down her empty carton of juice and looked serious. "I mean, if he did hurt them . . ."

"I can't see it. He's practically an old man!" Blair mocked.

"He's not *that* old," Tina countered. "But, yeah, it's pretty scary. It goes to show you can't trust men."

"Especially good-looking, middle-aged professors." Tina chuckled, stopping abruptly when Erica glared at her again. "Sorry."

"But what if it's not Dr. Daniels. What if . . ." Daisy paused, a look of pure terror on her face.

"What, Daisy?" Blair whispered. Everyone was on a fearful alert.

"What if it's . . . someone else? Someone watching and waiting for us?" There was a collective intake of air.

Not this again.

My head was pounding and this was the last thing I wanted to listen to.

"Come on, Daisy, be real. There's no one out there preying on college coeds. I think seeing *Scream* so many times has
gone to your head," I laughed. There was a hard edge to my
voice that everyone seemed surprised by.

"Yeah, who's to say anything happened to them?" Tina
agreed, eager, like me, to put this nastiness out of our minds.

Daisy didn't seem convinced. "I don't know . . . things
aren't making sense. Especially with Phoebe . . ."

I felt the room closing in around me. The drone of voices
buzzed like flies in my ears. I needed to get up. I needed to
move. My skin was slick with sweat from the alcohol that was
trying to leave my system.

"Seriously, that's enough, Daisy!" I snapped. At my
roommate's shocked—and hurt—expression, I forced myself
to calm down. "Stop freaking everyone out, okay? It's not
cool. Go to the health office if you need to talk to
someone."

Erica whistled under her breath and I knew I had crossed
a line. Daisy wouldn't meet my eyes. I had never spoken to
her—or *anyone*—like that.

"Daisy, I'm sorry. I didn't mean it. I'm just hungover—"
I started to say, but she waved a hand, cutting me off.

Daisy's smile was a little wobbly as she addressed the
other girls. "Sorry, guys. I didn't mean to go all conspiracy
theorist on you."

She glanced at me, her face troubled. I had to fix this, but
my headache and nausea, which wasn't entirely from my
hangover, kept me from saying anything.

I stood, needing some space from everything. "I'm going
to get a coffee. Anyone want anything?" I glanced at my
roommate. "Daisy? Can I get you something? My treat."

Would she take the olive branch I was extending?

"Uh, yeah, can you grab me another cranberry juice?"
Daisy asked a little more normally.

"Of course." I felt a wave of relief and gave her arm a
squeeze. "I know all this stuff about Tammy and Phoebe is
worrying," I said softly, "but I really don't think we have anything to be concerned about. It's not like any of us are

sleeping around with married men, right?" I straightened and grinned at my pledge sisters, most of whom giggled and smiled back.

"No, thank you. There's plenty of hot, *single* men on campus to focus on," Blair said, flipping her hair over her shoulder.

Then the conversation changed and everyone was rating the hottest frat guys. It didn't take much for them to forget Tammy and Phoebe. To forget the very real pall of dread that had descended over everything.

I hurried to get in line, standing behind a guy with familiar bleached-blonde streaks in his dark hair. As if sensing me, he turned around, our eyes meeting. There was instant recognition.

"You," he breathed, his full lips spreading into a contagious smile.

I found myself grinning back, thoughts of Phoebe and Daisy's constant suspicions gone for the moment. "Hey, stranger."

"I've been asking everyone about you. You're a hard woman to find," he grumbled good-naturedly.

"You must not have tried very hard. You knew I was a pledge at Pi Gamma Delta," I teased.

We moved toward the front of the line. I filled a to-go cup with coffee and Mr. Cute grabbed a tray. "I swear, I've asked around. My brothers have been no help. I was about to start knocking on every door in Westwood."

"That would have pissed a few people off," I laughed.

He took a hamburger and two slices of chocolate cake. The smell of the food made my stomach roil.

"You're looking a little green around the gills. You okay?" he asked.

"Keg stands on a Wednesday night seemed like a good idea at the time," I groaned.

"We've all been there." He snapped his fingers. "That was you? I heard about the hot chick doing keg stands at the Phi Lam house last night."

I flushed with delight. "Oh, you heard about that?"

He snorted. "Every frat guy on campus is talking about how you drank Dave Lingus under the table. I have a feeling you'll be getting invites to every party until the end of the year." He reached around me and grabbed a bottle of ginger ale and handed it to me. "Trust me, you'll need this."

"Thanks," I said sincerely.

Once he reached the cash register, he handed the lady his student ID. "I'm paying for both of us."

"No, that's not necessary," I protested.

"I'm sorry, I can't hear you. What was that?" He purposefully turned away from me while he paid for my drinks. When he was done, he followed me toward the table where I had been sitting with my pledge sisters. We both stopped a few feet away.

"Can I join you guys?" he asked.

"Why?" I suddenly felt nervous.

"Because I like you and want to get to know you more," he said, uncharacteristically serious.

We stood in the middle of the busy cafeteria, and I stared up at him, at a loss as to what to say. There wasn't an ounce of shyness about him and his easy confidence was incredibly tempting. And even though I felt awful, being around him was nice.

"My name's Ryan McKay." There was that smile again. Charming and sweet.

I glanced at my friends, who weren't even trying to be discreet as they openly gaped at us. "I'm Jess."

"Just Jess?" he titled his head, his smile widening.

"Jess Fadley." I chuckled awkwardly. "So, what now? Do we shake hands? Hug?"

He waggled his eyebrows. "Make out?"

"Let's not get ahead of ourselves."

"Well, you didn't shoot me down entirely. I take that as a good sign." He leaned in close, his voice dropping to a seductive whisper. "You're giving me hope, Jess. And that's a dangerous thing."

Just the sound of his voice so close had my nerve endings on fire. I had a feeling he knew exactly what he was doing. A guy didn't look like Ryan McKay and not get what he wanted when he wanted it.

It made me feel special that he seemed to want me. And that was my catnip.

I looked over at my pledge sisters again and dreaded the inevitable interrogation if he sat with us. The endless questions, the embarrassing innuendo. I couldn't deal with all that today. The last thing I wanted was to be the source of discussion.

"I don't think sitting with us is such a great idea. You seem like a decent guy, Ryan, I can't throw you to the wolves like that."

Ryan looked disappointed. "I think I can handle myself."

"Seriously, maybe another time," I said quickly before he could move past me toward the table.

Ryan seemed to finally pick up on my hesitation. He glanced again at the table full of my friends. "Fine, but that means you have to give me a raincheck."

I felt myself relax again, glad he didn't push it. If he had, I would have inevitably backed down. I was no match for men who wanted something. "Oh yeah? Says who?"

Ryan tucked a piece of my hair behind my ear and grinned. "Says the red flush on your neck."

I rolled my eyes, but could feel my skin growing hotter. "You really are full of yourself."

"Sorry to interrupt you guys, but we have to head back to the dorm, Jess," Daisy called out, clearly trying to get my attention. I didn't want to keep her waiting, particularly after our earlier disagreement.

"I should get going."

"Can I get your number? Maybe we can go see a movie tomorrow—"

"I'm leaving to head home for Christmas break first thing in the morning," I interrupted, my insides tripping over themselves. "But . . . call me when break is over."

Ryan put his tray down and fished a piece of paper and a pen from his backpack. I hastily rattled off the number to my room. When he had written it down, he carefully folded it and put it in his pocket, patting it with a smile.

"I'm calling you as soon as we get back."

"Is that a threat?" He was so easy to talk to. He made me feel as if a regular kind of life was possible.

He leaned in close, his lips deliciously close to my own. "Only if you want it to be."

Then he walked away. And I was left flustered and full of anticipation. I hoped the feelings would last.

* * *

I traveled the normal streets that would lead me home. It would be a short journey, barely enough time to drink my coffee. I should have turned left at the light onto Meadow Lane, then right onto Franklin Boulevard.

Instead I headed straight on Plymouth Avenue, passing the old movie theater with its 1950s style marquee and the empty flower stall outside the florist. All the houses looked the same, having been built in the same cookie-cutter style sometime after the turn of the century. Pale colored siding, dark shutters, four windows, and a door at the front.

I glimpsed the same old buildings I had seen every day of my short life. The still-broken fence in front of my doctor's office that had blown down in a hurricane three years ago. The overgrown field behind my old elementary school that we used to run through after the last bell.

Plain. Small. Nondescript. Tired. Confined.

Mt. Randall was many things, not many of them good.

I glanced in my rearview mirror at Southern State University sitting proudly on top of its hill.

This town was my whole world. For better or for worse.

I kept driving until I reached the blue sign with its whimsical script. A bright red cardinal sat on the limb of a pine tree above an official goodbye.

> *'You are now leaving Mt. Randall.*
> *Come back soon!'*

I headed out of town.

Five miles later I took a hard left, down a well-worn gravel road flanked on either side by a thicket of trees. The weeds and grass had been flattened by decades worth of tires. It was a recognizable spot, yet hidden.

If you weren't from Mt. Randall, you'd never find it. But if you were from Mt. Randall, you knew it well.

My car skidded to a stop at the edge of a large meadow. The massive body of water lay still and unmoving. It wasn't quite large enough to be considered a lake, yet that's how people around here described it. In actuality though, it was a man-made reservoir that had been there for close to a hundred years.

The water was ringed by an abundance of red-berried Banberry plants, or Doll's Eyes which they were sometimes called and for which the locals named the lake. In the fall, the berries turned bright white with a black spot in the middle, making them look exactly like creepy little eyeballs. Most people had no idea the pretty plant was, in fact, incredibly poisonous.

Doll's Eye Lake was a place heavy with shadows, tucked away from the main road. It was easy to see why it had given birth to a number of urban legends over the years. Kids swore it was haunted, daring each other to venture out to the dark trees late at night, hoping to see the apparitions that supposedly lingered there.

Wailing women. Crying children. Angry men.

Anonymous specters waiting to terrify unsuspecting visitors.

And they weren't the only stories.

In Mt. Randall, adults whispered of bodies wrapped in cloth and weighed down by bricks at the bottom of Doll's Eye Lake. None—or all—of it could be true. No one knew. But the tales frightened people all the same.

Dad would bring me to the lake when I was little. We'd take our small orange paddle boat out to the center, fishing gear propped between us. He'd tell me to look into the water. He'd ask me if I could see the tops of the houses that were said to be down there.

We'd float along, our fishing lines bobbing lazily. We never caught a thing. But that wasn't the point. This was our place. Just Dad and me. Mom never came and we stopped going by the time Lindsey came along. But for a few years, it was special to us.

*   *   *

"It's too heavy," I complained, dragging my fishing pole in the dirt as I followed Dad to the edge of the lake. He immediately came over and took the yellow pole he had bought me, carrying it to the boat.

"You only have to ask for my help, Jess, and I'll always be there. I'm your own personal superhero." He lifted me up, zooming me around like an airplane, making me giggle uncontrollably.

He put me down gently in the paddleboat. "Buckle up your life preserver, sweetheart," he instructed before pushing the boat into the water and hopping inside, making it teeter precariously.

I shrieked in delighted terror. "Don't make us fall in, Daddy!"

He sat down and used his arms to balance the boat. "Better?"

He handed me my fishing pole and carefully attached the brightly colored plastic used as a lure. "It's not real is it?" I asked, peering at the fish hanging from the hook, my lower lip trembling.

He chucked under my chin. "Of course not. It's just a pretty piece of plastic," he assured me.

"What will we do if we catch a real fish? Will we have to eat it?" I sounded horrified.

"We'll throw it back into the water. I promise." Dad kissed the top of my head and I leaned into him.

"We can't take the baby fish from her daddy fish!" I exclaimed, not able to think of anything worse than a child being taken away from their father.

Dad looked at me with grave seriousness. "Absolutely not. Baby girl fishes belong with their dads."

We never caught anything. But that wasn't the point. I loved spending hours listening to my father's stories. Hearing his voice, calm and comforting. There was nowhere I'd rather be than by his side. It's where I thought I would always belong.

*   *   *

I parked my car and sat there for a time, staring out the window, trying to remember what it felt like to be young and carefree. Before life led you down ugly paths and the people you loved twisted into someone unrecognizable.

My heart started beating fast and my breathing became shallow. Tears pricked my eyes and I felt an anger that frightened me.

The wind picked up and I watched the empty branches sway. I had never been scared of Doll's Eye Lake. I never listened to the tales, and I definitely never believed them. Being at the lake made me feel at peace once upon a time. Even after I had stopped sitting in a paddleboat with my dad, I still came here. Which is why, in my bleakest hour, I came back.

The dark, still water had watched me grow up. It had stood silent witness to the steady passage of time, forever constant. It watched me shed the old Jess like a snake sheds its skin. And then it watched the new Jess emerge.

What did the dark, still water think of her?

I didn't want to know.

I hated coming here now, but I was compelled all the same. It drew me to its quiet solitude for reasons that were grim and complicated.

I caught movement out of the corner of my eye. I could see a yellow 1965 Boss 429 Mustang parked beyond the tree line. I went still, watching the car . . . waiting. Acid burned in my stomach, my ears filled with a loud sort of whooshing noise.

Why here?

Rage ripped through my insides like a wildfire. Hate and a desperate sort of love warred against each other in my heart.

I spun the silver ring on my finger, hating the cool feel of it against my skin. I suddenly ripped it off, gripping it in my fist, tempted to hurl it into the lake.

But I didn't. I shoved it in my pocket instead.

I watched the two people in the car. They were oblivious to everything but each other. They had no idea that anyone else existed.

I felt dead inside.

It was the only comfort I could take.

Ten Seconds to Vanish: The Unsolved Disappearance of Jessica Fadley

Episode 5

Stella: It's another week, babes, and we are so excited to be here, giving you more piping hot, true crime tea. I'm Stella.

Rachel: And I'm Rachel.

Stella: And this is *Ten Seconds to Vanish: The Unsolved Disappearance of Jessica Fadley*.

Theme music plays

Stella: You'll never guess who we got a message from on Insta.

Rachel: Ooh, do tell! I know some very famous people have been listening from the tweets I've read.

Stella: I know! I can't quite believe it, but it's not someone famous . . . it was actually Stephanie Baker, Phoebe Baker's sister, who messaged us. She wanted to thank us for bringing light to her sister's case.

Rachel: Aww, that's so amazing. And that, right there, is why we are doing this, isn't that right, Stel?

Stella: Absolutely. These women have been relegated to the shadows for far too long. We're going to pull their stories kicking and screaming out into the sun. And there are people who won't like that.

Rachel: What do you mean?

Stella: While the reception we've received for our podcast has been overwhelmingly positive, we do get a few messages that are little out there.

Rachel: You're talking about the *"or else"* DM.

Stella: Yes, I am. It seems that there's someone out there who isn't too happy with the focus being given to our girls. Someone who wanted to let me know that if we knew what's good for us, we'd shut up *or else*.

Rachel: It's so scary.

Stella: I mean, we have to expect messages like that. It's the modern-day prank call. But, unfortunately for them, we don't scare easily. You hear that anonymous creeper?

Rachel: Whoever you are, we're still going to tell this story. We're going to do all we can to get our girls some justice.

Stella: Well, now that we have that out of the way, let's have a little chat about sweet, studious, quiet-as-a-mouse Phoebe Baker.

Rachel: It's always the quiet ones you have to watch out for, Stel.

Stella: You're absolutely right. Because our sweet, studious Phoebe, like responsible, reliable Tammy, was shagging the same too-friendly neighborhood pervy teacher.

Rachel: Ugh, can we say his name already?

Stella: No, but I really wish we could.

8

LINDSEY

Present Day

"I UNDERSTAND THAT YOU'RE angry Mr. Fadley—"

"Don't patronize me, damn it," Dad bellowed. "We've been dealing with the police and their condescending bullshit for twenty-four years. And I'm not someone who needs to be handled. We still have no idea who you found at the lake. The papers have been plastering my daughter's name everywhere."

"As I said when I spoke to you several weeks ago, the press somehow got wind of things—"

"And how the hell did that happen?" Dad demanded. "How is it that a bunch of reporters figured out something like this before we had been told anything?"

Lead detective, Lieutenant Jane Higgins looked contrite. "That's one of the things we're looking into. We take leaks in our department very seriously." She sounded pissed off.

"Leaks?" Dad scoffed. "It's more like a fire hydrant. Though, I shouldn't be surprised. Mt. Randall's police department's ineptitude is as well known as the town's god-damned Apple Festival."

"Your daughter's case has always been taken with absolute seriousness, Mr. Fadley. I can assure you that my predecessor, Sergeant O'Neil, worked tirelessly to find Jessica. And

I will do the same. I *will* find answers." Lieutenant Higgins looked at my mother and me, her somber expression kind. I liked her, even if my dad didn't seem to. She turned back to Dad. "I told you that as soon as the DNA test and autopsy came back I would contact you and your wife, and that *is* what I did."

Lieutenant Higgins was relatively calm, despite her obvious frustration. It was her frustration that I found encouraging.

She was on the smaller side—barely five foot five and probably weighed less than 120 pounds. But she had a demeanor that commanded discipline. She reminded me of my high school gym teacher, Ms. Phelps—short and feisty. She came across like a woman who got stuff done. She had the air of someone who was tenacious and methodical. I had done some Googling after hearing she had taken over my sister's case and she had a decorated career. She had come to Mt. Randall after a decade of work in the aggravated assault unit in Raleigh. She had been awarded the Criminal Investigation Award and the Honor Award for Public Service. She had been promoted to lieutenant and for some reason, thought tiny Mt. Randall was a good place to transfer to, though I couldn't figure out why.

Things had been in chaos since Mom called me. I had gone home instead of going back to work. I had called Marnie in a daze, telling her I was sick. I felt numb and hadn't been thinking straight.

The remains weren't Jess's.

They hadn't found her.

Even though it was late, I had found Lieutenant Higgins and another officer who introduced himself as Stanley James, the Family Liaison Officer, already at the house talking to my parents.

Mom was a mixture of devastated and relieved. Dad, on the other hand, was furious. I had never seen him act like this. Dad didn't express extreme emotions. He was calm, agreeable, usually a little distant. But Jess seemed to bring out the lion in him. This was a side to my father I had never experienced before. He was normally smooth-talking and relaxed, while Mom was high-strung and overprotective.

"Mr. Fadley, I acknowledge that a lot of mistakes were made in the early days of your daughter's disappearance—"

"Hmph, that's an understatement," Dad muttered and I was a little embarrassed at how blatantly rude he was being.

Lieutenant Higgins was calm. "Precious time was lost due to delays in reporting. There was a communication breakdown between departments. The FBI should have been called in. But I can assure you, things are different now."

Dad crossed his arms, his expression unyielding. When he didn't respond, Lieutenant Higgins continued.

"We're going back to square one in terms of the search. Now that remains have been found, we need to be incredibly thorough, particularly at Baneberry Lake. The usual things like dogs and sonar equipment weren't used back then because the police were looking for a missing woman, not a murdered one," Lieutenant Higgins said gently. She appeared regretful as soon as the words left her mouth, and my mom let out an anguished wail.

I wanted to intervene. Not only because Dad seemed ready to lunge at the well-meaning lieutenant, but also because Mom was getting more and more upset. I had never been put into this position before—where I was the one who would have to keep things together. I often left it to my parents, particularly my mom, but now, they were barely functioning. I wondered if this was what it had been like twenty-four years ago. I had been kept away from this part, but I felt a twinge of déjà vu all the same.

"You police don't know your asses from your—"

"Dad, don't," I interrupted. Dad acquiesced and didn't finish what he was about to say.

"As I said, Mr. Fadley, I understand your anger. If it were me, I'd be mad as hell." Lieutenant Higgins had a soothing way about her. I could tell she had, unfortunately, been in this position a lot. I imagined speaking to a victim's family was never easy, but she handled it well. "But, please remember, I am not the officer who originally dealt with Jessica's case. And you're absolutely right about how things were handled back then. But, I assure you that I don't operate that way. Technology has come a long way since 1999. Investigative procedure too. I promise I'm doing everything I can to find your daughter."

At her words, the fight seemed to leave my dad. He sat down in his chair with a heavy sigh. He ran his hands through his hair, gripping it at the scalp as if ready to pull it from his head. He stared down at the ground, his face ashen. If possible, he looked more horrified than before.

Mom had finally stopped crying. She wiped her now red, puffy eyes and turned to the lieutenant. "Can you tell us anything at all?" she begged. "Who was it, if it wasn't Jessica? What poor soul was left out there for all this time?"

The truth sat poised on the tip of my tongue, but I held it back.

Lieutenant Higgins's face softened. "I hope you understand, Mrs. Fadley, that I'm not at liberty to disclose that information. Another family has to be notified first. What I *can* tell you is that the remains we found were 100% not your daughter's." She once again addressed my father, as if to placate him. "We have an underwater forensic team coming in from Wilmington tomorrow. They'll search Baneberry Lake with specialist sonar equipment that wasn't available twenty-four years ago. We have a team out there right now, combing the woods. If there's anything else out there, we *will* find it."

We will find *it*.

I wanted to scream.

They were talking about my sister as if she were an object. Not someone's daughter. Not someone's sister. They were speaking about Jess, as if she wasn't a person at all.

"It's Tammy Estep," I said, unable to stop myself from revealing what I already knew.

Everyone in the room turned to me in surprise. Lieutenant Higgins' eyes widened imperceptibly.

I should have shut up. I'd already said too much. I had promised Ryan I wouldn't tell anyone the things he told me. I wondered if he could get in trouble—if *I* could get in trouble. But I needed to let my parents, let Lieutenant Higgins, know that I wasn't ignorant. That I had been finding things out, too.

"It was a blow to the head that killed her, right?" I said, my voice sounding surprisingly calm even to my own ears. But I hadn't felt calm when Ryan had told me what his source had reported.

"Tammy died from blunt force trauma. There were clear fractures to the occipital bone at the base of the skull. According to the medical examiner, her head was practically caved in. Skeletal weathering and tissue markers put her date of death sometime in 1998. So she most likely died almost as soon as she went missing."

"Lindsey?" Mom said my name as a question. I realized everyone was staring at me in confusion.

"I need to know how you got that information, Miss Fadley." It was the first time that Lieutenant Higgins sounded aggravated. Her calm fractured slightly.

"I . . . I uh have my sources," I stammered, inwardly cringing at how flippant I sounded.

"Tammy's remains were found not far from Doll's Eye Lake. Her body had been buried about four feet down, wrapped in an old, plaid wool blanket. The body was badly decomposed and was little more than bones, a few scraps of tissue and fabric strands that were clothing at one time. It was pure chance that she was found. This area has seen unprecedented wet weather. There's been significant flooding and runoff into the lake. According to my source, the lieutenant in charge believes the body simply rose to the surface due to the ground being oversaturated. A couple of boys were out there fishing and one of them went to dig up some nightcrawlers to use as bait. Poor kid found a lot more than nightcrawlers."

Ryan had sounded giddy as he relayed the facts he had been given. He'd been working on this story for so many years, to finally have new information was probably thrilling for him.

"They haven't been able to find a murder weapon. But they're looking in Doll's Eye Lake itself again. I know they gave it a cursory inspection back in '99, but this time they're going to do it properly."

There wasn't time to hear anything else because I had needed to get to my family. Ryan seemed like he wanted to talk more about what all this meant. He was energized. Frantic even.

It's not Jess, Lindsey." He repeated that sentence several times, as if hardly able to believe it.

Lieutenant Higgins was angry. The vein in the middle of her forehead was standing prominent. "This is a very big problem, Miss Fadley. If someone's feeding you confidential police information, I'm going to have to insist you tell me who."

Crap, crap, crap. I was such an idiot.

"I . . . I don't know—"

"Whose Tammy Estep? What does this have to do with Jessica?" Mom interjected, her voice quivering, taking the heat off me.

I waited for Lieutenant Higgins to insist I talk to her, but she never did. The issue with how I got my information seemed to be dropped for the time being. She glanced at Stan James, and there was an unspoken communication between them.

She turned to us, her expression guarded yet determined. "I want to be straight with you, Mr. and Mrs. Fadley. There are a lot of pieces to this puzzle. We are coming at this from many different angles." She looked at my dad who was still staring at the floor, his body tense. I couldn't figure out what was going on with him. "Have you heard of the new podcast that's out right now about Jessica's case?"

Mom appeared puzzled, but I answered affirmatively. "Yes, I've listened to it."

Lieutenant Higgins looked between my mom and me. "It's great that people are invested in these cases, it helps keep pressure on to solve them. But it's getting a little wild out there. The department is dealing with a lot of crackpots who fancy themselves detectives." Lieutenant Higgins pursed her lips. "But they do highlight some interesting things. Such as the long-standing theory that Jessica's disappearance is tied to the disappearances of the other missing girls from Southern State University, Tammy included. Unfortunately, back then, the idea that the disappearances were connected was disregarded, which makes no sense to me. But that means lines of questioning weren't followed and evidence was definitely overlooked. I'm coming at this with a fresh pair of eyes, and I am finding links that investigators at the time didn't. These cases needed a modern take to view it all clearly. And I can tell you that now we've found Tammy, I believe it's only a matter of time until we find the others. It's my opinion that whoever did this put them all in the same place. And the place matters—it holds personal significance to the perpetrator. More importantly, I think that these women all had a connection, not only to each other, but to the person responsible. These aren't random crimes."

Her words came down like a hammer. Lieutenant Higgins had admitted they weren't looking for girls who were still alive. They were looking for bodies. And she expected Jessica's to be one of them. And the person who took her from us was most likely someone she knew.

"Oh my god. Ben, are you hearing this?" Mom whimpered.

Dad finally looked up, his eyes hollow, as if his soul had been sucked out of him. "Yes, I'm listening." His voice was devoid of emotion.

"You think they're all out there at the lake? Including my Jessica? That's what I told that detective back then. I knew my baby was there." Mom was getting worked up again.

Lieutenant Higgins put a hand on my mom's shoulder and it had an instant, soothing effect. "I want you to know,

Mrs. Fadley, that finding Tammy has allowed the department to put resources into these cases for the first time in decades. It's no longer a cold case. It's been moved to active status. This is good news."

Dad had gone deathly pale. "You think you can solve this?" he asked, his voice cracking.

Lieutenant Higgins gave him a kind but firm look. "I don't *think*, Mr. Fadley, I *know*."

Stan James spoke briefly to my mom, handing her a card, and telling her to call him if she needed anything. Then the two police officers walked to the door, Lieutenant Higgins opening it. A waft of cold night air blew in and I shivered.

Lieutenant Higgins looked first at me, then my mother, before her eyes settled on Dad. "As soon as I know more, I'll be in touch but, I promise you, I *will* find out what happened to your daughter."

* * *

Later, after my parents had gone to bed, I found myself standing outside my sister's bedroom.

I had promised Ryan I would go through the boxes of her stuff to see if there was anything that might have been missed. But I didn't want to take anything to him. Not yet anyway. The image of his eager demeanor when he asked if he could see Jess's things had stuck with me. And not in a good way.

So, I crept into Jess's room and pulled three large boxes from her closet. I knew, from what I overheard my parents say years ago, that police had taken possession of the stuff in her dorm room right after her disappearance. They obviously didn't think there was anything of note and so had quickly released the effects to my parents. But given how poorly they managed the case, I knew I needed to look for myself because it would only be a matter of time before Lieutenant Higgins would want them.

It felt strange being in her room. Everything was as it had been left all those years ago. Her stuffed toys were still on her bed, her clothes still hung in the closet, now out of fashion and moth-eaten. Her books were still lined up on the shelf waiting for someone to read them again. Everything remained, and would remain, untouched.

Given how obsessed I had always been with the sister I barely remembered, it would have been so easy to cross the hall and enter her sanctum in order to learn everything I yearned to know. Yet I had only ever dared a handful of times. It felt wrong to invade her space when she was no longer around to allow or deny it. It felt like wandering into a sacred space, not to be disrupted. As if the room were sleeping, on the verge of waking up. And there was a presence there that never went away. It disturbed me.

I went in, stopping once I reached the middle of the room, almost too frightened to move.

Panic unfurled in my gut and I felt a cold breeze on my bare arms even though the windows were closed.

There was rustling from somewhere followed by what sounded like something moving around in the closet. What was it? A mouse? Somehow the idea of a rodent was more appealing than the alternative.

And what was the alternative? That my sister's room was haunted?

I wanted to laugh at the ludicrousness of the idea, but I couldn't. Because right then, I swore I caught the cloying scent of jasmine in the air.

A gasp caught in my throat as the door slammed shut behind me and I jumped. I rushed over and pulled it back open, not wanting to be shut inside.

Wide-eyed with dread, I stood on the threshold, staring out into the silent hallway, willing myself to calm down. I was being ridiculous.

Taking a steadying breath, I turned and faced Jess's room once again, giving myself a mental pep talk. I crossed the floor and turned on the bedside lamp. The filtered hazy pink light from the lamp shade made the shadows even deeper, but I didn't dare turn on the ceiling light for fear of waking my parents up.

I forced myself to focus on what I came in here for and got to work. After a while, I realized searching through Jess's things was futile. I hadn't found anything that seemed to hold a clue as to what happened to her.

I was about ready to give up when I discovered a small photo album at the bottom of the last box. Given how scarce pictures of my sister were, I pounced on it immediately.

I sat down on her bed, flipping through the pages of the small, fabric-bound book, seeing pictures of Jess posing with women I presumed were from Southern State. Blurry photos of dim dorm rooms and the sunlit quad in the middle of campus. Pictures of a group of laughing girls laid out on the grass.

There was a photograph of Jess in a short cocktail dress, her dark hair layered around her face. Her arm was slung around a pretty girl with beautiful bronze blonde hair.

I didn't quite know how to feel seeing proof of my sister's life. My eyes stung and I blinked away tears, feeling incredibly emotional. Jess looked happy, though at times, I noticed, her smile didn't quite reach her eyes. And there was a tension about her features that was at odds with the laid-back nature of the friends beside her.

Toward the back, there were other photographs. Ones of our family. These were pictures I had never seen before. There were several of me as a little girl, staring up at my big sister with wide, adoring eyes. I struggled to breathe around the lump that had formed in my throat. It was clear that Jess and I loved each other. No one could doubt that by seeing how she held me close and how I hugged her tight. I wished so much that I could remember her better.

I turned the pages, finding photos of random things that must have mattered to Jess. There was a teddy bear on a swing, a tree, a flower. Then there was a close-up of my dad. It was so close I could see the tiny flecks in his brown eyes.

There were so many pictures of my dad.

Even more of my dad *with* Jess.

Mostly, they were from around our house. Simple captures of simple times. There was one of Jess eating a huge ice cream sundae at Carina's Custard Stand downtown. It had been a Mt. Randall institution, only closing a few years ago. I knew that my sister had loved Carina's hot fudge brownies and dad would take her frequently. I only knew this because my paternal grandmother made a comment about it once before she died. She asked me if Dad took me to Carina's Custard, too, and I didn't know what to say. Because no, he had never taken me.

There were a few that were taken at Doll's Eye Lake, Jess holding a fishing pole, with an excited smile, an orange paddleboat bobbing in the water behind her. I knew she and Dad used to spend hours out on that boat when Jess was little. Mom said once, as if by accident, that it was their "special time."

After Jess went missing, I had been desperate to go fishing with my dad. To spend time with him. I wanted to paddle out to the middle of the lake like he had done with my sister a hundred times. I begged him. I had even cried. But he always refused. Mom scolded me, saying it made him too sad to go back there and to stop bothering him about it. So I never mentioned the boat, or going fishing, ever again. And now his boat—*their boat*—stayed in the garage, rusting beneath an old blue tarp.

Once, when I was around fourteen, Dad had been working late and Mom had too much to drink, she told me how inseparable Jess and Dad had been. I knew, on some level, that their connection had been deep. It was the way his face crumpled at the smallest mention of my sister. It was how he hardly ever came to the end of the house where my room, and Jess's, were. Sometimes he'd stand at one end of the hallway, his body sagging, as if he desperately wanted to venture there, but couldn't make himself.

And it was in the way that he loved me—a superficial kind of affection—never the deep, abiding tenderness I longed for from my father. In some ways, it felt like he was too scared to love me fully in case something happened to me, too. Or at least that's what I told myself.

Mom said they were always together, at least up until Jess went to college. She blubbered that that had been when everything changed. Jess stopped calling home. She refused to see Dad. Mom said she changed almost from the moment she moved into her dorm. She only came home briefly from time to time. And when she did, she'd go up to her room for a while and then leave without saying anything. That's why it was such a pleasant surprise when Jess announced she was coming home for my sixth birthday.

She whispered, her words slurring, "Your father has never gotten over her rejection. He wouldn't say it, but Jess destroyed him. She broke his heart. He's never been the same since she went missing. He took it personally. Like he should have saved her. Like it was all his fault she was gone."

She had passed out soon after that and it was the last time she ever dared mention Jess and her relationship with Dad.

I hated to admit that hearing confirmation of the bond between Jess and Dad had made me jealous. I wanted what they'd had. I wanted the fishing trips and Carina's hot fudge brownies. During my preteen years, I tried to build that same kind of relationship with him. But it wasn't the same. Sure, he always told me he loved me. He dutifully came to my school plays and attended every parent/teacher night, but there was a distance that I could never bridge. It felt as if he was doing what was expected of a father, rather than out of any real desire for closeness. We never had anything that was only for us like he'd had with Jess. We didn't have special trips or inside jokes. On paper, we looked the part, but scratch the surface and there was nothing really there.

Jess and Dad had been so much more, and it was hard knowing I'd never have it. In many ways, I never felt good enough because I wasn't *her*. His perfect Jess.

So, I forced myself to focus on the good stuff. To find a way to enjoy the relationship we *did* have, even if it lacked substance. But it was difficult. The jealousy, the feeling of inadequacy, was always there in the back of my mind. And it didn't stop me from missing what I could have had if it weren't for my sister.

Dad loved me in his own way, but it was more than obvious as the years went by that it wasn't as much as he loved Jess.

I closed the photo album, not finding anything but heartache in its pages. Yet I couldn't help but feel I was missing something. It was driving me nuts.

I put the tiny book in the box and started to lug it back into the closet.

I shoved it into the farthest corner. One of them—the heaviest box—hit the wall with a hollow thud.

"What the—?"

I dropped to my knees and pulled the box back out of the way. I lightly tapped the wall, searching for the hollow sound. I knocked a little lower until I heard the sound again. There was a definite void behind the drywall. I knelt closer, noticing a small square cut out, barely visible to the naked eye, as it blended in with the rest of the wall.

Using my fingernail, I ran it along the grooves and slowly pried a thin piece of drywall away, revealing a small cavity.

"Jessie, you sneaky girl."

I turned on the flashlight on my phone and peered inside. There wasn't much, only a small pile of papers. I pulled them out. Then, sitting on the floor of Jess's closet, I looked through them.

On top was a faded printout of what must have been Jess's classes at Southern State. Next to them were grades. The report was dated December 12, 1998. It seemed my academic, straight-A sister was struggling to get Cs and Ds. She was even failing her English class. There was also a letter from Pi Gamma Delta dated March 14, 1999, stating she was on suspension because of her low GPA and she was no longer an active pledge. There was another letter dated the following month from the administrator's office informing her that she had a scheduled meeting to discuss her academic probation.

I put the report and the letters aside and saw a receipt from the registrar's office. According to the slip of paper, she had audited Introduction to Statistics for the spring semester of 1999. I looked at the professor's name and felt my stomach drop.

"Dr. Clement Daniels," I whispered.

That was the name of the professor Ryan had said was involved with the other missing women. The same professor who, it looked like, had taught Jess statistics. Seeing his name among my sister's secret things felt uncomfortable. My heart started to pound as I went through the rest of the items that had been hidden away.

There were tons of pictures. I didn't understand at first why she hadn't put these in her photo album until I realized what I was seeing. These were pictures of Jess, clearly intoxicated.

This wasn't the Jess my parents knew and remembered.

I had no doubt she had put them in her hiding spot so our mom wouldn't find them. Lord knows what would have happened if she had.

In one photo, she held an overturned Silo cup over her head, her top practically see-through with what must be beer, and her head thrown back in laughter. In another, her eyes were glassy and she was clearly drunk. She held up a shot glass to the camera.

I flipped to the last few pictures and I froze.

It showed Jess in a messy dorm room, a radiant smile on her gorgeous face. Her arms were wrapped tightly around the neck of a handsome boy with dark hair and a contagious, familiar grin.

My entire body started to tremble.

There was another photo of the young couple. The boy's lips pressed to the side of Jess's neck, his hands tucked into the pockets of her jeans. They were obviously smitten with each other.

And yet another of the two kissing at the edge of a large, very recognizable body of water. It was taken at an angle that they had obviously propped up the camera and put it on a timer. The Doll's Eyes' red berries grew at their feet. You could tell that, to each other, no one else existed.

I let out a sob and pushed the pictures away.

I should have taken solace in seeing my sister happy.

But I couldn't. Seeing them filled me with a sadness that consumed me.

Because yes, my sister had obviously been in love.

Deeply in love.

With Ryan McKay.

Stephanie Baker is with Where is Phoebe Baker?
Yesterday at 8:02 PM 🌐

It's been 24 years since I last saw Phoebe. Who would have thought
these two girls would only have 18 years together? I'm sick of people
saying she ran off. Phoebe would NEVER do that! She wasn't the kind
of person to abandon her family and friends. Mom and Dad were never
taken seriously when they said someone has hurt her. The police kept
blowing them off and they dies never knowing what really happened.
I'm so thankful for the Ten Seconds to Vanish Podcast for shedding light
on my sister's case and maybe finally we'll get some answers. Because
I know there's someone out there getting away with murder. I've had
my suspicions for 24 years and if it's the last thing I do, I will find out the
thruth!

👍❤️😮340   11 Comments 7 Shares

👍 Like   ↪ Share

View more 16 Comments

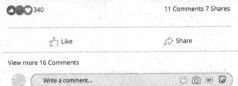

Write a comment...   😊 📷 GIF 🎁

9

JESSICA

Christmas Break 1998

I HAD BEEN HOME for over three weeks and I was losing my mind.

If it weren't for my little sister, I would have driven back to campus already. Or walked. Or run. Anything to get me away from here.

I lay on my bed, listening to music, staring at the ceiling. I took a drink from the bottle of vodka I had snuck from my parents' liquor cabinet. But not even the alcohol could numb the restless need to flee.

Nothing in my room had changed since I had left for college, yet things felt different. The walls were the same, the furniture the same, yet I wasn't.

I had changed.

More than my family could, or would, ever realize.

There was a knock at the door and I sat up, screwing the lid on the vodka bottle and shoving it beneath my pillow. I popped a mint in my mouth and put on a sweet smile, knowing that's what my parents would expect to see. The familiar smile of their eldest child—smart, capable, responsible.

A smile drowning in insincerity.

"Jessica, we need to talk." Mom opened the door and came inside without waiting for me to answer. I realized she never waited. She was always pushing. Always invading. My space was her space.

She was beautiful. Carefully put together and effortlessly stylish. People said we looked more like sisters than mother and daughter. I knew she loved that, even if it made me feel uncomfortable. She would loop her arm through mine and say we were a couple of girlfriends. I would laugh with her, all the while my chest constricting so tightly I could hardly breathe.

I never wanted her to be my friend. I had enough of those.

I wanted her to be someone I could talk to, someone who wouldn't judge me. Someone I could trust to protect me from the bad stuff.

But I didn't get that with Cara Fadley and I never would.

Mom sat down on my bed, holding out a copy of the local paper, pointing to the front page. "Did you know about this?"

I read the headline, my stomach dropping.

Another Girl Missing at Local College.

"It's nothing, Mom—"

"I don't think you should go back. Not with this going on." Her voice rose in pitch as her hysteria mounted.

I had been walking on tenterhooks since coming home, waiting—and dreading—this very moment. When Mom's overprotective tendencies swooped in and threatened to smother me completely.

Mom wasn't one for the news. She preferred glossy fashion magazines and daytime soap operas. She didn't typically know about national stories until months later. She and Dad's conversations usually revolved around Lindsey and me and little else.

"You can't keep me here," I said with a note of panic.

Mom's lovely face darkened. "I most certainly can, Jessica. Especially if I think you're not safe."

No, no, no . . .

"The whole thing has been blown out of proportion. The school believes those girls left on their own. Sure, it looks bad, but it's not anything to be worried about." I took a deep breath, trying to calm my nerves. "Plus, I can't exactly get a degree if I'm here, can I? Isn't that what you want for me? Isn't that why I'm in school?"

I knew all the right buttons to push when it came to ensuring my mother's compliance. I had learned long ago how to play the game—and win.

I saw it. The moment she let parental concern go, replacing it with her need for predictable contentment. Mom was big on not rocking the boat.

"You're right. But if you ever feel like campus isn't safe, you need to come home immediately." She folded the newspaper and dropped it in the trash can, the alarming article already forgotten.

"Where's Dad?" I asked, changing the subject.

Mom lifted her shoulder in a shrug. "Working late. He has an open house across town at six."

I hadn't seen much of my father since I'd been home. He was always busy at the real estate agency. He put in long hours and late nights. This was new for him. He had always been a family man, spending as much time as possible with Mom and especially me.

So, why did I feel as if he was busier since I had been home? I got the sense he didn't want to see me—didn't want to be around me. And that hurt. Particularly since that's not how things had ever been before.

Mom stood up and walked around my room, opening my jewelry box, rearranging the pictures on my dresser. Her hands were all over my things, moving them around to suit her taste. My room was as much a reflection of her as it was of me. She forced a dynamic that would never, ever exist between us. We weren't close. Not in the way she wanted. I couldn't help that I had never felt that intimacy with her that came so easily in my relationship with Dad. She was horrible at hiding her jealousy.

I loved my mother, but it was an obligatory love. And its shallowness sometimes hurt as much as my father's deep affection.

"You know, you still haven't told me your grades. I tried calling the school for a report, but they wouldn't give them to me." Mom sounded frustrated and I was mortified by her intrusion. "Your father and I pay for your schooling, we're entitled to know how you're doing." The change in tactics was instantaneous but expected. When she got tired of playing best friend, she tried her hand at strict parent. She switched and discarded her roles so fast it was hard to keep up. She was always trying to find a way into my inner circle. Poking and prodding, looking for weaknesses. She never found them.

"It probably has to do with the whole *I'm an adult thing*," I muttered, shocking both of us.

Mom's eyes narrowed. "What's gotten into you lately, Jessica? I don't think I like this new attitude you've come home with. Since when do you keep secrets from your parents?"

We had a silent standoff. Her demanding me to open up and me refusing to do so. At one time I would have given in, at least a little. Fed her scraps to appease her. But I couldn't be bothered to play the part any longer. I was tired. So, so tired.

"I'm doing fine," I lied. "All As and Bs." The truth was I was struggling for the first time in my academic career. I had scraped by with low Cs and a few Ds. And I failed Intro to English. I was looking into auditing a class next semester to try and get enough credits to ensure I could move on to sophomore year. But I couldn't tell her that. She would yank me out of Southern State so fast my head would spin. And I couldn't leave. Not now.

"Your father and I will want to see the grades for ourselves," Mom stated, and I had to suppress a sigh, purposefully not looking at my bookbag where I had put a printout of the very grades my mom was asking about.

"I'll send them to you when I get back to school." Another lie. I had no intention of sharing my grades with her and Dad. I needed to hide the grade slip as soon as she left.

"Did you bring home your books so you can study? I haven't seen you do any work over break." Mom unzipped my bookbag and I sucked in a breath, waiting for her to find the paper I had stashed away. I practically sagged in relief when she pulled out my school textbooks.

"Good. This will give you something to do this afternoon instead of lazing around." She patted my cheek. "I only want to see you succeed, darling."

"Jessie, will you play Barbies with me?" Lindsey came running into the room, her brown hair a mess of tangles. She had what looked like a smudge of ketchup across her cheek from lunch. She launched herself at me and we collapsed onto my bed in a fit of giggles.

"Lindsey-Bug, be careful," Mom fretted, lifting my little sister off the bed.

"It's okay. I like being her landing pad," I laughed, lightly pinching Lindsey's nose.

"You shouldn't encourage that kind of behavior, Jessica. She's likely to hurt herself." Mom sniffed with an air of disapproval. But she was all sweet smiles when she turned to my baby sister. "Lindsey-Bug, would you like me to make you Mommy's special hot chocolate?"

Lindsey's eyes widened and she nodded emphatically. "Yes, Mommy." Then she held her hand out to me. "Come on, Jessie, have some hot chocolate with me."

I started to stand up, smiling at my sister, but then Mom stepped between us. "Not today, Lindsey-Bug, Jessica has studying to do."

Mom took Lindsey's hand and started to lead her from the room. She looked back at me over her shoulder. "Remember what Albert Einstein said, *once you stop learning, you start dying.* Get to work. You'll thank me later." She looked pointedly at the books on my desk.

I didn't bother to say anything. What would be the point?

After she left, I jumped up and dug out the grade slip I had picked up from the registrar's office before coming home in December. I looked at the list of classes and the corresponding grades.

I was close to blowing it. If I didn't get my crap together, I would flunk out of college. What would Mom say to that?

How would my mother survive the complete annihilation of all her hopes and expectations?

I should have felt worried. I should have felt guilty. I should have felt anything other than a complete and total emptiness. It was hard to care about something that was quickly becoming less and less important.

I crumpled the paper in my hand, but instead of throwing it away, I hurried to my closet, pushing my clothes aside, revealing the tiny, barely visible cut out in the drywall I had made when I was twelve and wanted to hide candy from my health-conscious mother.

I popped it open and shoved my grades into the cavity on top of a few pictures I had already placed there when I got home. Photographs of a Jessica that my mother would never approve of, yet I wanted to remember all the same.

I pulled the ring from my father out of my pocket and thought about putting it in the wall. Leaving it there with all the other things I didn't want discovered. I hadn't been wearing it on my finger, yet I continued to carry it in my pocket. Unwilling to let go of the memory of how things used to be.

But I couldn't do it. I gritted my teeth and jammed it back in my pocket. Looking at it enraged me. It filled me with an acidic anger that incinerated everything in its wake. But I couldn't part with it—not yet.

I put the piece of dry wall back and shoved a pile of old books in front of it to hide it from my mother's prying eyes. Satisfied, I left the closet and closed the door. Figuring I'd make an effort to do what my mother expected, I sat down at my desk, opened a book, and pretended to study.

* * *

I woke up with a start. The phone on my bedside table was ringing. I wiped drool from my chin and sat up, grabbing the receiver before my mom could answer it.

"Hello?"

I looked tiredly at the open text book I had been using as a pillow.

"Jess! Oh my god, I miss you so much!" My roommate's shrill voice rang in my ear.

"Hey, Daisy, how are you?" I had spoken to Daisy a few times since being home. She seemed to have gotten over the momentary weirdness resulting from our almost-disagreement in the Commons. She carefully avoided mentioning Tammy and Phoebe or any of her paranoid suspicions. It had become a topic we resolutely didn't talk about. And I appreciated it. I valued Daisy's friendship. The last thing I wanted was to alienate her.

"Ugh, I'm so ready to get back to school. My parents are driving me nuts," she complained. I could hear kids screaming in the background, people laughing, glasses tinkling.

"Sounds like you're in the middle of a party," I laughed.

"No, that's how my house sounds *all* the time. Being the oldest of five kids means not having a moment's peace, ever. Hang on a sec." I could hear the sound of fabric rustling then a door closing. "Okay, I've hidden in the pantry. I should have all of three minutes before one of my demon siblings comes looking for me—or a snack."

"I'm guessing your Christmas break hasn't been very relaxing," I surmised.

"Are you kidding me? My aunt and uncle decided to visit from New Mexico, and they brought their two year old twins. Our house is cramped enough without adding that chaos. Then my grandparents flew in from Guadeloupe, so I was kicked out of my room and have been forced to sleep on the couch." Daisy sounded perturbed.

I couldn't imagine having such a large family. Both of my parents were only children, so I had never had cousins to play with. My mom's dad passed away before I was born and her mom not long after my first birthday. Dad's parents lived on the other side of town. We saw them occasionally, but they were the kind of people that mostly kept to themselves. They weren't particularly interested in being grandparents. So, it had only ever been Mom, Dad, and me until Lindsey was born.

"Please tell me you've been doing something fun while you've been home. Or *someone*?" I could practically hear her raising her eyebrows.

"Sorry to disappoint you, Daisy, but all I've been doing is sleeping and eating too much food. Though there's been a wild game of Monopoly or two."

"I suppose there's not much to do in good ol' Mt. Randall," Daisy commiserated. "But girl, do yourself a favor and get out of your house. Too much family time isn't good for anybody. But—"

"What?"

"Just be careful, okay."

I wanted to scream.

"Daisy . . ."

"I know, I know. I have to say it. I know you think I'm being ridiculous." This time her laughter was full of forced cheer that was painful to listen to.

I didn't know what to say.

"Have you heard from that cute frat pledge you were drooling over before we left?" Her change of subject was welcome, even if it was to grill me about Ryan.

"He said he'd call me when we're back on campus," I told her. I felt myself flushing as I remembered the way he'd looked at me.

"Okay, well, I asked around about him—"

"Daisy, seriously?" I groaned, cringing in mortification, but still eager for any information she had on him.

"Of course I did. I had to vet out the guy you seem interested in. That's what us gals have to do for each other. Anyway, it seems like he's a *popular* guy, if you know what I mean. His pledge nickname is Wam Bam McKay, and that's not all," Daisy cautioned.

"What is it?" Did I really want to know? I liked putting my head in the sand. It was safe there in the dark.

"Apparently he has a temper. Erica says—"

"Oh God," I groaned. "Are you really taking anything Miss Shit Stirrer says seriously?"

"This is legit, Jess. Don't be so dismissive. Because it's common knowledge that Ryan has a rage button. Erica's been hooking up with Dave Wendle for weeks and he's also a Sigma Kappa pledge. Anyway, he says everyone knows to give

Ryan a wide berth if something pisses him off. He told Erica that Ryan punched a hole in the wall after his favorite football team lost a big game. So be careful, okay?"

"So, he hit a wall. That doesn't mean—"

"Jess, a man that can destroy *things* can just as easily destroy *you*. That's all I'm saying."

"Okay, I get it." I didn't like the unsettled feeling the information gave me. And I hated the crushing disappointment that another man wasn't who he pretended to be.

"Anyway, Ryan seems okay, maybe not serious dating material, though. So, be careful if you do get up close and personal with him. A guy like that isn't worth ruining a good time for."

"Says the woman whose whole life is a good time," I joked good-naturedly.

"That's very true. Though I've seen you at the last couple of keggers. You're clearly vying for my flirty, party girl crown."

"I will never dethrone you, that's for sure." We both laughed.

"You won't be missing out on anything if you decide to forget about Ryan," Daisy went on. "Plus, it would probably be a little weird being with a guy who's been with not only Tammy but Phoebe, too."

My heart stuttered and the smile fell. "What?"

"Oh yeah. From what I heard, he hooked up with Tammy during the first week of school. And according to Dave, Ryan dated Phoebe in high school. And then there's the fact that he went around bad-mouthing Tammy, calling her a cocktease. Real classy. Sounds like Wam Bam McKay doesn't like a woman with agency. It seriously irritates me that his piggish behavior is forcing me to defend Tight Ass Tammy."

"He dated Tammy *and* Phoebe?" I asked, my voice shaky. The thought of him with both of them made me ill.

"Well, maybe dated is too strong a word. All I know is he was *involved* with both of them. I wonder what he has to say about them being missing?" Daisy pondered, her voice taking on that terrified edge that had become familiar.

"I guess we have some things to talk about when we get back to school," I finally said, sounding hoarse.

"Yeah, it sounds like you do." I heard a door opening on the other end of the line and Daisy shouting at someone to leave.

"Daisy?"

A few seconds later she came back. "Sorry, Jess, I've gotta go. My brother needs to use the phone."

She hung up before I could say goodbye.

I put the phone back on the cradle.

I could hear my mom and Lindsey singing along to a Britney Spears song downstairs. They sounded like they were having fun. I wished I could sit with my sister, drink my mother's hot chocolate, and forget everything.

But I couldn't. And that was a problem.

Daisy was right, I needed to get out of my house.

*　*　*

I decided to walk downtown instead of driving. It only took ten minutes and I enjoyed the cold air on my flushed skin.

Ryan had been involved with both Tammy and Phoebe. What were the odds?

A deep-rooted instinct wanted me to forget about him. Getting involved with a guy who had anything to do with either woman wasn't a great idea.

But then I remembered his smile and how I had felt when he kissed me, and for some inexplicable reason, I lost all sense.

Mom had asked me a dozen questions before I left the house. Lindsey had begged to come along. It had been difficult to extract myself, but I needed to be alone. I needed space.

I needed to *breathe*.

If Daisy could see me walking by myself, she would have a fit. She didn't understand that I had nothing to fear from Mt. Randall's streets.

Most of the houses were still lit up for Christmas, though it was now the first week of January. I knew no one would bother taking them down until the days became warmer. Mt. Randall held onto every holiday with an iron grip.

I smiled at the bright, seemingly random mailboxes that lined the sidewalk. The mailboxes were one of the more peculiar things about my hometown. There were no regular wooden or metal boxes for the homes in our tiny corner of North Carolina. Every person took it upon themselves to upstage their neighbors. The Wilsons on Partridge Drive had one in the shape of Godzilla. The Mercers on Dandelion Park had a green elephant. None were the same. All were strange enough to make you look twice.

I remembered picking out our own mailbox when I was no more than four. I had insisted on a bright red barn with a purple roof. Mom had wanted a more sedate black and white cow, but Dad had sided with me, as he had always done. So the tiny red barn had been sitting nailed to the thick wood stake at the bottom of our driveway for the past fourteen years.

The quiet, maple-lined streets eventually gave way to the main drag. The Dollar Store was the busiest spot in town, which wasn't saying much. With the college on winter break, the place felt empty. The town survived on the commerce generated by Southern State, and they hated that reliance.

It wasn't as if the college kids were particularly rowdy. They—*we*— kept to the top of the hill. But people complained about them—*us*—all the same. Growing up, I had heard the criticism and accusations thrown in the school's direction. Grumbling about Southern State was a Mt. Randall pastime in which almost everyone partook.

Yet one couldn't exist without the other.

My stomach growled and I realized I hadn't eaten since that morning. Checking the time on my watch I saw it was after four. Even though I knew Mom would be annoyed if I ate so close to dinner, I headed toward the Sunset Cafe.

I sat at the counter, not wanting to take up a whole booth for only myself. I picked up a menu and waited to place my order.

"Hi, Jessica. How's it going?"

A plain girl with long, brown hair tied back in a low ponytail approached me. She wore a stained apron and a tired smile.

"Not bad, Bianca. How are you?"

"Ah, you know, doing the Mt. Randall thing until I die." She laughed and then I laughed, though it was clear neither of us found it particularly funny.

Bianca Simmons and I had graduated high school together. We were two out of the eighty-five kids who had all grown up on the same streets and graduated the same year. Bianca and I weren't exactly friends, but we knew each other well.

"How's college life?" Bianca asked with a note of envy.

"College is good," I told her.

"You go up there, right?" She inclined her head in the direction of Southern State, its brick buildings visible for miles.

"I do."

"Strange about those girls, huh." Bianca chewed on her bottom lip, the skin cracked and peeling. "I was reading about it in the paper this morning. Two girls in two months. That's something."

"I don't really know anything—"

"What's that school doing to find them?" An elderly man spoke up from further down the counter, turning in his chair to face me. I recognized Mr. Warner from when he owned the old hardware store. Dad took me there several times over the years to get parts for our paddleboat. The store closed after he retired. Yet despite the nearest hardware store now being a thirty-minute drive away, no one had opened another one. That's what happened in towns like Mt. Randall. Places closed and stayed closed.

I shrugged, feeling a familiar kind of restless defensiveness. "I'm not exactly sure. I'm only a student."

Mr. Warner made a noise of derision. "Those kids are ruining our town," he muttered under his breath.

"At least they're not Mt. Randall girls or anything," Bianca remarked dismissively. As if they mattered less because of it.

Mr. Warner grunted in agreement.

"No, not Mt. Randall girls," I parroted. I didn't know what else to say. Bianca had already lost interest in the fate of Tammy and Phoebe and moved on to taking my order—a slice of sweet potato pie and a coffee.

Bianca and Mr. Warner didn't particularly care about Phoebe or Tammy. Neither did any of the others born and bred here.

Two missing college girls—girls from other places—didn't really impact them at all. Though if students stopped enrolling because their parents thought this place was too dangerous, the town would slowly wither and die. Without the financial help from "those kids ruining the town," Mt. Randall would lose what little life it had. And it was already struggling.

I stared out the window as I waited for my food. I never ventured far from these safe and familiar roads. I wondered, deep down, if I'd ever escape. If I'd ever build a life outside of Mt. Randall. I felt destined to remain. Forever a part of the dirt and trees. Maybe that's all I deserved.

I watched the entrance of the old movie theater across the street. The marquee was lit up, showcasing that week's feature—the original *Planet of the Apes*. It was one of my dad's favorites. I remembered watching it with him when I was a kid. I thought about asking him to go see it again. It would be like old times, before everything got so messed up. Before things got so warped and twisted between us. Missing my father was like a physical ache that never went away. But I held on to the pain as a reminder of him and what we used to have.

* * *

"Milk Duds, too, Dad," I insisted, standing beside my father as he put in our order for a large bucket of buttered popcorn.

"Can I get two boxes of Milk Duds? Oh, and a large Dr. Pepper," he added, giving me a smile.

Once we had our food we made our way to the theater. There were only three screens, the largest was currently showing a matinee of the original Planet of the Apes.

"We should go see it," Dad suggested when he saw it listed in the paper earlier in the week. *"It was my favorite when I was your age."*

"I don't know. It looks kind of scary." I sounded hesitant and unsure. At eleven, my favorite movie was Hook, followed by The Little Mermaid. *I hadn't yet graduated to more mature media.*

"It's not scary, I promise." He had tussled my hair and gave me a hug. And I believed him. He never lied to me.

We sat down in our seats. I wanted the middle row, right in front of the screen, so that's where we sat. Dad handed me the Milk Duds, making a face when I poured them into the bucket of popcorn.

"Gross, Jess." Dad stuck out his tongue and I giggled.

"Trust me, it's so good." I handed him the bucket and he took a mouthful.

"Hmm, not bad." He grabbed some more.

I pulled the bucket back. *"Hey, save some for the movie."*

We both laughed. Dad leaned over and kissed my temple. *"This is great. My favorite movie with my favorite girl."*

Then the lights went down and I was entranced. Planet of the Apes *became my favorite movie, too.*

* * *

As I stared, the doors opened and two people came out.

My mouth went dry. My heart began to race. Bitter tears stung my eyes.

I stood up and walked toward the door feeling numb.

"What about your coffee and pie?' Bianca called out. I didn't answer. I stepped outside. Nighttime was quickly approaching. The old streetlights flickered on.

I watched the older man and young woman hurry from the movie theater and quickly dart around the side of the building toward the cut-through that led to Beacon Road. The woman's coquettish giggles called out to me.

Without a moment's pause, I jogged after them.

No. He promised . . .

I wanted to stop and turn around. Go back to the cafe and eat my pie. Pretend I never saw anything.

Indignation, however, insisted I keep going.

I slipped down the narrow, dimly lit passageway that reeked of trash. I could hear the girl's breathless laughter. She sounded like a child. Probably because she practically was.

"Ben, we can't," I heard her say, though I could tell she didn't mean it. It was only the teasing protests of flirtation.

I kept my distance, far enough that they didn't see me. But close enough that I saw everything.

My hands became fists at my side.

My father—my beloved, doting father—pushed the girl against the brick wall, his hands sliding up her shirt. Her fingers were in his hair. Their mouths were fused together as if they couldn't get enough.

I heard her moan as his lips traveled the length of her neck. Her head fell back, her bright, blonde hair—the complete opposite of my mother's dark brown—fell over her shoulders, her eyes closed.

I recognized her. We went to school together, though she was a year behind me. She must be a senior now. No more than seventeen. Maybe eighteen.

Too young to be making out with my forty-two year old father in a dirty alleyway behind the local movie theater.

I took a step toward them, my foot accidentally kicking a can that clattered along the ground. It was loud in the oppressive silence.

They both looked up, startled. The girl fixed her tight-fitting sweater, smoothing her hair back from her face. She barely looked at me, instead grabbing my father's hand, pulling him away.

But not before he saw me. Our eyes met and there was a flash of anger. A hint of shame.

This wasn't the first time I found him like this. There had been so many of them. Too many. So, I knew this girl didn't matter to him. None of them ever did.

* * *

I walked into the fire escape, the door closing loudly behind me. I carried two empty boxes, taking them out to the trash. I was finally all moved into my dorm. I was exhausted and nervous, but excited, too. I could hear whispers further down the stairwell.

I had left Mom and Lindsey talking to my new roommate and her parents. Dad had gone to get us drinks a while ago and hadn't come back yet.

I wondered where he was.

My feet hit the bottom step and I could see two people tucked away in the shadow of the staircase. The man leaned in close toward the young girl, speaking softly in her ear. She looked nervous, but excited, her pale cheeks flushed. I had seen her earlier carrying a suitcase, a man and a woman who must be her parents right behind her. The man had been yelling at his wife, who appeared skittish and uncomfortable. Their daughter had either been oblivious to the familial discord or so used to it that she blocked it out.

I recognized the red-checkered shirt the man was wearing. And the perfectly styled brown hair.

I watched as he took the girl's hand, pulling her toward him. She tilted her face up to look up at him. She was pretty. They always were. He wouldn't bother with them if they weren't.

I felt sick watching them.

Not here. Not today.

I coughed loudly. My dad dropped the girl's hand. She looked like a deer in headlights. Without a word, she scrambled away, hurrying out the door and onto the quad.

Then it was just Dad and me.

"You promised." It was an accusation.

What if Mom had seen? Or Lindsey? Or anyone?

But that was part of the thrill for a man like my father. I got that now. It wasn't worth it if it wasn't dangerous.

"Jess." He said my name sadly. As if I didn't understand. As if I were the problem. As if I were a child, and not the same age as the young woman he was just flirting with.

"You promised," I repeated. I dropped the empty boxes and ran back up the stairs.

* * *

I stood there for a long time after they left.

I hated him. More than I thought it possible to hate anyone.

I loved him. More than I thought it possible to love anyone.

And then I cried. Because it was the only thing I could do.

**Mt. Randall Police Department Press Conference
Regarding the disappearances of Tammy Estep and Phoebe
Baker**

**January 15, 1999
10:15 AM**

"Good morning. My name is Sergeant Liam O'Neil with the Mt. Randall
police department. I want to start by thanking everyone for being here
and to thank the Mt. Randall Baptist Church for allowing us to use their
facility. I'm going to provide you an update on the recent disappearances of two women who both attend Southern State University. I know
there are a lot of rumors and speculation going around, and I wanted to
make sure you have the facts to put these stories to bed. It's true that
on December 11 a missing person's report was filed for Phoebe Baker
from Leonard's Creek, North Carolina, a freshman at Southern State
University. She was last seen on December 6 by her roommate at Marion Hall on campus. My team has interviewed a number of her friends
and acquaintances and have determined that, at this time, there is no
evidence of foul play. It is highly probable Phoebe left of her own voli-
tion. Tammy Estep, a junior from Baltimore, Maryland, was last seen on
November 12. It is important to note at this time that Tammy's disappearance is not being treated as a missing person's case, as neither her
parents, nor anyone else, have formally made a report. It is believed

that, like Phoebe, Tammy voluntarily left the school—again, there is no indication of foul play. Despite the lack of evidence, we at the Mt. Randall Police Department are using a methodical and committed approach to locating both girls in order to put their family and friends at ease. Because of this, we feel there is no danger to the greater community. These appear to be isolated incidents. That means there's no reason to believe a third party was involved at all, despite the talk going around to the contrary. The staff at Southern State University, particularly President Bradley Hamilton, have been working closely with our team to best support Phoebe's family. If you have any information regarding either Tammy's or Phoebe's whereabouts, please contact the Mt. Randall Police Department. I will not be taking questions at this time. Thank you."

10

LINDSEY

Present Day

I SAT ON MY bed watching my phone ring for the tenth time. And for the tenth time I ignored it.

Ignored *him*.

I wasn't able to sleep last night. I had lain awake until the early hours staring at the pictures of Ryan and Jess. I had looked at them for so long that when I closed my eyes, the images were burned on the inside of my eyelids.

Ryan and Jess had been together.

I couldn't come to terms with it. With what it meant for me.

Thankfully, today was my day off. I couldn't imagine having to plaster a fake smile on my face and deal with guests and my staff while my mind was reeling.

I had been purposefully avoiding my parents all morning. I didn't know what to say to them, so I chose to say nothing. Instead, I had sequestered myself in my room and thought of nothing else but Ryan. And Jess. And Ryan and Jess.

I needed someone to talk to. Someone who would understand. But I had no one. My isolation had never felt more pronounced.

I thought I could read people. I had always relied on my instincts. But he had duped me. How was that possible? I felt like an idiot who had been snowed by a good-looking man. Not just any man, either—my sister's boyfriend.

No wonder Ryan had been so invested in the story. He had wanted to find out what happened to her. Had he been in love with her all this time? Had her disappearance shaped his life like it had shaped mine?

I wanted to be angry with him. And I was. But the dominant emotion was sadness. A little for me, and even for him as well.

My phone chimed again and I almost ignored it. But then I saw it was an alert for the new episode of the *Ten Seconds to Vanish* podcast. I had become almost scared to listen to it. Their endless chatter and inappropriate jokes angered me. While I appreciated them shining a light on these cold cases, I wished they could do so with a little more respect.

Despite my criticisms about their behavior, they *were* uncovering a lot of information that was new to the investigation. And this week's podcast claimed they had found out some interesting information regarding Jess's boyfriend. But for once, I knew the scoop before hearing it from the hosts.

Because I now knew who the boyfriend was . . . Ryan.

"Linds!" Dad hollered up the stairs. "You've got a visitor."

I got off the bed and headed toward the door. I had no idea who it was, but briefly wondered if I could tell Dad to send whoever it was away.

I sighed heavily as I made my way downstairs, already knowing I couldn't do that. Dad was the type of man who thought you should face life, own up to your mistakes, take accountability. And he had raised me to never shy away from anything.

When I reached the middle of the stairs, I was shocked to see Ryan standing by the front door.

I wondered what Dad would do if he knew that the man in his home was Jess's old boyfriend. That he had tracked me down and lied about who he was in order to gain my trust.

Even after Jess disappeared, Dad had never been one of those shotgun you-can't-date-my-daughter kind of fathers. He left me to make my own decisions, saying he trusted me to make the right choices. Though sometimes it felt more like a lack of interest than trust. For my emotional well-being, I made it a point to never study his back-seat parenting too closely.

Despite this, I knew he'd be more than a little pissed off with this situation. More because of Ryan's connection to Jess than anything else.

I felt a violent clashing of emotions as I looked at Ryan. My body still responded at his nearness, yet it was at war with the devastating reality of who he was. His lies ripped away at my heart until all that was left was blood and pulp.

Both men turned to look up at me. My dad's smile was preoccupied as always, as if he had mentally exited the room before he had physically left.

I didn't want to look at Ryan, but I couldn't help it. Like the first time we met, I felt pulled in. I drank him in until I became sick.

It wasn't until that moment that our age difference became unmistakable. I had known he was quite a bit older than me, but seeing him standing next to my dad, it was blindingly obvious.

I focused on the crow's feet at the corners of Ryan's eyes. I noticed that his five o'clock shadow, as well as his dark-brown hair, was tinged with gray.

He was so handsome, and so much older than me.

And now all I could see—all I could feel—was betrayal and how if Jess were still here, Ryan would be waiting for her at the bottom of the stairs and not me.

"Hey, Lindsey," Ryan greeted, "I tried calling you a few times, but you didn't answer."

"I've been busy. What do you want?" He looked taken aback by the sharpness in my tone.

At my obvious annoyance, Dad seemed curious. He looked between us as if trying to get a read on the situation. As though trying to figure out how he would be expected to react.

"Maybe now isn't a great time for a visit," he remarked blandly.

Ryan ignored my dad entirely, instead appearing confused by my reaction to him. "Lindsey, are you okay?" He sounded worried.

"I . . . I uh, think you should go," Dad said, attempting to sound stern. It would have been comical if I hadn't been so upset. My dad wasn't the protective type, and it was clear he didn't quite know how to be where I was concerned. That wasn't our relationship. It felt like he was acting a part and fumbling over his lines.

Ryan's gaze slid to my dad before coming back to settle on me once more. "What's happened?"

Of course, he had no idea what was wrong. No idea why I was suddenly acting as if I didn't want to see him. The guy wasn't a mind reader after all.

It would be so easy to launch accusations at him like hand grenades, watching as they exploded in his dishonest face. But I didn't want to give him the chance to explain. I didn't want to hear the lies fall from his mouth.

Every part of me turned ice cold. "I have nothing to say to you."

My dad continued to watch us, though I noticed he had slowly started to make his way towards the kitchen as if the whole scene was making him uncomfortable. "Linds, do you need my help with this?" I didn't answer, my attention on Jess's boyfriend.

Ryan clenched his jaw as if he were trying to reign in his anger, his pleading eyes on mine. "I don't know what I've done to upset you, Lindsey, but I have something you'll want to hear. Please give me a few minutes. I won't stay any longer if you don't want me to."

I wasn't sure what to do. I wanted to confront him. I needed to unleash all this fury that had nowhere to go. He was my sister's boyfriend. I wanted him to know that I *knew*.

But what if, once he realized his cover was blown, he packed up his newly found information and left without ever sharing it with me? In that moment, my drive to find out what happened to Jess outweighed my desire to expose him.

But I didn't trust him. And even worse, I didn't trust *myself* with him.

"Lindsey?" My dad now seemed troubled, as if finally figuring out how he should proceed. He glanced at Ryan. "Maybe I should walk him out."

Ryan was openly scowling as he tried not to look at my father, yet somehow, I knew his anger was aimed at him. The amount of rage I felt emanating from him felt over the top given the situation. I didn't understand Ryan's level of antagonism.

Dad, however, seemed oblivious.

Feeling a bone-deep exhaustion, I came down the rest of the stairs. "It's okay, Dad, I'll talk to him." I felt like I was making the same mistakes over and over. I kept putting my trust in people who didn't deserve it.

Tell him. A voice whispered in my head. *Let him know that you're on to him.*

It was hard to ignore the impulse to shout in his face. But somehow, I swallowed it and kept it inside. For now.

"Alright, well, let me get out of your way." Dad seemed relieved that his assistance wouldn't be required and he hurriedly left the room.

I slid past Ryan, heading outside to the porch. He followed me and I closed the door behind us.

"What's going on?" Ryan demanded. "I've been calling you all damn day. I even went by the front desk and asked where you were, but they said you had the day off. Why didn't you tell me you were off today? You should have said something. I need to be able to get ahold of you, Lindsey. This is serious." He took a step toward me and I took a step back. He seemed intent on closing the distance between us, but I was determined to keep it. "Are you avoiding me?"

I started to turn away. I couldn't look at him. I needed to gather my thoughts. I hadn't prepared what I would say to him. I had barely been able to get my head around the whole thing myself.

Ryan reached for me, his hand wrapping around my bicep. He swung me back around to face him. "Listen, I don't know what I did or why you're ignoring me, but this isn't fair, okay. It's not fair, Lindsey. I have done everything you've asked of me. I've told you what I know. I've been completely open with you. But it's more than that." His eyes implored me to hear him out. "Lindsey, I like you." His hand slid down my arm to gently take my hand. And God help me, I let him. I loathed myself at how weak I was. "I never intended for this to happen when I came to Mt. Randall, but I'm so glad it did."

I felt paralyzed by his desperation. I wanted to forget everything I had learned. I wanted to go back to twenty-four hours ago when I felt on the verge of closure with Jess, and the potential of something with Ryan. I hated how quickly things could change for the worse. He continued to stare at me, his expression sad yet fierce.

"Goddamn it, say something!" he yelled suddenly. He grabbed my arms again and squeezed like he wanted to shake some sense into me.

I pulled out of his grip and took a step back, shock finally pushing me into action. "Don't *ever* yell at me."

Ryan was instantly remorseful. "I'm sorry, Lindsey—"

"You said you had information. Information so important you had to rush over here—" I stopped, my face hardening, though I already knew the answer to the question before it even left my mouth. "How did you even know where I live?"

The question took Ryan aback. "Oh, I looked you up—"

"You looked me up. Like you did when we met? What else do you know about me?" I pressed.

If I pushed hard enough, would he admit what I already knew? Could I make him tell me the truth? He *had* been dating Jess, so it made sense that he'd know where I lived–where *Jess* had lived.

"I, uh . . . nothing, it wasn't like that. I knew where you lived because—" He hesitated.

Was this it?

Was he going to reveal himself to be the lying bastard I already knew him to be?

Then the smile came back. The familiar easy one that made my insides quiver even as my stomach twisted into complicated knots. "I'm a journalist, remember? It's my job to know stuff."

I felt a crushing sense of disappointment. Deep down, I had hoped I was wrong about him. That maybe I got something wrong. But he wasn't going to admit anything.

I would have to bide my time to let it all out.

"You have two minutes and that's it."

He seemed frustrated. He looked tired and on edge. I wondered if it was hard for him to keep track of his lies.

"Can we sit?" he asked, indicating the steps.

I shook my head. "I'm fine standing. Just tell me what you came here to say."

He appeared dejected, but also annoyed. "Fine, I wanted you to know that I'm going to speak to Sergeant Liam O'Neil."

"Sergeant O'Neil? He worked on Jess's case," I said in confused surprise. Ryan nodded.

"He was the lead detective. I've talked to him a few times over the years. He's always danced around my questions. But last night after you left, after learning about Tammy, I called him again. I asked if I could finally see him in person and get him on the record." And there it was—his infectious enthusiasm that made it hard to remember the awful things I knew about him. "I want you to come with me, Lindsey. This is a real chance to dig into the case with someone who was there. Someone who knows the ins and outs of Jess's disappearance."

"But what could Sergeant O'Neil possibly say that would be of any use? Everyone knows the police screwed up the investigation back then," I argued, not willing myself to get excited . . . yet.

"I get that. But I think he has some real information. I'm not sure what's changed for him, but after all this time, he's finally letting me look at the old case files. Apparently, he made copies of everything when he retired, even though he obviously shouldn't have." Ryan was practically vibrating with anticipation.

"Okay, well, that's definitely good news." A thrilled jolt ran through me.

"I know, that's why I was trying to get ahold of you. So, what do you say? Will you come with me? I'm heading over there right now."

Ryan reached toward me as if to touch my face. It took me a second too long to evade him, his fingers brushing my skin before I pulled away.

What was wrong with me? Was I so pathetic that I craved the attention of a man I knew to be a liar? A man that had loved my missing sister? A man that was most likely using me?

"Will he even speak to you while I'm there?" I asked.

"Oh, I'm counting on you to be the one to make him spill everything." Ryan looked almost manic.

"Because I'm Jess's sister," I said, "and you think he'll feel guilty if I'm there and tell you what he knows." It wasn't a question. It was a fact, and one that Ryan readily agreed with.

"It sounded like he was more than ready to talk anyway, but what better way to ensure it happens than with you there. Jess's younger sister, still looking for answers all these years later."

"Spoken like a true journalist."

Ryan shrugged unapologetically. "But it'll work. Don't you see that? I *need* to see what he has. It could be a game changer. The answers *and* the mistakes that were made back then could be in those files. With the case being reopened, I think it's important to get ahead of everything so we can be ready." He reached for me again, his palm cupping my cheek. "And I know what this means to you. I want to help you get the closure you deserve. Maybe then we can move on from this."

I wanted to believe that in his eyes, I saw genuine affection. And yet, I had seen the photos. Ryan McKay was Jess's boyfriend.

And I was Jess's sister.

I turned away from him and I saw the hurt flash across his face.

"Let me grab my stuff." I went back inside and into the kitchen to gather my coat and purse.

"Is everything okay?" Dad barely glanced up from the car magazine in his hands.

"All good, Dad."

I couldn't tell him the truth.

I was too ashamed.

I was too embarrassed.

I hated that I had developed feelings for a man I barely knew. I should have known better. And, I hated that I needed him in order to learn more about Jess. It infuriated me that he held the keys to unlocking the mystery that was my sister.

"Where are you going? Your mom will want to know" he asked. I realized that he never inquired after me for himself. It was always for my mother. As if not for her, he wouldn't bother in the first place. The effort it took me to overlook the obvious was starting to wear me down.

"I have to head into work." *Lies.* "It will only be for an hour or so. I have some things to take care of." *More lies.* "Ryan said he'd drive me there and bring me home afterward."

I lied so easily.

Maybe Ryan and I were one and the same.

"Why don't you take your own car?" Dad asked.

I struggled to come up with a story on the spot, but I wasn't very good at it.

Dad regarded me closely for the first time. Was he actually paying attention for once? "What's going on, Linds? Who is this guy?"

"He's just a friend from work, Dad." I gave him a quick hug, wishing for a moment that I was still a kid so I could believe the delusion that my parents could fix my problems. "I'll only be a couple of hours. Tell Mom that I have my phone if she needs me for anything."

When I pulled away, Dad's eyes narrowed. "I don't like how he looks at you, Lindsey."

I swallowed thickly, unnerved by his unusual show of concern. "How does he look at me?"

My father stared at me, but I wasn't sure it was me he saw. "I know how men like that think. Please be careful."

Feeling touched, I kissed his cheek. I thought, rather optimistically, that maybe it wasn't too late to have the closeness between us I had always craved. Maybe, there was a chance for us to have our own bond. Feeling a little lighter, I headed back outside to where Ryan waited, not so patiently, for me.

My mood instantly soured at the sight of him.

"Let's get going," he said and I followed him to his car. I hesitated before getting in, wondering what other lies Ryan might have told me. Wondering who he really was. I knew I was right to be suspicious of him, but I also knew I had no choice but to go with him if I wanted to find answers. And I wanted answers more than anything.

Once he started the engine I felt him staring at me. I could tell that he wanted to say something, but was holding back.

"Where does he live?" I asked, filling the silent void between us.

"Not far. He moved away from Mt. Randall to the next town over not long after Jess's case went cold. He transferred to another police department, or was made to, I'm not sure which," he told me, turning onto the main road.

"I'm guessing he got a lot of heat for not solving Jess's case."

"The people in Mt. Randall weren't too happy. One of their local girls was gone and the police couldn't find her. They needed someone to blame." Ryan drove past the turnoff to Doll's Eye Lake. The police tape was still there. I wondered if they'd find anything else.

"And if the town turns against you, there's no coming back from that," I filled in.

"I know how it goes. I'm from a small town. too. Actually, I grew up in Leonard's Creek, which is only thirty miles from here and not much bigger than Mt. Randall. I came here a bunch of times as a kid. My grandmother lived right outside of town. She even took me to Doll's Eye Lake once."

"Oh really? Have you been there since then?" I raised my eyebrows. I already knew the answer. I had seen the picture of him and Jess there myself.

Just tell me!

"No, only the one time when I was younger," he answered tersely. I watched the bob of his Adam's apple as he swallowed.

"You've never said much about your life. So, you grew up not far from here?" I pushed. The fact that I knew so little about Ryan—that he had given away nothing about himself when he knew so much about me—should've been a huge red flag.

Ryan tensed up. "Yeah, I did, but there's not much to tell, really."

"Small towns can be hard, right?"

He side-eyed me warily at my probing "Sure are."

"Everyone always knows everyone else's business," I added.

"And they never let you forget a damn thing."

On some level, I understood. Growing up in Mt. Randall had been hard. I didn't really remember life before Jess vanished, only life after, and there was no escaping it. I would forever be known as the little sister of Jessica Fadley—the woman who vanished in ten seconds.

I wondered what Ryan was remembered for.

For the first time since meeting Ryan, I was a little afraid. What did I really know about this man?

"I drove out to Doll's Eye Lake a few weeks ago. It's been a long time since I'd been there," I found myself saying, more to fill the uncomfortable silence than anything else.

Talking was easier than thinking about the fact that I was in a car—alone—with him. With this man who I knew was holding things back from me. A man who had lied to me since the day we met.

His brow furrowed and his jaw stiffened. "You shouldn't have gone there."

I felt my hands tingle and my heart flutter.

I glanced at his handsome profile cautiously.

I had to believe he was only a liar and nothing more sinister.

But his next comment had me questioning my judgment once again.

"It's a pretty isolated spot. I'm not surprised Tammy was found there." He let out a heavy breath which was somewhere between a huff of annoyance and a humorless laugh. "To be honest, I'm surprised she was even found at all."

It was a strange thing to say. An awful thing, really. Ryan, realizing how it sounded, laughed again, this time with discomfort. "I mean, if you're going to dump a body, it's a good place to do it. Wouldn't you agree?"

"I . . . I guess." I looked out of the window, my pulse racing.

We lapsed into silence after that. Ryan lost in his thoughts and I lost in mine.

As we drove into Grantville, the town where Sergeant O'Neil lived, I broke the quiet.

"I can't be out too long or my dad will worry."

It was meant to be a warning, even if the words themselves weren't true. Dad wouldn't worry, but Ryan didn't know that. It was supposed to be a threat to not try anything because I was a woman that would be missed. I was taken aback by Ryan's sneer.

"Oh, I'm sure he will." The words dripped with a sarcasm I didn't understand.

I glowered at him, wondering where he got the audacity to be so openly hostile. He didn't know my dad. He knew nothing about my relationship with my parents. Not really. What he thought he knew about us ended when my sister went missing twenty-four years earlier.

Everything about my family had changed the day Jess went missing. Ryan only knew someone's memories of a family that no longer existed.

* * *

"Thanks for agreeing to speak to me on such short notice, Sergeant," Ryan said pleasantly. He held out his hand for the retired detective to shake.

"It's no problem. I've waited a long time for these cases to be solved. To know that at least one of those girls has been found is a light in all this darkness. I can only hope those poor families can get some closure once this is all said and done."

The retired police detective turned to me. "Hi, nice to meet you . . ." His words trailed off as his eyes widened. He drew in a shaky breath. "My god," he breathed. His eyes glistened and I thought he might cry. "You're the sister, aren't you." It wasn't a question.

"Hi, I'm Lindsey Fadley." I gave him a wan smile and held out my hand, but he didn't take it. He seemed to be in shock.

He wiped his eyes with the back of his weathered hand. "I recognize you. You were only a little girl when I saw you last, but I'd know you anywhere. Jessica was a beautiful young woman with so much life ahead of her. I had really hoped to find her. I'm sorry I didn't." He closed his eyes briefly, as if trying to get control of himself.

After a few seconds, Sergeant O'Neil composed himself and led us into the house. We sat down on the sagging sofa in the middle of his living room. The furniture smelled musty and every surface was covered in a thick layer of dust. He noticed me looking and gave a half embarrassed chuckle.

"I'm not one for housekeeping. That was always my wife's job. Since she passed away I've not had the heart to put her things away, or even clean up much. It's all I can do to get through each day."

"I'm sorry for your loss," I said softly.

"Thanks. It feels like yesterday, but actually it was two years ago next week. She was a good woman and we had a good life. Cancer got her, and it seems I won't be far behind." He didn't sound sad about it. "That's why I agreed to talk with you." He looked at Ryan and picked up a cardboard box from the table and handed it to me. It wasn't heavy.

"What's this?" I asked, opening the lid to see piles of paper inside. I drew in a sharp breath. "Is this—?"

"That's the old case file. Or at least a copy of everything I could get my hands on. Everything I have on those missing girls is in there," Sergeant O'Neil said as I put the box on the floor by my feet. "I know I shouldn't have taken it. If anyone knew I had this, I'd be in a lot of trouble. Especially since I'm now sharing it with you. But I need to go out with a clean conscience."

"Wanting to *go out with a clean conscience* makes it sound like you did something wrong," Ryan said, his words taking on an edge that hadn't been there before.

"I know how it sounds," the aging former police officer replied solemnly. "The thing is, you've been like a dog with a bone all these years—constant phone calls asking if there was anything new. Seems only right that I talk to you and tell you everything I know. And what I can't tell you, maybe you can figure out for yourself from what I have in there."

I could feel Ryan's eyes on me, but I wouldn't look at him.

Sergeant O'Neil leaned forward, regarding Ryan closely for the first time. "Do I know you? Have we met before? Because you look awfully familiar." He scratched his unshaven chin. The man had to be closing in on eighty, though he seemed much older than that. I could imagine that a job like the one he'd had would take its toll. The cases we'd come to ask him about probably aged him significantly. He still seemed sharp as a tack though.

Ryan looked uncomfortable. "Oh, I don't think so—" he started to say, but I interrupted him.

"He's Ryan McKay—he was Jess's boyfriend."

I wasn't sure why I had chosen that moment to reveal what I knew, but it felt good to let it out. And perhaps I felt safer in the company of someone else.

Ryan's head snapped up and I felt his shock. I avoided his gaze, instead focusing on Sergeant O'Neil. He was the one I wanted to talk to. I would speak to Ryan later.

"Oh yes, that's right. I remember interviewing you at the time." He picked up one of the notepads on his cluttered coffee table and flipped through a few pages before putting it down and picking up a different one and doing the same. "Ryan McKay . . . always thought you said Ryan *Kay* from the *Chicago Courier* when you called. Probably would have put two and two together otherwise. You had been dating Jessica for only a few months when she vanished, right?"

Once again, Ryan was silent, and when I looked at him, I found he was still staring at me, seemingly dazed. I wondered if Sergeant O'Neil had misheard him all these years, or if Ryan had purposefully given him the wrong name when they spoke. I wouldn't put anything past him at this point.

"That's right," he said, his voice hoarse.

My heart sank. I hated to admit that I hoped I had been wrong. That maybe, somehow, I had gotten things mixed up. Which was silly, given the pictures I had found, but that illogical hope was there all the same. But hearing the words from his mouth hurt more than I expected, or wanted, them to.

"I interviewed you several times. Definitely viewed you as a person of interest, no offense, but in cases like this, nine times out of ten it's the significant other." Sergeant O'Neil was flipping through the pages of his notepad now, unaware of the bombshell he'd dropped.

Ryan had been a suspect. Of course he had been. It made sense.

"You had an argument right before she went to her parents' house for her little sister's birthday party." He gave me a kind smile of acknowledgment. "By all accounts, it was loud and public." He tapped the side of his head and smiled. "See, I might be old, but it's all still up here."

"You said in '98 that you didn't think an unknown serial killer was involved in the women's disappearances. Do you still believe that?" I asked him, before he got sidetracked.

When you're leading an investigation, you can't let rumors dictate things. I know there were a lot of stories swirling around. We had a scared town that we had to keep calm. That was my priority." Sergeant O'Neil sucked on his teeth noisily. "And I can't say I ever bought the idea that the North Carolina Boogie Man or some other killer was responsible."

"Why not?" I prodded.

Sergeant O'Neil patted his oversized belly. "My guts never lie. I knew we weren't looking for one of those movie-style killers. This was something else. This was personal."

"What about Dr. Daniels? Did you ever look at him?" I asked, remembering Ryan's suspicions about the professor, though now I had to wonder why he was so keen to point the finger at someone else. My heart was beating too fast. The information about Ryan and Jess's argument was another surprise. Once again I was faced with facts that the man beside me had purposefully kept from me.

Sergeant O'Neil looked unsure. "We did, but he was written off pretty quickly. I need you to understand some things about the case back then. Those girls were only missing at the time. No one suspected any foul play. At least not at first. Girls run away all the time. What was there to even look into? But Phoebe Baker's parents wouldn't stop calling and calling, so we had to check things out. Hell, we never even linked them together. There didn't seem to be any connection at all. Different women, different looks, different social circles. The only connection they had was they all went to Southern State. That's hardly a red flag, now is it?"

"A lot of people said you should have called in the FBI to take over, yet you never did. You continued to investigate the disappearances yourself," Ryan began to talk. "It's been said that you overlooked obvious suspects like Dr. Daniels from the beginning."

Sergeant O'Neil inclined his head in agreement. "Maybe so. But no one wanted to look the professor's way. He was well respected up at that school. And things run differently there. It has its own way of doing things. We were frozen out early on. Everyone was tight-lipped about him, so it was hard to run a decent investigation." He sounded frustrated as he sat upright in his chair.

"Yeah, there's Mt. Randall and there's Southern State University. The two don't often intersect, and when they do, it never goes well," I agreed.

Sergeant O'Neil sighed wearily. "It was an uphill battle. The president of that school, what's his name," he flipped through his notebook again, "Bradley Hamilton—going through him was like trying to bust down a brick wall. He circled the wagons around Dr. Daniels, and we couldn't really get near him after our initial questioning. So it was easier to drop him as a line of inquiry." He put his notebook back down on the table. "I backed off when I admit I should have pushed more." He twisted his gnarled hands together, his piercing eyes never wavering. "The truth is, Dr. Daniels's alibi was his wife. And we all know that a spouse's alibi isn't worth the paper it's written on."

He slowly got to his feet, bracing himself on the armchair. He stretched out his back and then carefully made his way over to the fireplace. He picked up a black-and-white photo that looked like it was of him and his wife. I stood up and joined him.

In that moment, I hated him. Hated him for not doing more. For being weak. For not finding those women.

"So, his wife was his alibi," I repeated. Sergeant O'Neil grunted in assent. "She claimed to have been with her husband the night Jess went missing?"

Another grunt.

"And you think she lied, yet you never followed up on it?"

Sergeant O'Neil brow furrowed as his voice took on a note of hard defensiveness. "You have to understand. He was a well-educated man. He had been teaching at Southern State University for years. It made no sense for him to have done those girls any harm. I couldn't go around pointing fingers at men like him. Certainly not without some real evidence. Particularly given the way the college shut us down and made it damn near impossible to get answers. And I had no *real* evidence, only my instinct, which wouldn't exactly hold up in court."

"What makes you think his wife lied, Sergeant O'Neil?" Ryan asked as he joined us by the fireplace.

"It's that gut of mine talking again. Like I said, I knew something wasn't right." His body seemed to sag under the weight of his confession. "But, the truth is—" He hesitated.

"What is it?" I urged.

Sergeant O'Neil bowed his head. "The truth is, I didn't corroborate his alibi. I never dug any deeper into him. I never went to the restaurant where Mrs. Daniels said they were that night. I never did any of the things I should have done to officially eliminate him as a suspect."

I was horrified. I knew that police incompetence had been largely to blame for the reason my sister's, and the other girls', cases were never solved. But hearing it admitted by the lead detective was like a punch to the face.

Then the rage set in.

The man was lucky he was already on death's door because I was having very violent thoughts.

Sergeant O'Neil looked repentant. "I made the wrong choices back then. A lot of them. I know that now. Hindsight is always twenty-twenty. Because it was well known around the campus that he . . . well, he had several interactions that weren't entirely wholesome with some of his female students. But that doesn't make him a murderer, right? A pervert, yes, but a killer? I told myself it wasn't possible. I purposefully didn't listen to my hunch. Because if I had corroborated that alibi and it hadn't added up then everything would have come out. I would have had to formally name him. The man would have lost everything. His reputation would have been ruined. And he had a family. Young children. What would that have done to them?"

"What about those missing girls?" Ryan demanded. "What about Jess?"

Sergeant O'Neil looked stricken. "If I had gone down that road, the school would have come after me. Southern State has a lot of power in that community. I was worried I'd lose my job." He placed the photograph back on the mantle, his lips pressed into a thin line.

"So you cared more about your job than those missing girls. Got it," Ryan snapped, losing all sense of journalistic neutrality.

"I've felt more than enough shame about my choices back then. Because I was pushed out anyway, once it became clear I wasn't going to find Jessica. It was one thing when they were only a few girls from up on the hill, but once it was one of their own," Sergeant O'Neil's face took on a faraway expression, "it mattered a hell of a lot more."

"Let's say you had listened to your instincts about Dr. Daniels? What then?" I asked.

"Well then," he stated matter-of-factly, the fierceness returning. "he would have been my number one suspect."

**Ten Seconds to Vanish: The Unsolved
Disappearance of Jessica Fadley**

Episode 6

Stella: Welcome back, true crime lovers, I'm your
host Stella—
Rachel: And I'm Rachel.
Stella: And this is *Ten Seconds to Vanish: The Unsolved
Disappearance of Jessica Fadley*.
Theme music plays
Stella: Guys, we've been the number one true crime
podcast on iTunes and Spotify for the past month!
Rachel: I can't believe how people have taken to our
show. I know it has everything to do with our girl
Jessica.
Stella: I've opened a brand new bottle of red. You
want some, Rach?
Rachel: Absolutely, and then let's jump right into it,
because things have really taken a turn this past
week.
Stella: Have they ever! I'm having a hard time
keeping up with the twists and turns in this case.
So, my murder-loving beauties, I'm sure you've
all heard that the police have finally issued a

statement about those remains found at Doll's
Eye Lake outside of Mt. Randall.

Rachel: Who the hell names a lake, "Doll's Eye"? What
kind of crazy, nightmare fuel is that?

Stella: I know, it sounds like something straight from
a Stephen King novel.

Rachel: Okay, so this new detective seems to actually
have her shit together, which is a nice change
from the sloppy police work that has dogged this
case so far.

Stella: You can tell Detective Higgins is a bad-ass
bitch. And that lady is *on it*. No stone unturned
and all that.

Rachel: Detective Higgins has come out and said
that those remains—the ones that we were all so
convinced were Jessica's—they're not Jessica.

Stella: Nope. And it turns out that the bones found
at the lake—this place that was one of Jessica's
favorite spots–well, it's none other than Tammy
freaking Estep.

Rachel: What the actual crap is going on here?

Stella: And that's not all. It turns out Tammy was killed
by a blow to the head! And, the underwater
forensic team is now on site, diving into Doll's Eye
Lake to look for more remains. And guess what . . .
sources say they've found something.

Rachel: More bodies?

Stella: Maybe. Police are being tight-lipped about it,
which is really annoying. But I think we can
deduce that more bodies have been found. Now,
whether they're connected to Tammy and Jessica
has yet to be determined.

Rachel: It could be anybody floating around down
there.

Stella: Maybe it's one of our other missing girls.

Rachel: Maybe it's Jessica.

Stella: Maybe. But back to Tammy. Why were her
bones at this lake? From what I've read, this place

is really off the beaten path. You'd have to know it's there to find it, and Tammy wasn't from the area. To me, that obviously shows she was dumped there.

Rachel: If this is a place only known by locals, it narrows down the suspect pool considerably.

Stella: It sure does. But let's move on because there's another girl we need to talk about.

Rachel: That's right. We've talked about Jessica, Tammy, and Phoebe. So that only leaves . . .

Rachel and Stella in unison: Meghan Lambert.

CHAPTER

11

JESSICA

Late January 1999

I KNOCKED ON THE closed office door. The name *Dr. Clement Daniels* was engraved on a shiny brass plate below the frosted glass pane.

"Come in."

I turned the doorknob and went in, pulling the door closed behind me.

"Hi, Dr. Daniels, I'm Jessica Fadley. I'm interested in auditing your 6:30 Introduction to Statistics class." I sounded nervous. And who would blame me? If he didn't sign off on the class, I was at risk of losing my scholarship and being kicked out of not only Pi Gamma Delta, but school as well. I needed the class credits to become a sophomore because I knew I could never ask my parents to pay for summer school to make up the difference.

His head was bent over his desk as he wrote, his sandy blonde hair unruly. "Leave it on my desk and I'll see if I have room," he answered dismissively, not even looking up.

"I really hate to bother you, sir, but can you sign off on it now? I need to arrange my schedule and return the slip to the registrar's office before it closes." It wasn't usually in my nature to be pushy, but my future at Southern State University depended on it.

"I said leave it on my desk—" Dr. Daniels looked up and his words abruptly ended. There was a flash of recognition. This was the same man I had almost run into back in the fall semester.

He was also the same man I had seen in the car with Phoebe.

And he remembered me as well.

His hazel eyes met mine and there was a moment. He felt it. I felt it. It hung in the air between us. I was someone easily consumed by the desire for single, focused attention. Dr. Clement Daniels looked at me like I deserved his consideration. It was a heady feeling.

His full lips spread into a smile. "Here, let me see." He held out his hand and I gave him the registrar slip, our fingers brushing.

He turned to his computer, his attention now on the screen, giving me a brief reprieve from whatever that had been.

This was Dr. Daniels. The same Dr. Daniels that had been involved with Phoebe and Tammy.

Yet I wanted him to look at me again like I was worth something.

I watched his face as he squinted at the computer screen, clicking his mouse. When he was finished he grabbed a pen and signed the paper, holding it out for me to take. "Here you go, Jessica. You're all set."

This time, I made sure to take the slip without touching him.

"So there's room?" I asked.

Dr. Daniels sat back in his chair, folding his hands in his lap. He had the casual charm that I could see would be very appealing. He was classically handsome, with eyes that were both compassionate and heated. His mouth was full and seductive. His nose was straight and just about perfect. He reminded me of my dad in many ways. I understood why most of the female coeds on campus lusted after him. It was why it was so easy for Dr. Daniels, my dad, and all the men like them, to do what they did. Men like them made it easy.

"Of course, Jessica." My name sounded like an invitation.

"Oh, well thank you." I hefted my bookbag on my shoulder and turned toward the door. "I guess I'll see you in class."

"I make it a point to help students, particularly when they're struggling." His tone changed to that of a concerned teacher.

"Yeah, I guess my grades aren't where they should be." My face flushed with shame.

Dr. Daniels leaned forward and he was full of attentive kindness. "Freshman year is an adjustment for most students. The sudden independence can be tough. I've seen more than a few kids pass through this office right where you are."

I found myself relaxing marginally. He had a soothing effect on my anxiety.

"It's been hard," I found myself admitting.

I thought of all the classes I had missed. The now-nightly drunken partying. Even Daisy had expressed concern about the change in me. What I couldn't tell her was being wasted was better than having to deal with my thoughts. My memories.

Dr. Daniels stood up and walked around his desk. "Well, let's work together and get you back on track." He reached past me, his chest brushing against my arm, as he opened the door. "Don't be too hard on yourself, Jessica. We've all been there." His smile hit a nerve I didn't know was there. His confidence in me, his complete focus—it was a balm to a wound inside me that was oozing and raw.

I found myself wanting to lean against him as I would my dad. To let him comfort me and tell me everything was going to be okay. He was so close I could smell his aftershave and the mint of his mouthwash.

"You know, my classes aren't easy. A lot of students struggle. If you find yourself having a hard time keeping up, I offer one-on-one tutoring." He spoke softly, his voice altering almost imperceptibly. There was something there that I knew I should heed.

"Okay, I may take you up on that," I said just as softly.

"Good. I only want what's best for you—for all my students," Dr. Daniels murmured. And there it was. A flash of desire in his eyes. But then it was gone, almost as if it hadn't been there at all.

My stomach rolled and I felt my skin warm up.

"Thanks, Dr. Daniels." My voice was weak. Barely audible.

Dr. Daniels straightened up, taking a step back, his affect completely professional. It was a blink-and-you'd-miss-it transformation. "Please, call me Clement. I like to be on a first-name basis with my students. We're all on the same journey, after all."

A young woman was waiting in the hallway, leaning against the wall. When she saw me coming out of Dr. Daniels's— Clement's— office she appeared upset, though she tried to hide it. She looked from Dr. Daniels then to me, then back to Dr. Daniels.

"Meghan, right on time," Dr. Daniels said to her.

She walked toward us and for a second, our eyes met. I knew her. Or at least, I had seen her before. I could tell by the way she looked away from me that she recognized me as well.

She was the same girl my dad had been flirting with on move-in day.

I immediately felt lightheaded.

I moved aside so she could walk into Dr. Daniels's office. I turned to look at them, expecting to say goodbye to my new professor, but his attention was solely on Meghan now, making her feel like the center of his world, if only for a short time. Girls like Meghan—and me—chased a feeling only men like Dr. Daniels could provide.

For a brief second, he turned back, lifting his hand in a wave. "Bye, Jessica. See you soon."

And there it was. The note of intention I *wasn't* imagining.

I felt a strange sort of tugging in my stomach as I hurried out of Roosevelt Hall, making my way across the quad toward the administration building. I wanted to quickly hand in the signed audit slip and get back to the dorm. I had a free period and knew Daisy would be in class, so for once I would have the room to myself.

I was practically sprinting, as if I could outrun the mess my life had become.

The wind picked up and with it a creeping sensation I had become all too familiar with tip toed its way up my back.

I abruptly stopped, rooted to the spot.

Across the quad, in a small grove of trees, bright-red hair flickered in and out of sight.

My mouth went dry and my eyes burned.

"Jess! Hey, Jess!"

Distracted, the image disappeared as Ryan McKay jogged toward me. He had gotten a haircut over Christmas break and the bleached-blonde streaks were starting to grow out. He was more clean-cut than he had been the last time I saw him.

I pressed a hand to my thumping heart, willing myself to calm down. What was wrong with me? I needed to get myself together.

"I'm glad I found you," Ryan said once he reached me. He had called the room almost as soon as we got back to campus, though I had Daisy take a message. I wanted to see him, but I was still obsessing over the thought of him with Tammy and Phoebe. And I knew that when I spoke to him, my will would crumble.

"You're a hard woman to track down. If I wasn't so sure of myself, I'd think you were avoiding me." He was joking, but there was a note of something else in his tone. Angry frustration. I got the sense Ryan wasn't used to not getting his way.

"Confidence is great, Ryan, but *overconfidence* is a huge turn off." My smile was brittle as I went to walk around him.

He grabbed my upper arm, his fingers wrapping around my bicep. "What's going on? I thought we were going to hang out when we got back to school." He scowled at me, though tried to play it off like he was being funny.

I instantly froze. "Yeah, I've had stuff going on. I'm sorry. I would have called you back." I looked down at his tight grip on my arm and then back to his face. I felt myself instinctively become placid. Submissive. I backed down so easily when a force more powerful than myself pushed hard enough.

Ryan released me and took my hand instead. "I didn't think I'd have to track you down. I thought you *wanted* to hang out."

I let him hold my hand. It was easy to give in to him. To let him smile and make my insides flutter and pretend that this could go somewhere. And maybe it could. Didn't I deserve that?

But then Daisy's words about Ryan came back to me. The things she had told me about him. I thought of Dr. Daniels. I thought of my father. I thought of all these men that thought they could do whatever they wanted. I slowly, carefully extracted my hand from his grip even as the nerve endings ached for the contact.

"I found out about your pledge nickname." I tried to sound angry, but the words came out sad. As much as I hated it, I wasn't tough and in charge when it came to the men I wanted in my life.

"Nickname? What nick—," Ryan groaned and briefly closed his eyes. "Shit, okay, I know it sounds bad—"

"Wam Bam McKay?" It wasn't quite an accusation. I was walking a fine line. I lowered my eyes, my body sagging. I needed him to see how it hurt me. How much I suffered because of his behavior. Maybe then he would tell me all the things I longed to hear.

His cheeks flushed red. "It's not like that. I promise." He sounded sincere. God, how I wanted to believe him. Maybe I'd let myself.

"What about Tammy Estep?" I had to ask. I would despise myself if I didn't. "And Phoebe Baker?"

Saying their names out loud felt awful.

"It sounds like there have been a lot of girls," I continued.

He held up his hands in defense. "Okay, okay . . . I'm a piece of shit, I get it. But they were before I even met you—"

"And who comes after me, Ryan?" I asked softly.

I could never summon my anger when it counted. It only ever came out in wild, unpredictable ways. But the people, the *men*, who deserved my rage, never received it. I was conditioned to want their regard. Their tenderness. As much as I loathed to admit it, I would turn myself inside out in my desire to claim it.

His eyebrows drew together. "They were—" he shook his head, "—they were just fillers. Women to pass time with. You're not them. You're special."

He seemed so sincere. But I had heard these sentiments before. Men like him threw around words never knowing their true meaning. They did it to conquer. To make themselves feel better. To get what they wanted and damn the consequences. Damn the victims.

Men like Ryan were ruining my life.

Ryan reached for my hand again, a playful, hopeful smile tugging at the corners of his mouth. "That sounded corny."

"Maybe a little," I teased breathlessly, eager to put aside the ugliness. I was greedy for his attention and affection. It echoed the craving I experienced with Dr. Daniels. This impatient hunger that engulfed better sense.

"I wish you were the first, Jess. I really do. I want to pretend that there has never been anyone but you." He laid it on thick. He was a shark circling in the water and he could smell blood.

I let him pull me into his arms, his lips pressed against my temple. I felt the tension drain out of me. How quickly I dismissed all the reasons to keep my distance.

I had a hard time doing what was best for me.

Needing to be loved above all others would be my downfall.

* * *

The phone rang and this time he picked up right away.

"Hello?" He sounded distracted. He always sounded distracted these days. I wanted to scream, but I wouldn't.

There was a time when I had all his attention. It hurt so much that I had to share it now.

With all the others.

"Hi, Dad."

"Jess." He said my name flatly, as if he regretted answering the phone.

There was complete silence, neither of us saying anything for an uncomfortably long period of time.

"What do you need?" he asked, bracing himself.

"Aren't you going to ask how I'm doing?" I couldn't hide the pain in my voice.

"I'm sorry, sweetheart," he placated. "How are things? I hope they're better. Your mom and I have been worried that you're running yourself down. You were so distant at Christmas—"

"I wonder why," I interrupted, for once, summoning some bite.

Dad sighed as if annoyed. Irritated at having to explain himself. "Jess, it's not what you think."

"Stop it. Please, just stop it! For me!" I felt myself becoming unreasonable. My emotions were cresting like a wave. I couldn't find my anger, but my fear and misery were enough to destroy everything.

"Jess, don't be upset. I can't bear it." My dad's voice was wet with tears.

"I saw her." I felt sick. I had to take long deep breaths so I wouldn't throw up. I didn't want to bring her up, but I had to.

"What are you talking about? Who did you see?"

"The girl, Dad. The one from move-in day." I started crying. It's what I always did when faced with the awful truths I couldn't run away from. Like with Ryan earlier, and Dr. Daniels before that, I felt myself cave under the weight of this unbearable *need*.

"Don't cry, darling. This is all my fault."

He was right. This was his fault.

All of it.

I felt the ring in my pocket. I wanted to throw it away, but I wouldn't let myself. It was there for a reason.

It used to be a reminder of my father's affection.

Now it was a reminder of all the pain he inflicted.

"Jess, listen to me. We can make things better." He sounded as if he were talking from the bottom of a well. I barely heard him.

You're a liar.

I wanted to shout it into the phone. But I didn't. The recriminations reverberated around my skull.

"I have to go, Daddy."

His broken promises pierced my shattered heart.

"Okay, sweetheart. I'm here. Always."

You're a liar.

I hung up and the cavernous dark pit opened up inside me swallowing me whole.

*   *   *

The campus was quiet at night. It was Wednesday, so it was devoid of weekend partygoers. The drinking and debauchery would be reserved for dorm rooms.

For the first time in weeks, I was stone-cold sober. I had gotten used to the welcome numbness that took my mind off . . . everything.

But, Daisy had asked to have the room for the next hour, so here I was, wandering the darkness—on edge, restless, not quite alone.

Figures moved in and out of the shadows, and I forced myself not to look every time I caught something out of the corner of my eye.

I was terrified I'd see them again. I was scared of the other eyes I felt watching me.

Dad said to be careful. Daisy told me to stay in well-lit places.

Neither knew what real terror felt like.

I found myself wandering over to Roosevelt Hall. I looked up at the imposing building and noticed a light still on in Dr. Daniels's office.

"Jess." I nearly jumped out of my skin.

I pressed a hand to my chest. "Jesus, Ryan, you scared the crap out of me."

Ryan had his hands tucked into his jeans pockets, an orange-and-white-striped beanie pulled down over his ears. It had only been ten hours since our conversation and I could tell he wasn't sure what to say to me.

I was still wary of him, but there was an indescribable something about Ryan McKay that had me throwing caution to the wind.

"Sorry, I saw you walking alone, so thought I'd make sure you were okay." Ryan's eyes met mine, never wavering. There was a solidity there that I yearned for desperately.

"Why wouldn't I be okay?" I asked.

"With everything going on, I know people are freaked out." He glanced around the quad. "The guys on my floor keep saying there's a killer on campus. I think they're using it to get girls to let them in their dorm rooms." His smile was brief and lopsided.

I laughed, though I didn't think it was at all funny.

Ryan cocked his head to the side as he regarded me. "You never answered my question earlier." There was a thread of frustration in his tone that should have given me pause. "I hate being strung along, Jess."

Had Tammy strung him along? Is that why he called her a cocktease? I was nothing like Tammy. Or Phoebe.

"I'm not trying to string you along," I told him honestly.

His dark look brightened, marginally. "So, maybe I can take you on a date sometime." It wasn't a question. He knew my answer.

I bit my bottom lip to stop them from trembling. "Sure. I'd like that."

Ryan moved closer and confidently took my hand. My cold fingers laced with his. "Do you think we can schedule that rain-checked date—?"

The door of Roosevelt Hall opened, the heavy wood crashing against the brick wall.

"Come on." Ryan pulled on my hand as we ran around the side of the building, both of us hidden among the overgrown ivy.

"Meghan!" I heard a man yelling.

We peered around the corner to watch the drama unfold. It was Dr. Daniels. He was rushing after the same woman from earlier. Meghan ran down the steps, wiping at her face as if she were crying.

"What the hell?" Ryan whispered beside me. I could feel his warm breath on my cheek as I pressed into him so we wouldn't be seen.

We watched as Dr. Daniels grabbed hold of Meghan before she could get away. She pulled back, clearly fighting against him.

"Stop it, Clement, please stop!" she shouted, her voice wavering and broken.

"Shut up!" he barked, giving her arm a shake. He darted a look around and Ryan and I automatically moved back into the ivy, obscuring us from his view. I felt my body stiffen as I watched them. Ryan was a bundle of tension beside me. I felt it radiating off him.

Meghan was really struggling, but the professor continued to hold her tightly. He leaned in, his lips close to her ear, and spoke softly. Whatever he said had an immediate effect. She went limp, her head bowing. Dr. Daniels lifted her chin and kissed her.

I felt my insides lurch, but neither Ryan nor I said anything. I felt like I shouldn't be watching, but I couldn't help myself.

This is wrong!

I wanted to stop them. I wanted to pull her away from him. I wanted to . . .

Dr. Daniels broke the kiss first, his voice still too low for us to hear. Meghan was clearly unhappy with his words. She shook her head and tried to back away. Dr. Daniels looked furious. This was a far cry from the kind man I had spoken to earlier.

Finally she pushed away from him. He yelled after her, and this time, he was very clear.

"You stupid girl. I won't let you ruin my life." His words were like gunshots.

She let out a strangled sob and ran in the direction of the freshmen dorms. Dr. Daniels stared after her for a few more moments, his fingers combing through his hair, before heading back into Roosevelt Hall.

As soon as the older man was gone, Ryan moved away from me. "She's such an idiot." He sounded horrified. Outraged. He was clenching his teeth hard enough to break bone. "I should go talk to her."

I frowned in confusion—and irritation. "Do you know her?"

Ryan's wouldn't quite meet my eyes. "That's Meghan Lambert. She . . . uh . . . yeah, I know her."

I wanted to get indignant. The implication was obvious. Instead, I remained quiet. Stewing on my bitter thoughts.

Ryan's expression was shuttered. "I can't believe her." He shook his head. "Why would she get involved with him? What the hell?" He ran his hands through his short hair, he was a muddied mixture of aggrieved and furious. "I need to talk to her."

My chest felt like ice. "Fine." I couldn't help but sound devastated.

His eyes softened, his anger abating slightly. "Jess," he murmured my name and reached for me again. "Please don't read more into this—"

I forced myself to smile. To relax. "I said it's fine. You obviously need to talk to her, so go."

He seemed momentarily conflicted. "I'll call you tomorrow, okay?"

"Sure." My mouth ached with the effort it took to look unaffected. The smile stayed in place. Inside I was howling.

Then he kissed me. A brief touch of lips that felt distracted rather than passionate. His thoughts were elsewhere. Then he was gone. Off to check on a girl that wasn't me. I stared after Ryan, wishing that he'd come back, and furious at Meghan for putting me in this position.

* * *

Five Days Later

"Oh my god!" Daisy gasped, pointing to the TV. I was lying on my bed, legs stretched out in front of me, pretending to read *Great Expectations* for my Victorian Literature class. I knew, deep down, it was another assignment I'd never complete.

I looked up and froze. A young woman's face filled the screen. A face I recognized immediately.

Daisy turned the volume up. *"Nineteen-year-old Meghan Lambert, a freshman at Southern State University, has been reported missing by her family."*

Daisy turned to me. "She lives in our dorm. I think she's on the second floor."

I couldn't look at the TV. "We don't know what this means—"

"Listen," Daisy interrupted, glued to the news report.

"Meghan is the third girl to go missing since November. Tammy Estep, who has only recently been named a missing person, was last seen on November 12. Phoebe Baker, also a freshman at Southern State University, was reported missing on December 8 by her parents. While authorities have yet to make a statement regarding Meghan Lambert, speculation is rife over the potential connections between the three women, and police are keen to know Meghan's last whereabouts. Links to the morbidly named North Carolina Boogie Man have been mentioned in connection to the three women, though authorities refuse to comment."

"Daisy, turn that off," I pleaded, closing my book and putting it on my desk. My heart was pounding in my chest, a sick feeling clawing at me.

My roommate muted the TV, the images of the college and missing Meghan still bright on the screen.

She came over and sat on my bed. "Seriously, this is getting really scary. You can't dismiss my idea that it's a serial killer, now. That's three girls, Jess. Something horrible is going on." Daisy's distress was obvious. She bunched my new comforter in her hands, her pupils dilated in fear.

I wanted to make her feel better. I wanted to calm her. But the truth was, I was worried too. This wasn't something that could be mistaken anymore. These were clear and obvious crimes.

The overwhelming desire to call my dad left me shaky. I needed his reassurance. He was the only one who could make this better.

Or he'd make things a whole lot worse.

"No, I don't think there's a serial killer," I began, "there's no indication anything even happened to them." I felt a heaviness in my limbs. A sinking feeling as if I was being dragged down.

Daisy cuddled against me. "I don't know, Jess. What if we're next? I'm starting to think maybe I should go home."

I put my arms around my friend, hoping to comfort her despite the anxiety I was also feeling. "You have nothing to worry about, Daisy. I promise," I assured her.

Daisy looked up at me. "But you can't possibly know that. You can't say we're safe when it's becoming more and more obvious that we're not."

I didn't know what to say, so I defaulted to my tried-and-true response. Silence.

When I did nothing to assuage her fear, Daisy moved to her own bed as if she needed the space between us. "Seriously, Jess, we should stick together from now on, okay? I'm going to suggest a buddy system with the other pledges."

"The police think Tammy and Phoebe took off. Maybe Meghan did, too." My theory fell flat. "But if it'll make you feel better, I'll escort you to every class." I tried to sound airy and unconcerned. I was pretty sure I wasn't succeeding.

Daisy gave me an opaque look that bothered me. "Thanks, Jess. I hope you're right." She stood up and reached for her shower caddy. "I'm gonna go get a shower before dinner."

"Want me to stand guard?" I joked half-heartedly.

"Nah, I think I'll be okay," she remarked weakly before leaving the room.

I grabbed the remote, pointing it at the TV to turn it off when a picture of a yellow muscle car filled the screen. Against my better judgment, I turned up the volume again.

"An eyewitness has come forward claiming to have seen Meghan Lambert in a car similar to this one, a Boss 429 Mustang, on the day she went missing. Police are now looking for any information regarding this vehicle . . ."

I dropped the remote control and it clattered to the floor. I stood frozen in a state of horror with the image of a car, nearly identical to my father's Mustang, on the television.

Ten Seconds to Vanish Podcast
@TenSecondPod

Things are heating up! How are our 4 girls connected? Find out in the new episode dropping today! Get your thinking caps on because we're headed to class. #tensecondstovanish #truecrime #podcast #ItsAllAboutTheTeacher

9:22 AM Mar 14, 2023

⟲ 2.1k 💬 2.3k ♡ 12.7k

12

LINDSEY

Present Day

R YAN DROVE IN silence for several miles, and I was glad. I
didn't know whom to trust. All I knew was that I sure as
hell couldn't trust Ryan McKay. I felt like such a moron for
ever thinking I could.

I gripped the cardboard box on my lap. I didn't want to
let it out of my sight.

"There's a great little greasy spoon up ahead. Should I
stop so we can get something to eat? Maybe go through the
file together?" Ryan suggested cautiously.

He hadn't said anything about what I had revealed at
Sergeant O'Neil's house. He hadn't asked how I knew he had
dated Jess. He hadn't tried to explain himself. He simply let
the dark truth dangle between us, not acknowledging it.
How could he act like everything was the same, when it
clearly wasn't?

I scoffed at the very idea that he would think I would
want to go anywhere with him ever again, even a crappy
diner.

Perhaps he was too focused on getting his hands on Sergeant O'Neil's file. The thought of letting him have it was
abhorrent. I had to protect whatever it contained, which
meant keeping him away from it.

I refused to look at him, keeping my attention outside the window.

I was grateful to Sergeant O'Neil for finally doing the right thing after all this time, but I was angry with him, too. He had ignored obvious leads. He had purposefully looked the other way when suspects were practically thrown in his face. If he had actually done his job decades ago, then maybe it would have saved us all a lot of pain.

And while I was glad the retired detective had decided to try and help now, it would never make up for how little he had done when it actually mattered.

A clear conscience was something he would *never* have.

Ryan pulled into the parking lot of a small, rundown diner.

"What are you doing?" I snapped. I glared at him, my disgust for Ryan and the aging detective blending together. "Take me home, now."

Ryan put the car into park and turned to me, his brown eyes pleading. "Like I said, I thought we could get something to eat and look through the file . . . together. Maybe we'll get lucky and find something he missed. Sergeant O'Neil clearly never took the cases seriously enough."

I hugged the box to my chest, my eyes widening in disbelief. "Are you serious? I don't want to be anywhere near you. How can you think everything is fine between us?"

"But—"

"You lied to me, Ryan," I yelled. "From day one, you were dishonest. Right from that very first meeting. You could have come clean and told me who you really were, but you didn't. You chose to keep me in the dark about everything." It was too much. I was overcome by a combination of rage, sadness and grief.

"Lindsey—" He reached for me and I pulled away.

"Don't you dare touch me," I hissed. "You've been flirting with me. Making me think you . . . *liked* me," I hissed. "What is *wrong* with you? How could you do that to me?" I broke down, wrenching sobs left me gasping. "How could you do that to *her*?"

"Jess hasn't been my girlfriend in a very long time," Ryan tried to explain, as if that made this any better.

"You purposefully deceived me," I spat out.

Ryan looked appalled. But there was nothing he could say to justify his behavior.

"You and Jess fought on the day she disappeared. That doesn't look great for you," I accused. I realized, almost as soon as the words left my mouth, how precarious my position was. I was confronting a man I was beginning to suspect of horrible things, and we were alone . . . in his car.

Ryan threw his hands in the air in frustration. "We always fought, Lindsey. That's how our relationship worked. We'd fight. Then we'd . . ." he swallowed, "then we'd make up."

I thought I was going to vomit. "What were you fighting about that day?"

Ryan stared out the window. "I really don't remember."

He was lying. I could see that, clear as day.

He turned back to me. "Our relationship was like a roller coaster. We were up and we were down. At the time, I loved the ride. But now that I'm older, I can see how toxic it was. We weren't good for each other. No one should love so hard it hurts."

Hearing him talk about Jess like this wounded me in a way I wasn't sure I could stand. Sure, we weren't really involved, but I had come to think of him as *mine*. My potential *something*. It was a blow to my heart—and my pride—to know he never really had been.

"You love her." It was a statement of total truth.

Ryan looked contrite and almost sad. "It's hard to get over someone when there's no real closure. It took me a long time to mend what she broke."

I didn't believe him. I didn't think I ever would again.

"What can I do to help make this better?" he asked, his voice thick with emotion.

"You can't do *anything*." The space inside the car felt too small. Suffocating. I felt trapped by his guilt and lies with nowhere to go.

"I do like you, Lindsey. I really like you. And I know you like me, too." The words seemed to choke him. "I know what I did was wrong. I should have said something. But I was scared. Particularly after I got to know you and I felt all of these things I haven't felt since . . ." He hesitated.

"Since Jess?" My voice sounded flat.

Ryan lowered his head, staring into his lap. "I miss Jess—I always have, and I always will. But being with you . . ." He lifted his eyes to look at me and I wanted to slap him and kiss him all at the same time. It made me sick. "I can't explain it. I felt like *me* again. Like the man I used to be before all of this consumed my life. Before *she* consumed my life." His smile was mournful. "It felt like maybe, I could finally move on." He was close to crying. He was clearly having a deeply profound moment. But his words had the opposite effect on me.

I didn't feel like crying. I felt like hitting something . . . hard.

"I'm not her, Ryan. I'm not Jess. I'm my own person. I'm not some placeholder for the woman you really love. That's not fair to me and it's certainly not fair to her." His pupils dilated as he watched me warily. "She's not coming back. Ever. She's gone. Accept it." I opened the door to get out of the car, but before I could, Ryan grabbed my wrist.

"I don't want you to be her, Lindsey. Please don't go," he begged.

I extracted myself from his grip and got out, struggling to hold onto the box. "Do *not* follow me. I'll find my own way home."

"Let me take you—I'll drive you straight there, I promise."

I let out a short, humorless laugh. "As if your promises mean anything. Stay away from me, Ryan. I'll call my dad to pick me up, and if you're still here when he arrives, I don't know what he'll do."

"Your dad?" he chuckled darkly, "because he's such a stand-up guy."

"You don't know anything about him, or me."

"I know enough," he seethed. "I know that he can't be trusted."

I wanted to scream at him, but somehow I held it together. "You're in no position to talk about trust."

His mouth thinned with contempt. "He's not who you think he is, Lindsey."

"And neither are you." I slammed the door shut without waiting for a response. I backed away, waiting for him to get out and follow me, even though I told him not to.

But he didn't. Instead he put his car in drive and peeled out of the parking lot.

I watched him speed off down the road and then I walked into the diner.

I sat down at a booth, putting the box down beside me, and pulled my cell phone out of my pocket. I needed to call my dad to come get me because I knew he would ask me a lot fewer questions than my mother would. At the moment, he was the lesser of the two evils. With a deep breath, I dialed his number and felt disappointment when he didn't pick up.

I knew I had to call my mom, but I wasn't in a rush to face the inquisition that I would have escaped if I had gotten ahold of my dad. So, instead I lifted the lid off the box and pulled out a pile of papers, placing them on the table in front of me. A waitress came over with a menu and I ordered a coffee and a slice of sweet potato pie.

The older woman gave my shoulder a gentle squeeze. "Whoever he is, he ain't worth the tears," she said and I quickly wiped my face, realizing I was crying.

She was right. Ryan wasn't worth it. But I wasn't only crying about him. I was crying for the four missing women and how everyone had failed them. The police, the college, even their loved ones. What chance did they have when no one listened? The injustice was too much to think about. I could only hope that Lieutenant Jane Higgins kept her promise and solved their cases.

Tammy, Phoebe, Meghan, and Jess deserved it.

After the waitress left to get my coffee and pie, I turned my attention to the file, expecting piles of useless information, given the ineptitude Sergeant O'Neil had displayed in his investigation. To my surprise, there was much more than that.

The detective had, in some respects, been very thorough. There were photocopies of all of his notes. There were copies of official statements on old police forms. There were transcripts of interviews, some dozens of pages long.

And there were photographs. Lots and lots of photographs.

There were pictures of all the missing girls. A glamor shot of Tammy Estep with her frizzy brown hair. Meghan Lambert holding a hockey stick for an official school photo. A picture of Phoebe Baker smiling in her high school cap and gown. And there were pictures of Jess. So many pictures.

But there were also police photos of things the detective had thought relevant at the time. Snapshots of dorm rooms. Photographs of Doll's Eye Lake haphazardly marked off with police tape. Pictures of Jess's car, an older model of my own Toyota, parked in front of our house.

I flipped through the pages hoping to find something glaringly obvious. But there was so much that I decided to start at the beginning and work my way through it methodically.

A paper near the front of the stack caught my eye.

It was Ryan's police interview. I skimmed the page and wasn't surprised to find it disorganized and aimless. Sergeant O'Neil never followed up on anything that Ryan said. There were no probing questions. And given that Ryan hadn't even bothered to have an attorney present, it was clear he didn't feel that he needed one. Even though Ryan was a potential suspect, the whole thing read like it was merely a formality.

Mt. Randall Police Department
Official Interview: Ryan James McKay
Report Date: 04/28/1999
Time stamp: 14:45

Description: Interview with Ryan James McKay
Occurrence From: 04/28/1999, 14:45
Occurrence To: 04/28/1999, 15:50

Reporting Officer: O'Neil, Liam (Sergeant, lead detective of Mt. Randall Police Department)
Case/File Number: A413TR5

Sergeant L. O'Neil: Okay, Ryan, let me start by thanking you for coming down to the station today. I know things are probably real busy for you at school.

Ryan McKay: Yeah, it is, but of course, I wanted to come.

Sergeant L. O'Neil: Great, well let's get started. First off, can you tell me what your relationship is with Jessica Fadley?

Ryan McKay: Jess is my girlfriend.

Sergeant L. O'Neil: And how long had the two of you been dating?

Ryan McKay: I don't know, a couple of months.

Sergeant L. O'Neil: And were the two of you monogamous?

Ryan McKay: Yes, sir, we're as serious as you can get.

Sergeant L. O'Neil: Did Jessica have any other boyfriends?

Ryan McKay: No, sir, only me.

Sergeant L. O'Neil: How certain can you be about that?

Ryan McKay: Come on, a guy knows when his woman is stepping out on him, don't you agree detective?

Sergeant L. O'Neil: You're right, son. There are things a man just knows.

Ryan McKay: Men like us don't mess around with women like that, right?

Sergeant L. O'Neil: Sure, sure.

Ryan McKay: And Jess definitely wasn't like that.

Sergeant L. O'Neil: Okay, when was the last time you saw Jessica Fadley?

Ryan McKay: I think it was the night she went home for her sister's birthday party.

Sergeant L. O'Neil: April 23?

Ryan McKay: Yeah, that's right.

Sergeant L. O'Neil: Where did you see her?

Ryan McKay: Out in front of her dorm.

Sergeant L. O'Neil: And how did Jessica seem?

Ryan McKay: Umm, anxious . . . like, nervous, I guess

Sergeant L. O'Neil: Why do you think that?

Ryan McKay: She didn't like going back home. She didn't like her mom and dad. She didn't really get along with either of them, but particularly her father. It was a strained relationship.

Sergeant L. O'Neil: So why go home then? If the relationship was strained, why would she go back there?

Ryan McKay: Because she loved her little sister.

It seemed that Ryan had always been a liar. What he said about our family wasn't remotely true. Jess loved us. Everything I had ever known about her proved that she was a family girl through and through.

But then I thought about what I had found hidden in her room. Her failing grades and photos of a lifestyle far from the straight-laced girl she had been when she was younger. She had clearly gone buck wild after she'd left home, but a lot of kids did that. And it wasn't uncommon for a teenager to keep secrets from her parents—especially ones they wouldn't approve of. It didn't *mean* anything.

I flipped the page.

Description: Interview with Ryan James McKay

Occurrence From: 05/01/1999, 11:23

Occurrence To: 05/01/1999, 12:05

Reporting Officer: O'Neil, Liam (Sergeant, lead detective of Mt. Randall Police Department)

Case/File Number: A413TR5

Sergeant L. O'Neil: Thanks for coming back in, Ryan. I have a few more questions to ask you.

Ryan McKay: Sure, no problem. Anything to help, Sergeant.

Sergeant L. O'Neil: Can you tell me what you and Jessica talked about the last time you saw her?

Ryan McKay: I don't really remember.

Sergeant L. O'Neil: That's interesting. Because she's your girlfriend. You two are close, right? That's what you told me the last time you were in here.

Ryan McKay: Yes, we are.

Sergeant L. O'Neil: Then it should be easy for you to remember what you talked about the last time you saw her.

Ryan McKay:

Sergeant L. O'Neil: Let the record show that Ryan McKay did not answer the question.

Ryan McKay: No, I can answer. I just had to think—

Sergeant L. O'Neil: It's not really something you need to think long and hard about, Ryan. I'm not asking you to solve algebra, I'm simply asking what you spoke to Jessica, your girlfriend, about, on April 23.

Ryan McKay: It was no big deal. I was annoyed that she ditched our date. I was asking her about it.

Sergeant L. O'Neil: You were only asking her about it? You sure?

Ryan McKay: It really wasn't anything important—

Sergeant L. O'Neil: Because I have an eyewitness statement who says you two were seen fighting in front of Westwood Hall. This was around three in the afternoon, which is only a few hours before she went home.

Ryan McKay: I don't know if you could call it a fight—

Sergeant L. O'Neil: Well, according to this eye witness, it was a very heated argument and you grabbed her arm.

Ryan McKay: No, it wasn't like that.

Sergeant L. O'Neil: Did you or did you not put your hands on Jessica Fadley in an aggressive manner?

Ryan McKay: I would never hurt Jess!

Sergeant L. O'Neil: No one's saying you hurt her,
Ryan. Let's not get ahead of ourselves.

I stared at the words in front of me, but my mind was thinking back to earlier when Ryan had grabbed me in a fit of anger. I subconsciously rubbed my wrist still feeling the ghost of his touch on my skin. It was clear he had a temper—I had seen it several times already. But did having a temper equal hurting my sister?

Sergeant L. O'Neil: So. tell me more about this
argument. Did her ditching your date really make
you so angry that you grabbed her?

Ryan McKay: It was nothing.

Sergeant L. O'Neil: So, do you remember?

Ryan McKay: No comment.

Sergeant L. O'Neil: No comment? Son, that doesn't
work here, not with me. This isn't TV and I'm not
the FBI. Now, answer the damn question, or I will
make you answer it. What else were you two
arguing about?

Ryan McKay: She . . . she wanted to break up with
me.

Sergeant L. O'Neil: Did she say why?

Ryan McKay: She said she wasn't who I thought she
was. That she didn't think she was good enough
for me.

Sergeant L. O'Neil: And what did you say to that?

Ryan McKay: Jess is the best person I know. I love
her. I will always love her. That's what I told her.
Then she left and I went and got drunk.

Sergeant L. O'Neil: Can anyone corroborate that?

Ryan McKay: Yes. I was with Daisy. I spent the night
with her.

Sergeant L. O'Neil: Daisy Molina? Jessica's
roommate?

Ryan McKay: Yes.

Sergeant L. O'Neil: And she can vouch for your
     whereabouts?
Ryan McKay: Yes, I never left her room.
Sergeant L. O'Neil: So, your girlfriend, who you're
     madly in love with, dumps you and you then go
     and take up with her best friend? And then later,
     the now ex-girlfriend goes missing? Am I getting
     this right? Sounds like a bad made-for-TV movie,
     if you ask me.

That clinched it for me. Ryan was a grade-A liar. There was
no way in hell he didn't remember what he and Jess had argued
about. How could he forget that the woman he loved had
dumped him without warning on the day she disappeared?

As for his alibi . . . I was shocked. I wondered how close
Daisy and my sister could have actually been, for her to sleep
with Ryan. It was definitely implied that's what had
happened.

I noticed that Sergeant O'Neil never bothered to follow
up on the argument between Ryan and Jess. It had seemed
like he was on to something, then unceremoniously dropped
it and never brought it up again. It was incredibly frustrating.
Sergeant O'Neil never seemed to ask anything of importance
after that. It was almost like he wanted the interview done
with as quickly as possible. Ryan must have been convincing,
because that was his last interview.

I put the papers down, needing a breather. This was all
so much worse than I had expected it to be. There were so
many more questions that should have been asked but
weren't. How could the detective let so many things fall
through the cracks?

Those women never stood a chance of being found.

What did stand out to me was that Ryan had gotten
drunk and spent the night with Daisy. He was nowhere near
our house when Jess went missing. Though, that's not saying
he couldn't have ditched Daisy at some point.

I flipped through more pages, coming across photographs taken of possible evidence. There was a photograph

of Jess's car, the trunk still open. There were separate pictures of the contents, including a wrapped present I knew was for me and a three-tier cake. There was a photo of a black duffle bag sitting on a table, and placed beside it the items that must have been inside. It was all fairly common stuff; pajamas, a spare set of clothing, a makeup bag—all things one would expect to be packed for a couple of nights away.

There were copies of letters from the parents of Phoebe Baker and Meghan Lambert. I didn't spend much time reading them, as they were only the enraged sentiments of sidelined families demanding answers. I did notice there was no correspondence from Tammy's family. Or from mine.

Eventually, I found my own transcripted interview. It was strange how I could remember so little of my life before and directly after Jess went missing, but this one moment, I recalled with total clarity.

I couldn't be sure how long it was after Mom called the police that they came to the house. What I do remember was sitting at the dining table, asking when I could open my gifts. I was upset that my party had been canceled.

I'd been asked over and over if I had seen where Jess had gone. I tried to recall but there wasn't much to say. I had been watching her from the living room window. She said she was going to get a surprise for me from the car. I had gotten distracted—I couldn't say by what—and when I looked back, she was gone. It was then that I became upset, a sliver of the awful reality setting in. I had cried, wanting to see my sister. I howled that I had only looked away for ten seconds—but in truth it was probably much longer than that. I hated everyone's questions. I wanted them to leave.

I wanted Jessie.

The next report was my mom's statement. From the Sergeant's notes, she had been "hysterical and inconsolable." He wrote, *"Unable to extract any information. Mrs. Fadley was unable to answer questions, no matter how many times she is asked. Not sure if she understands what's going on."* I rolled my eyes at the Sergeant's condescending tone. Then I found my dad's statement. The questions all seemed pretty standard—nothing of note—until I saw a barely legible scrawl at the bottom in what I had come to recognize as Sergeant O'Neil's handwriting.

It read, 'Possible suspect—Meghan Lambert.'

I frowned, not understanding.

Possible suspect—Meghan Lambert?

It had been written on my dad's statement, so there was no mistaking what Sergeant O'Neil was thinking at the time and who the suspicion was directed at. But why?

How was my father connected to Meghan Lambert, let alone how was he a potential suspect in her disappearance?

That couldn't be right.

I leafed through more of the pages, coming across a photograph of a 1965 yellow Boss 429 Mustang. The photo was paperclipped to a statement from an eyewitness who claimed to have seen Meghan getting in this car on the same day she was reported missing by her friends.

And there was yet another picture of the same car, only this time parked in front of my house.

I found an official police evidence report covered in handwritten notes.

Description of Evidence retrieved from vehicle belonging to Benjamin Fadley:

1. Hair sample taken. *DNA to be confirmed.*
2. Semen sample collected from seat fabric. *DNA to be confirmed.*
3. One adult female's bra, white lace.

My stomach plummeted.

I would know that car anywhere, despite my dad never driving it. He still cleaned it and waxed it monthly. And I would often find him sitting in the driver's seat while it was parked in our garage, staring out of the window absently, listening to the same cassette tape over and over. I'd asked him a million times why he never drove it anymore, but he could never give me a straight answer.

Was this why?

Had my father really been involved with Meghan Lambert?

The idea didn't align with what I knew of my dad. Of his relationship with my mom. While he may be distant with me, he deferred to her in all things. He wouldn't cheat on her and definitely not with someone so much younger than him.

It didn't make sense.

But why were police searching his car? And why was there an eyewitness putting Meghan Lambert in the Mustang on the same day she disappeared?

What about the semen sample taken from the fabric seats?

There was only one reason something like that would be found next to a woman's bra. I had always thought my dad to be a great guy. Easygoing, if distantly loving. And while he seemed to keep me at arm's length, I excused it as a heartbroken father grieving the loss of his first child. He wasn't creepy. He didn't put people on edge. He was your average American dad who worked too much and was obsessed with cars.

But this . . . this changed everything.

Just after the picture of the Mustang was a five-page interview transcript.

Description: Interview with Benjamin Fadley
Occurrence From: 02/11/1999, 09:32
Occurrence To: 02/11/1999, 10:15
Reporting Officer: O'Neil, Liam (Sergeant, lead detective of Mt. Randall Police Department)
Case/File Number: A313TR7

Sergeant L. O'Neil: This will only take a few minutes, Mr. Fadley. But I need to talk to you about your whereabouts on February 8.

Benjamin Fadley: I was with my wife and daughter, Lindsey, at home all day.

Sergeant L. O'Neil: I will corroborate that with your wife, of course.

Benjamin Fadley: Actually, I'd appreciate it if you didn't speak to Cara about this. It's . . . a bit sensitive.

Sergeant L. O'Neil: I'm not in the business of busting up families, Mr. Fadley, but I need to know if you were having a sexual relationship with Meghan Lambert.

Benjamin Fadley: If I can keep this from my wife and family, I'll tell you what you want to know.

Sergeant L. O'Neil: Mr. Fadley, please answer the question.

Benjamin Fadley: Yes, I was having a sexual relationship with Meghan Lambert.

I couldn't read anymore, the words blurring on the page. I felt hot and sweaty, and tears pricked my eyes. My father had been sleeping with one of the missing girls. He had seen her the day she went missing.

Was he involved with the other missing girls, too?

It seemed like Mt. Randall had an overabundance of creeps perving on young women, my father being one of them.

Had Jess known this? Is that why she stopped calling my parents as my mom had claimed? Is that why she rejected our dad?

Ryan's words from earlier echoed back to me. *"He's not who you think he is."*

What did he know?

One thing was for sure, according to Sergeant O'Neil's notes, my dad was also a suspect. At least when it came to Meghan Lambert.

I flipped over the piece of paper to find more of Sergeant O'Neil's messy handwriting on the back.

Respectable family man. Doesn't fit any kind of profile. No further investigation required.

I shuffled through the rest of the items in the file, trying to see if my dad was ever questioned again. But it seemed after his less-than-forthcoming interview, as with Clement Daniels and Ryan, he was dropped as a suspect for no other reason than he seemed like a good guy incapable of hurting young women.

It was disgusting.

With a frustrated sigh, I started to put the lid back on the box but stopped. A photo of Jess stared back at me, her blue eyes piercing.

I lifted it, touching the glossy surface. I didn't know this woman, not really. She was my sister, and we shared blood, but she was a mystery.

"I will find out what happened to you, Jess," I whispered to her. "I will bring you home, one way or another."

A chill ran up my spine. The sensation of being watched made me shift in my seat. I chanced a look around, but no one seemed to be paying me any attention. Yet I couldn't shake the feeling.

I finished putting everything back in the file and then called my mom. She answered quickly, as she always did.

"Please, don't worry, but I need you to come and get me." I hated having to ask her, but what choice did I have? I couldn't exactly try calling my dad again. Not now that I had seen the file and knew what I knew.

How would I ever be able to face him again?

"Are you safe?" she asked as calmly as she could. I appreciated the effort.

"I'm absolutely fine. I went out with a friend and we got into an argument. I'm at a diner outside of town, but I don't have my car." I kept my voice as neutral as possible.

"I'll be right there."

I gave her directions and hung up. Knowing my mom and her penchant for worrying over me, I expected her to be there in a matter of minutes. She would no doubt drive through every red light.

I finished my coffee, which was now lukewarm, and pushed aside my uneaten pie, letting my thoughts consume me. Finally, I looked up at the TV mounted on the wall. A local news show was playing. The location of the report caught my attention.

"Do you mind turning that up?" I asked the waitress behind the counter. She pointed the remote at the TV. A camera panned around Doll's Eye Lake. Police vans were parked beneath the trees. Masked divers came up from the water. Something was placed on a black tarp on the ground.

"We're standing by at Baneberry Lake in Mt. Randall, North Carolina, where a second body was recovered only two days ago. The remains of Tammy Estep were found buried here, several feet from the water, last month. Now a dive team has found more remains in the reservoir previously searched twenty-four years ago," A reporter stated, looking directly into the camera.

Another body.

"While DNA testing needs to be conducted to officially identify the remains, sources say that preliminary tests, including the use of dental records, show that the body is that of missing Southern State student, Phoebe Baker, of Leonard's Creek."

"Hey Lindsey-bug," Mom said as she sat down across from me. She was out of breath, almost as if she ran the whole way. "Are you going to tell me what on Earth you are doing half way to Grantville?"

I couldn't answer her. My eyes were glued to the news report.

"Lindsey?" She said my name when I didn't respond. "What is it?" She turned in her seat to watch the TV.

We watched together in silence as the screen cut away to pictures of items on a white examining table. There was a close-up of a decomposed blanket the reporter stated had been wrapped around Tammy's body. There were only scraps left, but it was obvious that at one time it had been a colorful plaid pattern of blue and green.

Mom made a strange mewling sound and I tore my gaze away from the television to look at her. Her hand was clasped over her mouth.

"It can't be," Mom murmured, her chin trembling. "How in God's name did it end up there?"

"What is it?" I asked, growing concerned as her face went white.

Mom's eyes seemed deadened with shock. "I would know that blanket anywhere. My mother made it when I was pregnant with Jessica."

Then the memory hit me. A memory of that same plaid blanket in Jess's room at home. The one mom had draped over the end of her bed for years.

The very same blanket Jess had taken with her to college.

**Ten Seconds to Vanish: The Unsolved
Disappearance of Jessica Fadley**

Episode 7

Stella: Welcome back true crime, babes. I'm your
host Stella—

Rachel: And I'm Rachel.

Stella: And this is *Ten Seconds to Vanish: The Unsolved
Disappearance of Jessica Fadley*.

Theme music plays

Stella: It's been a wild seven weeks. So much has
happened!

Rachel: I know! I definitely wasn't prepared to be
solving this in real time, that's for sure.

Stella: Did you see the news report last night? This
story has gained some serious national attention.
It was even on the BBC!

Rachel: And CNN. I had popped my popcorn and
was glued to my screen. Another body, Stel, and
it sounds like it's Phoebe!

Stella: I know, and that's not all. I've heard that there
are even more remains, if you can believe it.
Right after they pulled one body up from the
water, divers found another.

Rachel: Goes to show you that the police really did a crappy job during that initial investigation. Because didn't they search Doll's Eye Lake before?

Stella: Yes, though from all accounts, it was a quick in-and-out job. They didn't even look in the water.

Rachel: But now they've found three bodies there. What the hell is going on in Mt. Randall? Remind me to never vacation there.

Stella: We've been methodically pulling these cases apart, so let's do a quick rundown on what we've uncovered so far. Take it away, Rach.

Rachel: We've established that Tammy, Phoebe, Meghan, and Jess all had connections to the same math professor. *And* . . .

Stella: And this same professor is reportedly a massive predator. He's been pervy toward his students since before I was a gleam in my mum's eye.

Rachel: Ew, gross Stel.

Stella: And listen to this, after talking to a few people who went to school with Jess and the other girls at Southern State University, we've found out that there's more than the creepy teacher connecting all these women together.

Rachel: Like another guy?

Stella: That's right Rach. This has turned into a case with more than one potential suspect. So, you know that hottie boyfriend we talked about in the early episodes? The one Jessica was seeing when she disappeared?

Rachel: Yeah . . .

Stella: well, I interviewed a couple of Jessica's sorority sisters, and it turns out that the hottie boyfriend dated Phoebe Baker in high school. We were lucky to talk with Erica Stead, who pledged with Jessica back in 1998. We'll be playing part of that interview next week.

Rachel: Why is it always the hot ones that are bad?

Stella: And that's not all, get this, he also shagged Tammy Estep and Meghan Lambert.

Rachel: The dude got around.

Stella: He clearly waved his man-whore flag with pride.

Rachel: You know what people would be saying if he was a girl.

Rachel & Stella: Mm-hmm.

Rachel: I really wish you could tell us these guys' names.

Stella: I know, but no one's looking to get sued here. All I can say is you can probably figure out who they are if you Google for more than thirty seconds.

Rachel: So, we have not one, but *two* sketchy men circling around the female coeds of Southern State University in the late nineties. And these men are like fleas, where there's one, there's always more.

Stella: What do you think about the theory that these girls were victims of a serial killer? Do you think it has any merit?

Rachel: I don't know. It's easy to point the finger in that direction, as there were killers operating in the area at the time, but when it comes to murder, it's often best to look close to home.

Stella: Right, like someone the girls all knew.

Rachel: Exactly. Though I don't want us to rule out the serial-killer angle, I think we need to dig deeper into these other dudes. Because it seems like there's something there.

Stella: And one thing we've learned since starting this podcast is there's *always* more to the story than we think.

CHAPTER

13

JESS

Early April, 1999

I WAS SUPPOSED TO be studying for exams, but neither my head nor my heart was in it. The soft drones of the Dave Matthews Band played through the speakers of my stereo. Daisy was at a pledge meeting and wouldn't be back for a few hours, leaving me all alone.

I had been officially put on probation with Pi Gamma Delta. I had been relieved of my pledge duties and wouldn't be inducted at the end of the month. I hadn't quite been kicked out, but I was on thin ice until I could pull my GPA up.

Who knew sororities were such sticklers for grades?

Daisy had been practically inconsolable when I told her. I couldn't tell her that I didn't care one bit about being in Pi Gamma Delta. That as the months passed and my life continued to teeter on the edge of the abyss, the things that had mattered only a short time ago no longer did.

Sometimes, I wondered what it would be like to disappear.

Not a *poof* and you're gone kind of moment, but a slow fade.

Is that what I was doing now?

Would no one notice until I was no longer here?

I looked around the tiny dorm room trying to remember the girl who had taped posters to the walls in August. What happened to her? When had I stopped trying and fallen into barely existing? I wanted to blame my dad for everything. Lord knows he had been the primary villain for a while now. But when would I accept that this chaos was partly my own doing?

My father and I really did make a perfect team. We were both masters at self-sabotage.

My dad had ruined everything.

He had ruined *me*.

And I, in turn, had destroyed any chance at a normal life.

This is why I hated being alone.

I couldn't trust myself—my thoughts. They always went to dark, uncomfortable places.

I had been trying to read the same passage in my biology textbook for the past twenty minutes, But I was having a hard time focusing. Every time I tried to concentrate, my thoughts would wander to Tammy. And Phoebe. And Meghan.

They were everywhere. I couldn't escape them. I tried to act like I wasn't worried. That their disappearances didn't affect me, but it was all a lie, and not so deep down, I was terrified.

I had become quite adept at dishonesty.

I slammed my book closed with a loud sigh.

My head wasn't on academics. I was failing everything. I hadn't turned in a homework assignment in weeks.

The only class I was passing was Intro to Statistics and that's because Dr. Daniels had been making it a point to help me. I had grown dependent on his tutoring, knowing I'd fail his class as well, without his assistance. Yet he never made me feel like an idiot for how much I didn't know. He made me feel, for a brief moment, capable. Almost like the old Jess. But then his hand would graze my knee or he'd scoot his chair in closer, and I was reminded why he was taking such a personal interest in my performance.

But he listened to me. It was easy to talk to him. When I was with him, I knew that his focus was entirely on me. That kind of attention was addictive. And even though I wasn't fooled by his deceptively benign preoccupation, I found myself craving his approval.

Then I'd get angry with myself, because I knew better.

Just as Tammy should have. And Phoebe. And Meghan.

Yet Dr. Daniels' insidious affection was hard to resist.

Ryan didn't understand why I was spending so much time with my teacher.

"How can you be alone with that creep after we saw him with Meghan?" he had demanded one day last week. He had been particularly edgy once Meghan was labeled a missing person, at times snapping at me and then asking for forgiveness. It was a cycle we fell into almost immediately after we started dating.

When things were good between us, I thought of nothing but him. There were no intrusive thoughts. No soul-destroying depression. No gut-wrenching anxiety.

There was only Ryan McKay.

But when things were bad . . .

That kind of intensity didn't come without consequences. Because Ryan was as obsessed with being with me as I was with him. We spent most of our free time together. And when we weren't together, we were both tangled up in irrational jealousy. We loved each other . . . but at a horrible price. And his temper was something awful to behold.

As much as I tried, I couldn't get the thought of him with those other girls—Tammy, Phoebe, and Meghan—out of my mind. I couldn't stop imagining him touching them. Kissing them. It filled me with a resentment that I couldn't explain, but also with a grim satisfaction knowing I no longer had to share him with them. It was an evil thought, I knew that, but I had it all the same. It was another way in which I had changed. The old Jessica would be appalled.

I was a stranger, even to myself.

What happened to the diligent student who had been accepted to college on a partial scholarship?

It seemed I had buried her deep in the ground where no one could find her.

The phone in my room rang. It sounded muffled and far away. I stared down at it unblinking, before finally snapping out of my thoughts.

"Hello?" my voice sounded anemic. Sad. Lonely.

"Jess, I'm so glad you answered. We need to talk. Please, this is getting serious—"

I hung up.

When it immediately started ringing again, I stood up, stumbling back from my desk chair. Why couldn't he leave me alone? The phone stopped ringing and then immediately started again. I covered my ears with my hands, letting out a soft, anguished sob.

I *wanted* to talk to him. The pull was immense. The love was there . . . my god, the love. But it was tainted with heinous things.

"Leave me alone," I keened.

When it continued to ring nonstop, I pulled the cord from the wall.

I knew what he would say and I didn't want to hear it.

It would be a cold day in hell before my father would become my conscience.

A knock at the door startled me.

I opened it slowly only to find Ryan standing on the other side holding a plastic bag from a local convenience store.

He took a step toward me, wrapping an arm around my waist and pulled me close. He kissed me long and deep. When he pulled away I was slightly out of breath. "I'm kidnapping you," he murmured, tucking a strand of hair behind my ear.

"I have a lot of stuff to do—" I started to protest.

"It's nothing that can't wait." He lifted the bag. "I got us sandwiches because I have a feeling you haven't eaten since the donuts at breakfast."

I couldn't help but smile. "You know me so well."

I glanced back over my shoulder at the pile of work on my desk. "Honestly, Ryan, I really have a lot to do. I'm . . . I'm flunking my classes. It'll be bad if I don't pull my grades up soon." My protests were weak and ineffectual. I would give in. I could never say no to Ryan McKay, no matter how much I wanted to.

"Hey, it's okay. Come take a short break and when we get back I'll help you study." He tipped my chin up and placed a gentle kiss on my lips.

"Okay," I relented, and he smiled widely, like he'd won the lottery. I shoved my feet in my sneakers and grabbed my keys. As I went to shut the door Ryan pulled something out of his back pocket and held it out to me. "Oh, I found this in the hallway outside my room. It's Daisy's. Not sure how it got there, but I'm being a good boy scout and returning it."

I startled at the sight of it. I took the campus ID card from him. "Thanks."

I went back into my room and dropped it on Daisy's desk before joining him in the hallway.

Ryan closed the door behind me. "Come on then."

Once in the parking lot, Ryan unlocked the passenger side door of a brown Ford Explorer. He pressed me against the side of the car, cupping my face in his hands. "I can't stay away from you, Jessica Fadley," he whispered against my lips. "What have you done to me? I'm half crazed over you."

My insides felt shaky. I was both flattered and suffocated. I wanted his love and attention, but sometimes it could be too much. There was no such thing as space with him. Boundaries were blurred and pushed.

All of my misgiving melted away at the feel of his mouth against mine.

I knew what Ryan wanted from me today. I could tell by his desperate kisses and urgent touches. That was okay, though. I wanted it, too. I needed him to help me forget even for a little bit.

Yet, I couldn't shake the sense of foreboding as we made our way through Mt. Randall. I felt off balance the further we drove from campus.

"Where are you taking me?" I asked as we cut through the main part of town.

"You'll see." He gave me a sideways glance. "Nothing to be nervous about. I wanted somewhere romantic. There's a place I know from when I was a kid. It's perfect."

I turned on the radio so I wouldn't have to talk. Then I wished I hadn't. It was a news report about Meghan. I noticed the way Ryan's face turned thunderous.

"Turn that off," he commanded, his eyes dark.

"I'm . . . I'm sorry." I fumbled with the knob. Ryan could be the most loving, gentle boyfriend, but I also knew he had a temper. Daisy had warned me. Sometimes a switch would flip and he was like a different person.

"You never did tell me if you ended up speaking to her that night." I broached the subject tentatively. It was like walking on eggshells on top of land mines.

"Uh, yeah. Only briefly, though." He sounded dismissive. He reached for the radio and turned it off more aggressively than was warranted.

"What did you talk about? Did she say anything about Dr. Daniels?" I was pushing. I knew he hated that. It was in my nature to back down, but I wanted to press and prod. It was so out of character that it rattled me.

And like every single time the subject came up, Ryan effectively shut it down. "I don't want to talk about that."

"Okay, I just—"

His nostrils flared. "I can't believe she would get involved with someone like that. Not after the shit she went through with her parents. She's dealt with a lot. It's why we clicked when we met at the beginning of the school year. She has a shitty dad, I have a shitty dad. That's why it pisses me off so damn much. She should know better." He spoke with authority. It made the blood in my veins turn to ice.

"What do you mean?"

Ryan kept his eyes firmly on the road. "Women like that, the vulnerable ones, are easy pickings." It was an angry, definitive statement.

His words had been brutal, and direct.

I was unnerved.

Neither of us said anything for an uncomfortably long period of time.

Finally, he took my hand, lacing our fingers together and pressing them to his thigh. "I'm sorry. I didn't mean to upset you."

My stomach twisted into knots, but not with excitement.

"It's really upsetting. The whole thing, Jess." He paused before continuing. "Look, can we not talk about it? It's all anyone ever seems to want to talk about. Everywhere I go it's Meghan this, Phoebe that, did you hear about Tammy? I . . . I can't, okay. I need to not think about them for a while. I want to think about you and me. I want a couple of hours for us and no one else. Is that cool?"

I felt numb. "Sure, Ryan. I want that, too. You and me and no one else."

He seemed to brighten.

All I felt was dread.

The feeling got worse when I realized where Ryan was going.

I was paralyzed, unable to speak, when he turned off the main road, driving over the bumpy gravel before finally coming to a stop beneath a thick overhang of trees at the edge of Doll's Eye Lake.

He turned off the ignition and grabbed the plastic bag from the back seat before opening the door. When I made no move to follow him, he looked at me in confusion. "What's wrong?"

I stared out at the glistening surface of the lake. My heart thumped loudly in my ears.

"Why did you bring me here? How do you even know about this place?" I croaked. I sounded as if I had swallowed broken glass. My bones felt leaden. My muscles turned to jelly.

I should have felt comforted to be here. This special place that resided in my best childhood memories.

Yet I wasn't. This place reminded me of everything that I had lost. And of a father who had become a stranger. It was now filled with nightmares.

"I told you, I came here a couple of times as a kid. My grandma used to live in town and I'd come to the lake to fish when I'd visit. I remember it being secluded and out of the way. I thought some privacy might be nice." He sounded strange. Almost excited.

My heart fluttered wildly. "I don't know . . ."

Ryan's eyes were pleading. "I want to be alone with you."

"We can be alone in my dorm room," I countered, still not getting out of the car.

"Yeah, but here no one can hear you scream," he chuckled, kissing the side of my neck, brushing his nose along the underside of my jaw.

I knew he was trying to be sexy, but his words made me uneasy.

He had no idea why I hated Doll's Eye Lake so much. Somewhere I had once loved was now the last place I wanted to be. Not after everything.

"Jess, stop being weird and get out of the car." He sounded impatient.

"I . . ." I looked around us, realizing how alone we were.

"Jess, damn it, get out!"

My hand was trembling as I reached for the handle. I didn't want to get out. I wanted to go back home. I wanted to have never opened the door to Ryan McKay. I wished I could go back in time.

Ryan came around to my side of the car and opened the door for me. He held out a hand and I took it. He tugged me out, pulling me close to his body.

He smiled down at me. "Now I have you all to myself with no interruptions."

Ryan kissed me rougher than usual. He seemed irritated by my lackluster response.

We walked closer to the edge of the lake. My legs were shaky and I stumbled twice. Ryan's arms were there to catch me each and every time.

I noticed a car parked a few feet away from us and relief flooded through me.

"Looks like we'll have to forget about being alone. Maybe we should scrap this idea and head back to campus" I pointed to the shiny Chevy Impala.

Ryan scowled. "God damn it!"

He was still holding my hand. It felt restrictive.

I wanted to scream.

This all felt so wrong.

I shouldn't be here.

"Nah, we can still enjoy ourselves. Though, I guess we'll have to stick with eating. The other stuff can wait until later." He waggled his eyebrows.

A man was walking along the perimeter of the lake, making his way toward us. It was only when he was within a few feet that both Ryan and I recognized him.

Ryan stiffened and I felt lightheaded.

"Dr. Daniels, hi," I greeted once he was within earshot.

He looked up at me in surprise, clearly not having noticed us there.

"Jessica, hello."

Ryan's face went stony. I recognized the possessive glint in his eyes.

"What are you doing out here?" I asked him.

Dr. Daniels peered out over the water. "I live nearby and I come here sometimes when I need to think." He turned back to me and I felt my cheeks heat up. "When I want to make important decisions."

"Oh," was all I could say.

"It feels like a good omen to meet you out here, Jessica," Dr. Daniels's smile broadened.

Ryan cleared his throat, as if reminding Dr. Daniels—and me—that he was there.

"This is Ryan," I said by way of introduction.

Ryan glared at me before turning to my teacher. "I'm Jess's boyfriend." He clutched my hand so tight it hurt.

Dr. Daniels raised his eyebrows at that but didn't respond. Instead he looked at me again. "Well, I'll see you tomorrow for our tutoring session." His gaze lingered, but only for a moment. It was so quick you could almost convince yourself that he was simply being nice. "Enjoy your evening."

"You, too," I replied softly as the older man walked away.

As soon as Dr. Daniels was out of earshot, I felt Ryan's anger unleash like a hurricane.

"What the hell was that, Jess?"

"I don't know what you're talking about."

"That man looked at you like he was the cat and you were the goddamned cream."

"You're seeing things."

"I'm seeing what's pretty obvious, Jess. You liked it. You liked the way he looked at you, didn't you?" Ryan was enraged.

I shook my head profusely. But I knew it was no good. There was no calming him down.

I pulled Ryan close, staring up into his face, beseeching him. I hated it when he was angry with me. Like all the men in my life, Ryan wasn't good for me, yet I couldn't stay away. "I don't want to fight," I whispered.

He seemed to relax slightly, though his anger was still palpable.

"Me neither."

I tipped my face up to him and he kissed me. And all thoughts drifted away as the water, with its hidden secrets, lapped at our feet. Somewhere close by, I knew Dr. Daniels would be watching.

* * *

I felt better, more settled, by the time Ryan dropped me off at the dorm. I fumbled with my keys in the lock when the door flung open suddenly and Daisy stood there, seeming frazzled.

"There you are!" she exclaimed.

Daisy pulled me into our room and quickly closed the door behind me.

"What is it? Did you lose your lip gloss again?" I joked.

Daisy looked like she was about to have a panic attack. "This is serious, Jess." She walked to her desk and picked up her ID. "Where did you find this?"

"What are you talking about?"

Daisy shook the ID card. "My campus ID, Jess. Where was it? It's been missing for like three months. I've not seen it since before Christmas."

"Oh, Ryan returned it earlier."

"What? Why did Ryan have my ID?" She was gnawing at her bottom lip.

"He said he found it so he brought it back." I shrugged nonchalantly.

"That doesn't make any sense," she murmured. She seemed close to tears. "Where did he find it?"

"What's going on, Daisy?" I asked, getting to my feet and crossing the room to my frantic roommate. I reached out and took ahold of her shoulders. "You need to calm down. Tell me what happened."

She sat down on her bed, covering her face with her hands. "I was called to the police station in town."

My stomach dropped. "What? Why?"

Daisy looked up at me with red-rimmed eyes. "Because, apparently, my student ID was the only one used in all the last locations where Tammy, Phoebe, and Meghan were seen."

I swallowed. Anxiety rising in me. "That doesn't mean anything."

Daisy's eyes took on a wild look. "Don't you get it, Jess? My card was used to check out a computer in the computer lab within ten minutes of Tammy checking into that *same* computer lab." She ran her hands through her hair. "My ID card was used to check out a book at the library, at the same damn kiosk as Phoebe's. At almost the same time!" She was getting worked up again. I could see she was spiraling.

"Daisy, take a breath—"

"And at the gym, too. At like one in the morning. Guess who was also at the gym at one in the morning on

February 8?" She looked at me, her eyes unwavering. "Meghan Lambert."

"Okay . . ."

"I don't go to the gym, Jess," Daisy went on. "And I sure as hell have never set foot in the library. But the police have proof that my card, at least, has been to those places, coincidentally around the same time as Tammy, Phoebe, and Meghan. And wouldn't you know it, it happened to be the last place anyone ever saw them."

"I don't understand what you're saying."

But I did.

Daisy's eyes welled up with tears. "They were interrogating me, Jess. Like I had done something to those women. Me—as if I'd ever do something like that."

I sat down beside her and put my arm around her shoulders. "I know you would never hurt a fly, Daisy."

For once, she didn't lean into me. "I don't understand what's going on. How could my card be used at all those places? You know it's been missing for months. I've been borrowing Erica and Tina's IDs."

"Maybe it's some kind of technology error. I can't imagine Mt. Randall's police force being too skilled in that area," I offered.

Daisy wiped her face. "Yeah, maybe. But it's so weird." She looked down at the ID in question. "Where did Ryan find it?" She seemed to be bordering on hysteria.

I hugged her and this time she let me. "I'm sure it will all be okay. It's just a misunderstanding. Don't worry so much."

Daisy placed the plastic card back on the desk. "What if they think I did something to them?

This time I did laugh. "Come on, Daisy, what motive would you possibly have? I mean, Tammy maybe, but Phoebe and Meghan?"

My roommate gave me a wobbly smile. "Yeah, I mean, come on, I'm too hot to be a serial killer." She flipped her hair over her shoulder. "And I'm sure as hell not going to jail because of Tammy Estep. God, she'd love that wouldn't she."

"Exactly." I took a deep breath, steadying myself. "Don't give it another thought. It will all get figured out."

Daisy gave me a strange look. "Did you ever find *your* ID card? I remember you kept borrowing mine."

"I only used your card that one time, Daisy."

Her eyes looked doubtful. "No, you used it a bunch because you kept misplacing yours."

"Nope, I found mine. See." I dug into my bag and produced my ID card on its bright pink lanyard.

"Jess, you used my card more than once. Why are you lying?" Daisy insisted, frowning. She was stressed and upset, her tone accusatory.

I felt my hands start to shake. "I'm not lying . . . but you're right. Maybe I used it a few more times than I remembered. But, Daisy, that was way before Christmas break and I always returned it. Promise."

Daisy stared at me for a moment too long before she got to her feet. "Right. Yeah, okay." She picked at the corner of her mouth. "I don't know what's going on. Things have been so messed up this entire year. Freshman year was supposed to be amazing." She let out a little sob. "This is not how things were meant to be."

I stood up and started to go to my friend. "Daisy, everything will be fine—"

Daisy held up her hands, as if to ward me off. "Before you say anything, I know I'm being overly dramatic again." She seemed angry now. And that anger was clearly directed at me. And I didn't know how to fix it. She picked up her purse and turned away from me. "I have to meet up with the other pledges to plan Big/Little activities for the weekend." For the first time she didn't complain about the fact that I wasn't joining her. Her demeanor had gone cold, leaving me firmly on the outside.

"Don't forget I'm going home on Friday for Lindsey's birthday party," I reminded her before she left.

"Oh right. I forgot about that. Well, that should be fun." Daisy barely looked at me as she opened the door.

"Yeah. Fun." My voice was monotone and Daisy would normally ask if I was okay. She didn't this time.

Truthfully, she seemed eager to leave the room.

To leave me.

And I, too, was glad when she was gone.

True Crime Crazy Blog
Post 814
Southern State University's Missing Coeds UPDATE
2023

It's been a long time since I've added anything to my coverage of this case. Probably because for two decades, nothing new has been revealed. There were no leads. No evidence. It was a giant, black hole of nothingness and the police weren't in a rush to do anything about it.

I've called out the lack of virtues of small town police forces many times on my blog and Mt. Randall's police are no exception. They screwed up this case in every way they could. Like most crime watchers, I gave up on anything ever coming to light in the case of the missing Southern State coeds.

So, color me shocked when only two months ago bones were found near a lake only twelve miles from campus. First, Tammy Estep was found. Then later, Phoebe Baker. And as I sit here typing this, testing is being conducted on another set of remains, and most think they belong to Meghan Lambert.

That's three of the four missing girls all found and accounted for twenty-four years after they were last seen.

So that leaves the important question—where is Jessica Fadley?

Are her bones, like the others, languishing at the bottom of the lake waiting to be found? If so, why haven't they recovered her yet?

At this point, divers have scoured every inch of that underwater world on the outskirts of a tiny town in North Carolina.

So, where is Jessica Fadley?

When will her body be found? Because at this point, there is surely no doubt that it is a body that is being searched for.

And who killed these women? Because each set of remains bear marks consistent with a violent death. These girls were murdered in the prime of their lives and left to rot in some backwater town where they went unnoticed indefinitely.

Whoever killed them was angry. These weren't crimes of cold calculation. These were crimes of rage and passion.

Was it the professor? Or perhaps the fellow student that online communities speculate dated all four?

Or was it someone else entirely? The elusive serial killer so many people have speculated about perhaps? The North Carolina Boogie Man? The SeaSide Strangler?

Or someone else who has been overlooked all these years?

Whoever it is should be scared. The secrets are coming out. Their days in obscurity are almost over.

It's almost time for them to pay the piper.

14

LINDSEY

Present Day

Mom had been inconsolable at the diner. So much so that I had to be the one to drive us home. When we pulled up in front of our house, she opened the car door and leapt out before I fully came to a stop.

She was inside and up the stairs by the time I got to the door.

I could hear her tearing through Jess's room.

"Mom?" I called out, hurrying upstairs after her.

She was frantic. "It has to be here. It has to be!" she cried from inside Jess's closet.

"Mom, calm down," I pleaded, watching as she opened the boxes I had only recently gone through.

"How had I not noticed it missing? What kind of mother am I?" She pulled items out of the boxes, tossing them on the floor.

"Mom, please, calm down, we'll figure it out—"

"No!" she yelled, startling me, "I *can't*. Don't you see? If that's her blanket then . . . then she's down there too. My baby is down in that water with those other girls. Or maybe she's buried in the woods," she wailed, her body suddenly going limp.

I dropped to my knees beside her, pulling her to me. She sagged, and I had to support all of her weight. She cried, her words unintelligible. I gently rocked her back and forth like she was the child and I was the parent.

After a few minutes, she sat up, wiping her face. She seemed to have gotten herself together somewhat. "Will you help me look?" she asked, her voice gravelly.

So, we sat on the floor of Jess's closet, going through all of the boxes carefully. We were meticulous and methodical. Pulling out each and every item. But I already knew the blanket wouldn't be here. I'd been through these boxes already.

"We need to go and speak to that lieutenant," Mom said, finally giving up on the search.

She stood up, leaving Jess's things scattered across the floor, and hurriedly left the room, practically flying down the stairs.

"Where are my keys?" she exclaimed in a panic.

"I'll drive," I offered, grabbing my purse. There was no question I would take her. We needed to go to the police with what we suspected. I was due in to work later that night, but I would call them on the way to the station and tell them I needed to take some personal days. I'd barely had a handful of days off from that place since I'd started, so I knew it wouldn't be a problem.

We pulled up in front of the police station ten minutes later. We sat in the car for a moment, both of us needing to prepare ourselves.

"Why was her blanket with that other girl?" Mom asked for the hundredth time since seeing the news broadcast. And for the hundredth time, I had no answer.

Finally, we headed inside. I wondered why Mom hadn't called Dad. It was usually her de facto response in an emergency. Yet she hadn't. And secretly, I was glad. After everything I had discovered, I wasn't sure when I'd be ready to face him.

My father was not the man I used to believe he was.

Inside, the station was quiet. Mom greeted the front-desk officer by name. Having grown up in Mt. Randall, she knew almost everyone.

"Hi, Randy, I need to speak to Lieutenant Higgins."

"Sure, Cara. Let me go get her. Have a seat." Randy said, giving my Mom a sympathetic smile.

Mom and I sat silently side by side. I had a thousand thoughts running through my mind.

My dad was a liar. He was a cheater, too. Did Mom know? I couldn't imagine her staying with him if she did, but I couldn't be sure. People could overlook horrible things if it meant maintaining the status quo.

And he had known Meghan—one of the missing girls—intimately. The ramifications of that were appalling.

Ryan was a liar, too. He had been Jess's boyfriend. He had been a suspect, too.

Both he and my dad had been questioned about the missing women.

I was surrounded by men of questionable character.

And then there was the blanket.

Jess's blanket.

Wrapped around Tammy Estep's decayed remains.

Just then, the Lieutenant came out, a folder clasped under her arm. She looked at us cautiously before indicating we were to follow her.

"Officer Paten said you needed to see me." She spoke as she walked, and I appreciated that she hadn't talked to us in front of everyone sitting in reception.

She opened a door at the end of the hallway and motioned for us to step inside. "Please, have a seat." She gestured to the chairs on either side of a large table in the center of the room. She closed the door and took a seat across from us.

"The blanket," my Mom began, "the one they showed on TV . . ."

I watched the lieutenant's face, noting how she kept her expression neutral. "The blanket we recovered with Miss Estep's remains?"

"Yes, that blanket." My mom took my hand, squeezing it tightly. "I'm positive it belonged to Jessica. I looked for hers today and it's not with her belongings, and I don't remember it being with the things from her dorm room."

Lieutenant Higgins nodded. "I suspected as much."

"You did?" I asked.

"In going through some old photographs entered into evidence at the time of the initial report, I saw a plaid throw in one of the pictures submitted by Jessica's roommate that was remarkably similar to the one we recovered at Baneberry Lake. I have since contacted Miss Molina for clarification, and she's stated that she remembers a blanket like this had indeed belonged to Jessica. I was planning to come by and ask you about it. But no need to now that you're here." The detective crossed her hands on top of the table. "Given the clear and obvious connections between the four girls' disappearances, I've put in a request for expedited testing." She looked at me, her eyes steady. "Unfortunately, I doubt there will be any residual DNA on the wool given how long it was in the ground, but we're testing anyway. Maybe we'll get lucky and we'll get some answers." She gave us a kind smile. "But, with what you're telling me, I believe my instincts were correct and the blanket *is* Jessica's."

Mom began crying again. My throat felt tight. Everything seemed to be happening quickly. I had gone so long without knowing anything about my sister and her disappearance and suddenly I was inundated with clues and information. It was almost too much to keep up with.

"Can you tell me more about this blanket, Mrs. Fadley?" Lieutenant Higgins asked.

Mom looked up, her face red and blotchy. But despite this, she was still beautiful when she smiled. "My mother made the knitted wool throw when I was pregnant with Jessica. I had been told I was having a boy." She chuckled briefly, dabbing her wet face with a tissue. "The nursery had been decorated in blues and greens. Ben, my husband, had hung framed pictures of trains and trucks on the walls. My mother had terminal cancer, but she worked for months on that blanket. She wanted her grandson to have something from her. I had kept it folded over the foot of the crib." I had never heard this story before. I was half terrified to make a noise, scared she'd stop speaking.

My mother's face suddenly brightened. "Then Jessica came along. Not a boy at all, but a perfectly healthy girl, and I wrapped her in that blue-and-green blanket when we brought her home from the hospital. Secretly, I was over the moon. I mean, I would have been happy with a boy, but deep down, I wanted a girl. Ben, too. He doted on our girl. Nothing else mattered to him. She was the apple of his eye from the moment he laid eyes on her."

"Your husband had a very close relationship with Jessica, didn't he?" Lieutenant Higgins asked, taking notes on a pad of paper.

"Yes, those two were as thick as thieves. They went everywhere and did everything together. Jessica and I had our own relationship, but it had nothing of the closeness she shared with Ben." Mom's voice sounded distant as she spoke, as if she weren't sitting beside me, but instead back in time with her one-time perfect family. "I may have been a little tough on Jessica. I only ever wanted her to succeed. Sure, I had high expectations, but she was my firstborn. Moms are always a bit harder on the oldest child." She gave me a watery smile. "But, there was no room for me in the relationship Jessica shared with Ben, that's why I had Lindsey." She patted my hand.

"What?" I gaped at her.

"Your dad didn't want any more children after Jessica. He said she was more than enough for him, but I wanted another one. Someone to love me more than anyone." She laughed again, but I didn't find it funny.

Mom had a wistful expression when she looked at me. "But this time, we knew right away that we were having a girl, and I was glad. This was my chance to get things right. To ensure you loved me like Jessica loved her dad. Didn't I deserve that?"

"God, Mom, that's so unhealthy. Didn't you think it was odd that Dad and Jess excluded everyone else?" I demanded, forgetting for a moment that Lieutenant Higgins was in the room.

Mom frowned. "What do you mean?"

"It's strange, Mom. You have to see that. Why would you want us to have a relationship like that?" I swallowed, feeling sick. It was all too much. My heart felt like it was going to collapse under the weight of each new revelation. My mind swirled with thoughts of the file Sergeant O'Neil had given me. The copy of the transcript of my dad's interview from 1999. The pictures of his car and the contents that had been found inside.

He had cheated on my mom with a girl Jess's age. You couldn't even describe it as an affair, given the age gap and power difference. He had preyed on her, plain and simple. Had there been more?

The Lieutenant opened the folder in front of her and pulled out some photographs. She laid them out in front of us.

Mom touched a photo of Jess with a shaking finger. These were pictures of a Jess that she didn't know. I couldn't tell her I had seen similar photos before—in the hiding place in my sister's closet.

In one of the pictures, Jess was propped against a wall, a dazed smile on her face. She was obviously drunk. In another she stood next to a keg holding a red Solo cup, a joint pinched between her fingers.

Mom flipped through the photos, making noises that sounded like whimpers. I wondered what she was thinking as she faced the reality of who her daughter had really been.

There was a picture of Jess and another girl with long golden brown hair in a dorm room hugging and smiling at the camera.

"That's Daisy Molina," Mom said to me. "That was Jessica's roommate."

"And that's the blanket?" Lieutenant Higgins asked, pointing at the bed in the background where a blue and green plaid throw was draped haphazardly.

Mom's eyes once again welled with tears. "Yes, that's Jessica's blanket."

"Okay, one more thing, Mrs. Fadley, can you tell me about this ring?" Lieutenant Higgins pointed to a barely noticeable band of silver on Jess's right ring finger.

Mom leaned closer, squinting at the photograph before looking up. "Ben gave Jessica that ring for her sixteenth birthday."

"Did it have any sort of engraving on it?" the detective pressed.

My mother sniffed, wiping her wet cheeks. "Yes it did. It was a swirling pattern. Ben picked it out because it looked like the curlicues on the cover of a book he used to read to her every night when she was a girl. And he had her initials engraved on the inside, if I remember correctly. Cost us an arm and a leg. It was from Tiffany's. But Ben insisted."

Lieutenant Higgins leafed through the file and pulled out another photograph and placed it on the table. "Did it look like this?"

Mom glanced at the picture briefly before covering her mouth with her hand and closing her eyes. She nodded and Lieutenant Higgins put the photograph away.

"Where did that ring come from? Is it Jess's?" I asked.

Lieutenant Higgins closed the file, her expression grim.

"We found this ring on the hand of another woman recovered from Baneberry Lake. The one we have in evidence also has initials carved on the inside," the detective explained.

"JAF?" Mom whispered.

"Yes, JAF," the detective confirmed solemnly.

"We compared dental records, and now have the DNA results from the state crime lab so I can say the body the ring was found on was *not* Jessica's."

Mom was shaking, her teeth practically chattering.

"First her blanket, now her ring?" Mom rasped, her voice barely audible. She lifted her face, her eyes meeting mine. "What's going on? Where's my baby?"

I stared at the lieutenant, but she gave nothing away.

"Can you tell us who you found?" I had to ask, though deep down, I already knew.

The lieutenant's face was somber as she answered. "It's the third missing girl. Meghan Lambert."

* * *

After seeing the pictures, Lieutenant Higgins asked us a few more questions. She asked Mom if Jess had ever said the blanket or the ring had gone missing. Mom stated that she had no idea the blanket had been missing, but the ring—Jess admitted to losing it before she disappeared.

I thought about telling Lieutenant Higgins about the things in Jess's hiding spot, but after seeing how exhausted Mom was, I knew she couldn't handle any more shocks. I would make sure to call the detective later and let her know.

Mom seemed unsettled once we were back in the car. As I drove us home, she looked out the window, her lips quivering. "I've devoted my entire life to my family. First, with my parents, and then later my husband. Then when Jessica came along I felt I had a new purpose." Tears slid down her cheeks. "But she never cuddled me. Never wanted to spend time with *only* me. It was always her dad from the moment she was born. I tried not to be hurt by it, but I was. She broke my heart day after day when she chose him over me. So I tried to be a different kind of mother to her. The kind that could be a friend. And when that didn't work, I was the disciplinarian." She pressed her fist to her mouth as if to choke back a sob. "It never mattered, though. Because she never loved me. Not like she loved him." She glanced at me, her eyes bloodshot and puffy. "I'm meant to be the backbone of our family. The foundation. That's who I'm supposed to be."

"And you are," I protested, trying to make her feel better, even if it wasn't the truth.

Lies were my family's love language.

"I'm not, Lindsey. And it's obvious I didn't know anything about Jessica," she whispered, pressing her face to the glass and closing her eyes.

Once back at the house I watched Mom sluggishly climb the stairs with barely a backward glance.

Despite Mom being kept out of Dad and Jess's relationship, I knew she had loved my sister deeply. She may have had me to fill some kind of void, but it was obvious that Jess had not only been the apple of my dad's eye, but my mom's, too. It was sad that three had been a crowd.

I went to Mom's car and retrieved the file box from the back seat. I sat down on the porch step and pulled out the stack of papers I had already gone through, stopping on the copy of the photograph of Jess and Daisy that Lieutenant Higgins had shown us earlier.

I flipped to another interview I had only skimmed. This one was with Daisy Molina, Jess's roommate.

I read it quickly. It wasn't long, it seemed to last only about ten minutes. Apparently, the police department was able to identify an ID card used at multiple locations around campus. It appeared they were trying to make a connection between the individual using this ID card and the last known sightings of each of the missing women.

I was surprised to see that the ID card belonged to Daisy.

She claimed that her card had been missing for months and she had no idea where it was. She became hysterical, and the interview ended abruptly. I flipped through the file trying to find where Sergeant O'Neil followed up on what seemed like a solid lead.

But, of course, he hadn't. Like with Ryan, Dr. Daniels, and even my dad, something that seemed important was dropped completely and never revisited.

Daisy's name obviously came up frequently in the file. Not only because she was Jess's roommate and Phoebe's pledge sister, but also because she was Ryan's alibi. She was intrinsically connected to these women and this case.

Of anyone, she was the person most likely to have some insight into what was going on back then. I couldn't count on Ryan to be honest, but maybe Jess's friend would give me some answers.

I pulled out my phone and googled Daisy. Daisy Molina wasn't a very common name, but unsurprisingly, there were more than a few matches. I started clicking on links, hoping it would point me to something useful.

Then, I found it.

It was an article from last year about a new dating violence prevention program at Southern State University that had received grant funding. There was a picture attached to the story of a woman in her forties with shoulder-length golden brown hair who apparently worked at the college. I recognized her immediately. She hadn't changed much.

Daisy Molina.

I went to Southern State University's website and looked up their current staff list, and sure enough, there was her name. She was listed as a college counselor at the Student Health Services Office on campus.

She was only a few miles away. It felt ironic that the one woman who could provide me answers had been so close this entire time.

I checked the time. It was just before five. Not wanting to waste another second, I decided to drive over there in the hopes that I may be able to catch her before she left for the day.

I got into my car and headed up the hill toward the school. If anyone could fill in the blanks from that time in my sister's life, it was her best friend.

Once there, I checked the map of the campus on my phone and made my way toward the Health Services office.

I had never stepped foot on the Southern State University campus before. It felt surreal to be there now, walking in my sister's footsteps. It had always been a distant point up on the hill. A chapter in my missing sister's story that seemed a million miles away.

I felt a shiver as I made my way along the same graveled paths as Jess once had. The air around me suddenly felt warm and something brushed against my hand. I stopped and looked around, but I was alone.

There was a whisper of breath against my ear and my heart started thudding erratically.

I could almost feel Jess. She was in the very molecules of this place. I could smell the jasmine blooming like echoes of her ghost.

I rubbed my arms, feeling both comforted and unnerved.

Eventually, I found the small, brick building that housed the health and counseling services for the college. Inside, the small reception area was empty, but I could hear the sound of raised voices coming from an office down the hall.

I slowly made my way in the direction of the arguing, stopping outside an open door with Daisy Molina's name embossed on the glass.

"I have nothing more to say about this, Ryan. I've told you what I needed to tell you and that's the end of it. Now, you need to leave," I heard a woman I suspected was Daisy say, her voice even and controlled.

I surreptitiously peeked around the door to find two people standing in the middle of the room. I knew one of them to be Daisy—and the other was Ryan McKay.

Daisy tried to move past Ryan, but he grabbed her arm, pulling her up short. He leaned in close, his face only an inch from hers. His features twisted in fury.

He looked scary, but Daisy remained calm, pulling her arm from his grip and giving him a shove.

"Don't you dare put your hands on me, Ryan. I am not the sort of woman who will stand for your bullshit," she threatened.

"For God's sake, we're supposed to be on the same side, Daisy!" he shouted in frustration.

"There's only one side, Ryan. The right side. And we've been on the wrong one long enough," Daisy exclaimed, her cheeks flushed. Ryan threw his hands up in the air and turned his face away from her and in that moment his eyes connected with mine.

"Lindsey," I heard him say, his voice reflecting his surprise.

I walked into Daisy's office and gave Ryan my best withering look. "I should have known you'd be doing whatever you could to cover your tracks."

"It's not what you think, Daisy contacted *me*." He sounded desperate and worried.

"I think you should go, Ryan," Daisy cut in. "I've told you there's nothing more for us to talk about."

Ryan looked like he wanted to argue. "Daisy—"

"Just go," I ordered. "I need to talk to Daisy," I gave him a pointed look, "alone."

"I know it looks bad," he said, his tone soft, "I know you think I—"

Daisy picked up the phone off her desk. "I think it's time I make that call to campus security."

"That's not necessary, I'm leaving." Ryan's jaw was stiff and I could tell he was barely reining in his frustration.

He looked at me again. "We need to talk, Lindsey."

"If Lindsey is at all like Jess, you should know you can't force her to do anything," Daisy interjected. She walked him to the door. "Goodbye, Ryan." And then she closed the door in his face.

I sighed in relief, glad that he was gone. Daisy turned around, her smile blinding. "Lindsey." She came toward me, her arms outstretched.

I let her hug me, feeling a little awkward. When she pulled back and patted my hand, I relaxed. Daisy had a comforting way about her. I understood why she and Jess had been friends.

"You really haven't changed much," she announced. I must have looked confused because. Daisy laughed. "That sounded weird, but I looked at your face every day for an entire school year. Jess kept a framed picture of you on her desk."

That was an unexpected gut punch.

"She did?"

Daisy nodded. "She talked about you a lot, so I feel like I almost know you. Or at least the younger you." She had no idea how much I needed the reminder that my sister had, in fact, loved me. Especially after all of the revelations from the past twenty-four hours.

"You handled Ryan nicely by the way," I commented as Daisy returned to her desk.

"I've dealt with bigger pains in the ass in my life than Ryan McKay. Please, Lindsey, have a seat." She pointed to the cushy armchair on the other side of her desk.

We both sat down, regarding each other intently.

"I was surprised to find you were still in Mt. Randall. And here at the college, no less." I looked around her office. It was a comfortable space meant to put people at ease. There was a small water fountain glowing with LED lights in the corner. Wind chimes tinkled in the breeze from the open window. Incense burned, giving off a soothing scent. There were thick, multicolored rugs on the floor and soft instrumental music piped through the speakers on Daisy's desk.

My sister's former roommate gave me a sad smile. "After what happened to Jess, I thought about leaving a hundred times. About transferring to another school. It had been awful after she went missing. Every girl on campus was terrified. We felt like sitting ducks. But, I decided then and there that enough was enough. I was sick of the endless cycle of fear that we, as women, live in. I stayed, I graduated, and then was accepted to the graduate program in counseling. After that, I applied as a counselor here because this was the one place where I knew I was needed." She looked out the window at the manicured lawns. "I wanted to do something important. I wanted to try and prevent what happened to your sister and to Phoebe, Tammy, and Meghan from ever happening again." She opened a drawer and pulled out a pack of cigarettes. "Do you mind if I smoke?"

I shook my head and she lit one and took a long drag, blowing the smoke out the open window. I waited for her to speak, though I had a thousand questions I wanted to ask her.

"I've been hoping for the day these cases would be reopened and for the authorities to take the disappearances seriously. I need to know what happened to Jess. And when the police called me asking about a blanket they found with Tammy's body, it felt like, finally, they could solve it."

"It's all I've ever wanted, too," I told her. "It's consumed me. I feel like I've lived half a life waiting for this day to come." Daisy made it easy to confide in her. I had no doubt she was a great counselor.

I knew she understood. After all, she had been Jess's friend. Her roommate. For a short period of time they had probably known each other better than anyone else. It was impossible to share a living space with someone and not know them intimately.

I had lost a sister, and Daisy had lost a friend.

"God, they're back again," Daisy groaned, watching a small group walking along the path, their phones out, obviously recording their surroundings.

"Who are they?" I asked. They appeared to be younger than me—maybe even college students themselves.

"Ever since that podcast came out, the campus has been crawling with social media hounds. Kids making videos, ambushing students and staff, trying to get interviews. It's like they forget real people live and work here. That real women are missing." Daisy was clearly disgusted.

"Yeah, it's been hard to deal with," I agreed.

"That podcast doesn't help. They've emailed me at least half a dozen times, trying to get me to do an interview. As if I'd talk to a bunch of ambulance chasers," she said with revulsion.

"If only everyone had your morals," I muttered.

Daisy looked at me sympathetically. "Yeah, I heard my old sorority sister, Erica, spoke to them. She's been posting about it nonstop on Facebook and Instagram for weeks. God only knows what she told them." She pressed her lips together in consternation. "But I know it'll be a bunch of bs. Erica and Jess weren't close. Hell, I don't think you can even call them friends. She doesn't know anything about what was going on with your sister."

"It won't matter, it seems the lies make a better story." We shared a look of frustrated agony.

Daisy watched the group as they headed down the hill. "It's all entertainment to people like them—like Erica. A scary story to tell in the dark. The actual victims get lost in all the noise. *Jess* is getting lost. It makes me so angry."

She picked up the phone on her desk and made a quick call to campus security, telling them about the group.

After she hung up, Daisy took another long drag of her cigarette. "We're not really supposed to smoke in here. It's a health-code violation and all." She chuckled dryly. "But given the things these kids tell me, I need my vices. So, I smoke, and I let students, too, if they need it, and if the college doesn't like it, then screw them."

She seemed agitated, but resolved. "Southern State," she sat back in her chair, the cigarette dangling between her fingers, "hasn't changed much in the past twenty-four years. There's a malignancy of silence in these institutions. The administration turns a blind eye to things they shouldn't. Young women are abused and violated, and the school is more worried about its reputation than about any inflicted trauma." She met my eyes, appearing determined. "That's why I'm here, Lindsey. I won't let them look the other way."

She was full of righteous anger. I believed if anyone could hold this school accountable for its history of harmful secrecy, it was Daisy Molina.

"Do you know what happened to my sister?" I asked. Daisy took another drag before stubbing it out in an ashtray by the window.

"*This place* happened to her." Her face darkened. "This place and these men, and the fucked-up world we live in where a woman's life is valued only by what she can provide to others. *That's* what happened to Jess."

Her outrage was justifiable, but I needed concrete answers, not a speech on a soapbox.

"Daisy, can you tell me something? Anything?" I couldn't hide my desperation. "They've found three girls at Doll's Eye Lake. Jess is the only one still left missing. I'm trying to piece together what happened to her. I could wait for the police, but damn it, I've been waiting most of my life for answers, and it's way past time I figured things out for myself. You knew Jess. You were her friend. *Please,* help me."

It had been a long day, and it seemed there was still so much of the day left to go. I was exhausted. My head throbbed with a migraine. I hadn't eaten since that morning, and my stomach ached with hunger. But none of that was as important as getting Daisy to talk to me.

"I'm not sure how I can help you. I was a lot less observant than I should have been back then. While girls were disappearing, I was too busy getting drunk with my sorority sisters." She seemed appalled with the behavior of nineteen-year-old Daisy.

"If I knew what happened to Jess, I would have said something. I want her found as much as you do."

I tried not to be disappointed, but I was. I wasn't sure what I expected, but I had hoped for . . . something.

Daisy regarded me kindly. "I always knew you'd come here one day asking questions." She looked away, lighting up another cigarette. "I've been both hoping for and dreading it. Because I wasn't sure what you knew about your sister—what your parents have told you. I knew she had a complicated relationship with them."

"I know," I agreed.

Daisy took a drag, blowing smoke out slowly. "She loved your parents, but it was . . . odd. Especially her relationship with your dad. It was like . . . she loved him, but she hated him, too. But that's from an outsider's perspective. My observations may be totally wrong. Hell, I come from a family that would rather take a bath in acid than give you a hug, so what do I know?" she hurried to add.

I opened my mouth to grill her further about Jess and my father, but she was still talking. Almost as if she were in a confessional and I was her priest. Her words had the note of disclosure, as though she had been holding in the truth for a long, long time.

"I have to accept the consequences of my actions. I've made some shitty choices. All I can say is I was young and I thought I was doing the right thing." When she turned back to me, her eyes were bright with tears. "I wouldn't blame you if you hated me. But you can't hate me anymore than I already hate myself."

"Why would I hate you?" I felt a shudder of apprehension.

Daisy shook her head, but otherwise didn't say anything. As if she couldn't bear to put the truth into words.

"Daisy, please. Tell me about Jess. About what you and Ryan were arguing about. Why did you call him?" I took a deep breath, "tell me why you slept with my sister's boyfriend."

Daisy looked as if I had slapped her.

"I didn't sleep with Ryan." The denial was swift and absolute. "I would never have done that to Jess. Even though things were strained between us those last few weeks, she was my best friend. I loved her like a sister."

"But you were his alibi. He said you spent the night together," I said, confused.

She stood up and faced the window, pressing her palm to the glass. "I know how it must sound, but I never slept with Ryan. And I wasn't with him the night Jess disappeared. I lied to the police."

The admission sat between us like an undetonated bomb.

Daisy turned around to face me. Her eyes filled with tears and her mouth pinched in anger.

Her self-recrimination covered her like a film.

"Why?" I barely managed to say, my voice quiet and rough. "Why would you lie for him?"

"Because I was young and naive and I thought I was doing what Jess would want me to do." She sighed. "Ryan told me he and Jess had argued. That she broke up with him, which had shocked me because I knew how much she loved him. Even though their relationship had so many ups and downs it gave *me* a headache." She laughed, but it died quickly as she became serious again. "He said he went back to his dorm, got drunk, and passed out—end of story. But the next day news broke that Jess was gone. The police were questioning everyone. It looked bad. It looked—"

"Like he could be a suspect," I finished.

"I knew Ryan pretty well by that point. He had been dating Jess for a few months and they spent so much time in our room that I joked he should move in." Her smile was full of nostalgia. "I thought he was a good guy, even though there were rumors about him. About his temper." I must have made a face because Daisy gave me a knowing look. "I'm getting the impression you already know that."

"I've seen him lose his cool a time or two," I admitted.

"Jess, too. But she was happy with him most of the time, and like I said, I knew how much he loved her. He would have walked over broken glass for her. So, in my mind, I knew there was no way he could have hurt her. And I had watched enough soap operas and Lifetime movies to know he would be suspect numero uno. I thought I was being noble," she argued.

"So you lied for him, but . . . I'm getting the sense that now you're not so sure?"

Daisy put out her second cigarette and immediately fished out another one. She was obviously a stress smoker. "Even after all this time I don't know what to believe. Not about Ryan. I guess I never fully bought his story. Something was off about what he claimed. Then again, something was off about the whole damn situation."

I let her words sink in for a moment, horrified and yet not entirely surprised either. I had the same feelings.

"But this isn't only about Ryan. It's about all the ways this school failed to protect those women but bent over backward to protect Dr. Daniels and its reputation." Daisy sat back down heavily in her chair. "Everyone has secrets. I'm no exception. Neither is Ryan. Or Jess." She paused, as if trying to decide how to proceed. "Jess was hiding something, Lindsey, something big. I hate to say this but at the end . . . I didn't trust her."

"You didn't trust her? Why?"

"She had changed so much. It was gradual at first, but when we came back from Christmas break it was like she was a different person. We had been close. Closer than I was with my own family. I thought we told each other everything." She shook her head. "But she stopped talking to me. She was failing her classes because she was barely going to any of them. She was partying almost every night, drinking more than most of the frat guys I knew. She was kicked out of Pi Gamma. It looked like she was going to be thrown out of school as well, but she didn't seem to care about any of it. Something was wrong with her. She would disappear for hours and never tell me where she went. I'd hear her sneak out of our room late at night. She was a shadow of the woman she used to be." Daisy sounded tormented and I felt a growing sense of dread.

"What was going on with her? Did it have to do with Ryan?" I sat forward, feeling my entire body tense in anticipation.

"I don't think so. I think it went deeper than that," Daisy mused, staring off into space again.

"Ryan insisted it was all Dr. Daniels, and he begged me to be his alibi. He said that if the police were busy looking at him, then Dr. Daniels would get away with it. And he's not wrong. Who would the police believe? A college kid or a respected teacher at the school?"

I frowned, frustrated because I knew she was right. Yet lying to the police about Ryan's alibi also felt incredibly wrong.

"Ryan was no saint, and I regret lying because, looking back now, I'm not entirely sure I believe that Ryan was actually passed out in his dorm. Something about his story didn't feel right to me," Daisy continued, "but he was right in that Dr. Daniels had been involved with all those girls—even Jess."

"So, it's true, Jess and Dr. Daniels were together?" I interrupted.

Daisy shrugged. "He was definitely calling the room for her, and she was seeing him one-on-one for tutoring. Everyone knew how he was with his students. It was an open secret. A scandal to laugh and gossip about. Though it wasn't so funny when it was someone I loved—when it was Jess." She bit her lip as if to stop herself from crying. "I thought perhaps that was why her behavior had changed so dramatically. That Dr. Daniels was preying on her like he had preyed on Tammy, Phoebe, and Meghan. Ryan and I both believed Dr. Daniels had something to do with Jess's disappearance. We became fixated on it. On him paying for his seemingly obvious crimes."

"But nothing happened. He didn't pay for anything."

Daisy's face flushed with anger. "No, he didn't. The police barely questioned him. The staff rallied around him, and his reputation, though slightly tarnished, remained intact. He continued to teach here, and prey on vulnerable women, until he retired five years ago. By the end, he stopped trying to hide what he was doing all together. What was the point when no one even tried to stop him?"

"It's wrong that he never faced the consequences for his actions." I felt the same simmering fury that Daisy clearly felt.

Daisy made a noise of revulsion. "It *is* wrong. And that's the kind of injustice I hear about every single day in this job. It's what made me become a youth advocate—because I was tired of people being taken advantage of and I was tired of places like Southern State University allowing it to continue." Her expression hardened. "You have to always be on your guard around men like Dr. Daniels. Around men like Ryan McKay. They make it easy to believe them." Her words held a note of warning. "You can't trust him, Lindsey. Whatever Ryan says is complete bullshit. He only knows how to lie and deceive."

My blood turned to ice. That same inexplicable presence that had shadowed me for weeks had returned. It was a whisper on the back of my neck. I couldn't stop myself from shivering. The feeling of being watched, ever present.

Daisy cast a wary look around, and I wondered if she felt it, too.

"Why are you so sure Ryan's lying about where he was that night?"

She blinked twice as if she'd forgotten I was there. But then, her face cleared and she took on a look of seriousness that had me on edge.

"A few months before we graduated, Ryan and I were both at a party. He was drunk. I hadn't really talked to him over the years. We had an unspoken understanding to avoid each other, which worked for me. I was trying hard to move on from what happened freshman year. That evening I found myself sitting in a back corner at a frat house and Ryan joined me." She hesitated, seeming unsure if she should continue.

I waited.

"It felt weird to be around him. For him, too, I think. He got really emotional. We started reminiscing about Jess.

Talking about the good times. It was all pretty nice, actually. But then . . ." she paused, "then he started babbling about how he knew something bad happened to her—that he saw her."

"What?" I gasped.

"I was confused, too, until he told me how angry he had been that night. He was crying hard by that point, I could barely understand him. But what I gleaned from his drunken ramblings was that Ryan had driven to Jess's house—*your* house—to confront her. She had broken up with him and he was pissed off."

"Ryan was at my house that night?" I repeated, needing confirmation.

"Yes, Ryan was there. And he saw your sister."

15

JESSICA

Mid April 1999

THE WALLS WERE closing in on me. I had no room to move. No way to escape.

Daisy was barely talking to me—not since the day the police had questioned her about her ID. I didn't dare ask her why. I didn't want to hear the truth.

I was dangerously close to losing everything.

Daisy had her headphones on while she worked on a paper for art history. I might as well not be there.

The phone rang, but I couldn't bring myself to pick it up.

When I didn't answer, Daisy finally stopped and gave me an irritated look. She answered it with a chirpy, "hello?"

Then she held out the receiver. "It's for you. Not sure why you didn't answer it." She wouldn't meet my eyes.

"Thanks," I muttered, taking the phone from her.

"Jessica," he said my name with a smile I could almost see.

"Hi." I turned my back to my roommate, though I knew she was listening. She hadn't put her headphones back on.

"I'm checking everything is still set for Friday," Dr. Daniels said.

"Yeah." I clenched the phone to stop my hand from shaking. Dr. Daniels had finally requested to see me *off campus*.

This had been building for weeks. It wasn't a race to the finish line like I expected. When I pictured this, I hadn't expected how gradually this man would sink beneath my skin. It actually took me by surprise. And even though I thought I was prepared, I had been almost seduced by his gentle persuasion.

Dr. Daniels hadn't kissed me or touched me beyond brief moments of fingers on skin. He was subtle. He was shrewd. There were only a few occasions when he made his true objective known. The rest of the time he was 100% professional.

It was then, when you could convince yourself you were imagining things, that he was most dangerous.

He told me to meet him this Friday. When I said I was going home for the weekend for my sister's birthday, he suggested we see each other beforehand. He explained he lived in Mt. Randall, not far from the lake where I spent so much time with Dad growing up. He wanted to spend some time with me, away from school, so we could "really relax." He said I had earned it.

What he meant was *he* had earned it.

He had put in the time and he aimed to collect.

Dr. Daniels had been helping me keep it together because I was failing everything. Barely holding on by my fingertips. If it wasn't for him, I would have already been kicked out. I felt a sense of obligation toward him that he had been meticulously grooming.

"I'm looking forward to it. I hope you are, too." His voice dropped and I felt it. The second when things between us crossed a line.

Is this how Tammy felt? Phoebe? Meghan? Had they vibrated with this anxious anticipation as they recklessly careened into him?

"I am."

I heard him let out a quiet breath. Soft, yet it filled my ears.

"See you Friday, Jessica." He liked to say my name.

"Bye." I quickly hung up, noticing Daisy watching me.

"Was that Dr. Daniels?" she asked.

"Yeah." It was my turn not to meet her eyes.

"What are you doing, Jess?" This wasn't my ditzy, party-loving roommate. This Daisy was too astute for my liking.

"Nothing—"

"I'm getting really sick and tired of you lying to me," she snapped. "You've been slinking off to meet that professor for weeks now."

"Are you following me or something?" I laughed, trying to lighten the mood, but Daisy wasn't having any of it. Our friendship had deteriorated to barely functioning.

It was clear Daisy no longer viewed me as a friend but as someone she couldn't trust. And it all started with that stupid ID.

"What about Ryan? Have you thought about him?" she asked, her voice tight. "And what about Tammy? And Phoebe and Meghan? They made the same mistake and where are they now?"

"They ran off, Daisy. I thought we agreed on that." I was trying to placate her. It wasn't working.

Daisy stood up and grabbed her book bag, slinging it over her shoulder. "And if you believe that, you're not only lying to me, but you're lying to yourself." She shook her head. "I need to get to the library."

"I thought you never went to the library." It was a poor attempt at a joke.

"Yeah, well, things change, don't they?"

"Daisy, why are you so angry with me?" I asked her before she could leave. My voice was husky. I could barely contain the panic that was ready to burst out of me.

She stopped, but didn't turn to face me as she answered. "Because I feel like I'm rooming with a stranger. Or—" she hesitated, "maybe I never knew you to begin with."

"What does that even mean? Of course you know me." After everything, the thought of losing Daisy's friendship was almost too much to bear.

She finally looked at me, but her eyes seemed to see something that she didn't like.

"There are things you aren't telling me, Jess. You think I'm some dumb airhead, but I notice stuff. And I know when stories aren't adding up." Her demeanor had become tough and unyielding.

"Is this still about the ID—?"

"No, it's not only that. It's whatever's going on with Dr. Daniels. It's those unaccounted hours when you disappear. It's the late-night phone calls to your dad. It's you failing your classes and getting drunk every night. You think that no one notices how much you've changed, but we do. *I do*."

I wanted to cry. I wanted to beg her to give me a chance to explain. But what would be the point? I couldn't explain what was happening. What had already happened. I could never tell anyone why my dad called me late at night. Why I snuck off to meet him.

I could never tell Daisy my secrets.

She became anguished. "You've been my best friend since we got here and I wish you'd be honest with me. Please, tell me if you've gotten into something you can't get out of. Maybe I can help."

I didn't like where this conversation was going. I had to reassure her somehow, but there were no words I could think of. There were only more lies.

So I stayed silent. I said absolutely nothing.

With a look of heartbreaking disappointment, she shook her head. "This is going to end badly, Jess, and I can't stand around watching it happen." With that, she left, closing the door behind her.

My despair instantly morphed into anger. I picked up my pillow, screaming into it as loud as I could.

I had lost control of my life, of my future. I couldn't see a way out of the mess I was in.

I couldn't breathe.

I grabbed my keys and left my room. I needed space. I needed air.

I didn't know where I was headed. I walked blindly. Without purpose. Without a destination. I had never felt so completely and utterly alone. I had no one to talk to. No one I could confide in. I was by myself in this awful darkness.

Eventually, I made my way toward the crest of the hill that overlooked Mt. Randall. When I first started college it felt good to be up here, with my old life out of reach down below. But it had all started to collide.

I sat down on a bench, wishing I could undo the past six months, but knowing it was impossible.

I had made my choices, no matter how rash they had been. And those decisions, made in the heat of the moment and fueled by pain and misery, were destroying me.

"Hey, babe."

I felt his arm slide around my shoulders, his warm body pressed into my side.

I turned my face into Ryan's solid chest, needing him desperately.

"Woah, what's wrong?" he murmured into my hair.

"Do you have a few hours?" I laughed half-heartedly.

Ryan cupped the side of my neck. "I'm here for you, Jess, always. I can tell something's wrong and has been for a while. I hope you know you can tell me anything and I will never judge you. Never turn my back on you." I knew he meant it. Even if his promises were hypotheticals. He would never make those kinds of assurances if he knew the truth.

I snuggled into him. "It's nothing. I'm being overly dramatic."

The pieces were falling apart. I couldn't even trust Ryan to put them back together.

He kissed the top of my head and we sat in silence for several minutes, watching the world go by.

Ryan eventually stood up. "Let's go to my room for a little while. My roommate is at lacrosse practice."

I let him take my hand and lead me back toward the dorms. Perhaps I could pretend for a little while.

"Jess?"

Every part of me froze. Ryan looked over his shoulder, frowning in confusion as my mom's blue-and-tan minivan pulled up beside us as we walked along the road.

"Just keep walking," I told him quietly.

"Jess, I need to talk to you," my dad called out. I heard the slam of a car door. "You can't keep avoiding me."

"Who is that?" Ryan asked, his voice steely, his grip tightening possessively.

"Jess!" my father yelled and I finally came to a stop.

I gave Ryan a tiny smile. "It's my dad. Give me a minute."

Fear and anger shadowed my steps as I left Ryan's side and walked toward my dad, who was striding towards me. He looked like a wreck. His normally perfectly styled hair was messy as if he hadn't brushed it in days. He had dark smudges beneath his eyes, and he clearly hadn't shaved in awhile. My mother must be having a fit at the sight of him.

How was he explaining the slip in his appearance? What lies was he spinning to get her off his back?

What reason did he give for driving her car instead of his own, very conspicuous, bright-yellow Mustang?

"You need to answer your phone when I call you, young lady." To anyone else he sounded like a stern father. They wouldn't hear the slight tremor in his voice—the barely concealed hysteria. I felt the instinct to morph into "old Jess." I looked down at my feet. I shrank in on myself until I was as nonthreatening as possible.

"I'm sorry, Dad," I said softly, my voice pitched low, like a child's. This was how I always was with him.

Then I looked over my shoulder at Ryan who was far enough away that he couldn't overhear our conversation. He was watching us with open concern.

Everything was so messed up. And it started with my father.

"Damn it, Jess. I needed to see you. Where have you been?" It came out as an accusation.

"There's nothing left to say to each other." I was tired. Incredibly tired. So, I forced that little girl inside me to disappear. In her place was a woman to be reckoned with. I stood up straighter. I felt my spine stiffen. Dad took a step back, as if to protect himself.

"Jess." My name sounded like agony. Like broken dreams and empty promises. I couldn't stand to look at him. He made me sick. But there was the part of me that wanted to hug him. I wanted everything to go back to how it used to be . . . even if that hurt, too.

"Leave me alone." It was both a plea and a demand.

Dad took a hold of my upper arms, his fingers digging into my skin.

"The police called me downtown to ask me questions about Meghan. Why would they do that?" He gave me a little shake.

I tried to pull out of his grasp. "So? What does that have to do with me?"

My father tightened his grip. "They said they got a tip about me. They tore apart my car. They took things into evidence. They think—" He cut himself off, looking away.

"They think you did something to her, right?" I filled in, trying hard not to be swayed by his misery. Trying not to be flayed open by my guilt.

Dad's face shattered. "You did this, Jess."

I clenched my teeth. "No, Dad, *you* did this. This is on you. You've dragged me into it." This time my anger was directed at the right target. I welcomed it with open arms. It decimated my conditioned submissiveness. It stomped my need to please into the ground.

"Jess." My father looked down at me, his eyes full of something that looked like hatred. I tried to take a step back, but he held me in place.

I had never doubted my father's love. He had made it clear that no matter what, he was there for me. He'd help me when I needed it. He loved me unconditionally.

But this wasn't the face of a man devoted to his child. This was a man who despised the person in front of him. Who blamed them for everything.

"If I go down, Jess, you go down, too. Remember that when you're stirring the pot. Think about your mother. Think about Lindsey. Think about what you're doing to *them.*"

"I don't need to think about *anything*," I spat. "And you won't make me feel guilty because of *your* mistakes."

He slapped me.

I stumbled backward, holding a hand to my cheek. My father seemed shocked. He looked down at his hand as if it were foreign to him.

"Jess!" Ryan ran to me, pulling me away. He turned to my dad. "You ever touch her again, I'll kick your ass, old man, you hear me?"

"Jess—" Dad started to say.

"Go. Just leave," I told him.

He looked between Ryan and me, his emotions torn. "Jess, please . . . I'm sorry."

Ryan put his hands on my dad's chest and shoved him backward. My dad stumbled. He looked like he wanted to cry. He looked broken.

"Get out of here!" Ryan yelled.

My father seemed conflicted, but with a final look at Ryan, he got in the van.

"What the hell was that all about?" Ryan was still angry, but he softened at the sight of my despondent expression. "Hey, it's okay." He put his arms around me and I pressed my face into his solid warmth, crying for the first time in as long as I could remember.

"Sometimes I hate him, Ryan. I really hate him," I sobbed, feeling ashamed of the words. I was being torn in two. The bone deep love was being quashed by harsher, more savage emotions.

He ran his hands up and down my back. "Wanna tell me about it?"

The desire to unload everything was tempting.

I wiped my face and pulled away. "I'm fine. It's only family drama."

Ryan glanced in the direction my dad had driven off. "That looked like more than simple family drama, Jess." He sounded worried.

"I have a complicated relationship with my Dad." I sighed. "We've always been close. He was my best friend.

There were no secrets between us . . . until there were." I closed my eyes. "He's cheating on my mom."

Ryan's eyes widened. "Crap, for real? That's a lot to carry around with you." He hugged me tighter and I breathed a little easier.

It seemed like he wanted to ask more questions.

"No, we're not talking about this," I said firmly, "come on, let's go watch some really bad daytime tv and take my mind off all the ways my life sucks."

"Except for me, right?" Ryan asked, sounding vulnerable.

"Except for you," I agreed and forced myself to be normal, at least for a little while.

Ten Seconds to Vanish: The Unsolved Disappearance of Jessica Fadley

Episode 10

The Interview

Stella: Hi all my true crime babes. Thanks for tuning in for another week of twists and turns and absolute madness! I'm your host Stella—

Rachel: And I'm Rachel

Stella: And this is *Ten Seconds to Vanish: The Unsolved Disappearance of Jessica Fadley.*

Theme music plays

Rachel: Today's episode is a big one because we have a special guest here with us. Someone who can give us firsthand insight into what it was like at Southern State University back then. Someone who knew all four of the victims.

Stella: We'd like to introduce Erica Stead. Hi Erica. Thanks so much for getting in touch and agreeing to come on our show.

Erica: Hi ladies. I absolutely love your podcast. I knew you two were the perfect ones to share my story with.

Rachel: And we're so glad you decided to. Because, girl, you've got quite the story to tell.

Erica: I'll say. I'm so thankful I'm here at all to talk to you.

Stella: Oh my god, of course. Because you could have been a victim, too!

Erica: Well, not really. *I* wasn't sleeping with my married professor.

Rachel: So it's true that Jessica was sleeping with the same professor who had been involved with Tammy, Phoebe, and Meghan?

Stella: Spill the tea.

Erica: It's true. Jessica would tell me everything. I knew all about her and Dr. . . . . can I say his name?

Stella: I wouldn't. Not until he's officially named as a person of interest.

Erica: Okay, well anyway, we were super close. She was a literal sister to me. You know, because we were both pledges of Pi Gamma Delta. I have to say hi to all my sisters out there! Love in our bond!

Rachel: That means you knew Phoebe, too. She was a pledge, right?

Erica: Phoebe was the sweetest. We had so much in common. We spent so much time together. I've been a wreck since they found her body.

Stella: Back to Jessica. You said she was definitely sleeping with her teacher?

Erica: Oh, absolutely. But that was the kind of girl Jessica was. I loved her, but she had her faults. Everyone knew Jessica was out of control. She was cheating on her boyfriend and she was even put on academic probation and kicked out of Pi Gam.

Rachel: Really? I thought she was a good student.

Erica: No way. She was a hot mess. If she hadn't disappeared, she would have been kicked out of school.

Stella: Wow, goes to show you never really know what's going on with people.

16

LINDSEY

Present Day

"WHAT DO YOU mean he was there?" I demanded.

Daisy lit another cigarette. The incessant smoke was making me ill.

"Ryan was at Jess's house—your house—that night. He admitted it to me. And given how mad he could get sometimes, and how jealous he was of Jess spending so much time with Dr. Daniels, I now wonder if he did something to her . . . even accidentally." She appeared apologetic for her bluntness. "I refused to see it then because I was so fixated on Dr. Daniels, and Ryan was right there, pushing me down that path. But hindsight is a bitch, and looking back now . . . I have to ask myself, is that really why he lied? My young, naive self accepted his story and filed it away as another justification for being his alibi. Because it reinforced the idea that he would have been unjustly labeled a suspect, but what if I was wrong?"

I was glad I was sitting down. The suspicions about Ryan had been sitting there, in the back of my mind, since finding out he had been Jess's boyfriend. But I hadn't fully accepted them.

But now I couldn't deny the real possibility of his guilt any longer. And I had been alone with him in his car. My foolishness was infuriating.

"What about Dr. Daniels? Isn't he as much of a suspect as Ryan?" I asked, my voice barely above a whisper.

"Of course. Or maybe he's simply your run-of-the-mill white, middle-class pervert. Being a sleaze doesn't mean you're a murderer," Daisy scoffed bitterly. "The only way this will ever be solved is if I tell the truth. If the police know everything. Because either way, he needs to be exposed. Whether he's responsible for Jess and the others is up to the police to figure out."

Had Ryan really hurt Jess?

Could he have killed all those women? Was he actually a serial killer who had gotten away with his crimes for over two decades?

I had believed him when he said he only wanted to find out the truth, yet he had lied to me from day one. Had I been completely bamboozled by a killer?

"You don't believe it was someone else?" I croaked.

"You mean those theories about a random serial killer stalking campus?" Daisy looked doubtful. "Not anymore. Look, at the time, everyone was terrified. Women couldn't go anywhere without thinking they were going to be snatched by some stranger. The fear was everywhere. In everything we did. You couldn't escape the idea that any one of us could be next."

"So what do you think now?" I asked, already knowing, and dreading, her reply.

"I think it's too easy to cast suspicion on a faceless villain. No one wants to blame the very real evil that may be right there in front of you. Oftentimes, the truth is something you don't want to admit to yourself. I've learned to stop putting my head in the sand. Which is why I'm going to the police with everything I know about Ryan *and* about Dr. Daniels."

"I never really believed it was a stranger either," I admitted. "We all have heard that when a woman is hurt, most of the time she knows her attacker. The police believe that as well. Lieutenant Higgins says that the women knew the perpetrator."

Daisy's shoulders drooped. "It makes sense. And by not telling the truth, I hampered the investigation. I messed up. I've been terrified of owning up to my mistakes for years, but not anymore. I'm going to tell the truth now. I'm going to the station to tell them that I lied. I'm trying to put this right. Jess deserves it. Tammy, Phoebe, and Meghan, too." Daisy sounded heartbroken, yet determined.

"Is that what you and Ryan were arguing about?" I asked her.

Daisy blew out a noisy breath. "I was an idiot and called him. I've been stewing on what I should do for days—since Lieutenant Higgins called me. She was asking about Jess's blanket and following up on my interview from back then. But I knew I needed to come clean. So, thinking I was being the better person, I reached out to let Ryan know my plans. I didn't want him to be blindsided." She raised her eyebrows. "To say he took it badly is an understatement."

"So, he came here to what? Stop you?" I asked, aghast.

"I had no idea he was even in town. The last time I had heard, he was living in Chicago. I was shocked when he showed up here, though perhaps I shouldn't have been surprised. If he thought they found Jess, of course he'd come. He could never stay away from your sister." Daisy looked pained. "He was all fired up, saying he didn't hurt her. And let me tell you, if I was still nineteen, I probably would have believed him. His sincerity is very convincing." She made a look of distaste. "He wanted me to hear the whole story before I went to the cops. As if that would stop me."

"What *was* his whole story?"

Daisy flicked ash out the window, watching students walk by. "He said that he went to her house and parked down the street. He said he saw her car out front so he knew she was there."

Daisy aggressively put out the cigarette before turning in her chair to face me again.

"Ryan said he didn't know how long he sat there. He was wasted. He claimed he'd had a fifth of vodka. The stupidity of driving while intoxicated alone should have convinced me to turn him in, but here we are." She briefly closed her eyes, obviously irritated with herself. "Eventually, Jess came out of the house and he started to get out of the car, but then he saw her talking to an older man he thought was Dr. Daniels."

"So, Jess *was* sleeping with him then," I stated matter-of-factly.

Daisy could sense my frustration. "Like I said, I honestly don't know. Ryan told me he saw Jess talking to an older man—he assumed it was Dr. Daniels, but it could have been anyone really. Ryan was drunk, it was dark, and he was upset, so who knows. He did say it looked, well . . . heated. That he felt like he was watching two people about to fight and make up if you know what I mean."

My empty stomach rolled. "And then what?"

"He said he dropped his keys on the floor and he reached down to get them. By the time he sat up again, Jess and the man were gone, the trunk of her car still open. He said he sat there for a little while longer, but when she didn't reappear, he decided to head back to school. He swears he didn't think anything was wrong. He went back to his dorm room and passed out."

I could hardly believe what I was hearing. "So, he was there when Jess disappeared. He saw her with a man he thinks was Dr. Daniels, and he didn't think it important to tell the police?" I sounded incredulous.

Daisy's jaw stiffened. "I know. That's exactly what I said to him when he showed up here to tell me a story that should have been shared twenty-four goddamned years ago."

I swallowed past the lump in my throat. "Do you believe his story?"

"I don't know. What I do know is that Ryan was scared."

"Scared? Why?"

"Because Dr. Daniels wasn't the only man to have been involved with all four women."

"What are you saying?"

Daisy looked conflicted. "Ryan slept with Tammy and Meghan. And he dated Phoebe in high school. And, of course, he was Jess's boyfriend. So yeah, if the police knew, then he would definitely be on their radar, that's for sure."

"Oh my god," I gasped.

Ryan was connected to all of the missing women.

Every.

Single.

One.

"The police need to know what Ryan saw," Daisy continued. "They need to know I lied for him. Then let the chips fall where they may." I could sense her growing agitation. "Ryan says if I go to the authorities with the information now, we'll both be charged with obstruction of justice and lose our jobs. But at this point, I don't even care. We've both lied for long enough."

I was still trying to process Daisy's revelations. "How can you be sure Ryan was even telling the truth about going to my house? I don't think he'd know how to be honest if his life depended on it."

"Because why would he implicate himself like that? Regardless, I can't keep what I know a secret any longer. If there's a chance—even a small one—that Ryan's story checks out, it could mean a killer, whether it's Ryan or Dr. Daniels, will finally be put away and those women will get some justice." Daisy looked at her watch. "I'm so sorry, Lindsey, but I need to head to the police station before it gets any later." She stood up and grabbed her jacket off the back of the door.

"Would you like me to come with you?" I got to my feet and watched as she gathered her things.

Daisy shook her head and then pulled me into a hug. "I have to do this on my own. I made a promise to Jess that I would make things right. And I'm promising you the same thing." She stepped back, taking my hands. "I'm going to admit that I lied for Ryan. I'm going to tell them what Ryan saw. And I'm going to tell them what I know about Dr. Daniels." She went to her desk drawer and retrieved a manila folder. "I've kept years of documentation about his predatory behavior and how the school has covered it up. And if the police won't do anything about it, I'm going to the press. It's way past time."

"You're definitely going to lose your job over that one," I warned.

Daisy opened the door to her office. "Then so be it. I need to put these ghosts to rest."

We stared at each other for a long moment. We were mirror images of grief and rage. Whatever had happened, I knew I couldn't blame Daisy. She had been young and scared, and quite possibly even deceived by the killer. I followed her out of the office. Once outside, Daisy turned to me, her lips trembling slightly.

"I'm sorry, Lindsey. I should have been honest a long time ago."

"You're doing the right thing now, and that's what counts," I assured her.

Daisy looked uncertain. "Before you go, there's something else. I'm not sure if I should even mention it, but I don't want to hold back anything ever again."

"Okay . . ." I felt myself bracing for impact once more.

"You know how I mentioned Jess was acting strange after Christmas break? How much she had changed?" I nodded. "And I told you I had stopped trusting her." I nodded again. "It has to do with my student ID card."

My mind went to the interview transcript I had read in the case file. It was the reason Daisy had been questioned by the police in the first place.

"It went missing sometime before we left in December. I didn't think much of it at the time because Jess would often use it when she couldn't find hers." She seemed to be struggling to piece things together. "Then the police called me downtown to ask about it. It wasn't long after Meghan Lambert went missing. The detective wanted to know why I was at these different locations at the same time as the missing girls. And the thing was, I hadn't seen that ID in months. I told the police that. I was freaking out by the time I left, thinking they were looking at me as a suspect or something."

"Understandably," I told her, imagining how terrifying that must have been for her.

"Yeah, well when I got back to my room after the interview, the ID was on my desk, like it had been there the whole time. And when I asked Jess about it she said Ryan brought it back. That he found it in his dorm."

"And it all comes back to Ryan again," I said.

Daisy seemed conflicted. "Yes, sure it makes Ryan look bad, but that wasn't the part that bothered me most." She hesitated.

"What was it?"

"When I asked Jess if she had been using it, as I knew she had done before, she denied it. In fact, she tried telling me she only used it once, which I knew was a lie. I remembered handing it to her myself at least half a dozen times. But she insisted. As if my memory was mistaken."

I frowned uncertainly, not sure what she was getting at.

"Even then, I knew when someone was trying to snow me. My bullshit meter has served me well over the years." She gave me a small smile.

I wasn't sure what her lying about using her roommate's ID card meant, but it seemed important to Daisy. As if it confirmed a suspicion she couldn't quite put into words.

"You know, I came to see you once," Daisy added before leaving.

"You did?" That surprised me.

She looked distraught. "I did. I'd been worrying about you for so long, I decided to come and check on you. I knew Jess would want me to. Especially with how strained things were between her and your dad. I knew she didn't really trust him. She loved him, yes, but trust him? Not so much." Again, with the pointed remarks about my father.

"I drove over to your house. I knocked on the door, but no one answered. I could hear music and I thought it was coming from the house. So, I knocked again. Then I started looking through the windows to see if someone was there."

"You're lucky Mrs. Lewis, next door, didn't see you. She would have turned the hose on you," I chuckled, thinking of my busybody elderly neighbor.

Daisy didn't laugh, she seemed . . . disturbed.

"Yeah, well, when I looked through the window of the garage, I could tell the music was coming from the yellow car inside. And I could make out someone, who I assumed was your dad, sitting in the driver's seat."

"So, he was sitting in the Mustang listening to music." It wasn't a question. I could picture what she had seen perfectly. I had seen it myself many times before.

"Yeah. He was just staring into space. Frankly, it creeped me out. I couldn't see him clearly, because the window was pretty dirty, but I got the impression he was upset. His shoulders were shaking like they do when someone is crying. I felt weird being there, so I left and could never bring myself to go back."

I thought about all the times I had found Dad doing the same thing. Sitting in his car, listening to music, staring out the window at nothing in particular. I'd always thought it was odd, but Mom never commented on it, so neither had I. But, obviously his behavior was peculiar, because Daisy was as bothered by it as I had always been.

"For what it's worth, I really am sorry. I hope that we finally find out what happened to Jess—to all of them." Daisy gave me one more hug before leaving. I watched her go, my mind running a million miles an hour.

I walked slowly back to my own car, not sure what to do now. I had no one that I could talk to about any of this. No one I could trust.

For the first time in my life, I felt truly alone.

Back in my car, I sat with the engine running. My mind felt too full to properly process anything. I had discovered so much—too much—and yet none of it made any sense.

But one thing was painfully clear—my dad was the worst kind of man. A person who could betray his wife and lie to his family. A man who preyed on young women.

When I thought back over the years, I could remember times when he had perhaps looked a little too long at some of my friends. Maybe flirted with a waitress or two. At the time, I hadn't thought it was anything sinister. It was only my charismatic dad being his friendly self. Mom said he'd always been a flirt, but that didn't necessarily make him a cheater.

Yet it seemed my father hadn't stopped at a wink and a comment. He had taken it to a place he shouldn't have.

My thoughts swirled in my head like sewage. The more I tried to push them away, the more they forced their way to the surface.

Then there was Ryan. He had no alibi for the night of Jess's disappearance. And neither did Dr. Daniels.

They were both connected to each of the missing women. One seemed as guilty as the other.

And, of course, there was my dad.

There were so many unanswered questions about these men, and I felt no closer to discovering any answers.

I pulled my car out of the parking lot and headed back down the hill towards town. Horror swirled inside me as I drove closer to home and the lies I had been raised on. I wondered what secrets Jess had held on to.

And what dark truths she had likely taken to her grave.

* * *

I woke early the next day with a terrible headache.

When I'd gotten home, I had taken a bottle of wine to my room and spent the night reading, and rereading, the case file.

Mom had already been in bed and Dad was presumably still at work.

I woke up around 3 AM to my parents arguing.

It wasn't a sound I was used to hearing. Except for that one time over Jess's room, I realized they never fought at all, which was strange. Because all married couples fought at one time or another. But not my mom and dad.

They seemed to exist in a delicate balance of real and pretend. I knew now they worked hard to keep up the image of a perfect couple. But it seemed the cracks were finally starting to show.

It was now early. The sun had barely risen when I dragged myself out of bed. I looked out the window and saw that Mom's car was gone. I remembered she had an early morning doctor's appointment followed by a few hours at the gym. She most likely wouldn't be home until sometime this afternoon. But my father was home. So, I opened the door slowly, listening for any sign of him before deciding it was safe to leave my room in search of food and painkillers.

I had barely eaten anything yesterday, and after drinking the entire bottle of wine on an empty stomach, I was feeling worse for the wear.

Downstairs, I put on a pot of coffee and sat at the kitchen table waiting for it to brew. I looked around the familiar room. A space once filled with, what I thought was, unconditional love. We had shared so much, but now I wondered if we had really shared anything at all. The pieces of my life, the parts I had trusted and counted on, now felt like a work of fiction.

Had I been purposefully blind to the reality of the people around me? When I thought about it, really thought about it, that picture perfect childhood I was so sure about, was anything but. My life had been constricted and restrained. I grew up feeling both smothered and an afterthought.

I had manipulated my own memories to make them palpable. To make them seem healthy and genuine.

Not only had my parents lied to me, but I had done a damn good job of lying to myself.

Dad hadn't wanted me at all, he had been content with his one, perfect daughter. And Mom had wanted someone to make her feel loved. The hurt and betrayal was overwhelming.

My hands were shaking and I balled them into fists to stop them.

A loud bang came from the garage, as if something had fallen over.

I walked toward the door at the back of the kitchen that led directly to the garage. It was painted the same color as the kitchen cabinets. Because of that, it blended in, making it hardly noticeable. Sometimes I forgot it was there altogether. No one, other than my dad, ever went out there anyway.

I retrieved the key from the hook and slipped it into the lock, the door clicked and I pushed it open. The air was cold. Much colder than one would expect given the temperature outside.

The garage was piled high with decades' worth of family clutter packed into plastic tubs, and bags. Fishing gear, paddles, Christmas decorations and old clothes I had long since outgrown. Stuff that was supposed to be donated to Goodwill or sold at yard sales, but instead had accumulated here, gathering dust.

The walls were lined with shelves filled with old tools I had never seen my dad use. I also noticed glass bowls from the vinegar he used years ago to eradicate the smell of rot from the dead animals that had died in the eaves. I recalled the rancid odor and Mom's loud complaints about the smell wafting under the door. Then one day the smell was gone, replaced by the overwhelming perfume of peppermint.

In the corner, underneath a large, blue tarp was the paddleboat. The same one Jess and Dad used to take to Doll's Eye Lake. The same paddle boat I had never been on. It had remained untouched since the last time the two of them had taken it out. It seemed sad and lonely, discarded with a hundred memories. I could only see the bottom rudder. It was otherwise covered.

And there, in the center of the garage, was Dad's beloved Boss 429 Mustang—once a vibrant yellow, now cracked and peeling. It was a far cry from its mint condition in the photographs in Sergeant O'Neil's case file.

My dad loved the car. Some of my earliest memories, the hazy, half-formed ones I could vaguely recollect from before Jess disappeared, involved standing at my father's side as he buffed and waxed its bright yellow surface.

Then one day, Dad declared it had broken down. A busted carburetor or something. He said it was an expensive part to replace in a retro vehicle, so he'd never had it fixed. I had never thought to question the obvious lie. How he could listen to music in a car that apparently didn't run. I felt foolish for my obliviousness. Now, like the unused boat, it sat in this cold dark space, rusting away.

I tried the door handle and found that it was open. Impulsively, I climbed inside, sitting in the driver's seat like I'd seen my dad do countless times before—like Daisy had seen that day long ago. The keys dangled from the ignition. I turned it on, surprised, though I shouldn't have been, when the engine turned over. I let it idle. I fiddled with the radio, turning it on. A slow, melodious voice whispered through the speakers like a phantom. I recognized the old fifties classic. An agonized ballad about love and death.

I looked at the small window in the garage door that Daisy must have looked through all those years ago. What the hell had he been doing sitting there, listening to sad music? I wondered, briefly, if he had been thinking about Meghan. Or maybe one of the other girls he had been involved with. The thought made my skin crawl.

A few minutes later, I turned off the engine and got out of the car, not wanting to be inside it any longer. Something about the garage and the Mustang didn't feel right.

As I turned to leave, I glanced back at the car, noticing that one of the taillights was broken. There was a black cavity where the glass had once been. I wasn't sure if it had always been like that but, I couldn't imagine my father not fixing something cosmetic and easily repaired. I looked at the floor and there was no broken glass anywhere.

I walked to the trunk of the car, gently brushing my fingers over the empty socket. I moved as if possessed, my hands hovering over the lever. The sudden need to see inside felt important.

Imperative even.

But when I tried to pop it open, it wouldn't budge. I pulled and pushed, frustrated, but it still wouldn't move.

A shudder went through me, and I wondered what could possibly be inside that he felt the need to lock away. I remembered the pictures from Sergeant O'Neil's case file. The list of items police had recovered from this very car. What secrets did it hold? I quickly grabbed the keys from the ignition and went to open the trunk. My hand trembled as I turned the key and lifted the lever. I peered inside, expecting to see the worst . . .

And it was empty.

I patted around to see if something was hidden, but there was nothing there.

With a sigh I slammed the trunk shut. What was I doing? Did I really think my father was hiding something nefarious in the trunk of his Mustang? I was letting my imagination run wild, looking for the worst in the people around me.

There was a rustling of movement out of the corner of my eye. I froze.

The tarp covering the boat slightly fell to the side revealing a portion of its faded orange hull.

Curious, I walked toward it. I couldn't remember ever having actually seen it before. It had always been hidden by plastic. I had only seen it in photos.

I reached out to pull the tarp from its worn body . . .

"Lindsey!"

I went completely still.

Looking over my shoulder, I felt my body go rigid with a fear that felt rooted in survival if not sense.

My father stood in the doorway, the light from the kitchen throwing him deep in shadow.

"What are you doing?" His voice sounded strained—almost breathless.

My hand still hovered over the tarp-covered boat.

"I—"

"Stop that, right now!" he roared, practically running across the garage and pulling me away.

He was shaking, his face flushed red. The vein on his forehead popping in a way it did only when he was angry.

But my dad didn't look angry.

He looked terrified.

Ten Seconds to Vanish: The Unsolved Disappearance of Jessica Fadley

Episode 12

Stella: Hi everyone. Welcome to our penultimate episode. I'm your host Stella—

Rachel: And I'm Rachel.

Stella: And this is *Ten Seconds to Vanish: The Unsolved Disappearance of Jessica Fadley.*

Theme music plays

Stella: We should address something before we get started. There's been a lot of blowback in regard to the interview we did with Erica Stead last week. It seems a lot of our listeners were pretty upset with how she characterized Jessica, a woman who isn't around to defend herself.

Rachel: We get it, guys. And we totally agree. As much as we loved having Erica on the show, it's important to note that those were *her* impressions, which are completely subjective.

Stella: And we received several emails from acquaintances of both Erica *and* Jessica who claim that many of the things Erica said during her interview were blatantly false. We are so sorry we didn't vet her better. But, we're human, and in the rush to get the scoop, we let you all down.

Rachel: More importantly, we let Jessica down. That's not to say Erica didn't provide some important insight. And it's always good to get an eyewitness account, no matter how skewed it may be.

Stella: That's right, because it turns out Erica did provide some accurate info. Like the fact that Jessica had, in fact, been kicked out of her sorority.

Rachel: And she had broken up with her boyfriend the same day she went missing.

Stella: That's a big one. Because all this time we've been looking at the professor. But we also need to look at the other men in Jessica's life. Men that were connected to the other missing girls as well. We mentioned earlier in this podcast that this hottie boyfriend had a history with our four girls, and Erica did confirm that.

Rachel: This is a week of big surprises. So let's get to it.

CHAPTER

17

JESSICA

April 23, 1999

The Day of the Birthday Party

E VERYTHING WAS FALLING apart.
　　I got the official letter telling me the school had put me on academic suspension. I wouldn't be able to return in the fall. I would have to complete any outstanding work for my current classes and then undergo a formal hearing before I'd be allowed to resume my studies in the spring.

How was I going to tell my parents?

I knew my mother's reaction would be extreme. But I couldn't summon the energy to care.

School no longer felt important. Grades didn't matter.

Because every decision I had made since coming to Southern State University was coming together to destroy me.

I packed my duffel bag, throwing items in, barely paying attention to what they were.

To my relief, Daisy wasn't there. Since our argument, she had been spending the night elsewhere.

I knew she didn't trust me. Didn't believe a word I said.

I didn't blame her.

I picked up the torn sheet of paper where I had written an address down after Dr. Daniels—Clement—had given it to me.

Was I really going to do this?

Was I really going to meet up with my professor outside of school and do . . . what?

I was sick and tired of my actions being dictated by selfish men. Every bad thing in my life had to do with *their* wants and desires consuming me.

I put my hand in my pocket to feel for the ring I always carried, only to remember it was no longer there. It was gone forever. My skin felt naked without it, but also free.

There was a knock at the door. I dropped the paper on my desk and covered it with a book.

I opened the door and had to swallow a groan. Ryan stood in the hallway looking like he hadn't slept in a week.

"Why won't you call me back? We were supposed to meet yesterday, but you never showed up." He looked lost and confused, and I understood why. I had been avoiding him. "Have I done something to piss you off?"

I wanted to tell him to leave. I didn't have the energy to fight right now, and that's what he seemed to be gearing up for. It's what we did, after all. But there would be no making up this time.

I felt a deep, conflicted sadness at the realization that our relationship had run its course.

I already mourned its death.

"I was busy," I lied. The truth was I had been with Dr. Daniels trying to figure out a way to save my life.

"I thought things were good between us, Jess. What changed?" His words became a challenge, the volume rising.

I couldn't tell him that he was getting too close. That every day it became harder and harder to keep my secrets from him. To hold things back.

I loved Ryan. I knew that with bone deep certainty. And that love meant the end of us.

"Stop being so clingy. It's not cute," I snapped cruelly.

Hurt flashed across his face and I wished, with everything I had, I could take the words back. I had never spoken to him like that before. But it was too late. The first shot had been fired.

I had forgotten how to be the version of Jess I had been before. I was morphing into someone else entirely.

Ryan picked at his thumbnail. "Can I at least come in so we can talk—?"

"No, I said I was busy. And I really don't have time for all this, Ryan. I'm trying to get my stuff together so I can go home." I pulled the door closed behind me, stepping into the hall.

"Are you sure you want to go home? Especially after the argument with your dad?" He was so concerned, I almost wavered.

"You don't know a thing about my dad."

"I know how much you hate him. You've made that clear enough."

I rolled my eyes. "You have no idea what you're talking about."

"You're the one who told me about—" he dropped his voice low, "him sleeping with those young women."

My face heated up. I wanted to scream at my lack of restraint.

"Jess, you said you were scared."

Why had I told Ryan so much? This is why he was dangerous. It was too easy to tell him things he had no right to know.

"Shut up about that," I hissed, letting some of my anger show itself. "It's none of your business."

Ryan looked taken aback. "What the hell, Jess?"

I pushed him toward the stairwell. "You need to leave. I have too much to do and I'm not in the mood to fight with you right now."

"I'm not going anywhere until you tell me what's going on," he insisted.

"I need you to go, Ryan." I was practically begging him. I needed him gone. I needed him to stop asking questions. "Please go. I want some space right now."

Ryan continued to stand there, clearly not sure what to do. With a huff of annoyance, I started down the stairs, knowing that he would follow me. Outside, I stopped in the middle of the quad in front of Westwood Hall. I realized with a twinge of regret that we stood in the same spot where we had our first kiss all those months ago.

That had been the first indication of how deluded I had been. To think I was capable of a normal relationship. A normal life.

"What's going on with you?" Ryan demanded. He grabbed my arm, his fingers digging into my skin. It hurt. I relished the pain. "Tell me why you're doing this to me." His voice cracked. His pain evident.

"I'm not doing anything—"

"Were you with him?" Ryan suddenly shouted. We had the full attention of everyone walking by.

"Who are you talking about?' I asked, but I knew exactly what he was asking me.

"Dr. Daniels. You've been ditching me constantly to see him."

I snorted. "For tutoring, Ryan. Are you serious?"

A couple walked by, their watchful eyes on us. I noticed my former pledge sister Erica on the other side of the quad not even trying to be discreet as she watched us.

Ryan let go of my arm and I instantly missed the feel of his touch, even in anger. "I'm sorry. I don't mean to act this way. I love you so much, Jess. I want us to be okay and I feel like we're definitely *not* okay and I want to know why."

The first tears started to fall and I couldn't stop them. "Ryan, I'm sorry. I'm not the person you think I am."

Ryan reached for me again, tenderly this time, the anger leaching out of him as he wiped my cheeks. "What are you talking about? You're the best person I know."

I shook my head and pulled away. "Stop it. You're making this harder than it needs to be. I'm not good enough for you. I never will be."

He finally caught on to what was happening. He looked distressed. "Jess, come on—"

"I'm sorry." I shook my head.

"Jess, please."

"We're done, Ryan. This is over." I took a step back, putting the necessary distance between us. "I can't do it anymore."

"Baby, don't. I have no idea why you're doing this, but you love me. I know you do." I hated the sound of his desperation. It broke my heart. It made me feel worse than I already did.

"You don't know a thing about how I feel," I snarled. "You don't even know me."

"I do—"

"You have no idea who I am!" I yelled.

Ryan's expression darkened. "What the hell, Jess?"

"Just go. Stay away from me, Ryan." I turned away, hoping he got the message. I couldn't bear to look at him anymore. It hurt too much.

He was quiet for a long time. I knew he was debating how to proceed. Part of me wanted him to fight for me. Part of me wanted him to leave and never look back—it would be better for both of us.

"You'll regret this, Jess. I swear to God, you're going to regret this." And then, finally, I heard him walk away.

My knees could barely support me as I hurried back to my room.

I wanted to sob into my pillow. I wanted to scream and smash everything I owned. My rage had no outlet. It needed direction before I made another horrible mistake.

I had ruined everything. *He* had ruined everything.

I gasped, feeling short of breath. My grief and anger were all-consuming. I was a pitiful mess. I had destroyed everything and there was no way back from that, but perhaps I could change my course.

I picked up the phone and dialed a number.

It rang once before he answered.

"Dr. Daniels's office."

"Hi, Clement." I breathed heavily into the phone.

"Jessica. What can I do for you?" He sounded surprised. I liked being able to throw him off balance.

"I can't see you later. I'm not . . ." I hesitated. "I'm not interested in whatever you think this is."

There, I had said it.

There was silence on the other end. I thought for a second he had hung up.

"Jessica." He said my name again, but this time it felt like a warning.

"I can't, Clement. It's not right. I can't do that to your wife. To your kids—"

"Don't," he cut me off with a note of finality. "Don't bring them into this."

"But they *are* in this, don't you get that?" My voice had a note of pleading. I was trying to get him to see reason. Maybe I could stop all this once and for all.

I thought of his daughter with her pink ball and pigtails.

She deserved better.

Just as I had.

"My family has nothing to do with this," he snapped. "Now listen to me. You started this, and I expect you to follow through." My jovial, charming teacher was gone. This was a man that meant to get what he wanted.

"I won't."

"Don't play coy with me, Jessica."

"What if I told her—your wife? What would you do then?" I was playing with fire, I knew that. But I couldn't stop myself. I had no sense of self-preservation.

"Don't even think about doing something so stupid. Who would believe you anyway?" he snarled.

"Clement—Dr. Daniels—this can't happen."

Then he laughed, his anger replaced by bemusement. "You think you have any say in that? I know you received your letter about your academic suspension. What if I were to tell you I can make that go away?"

"What?" Was he serious? He was obviously changing tactics, trying to find my weakness.

"I don't like being strung along, Jessica. In fact, it really pisses me off," he growled low in my ear. I felt a shiver of fear. "So, give me your parents' address. I'll pick you up there. This will work out well for both of us." He wasn't asking. The days of him playing nice were clearly over.

"What if someone sees you?" My mouth had gone dry.

"No one will see a thing," he promised.

"I don't want to." I tried one last time to end this.

"I don't really care what you want." His voice was darkly calm.

His words were final. His meaning clear.

I hung up the phone.

Things were spiraling fast.

I needed to get away. I grabbed my duffel bag and left.

Ten Seconds to Vanish Podcast
@TenSecondPod

The final episode is almost here! Who do you think did it? The teacher? The boyfriend? The North Carolina Boogie Man? Sound off in the comments! #justice #tensecondstovanish #podcast #finalepisode

10:17 PM Apr 4, 2023

37.8k 42.1k 89k

18

LINDSEY

"DAD!" I YELPED as he pulled me backward, away from the boat. His grip was tight—too tight. His fingers dug into my skin, hard enough that I knew there would be bruises tomorrow. "Dad, stop."

"What are you doing?" he yelled, but it wasn't anger in his voice, it was panic. "Why are you in here?" He shook me, his face tortured.

"Let go of me," I whimpered. I finally managed to free myself and staggered back, bumping into a shelf and knocking over a small glass bowl once filled with vinegar that had long since evaporated. It fell to the ground, shattering at my bare feet, but he barely seemed to notice.

I had never seen him like this before. My dad was usually cool and calm. He was the irresistible charmer who could smooth-talk his way into any restaurant or get our flights upgraded with only a smile. The man in front of me was a complete stranger. He was sweaty and red-faced. His eyes were wild.

Dad was in a tailspin.

It was the only way to describe what was happening with him.

"You shouldn't be in here." His voice shook. He leaned back against his beloved car, sliding to the floor, and buried his face in his hands. "You shouldn't be in here."

I wasn't sure whether to stay or go. I debated calling my mom, but my phone was upstairs in my room.

I took a step toward him, my hand reaching out. I couldn't leave him like this. This was my father. And for better or worse, I loved him.

But this was also the same man who preyed on young women. Who took advantage of girls young enough to be his daughter.

"Dad . . . what's going on?" My words were barely audible.

He was looking at me, but he wasn't seeing *me*.

"She was everything to me," he whispered.

"Jess?" I asked, but he didn't answer. I wasn't sure he had even heard me.

Dad's face contorted in pain. "I would have done anything for her. Absolutely anything. She was my whole world. I had never known love like that before. Not with my parents. Not with your mother. Not with—" He cut himself off but I knew what he was going to say.

Not with me.

I stared mutely at him sitting on the filthy garage floor, his back against his beloved Mustang. He lifted his knees and wrapped his arms around them. He looked like a pitiful child.

He was broken.

Dad's eyes were beseeching. "I *didn't* mean to do anything."

My heart stuttered and my stomach tightened into knots.

"What did you do?"

* * *

Jessica:

I drove away from Southern State University like the devil was on my heels.

The sun was low in the sky by the time I pulled up in front of my parents' house. I looked up at the pretty two-story home and tried to remember a time I felt happy there.

When I had been happy at all.

I was starting to forget what joy felt like.

I readied myself like a soldier going into battle. I took the keys out of the ignition and headed for the front door. It opened before I could turn the knob.

"Jessie!" Lindsey threw herself at me and for a brief second, I felt it . . . happiness.

I picked up my baby sister and hugged her tight, burying my face into her soft hair.

She wiggled in my arms, and I put her down with a watery laugh.

"All my friends are coming and Mommy put Christmas lights up in the backyard! Dad got me a bouncy castle, too! Come on!" She grabbed my hand and pulled me into the house.

Mom came out of the kitchen and gave me a quick hug. She tucked a strand of hair behind my ear and looked at me with concern.

"Jessica, are you okay? You look tired." She gave me a stern once over. "And you've lost weight. Too much weight. You're nothing but skin and bones."

Of course her worry was laced with criticism.

"I'm fine," I replied shortly, pulling away from her. I looked around, feeling my belly tighten. "Where's Dad?"

"He had to grab some extra paper plates from the garage. He'll be back any second." Her look became piercing. "Is everything okay between you two?"

I was taken aback, not used to my mother's perceptiveness. "Everything's fine." I said it too quickly. It sounded like the lie it was.

Her frown deepened. "Funny, he said the same thing, and I didn't believe him either."

Before I could say another word, Lindsey yelled for me from the back of the house.

"Go keep her entertained. She's been bouncing off the walls," Mom sighed in good-natured annoyance.

I went to find my sister, every step as heavy as lead.

*   *   *

Lindsey:

"What did you do?" I asked again. "Dad, please, tell me what happened."

"It's not as simple as that," he laughed humorlessly. Dad dragged his hands through his hair, standing it on end. "It never is."

I waited, my anxiety building as the seconds ticked by.

"Jess was a very mixed-up woman. She had her whole life in front of her, but she so quickly lost sight of what was right in front of her. She let her emotions rule her. She got carried away by misdirected anger. She always felt things so passionately." He wiped his eyes. "When she was little, I got her a pet bird, much to your mother's chagrin." We shared a brief smile, knowing how much Mom hated pets, which is why I never had one.

"It died after a few months. I think the pet store sold me one that was sick." He sniffed, his words wobbling. "Jess cried about that bird for weeks. She was so . . . *intense* about it. I loved how *much* she felt about everything in her life. Her fury was no different."

A cold draft blew through the garage and I shivered.

"What does that mean? Her fury?" I asked.

"I've not always been a good man, Lindsey. I'm selfish, I have needs—like all men," he began. His words sounded like an excuse. "I loved Jess—maybe too much. She wasn't the only one to feel things deeply. Perhaps my love was too big for both of us." I tried to suppress a shudder. "Everything I ever did was to protect her. To make her happy. To make her life perfect. But when she saw something in me she didn't like, she turned against me. She *hated* me as strongly as she loved me." He seemed to struggle to find the words he needed.

"It was easy for her to forget the good things I did. How much I gave up for my family. She disregarded all the times I stayed up with her when she was sick. Every T-ball team I coached and every fishing trip we took."

He sounded as if he had been the one betrayed. As if Jess had hurt *him*. It was all wrong. Their relationship, that I used to be so jealous of, was twisted and unhealthy. He spoke of my sister in a way that made my insides curdle. I didn't understand it. And I didn't want to.

He spoke of all the things he had done for Jess. *With* Jess. My sister had gotten a side of our father that I used to think I wanted. But not anymore. Those were *her* experiences, her affection, her love. He gave her all of it and left none for me. And for the first time, I was thankful. I didn't want this kind of love.

The kind that could choke you.

"She wanted to ruin me, but in the end, she ruined herself."

*   *   *

Jessica:

Walking through my childhood home felt odd this time.

Like I was already a stranger.

As if I didn't have a right to be there.

"Where's your ring?" Mom asked, coming out to the back-yard where I was pushing Lindsey on the swing.

I looked down at my naked finger and felt a flash of satisfied rage. "It's gone," was all I said.

"Gone? We spent good money on that ring and you lost it?" Mom shrieked. I saw the telltale signs of one of her lectures.

I leaned down toward Lindsey. "I need to go outside and get something from the car. I think you're going to be surprised."

Lindsey's eyes widened. "Ooh, what is it?" She hopped off the swing. "Come on, come on!"

I started to walk past Mom, but she grabbed my arm. "Where are you going? I'm not done talking to you."

"You don't listen, Mom, so I won't bother saying anything." I sounded sad, not angry. "I wish you would hear me out. Just for once."

The frustration drained from my mother's eyes, replaced with the same concern that had been there earlier. "Jessica . . ."

"I need to get Lindsey's cake out of the car. Don't want to mess up anything else." I couldn't stop the hostility. It bled into everything.

I opened the front door and I saw a red Mazda Miata parked behind my car. Dr. Daniels was sitting in the driver's seat.

Lindsey started to follow me outside, but I held her back. "You wait here. I don't want you to see the surprise until I bring it inside."

Lindsey pouted. "That's not fair," she whined, crossing her arms over her chest.

"I'll be quick. I promise." I ruffled her hair and she swatted my hand away, hurrying over to the front window, pulling back the curtain so she could watch me.

I cast a nervous glance toward the Miata as Dr. Daniels got out.

I closed the door, took a deep breath, and walked toward my fate.

* * *

Lindsey:

"Lindsey!"

A loud banging came from the front of the house.

"Lindsey! I know you're in there. I need to talk to you!" Ryan called out.

"Who is that?" Dad asked, getting to his feet, casting a furtive glance toward the garage door.

"I'll get rid of him. Give me a second," I promised, hurrying to the front door. I opened it to a frantic Ryan.

"I've been calling you for over an hour. I didn't know if you were still with Daisy so I took a chance and drove over . . ." His words tapered off as he looked past me into the house. He furrowed his brow, as if he could sense something was going on. He turned back to me, his expression tense. "We need to talk."

"We have nothing to talk about." I started to close the door, but he held it open. "Ryan, I need you to leave. Now."

He pushed past me. I grabbed his arm, holding him in place so he couldn't go any further.

"I want to see that case file," Ryan demanded. "It doesn't belong to you, Lindsey. Sergeant O'Neil gave it to *both* of us. I'm the one he's been talking to. You can't keep it from me any longer. I *need* to see what's in it."

"Are you scared about what the police will do now Daisy is finally going to tell them the truth?" I bit out angrily. I couldn't help it. Standing face to face with him after learning all the ways he had deceived me, I wanted to hurt him as he had hurt me.

Because he had made me feel important. And for a time, like I was more than simply Jessica Fadley's little sister. It obliterated me to know that, to him, that's all I'd ever be. After everything, there was no future for us, and never would be. He would always belong to Jess. There was no room for me in his heart. "It must be terrifying now that everyone will know you lied."

Ryan had lied.

Daisy had lied.

My dad had lied.

Everyone had lied.

The only thing left to know was *why.*

"I don't give a shit about that. Daisy can say whatever the hell she wants—I'm glad it's all going to come out."

I sneered at him. "Sure, that's why I found you yelling at her. That didn't sound like someone who was *glad it's all going to come out.*"

Ryan made a noise of frustration. "You have no idea what's really going on here, Lindsey. If you did, you wouldn't—"

"I wouldn't what?" I threw back at him. I was sick of everyone telling me that I didn't understand. "Tell me then. Tell me what happened."

"Lindsey?"

My dad came out of the garage. His face was red from crying. "What's going on? Do you . . . do you need me to do something?"

Ryan's lip curled in disdain. "What? Are *you* going to protect her?"

"Do I need to?" Dad countered, drawing himself upright.

Ryan laughed. "As if you could protect anyone. Where were you when your other daughter was falling apart?"

"You don't know anything about me or my family." Dad threw back contemptuously. "I think you should leave," Dad walked toward Ryan, his face darkening.

"And I think you should tell Lindsey what you did."

I stared between the two of them, anxiety gnawing at me.

"I . . . I," my father stuttered over his words. "I don't know what you're talking about."

"I'll tell her then. Your dad here was screwing around with girls Jess's age. Hell, he's probably still doing it. He's a disgusting, perverted old man who preys on vulnerable young women." It was Ryan's turn to take a threatening step toward my dad.

Dad stared at Ryan in shock. "What? How . . .?"

"Jess was destroyed by *your* actions." He pointed at my father. "That's what drove us apart in the end. I never understood the hold you had over her—why she felt the need to protect you. Your relationship twisted her up inside. It changed her. She became someone else. And it's this asshole's fault.

"Who are you?" Dad asked in confusion. Then his eyes cleared with recognition. "You're that boy Jess was dating." He turned to me, seeming horrified. "Did you know who he was? My god, Lindsey, what were you thinking getting involved with him?"

I opened my mouth to defend myself, but he had already turned back to Ryan. "I don't know what Jess told you—"

Ryan crossed his arms and glowered. "I was there that day on the street when you two argued, remember? I heard what you said to her. After you left, she told me all about what she caught you doing."

Dad let out an agonized groan. "I know what she thought and she made sure to punish me for it." He seemed to harden. "But Jess was my daughter. There wasn't a thing in this world I wouldn't do for her. You have to believe I did everything I could to make things better."

"I believe you, Dad." I realized, with absolute certainty, that I did. I may not understand the depths of his relationship with Jess, but I knew he loved her in his version of unfathomable affection.

But there was still something that he was keeping from me—from all of us.

I addressed Ryan again. "Daisy said that you got drunk and drove to our house. That you saw Jess with a man."

"I did. We fought earlier that day—she broke up with me—and I went and got drunk on a bottle of Grey Goose vodka I'd received for Christmas. Then, full of drunk courage, I had the stupid idea to drive over here and confront her. Maybe I was going to tell her she was wrong to leave me. Maybe I was going to beg her to take me back, who knows. I just needed to see her." He was picking at his thumbnail, looking torn.

"What were you planning to confront her about?" I asked.

"I thought she was sleeping with Dr. Daniels. That he had sucked her in like he had all the others," he replied. "So, yeah, I wanted to confront her. I don't know why I thought it would make me feel better to hear her confess it."

"What happened when you got here?" I asked.

There was a tick in Ryan's jaw. "I saw her with him—with Dr. Daniels—at least I thought it was him. It was dark and I was wasted. But I saw her arguing with an older man. His back was to me, so I couldn't see his face. Though, I know for certain that whatever was happening wasn't good. Then he grabbed her . . ."

* * *

Ryan:
April 23, 1999
6:20 PM

I turned the radio up. Bone Thugs-N-Harmony belted out of the speakers at full blast. I weaved too far to the right, running off the road.

"Shit," I muttered, overcorrecting myself, almost driving into oncoming traffic.

I rubbed my eyes, looking nervously in my rearview mirror to make sure I wasn't being tailed by the cops.

Maybe driving to Jess's parents' house when I was loaded wasn't such a great idea after all.

I thought about her face when she told me to leave. There was no way in hell she actually wanted that. Not when she was sleeping in my bed only two days ago. Girls can't fake that kind of thing. Or, at least, I hoped not.

So no, I had to see her. I'd beg her to come back to me. We'd fix what was wrong. I'd help her with whatever she was going through.

Because I really loved that girl and I couldn't stand the thought of us being apart.

My frat brothers told me I was whipped. Tomas, my big brother, said I should forget about her. He tried hooking me up with one of the Omega Mu girls. They didn't get it. Jess was it for me. She was the one.

Somehow, I made it to the right road. I had looked up Jess's address in the student directory before leaving, ripping the page out and taping it to the dashboard.

I recognized her Toyota Camry with the dented chrome from when she had driven into a ditch by campus. It was parked in front of house number forty-two.

I made sure to park a little way down the street. Far enough that she wouldn't notice me, but close enough I could see her house. I wasn't exactly sure what I was going to say to her, but even as hammered as I was, I knew she'd be pissed if she found out I'd driven here intoxicated.

I cupped my hand and smelled my breath. Damn, it was bad. I smelled like a distillery. I hit my hand against the steering wheel, knowing that I had to go home. I couldn't waltz up to her kid sister's birthday party drunk as a skunk. I was such an idiot.

Then I saw Jess. She was standing by her car, the trunk open.

My heart sped up. At the sight of her, every worry drifted away. I had to talk to her. Now.

I put a hand on the door, but before I could get out, I saw a man walk toward her. She stopped, turning to talk to him. Only they weren't talking, they were arguing. They were clearly both angry. I squinted, trying to make out who it was she was speaking to, but his back was to me. All I could tell was that he was older. It must be Dr. Daniels. Who else could it be?

I watched them for what felt like forever, their heated fight building, before finally getting up the courage to confront them.

"Screw this," I snarled under my breath.

I fumbled to get my keys out of the ignition, dropping them at my feet. With a string of curses, I reached down and picked them up, smacking my head painfully against the dashboard as I sat back up.

"Goddamn it," I grumbled, rubbing my head. I reached for the door handle and looked out the window.

Jess was gone.

The man she had been arguing with, too.

The trunk of her car was still wide open, like she only stepped away and would be back any minute.

I got out of my car and stood there in the middle of the street, looking around for her.

I waited. And waited.

I waited so long that eventually I got back in my car to wait some more.

Five minutes turned to twenty and she still wasn't back.

The front door of her house opened and a little girl stepped outside. "Jessie!" she shouted. "Where are you?'

The girl looked over to my car. I wasn't even sure if she could see me, but it unnerved me all the same. What would Jess say if she found out I was parked by her house, drunk? It looked weird. I looked weird. Like some freaky stalker or something.

"Christ." I sped away as fast as my drunk ass could go. And when I got back to my dorm room, I crashed on my bed, feeling too far gone to think properly.

I'd call Jess when I woke up.

Hell, maybe I'd even go back over there tomorrow. But sober this time.

19

LINDSEY

Present day

"SHE WAS GONE. I never saw where she went or what happened." Ryan looked around like he was still searching for her after all these years, expecting her to come through the door. "I should have gone over as soon as I saw her. I should have punched that old perv in the face and kissed my girl and told her that it was okay, that I still loved her, but I was so mad and so drunk . . . at that moment, I hated her. She broke my heart. I got out to speak to her, but when she didn't come back, I just . . . left. I panicked."

I was silent, trying to piece together everything I knew and everything that was missing.

"I should have stayed, I know that," Ryan said, his tone filled with crushing guilt. "I've always blamed myself. I imagine her sometimes. She's always there, by the house, dying. And I sat in my car like an asshole waiting while she suffered." He let out a choked cry. "And then I *left*. God, if I had only gotten out and gone over there, maybe I could have saved her."

I couldn't look at him. Of course, I couldn't remember seeing him. I had been too consumed with finding my sister because she shouldn't have been gone that long.

I wondered how differently things would have been if Ryan *had* gone to check on her. If he had knocked on the door and let us know as soon as he realized Jess was gone. If he'd broken up the fight between my sister and Dr. Daniels. But whatever had happened, it wasn't Ryan's fault. He hadn't hurt her. He had loved her. And he had spent his whole adult life trying to find her to make up for what he should have done back then.

"So, Dr. Daniels murdered Jess," I said, more to myself than to either of the men standing beside me.

Perhaps it was insensitive of me to blurt it out, but I was done trying to be gentle with everyone's feelings. This story was anything but gentle.

Ryan's shoulders tightened. "I've always thought so. He was a creep. He preyed on those women. They looked up to him because he was their teacher. He chose women who were vulnerable. Women who wouldn't fight him. Jess and I saw him with Phoebe and with Meghan. And I know he was making a move on Jess. But that school protects its own. It has protected him for decades. Rather than doing the right thing and turning him in, they covered everything up."

"That's what Daisy said, too." I chewed on my bottom lip. "So why did he murder Jess? How did it go from him trying to sleep with her to killing her? And the other girls, too. What made him take that leap?"

Dad was standing there, silently listening. I couldn't get a read on what he was thinking. He was being surprisingly quiet as Ryan and I discussed the details of his daughter's possible murder.

"Everyone said Tammy showed up to his office threatening to tell his wife. Maybe the others did the same thing," Ryan suggested.

I paced the hallway, a sinking feeling in my stomach. I was close, but I was missing something important.

* * *

Jessica:

I rushed down the stairs as Dr. Daniels closed his car door. I glanced over my shoulder. I could see Lindsey's face in the window. I smiled at her and made a shooing motion. I could see her laugh and then she turned, distracted by something inside.

"Jessica."

I shivered.

"I told you, I didn't want you to come." I approached my teacher, seeing him for the selfish, entitled bastard he really was. He didn't care that he was destroying his daughter's life. He only cared about getting what he wanted from me.

Dr. Daniels reached out and grabbed my arms, pulling me close. This wasn't slow and steady, this was fast and treacherous.

"And I told you it didn't matter what you wanted." He leaned in close to me, his breath melding with mine. "I know you want it. Admit it."

He wanted me to give him permission. He wanted me to succumb. But I was a different woman now than I had been that morning. I was no longer weak like Phoebe or Tammy. I was nothing like Meghan.

I pulled away from him with a cruel laugh. "What's wrong with you that you have to pant after a woman twenty years younger than you? Are you not getting it at home or something?"

Dr. Daniels looked shocked. He wasn't expecting my savagery. "Jessica, it has nothing to do with—you're special. You're—"

"Different? Unique? One of a kind?" I spat out. "Give me a break." I crossed my arms over my chest as I regarded him with a loathing I didn't bother to hide. "It amazes me that other women fall for this crap. I bet Tammy ate it up with a spoon."

At the mention of Tammy, Dr. Daniels went still. "I don't know what you're talking about . . ."

"Stop it. I'm not your wife. You don't need to lie to me. Everyone knows you and Tammy were sleeping together. You screwed in her dorm room, Clement." I rolled my eyes. "I know

about them all. Phoebe, too, and Meghan. And so many others . . . but not me. You'll never have me."

Dr. Daniels had gone deathly pale. "You don't know what you're talking about."

"I know enough to tell the police. I wonder what that detective would say if I told him all about this." I waved a hand between us. "How you tried to get me to sleep with you."

Dr. Daniels stared at me incredulously, and I laughed.

"The school might have protected you, but I wonder if the police would be so quick to dismiss it. Especially with all those missing girls." I crossed my arms and glared at him.

Dr. Daniels was backing up toward his car. "You need to shut your mouth."

"Or maybe I should give your wife a call."

Gone was the kind, self-assured man I was used to. He recognized the danger and was trying to make his exit. "No one will believe you over me. If you try to tell anyone, I won't be the one to get into trouble." His threat was weak, and maybe if I was any other woman it would have affected me. I, however, had nothing left to lose.

When I didn't respond he seemed satisfied that I would keep my mouth shut. Probably already thinking of the next stupid girl he had his sights on. "I can see I was wrong about you. Goodbye, Jessica."

I watched him drive away so fast, his tires squealed, giving away his lack of confidence.

I should have found some grim amusement at that, but it did little to alleviate the empty nothingness inside of me.

With heavy steps I made my way over to my car and popped the trunk. Inside sat the three tiered birthday cake my mom had ordered from a local bakery for Lindsey's party. I reached down to lift it up . . .

"Jess."

*   *   *

"So these girls threaten to out him and he what? Hits them over the head and drives them out to Doll's Eye Lake?" I was trying to put everything together, but it didn't feel right.

"Possibly. Jess and I even saw him out at the lake once. He definitely knew the area. Though . . ." He hesitated. "I hate to give this guy any benefit of the doubt, but surely there had to be a better way for him to keep them quiet than offing them. It always seemed like a huge risk for a guy who was big on protecting his own ass." He scowled at my Dad, and if looks could kill, my father would have been six feet under. "Though, it's hard to get into the mind of a perv. Maybe you can clue us in on how they think."

"That's enough," Dad snapped, making a move toward Ryan as if he were going to swing at him.

"Stop it, Dad." Then I turned to Ryan. "And enough with the insults already, it's not solving anything." Ryan had the sense to look chastised.

I rubbed my forehead, trying to think. "So Dr. Daniels comes to the house and what? Kills her right there?" It wasn't making any sense.

"They were arguing," Dad whispered, more to himself than to us.

Ryan and I shared a look. "What was that, Dad?"

Dad looked startled, as if he hadn't realized he had spoken aloud. "It's nothing—"

"It's *not* nothing. It sounds like you overheard something," Ryan barked with impatient frustration.

I held a hand up, silencing Ryan. "Tell me, Dad. What did you hear?"

"You don't understand," Dad said, backing away. "She was a mess. Then that man swooped in and scrambled her head. She wasn't seeing straight." He pressed the heels of his hands to his eyes and let out a wail that terrified me.

"Dad . . ."

My father held out his arms, keeping me at bay. "Stop, Lindsey. Don't touch me. This is all my fault."

* * *

Jessica:

"Jess."

My dad came around from the side of the house. I knew he wanted to speak to me and I had intended on trying to avoid him as much as possible. At this point, what was there left to say?

"Hi, Dad." Derision dripped from my lips. My revulsion hit him like a sledgehammer. It began to overpower the love that still simmered there, bubbling away under the surface.

"Who was that?" he asked softly, carefully, like he was worried I might break.

"No one," I answered, my hand still on the lid of the trunk. I didn't want to look at him.

"Are you seeing that man?" I continued to ignore him. "Answer me," he hissed.

I finally turned to him, coming around the side of the car. I looked back at the house, relieved that Lindsey was still somewhere else, far away from this.

"So what if I am?"

"He's too old for you . . ." His words trailed off as we both felt the hypocrisy of them.

"I guess I have Daddy issues," I taunted. The gloves had finally come off. I was no longer my father's little girl. I was a full grown woman, and I was angry.

Dad took me by the arm, pulling me toward the garage where he pushed me inside, slamming the door behind him. "Haven't you put me through enough?" he entreated with so much agony it gave me pause.

But then I remembered everything that had happened. Everything I had done.

Everything that led to this one awful moment.

"Of course, Dad, make this all about you," I challenged.

"This is about me, right? Isn't that what you've been telling me for months?" He wanted to yell, but he couldn't. Because then Mom would overhear him and what would he tell her?

What lies would he invent to cover us both?

"Yes, Dad. You're right. It is all your fault."

I hated him so much. No, I hated how much I didn't hate him.

"Jess, please," he begged, his pain almost visceral. "I miss you. I miss us. Please . . ."

I couldn't help it.

I couldn't stop myself.

For all of my rage, there was still so much love, no matter how much I wished there wasn't. Seeing him upset physically hurt me.

I wrapped my arms around him and started crying. Once I started, I couldn't stop. I needed my dad.

He stood like a statue for a long, endless moment before his arms came up to encircle me.

"Shh, Jess. I'll take care of this," he cooed and I wanted to have faith in his promise.

For the first time in a long time, I let myself believe him.

* * *

Lindsey:

I stared at my dad in shocked confusion. "I don't understand . . ."

"I saw him leave," Dad said with a heavy sigh. "I knew what was going on. How she was doing this to hurt me. She made it clear it was *always* about what I did."

He winced like the words were difficult to say. I knew this was the pivotal moment in this sordid story, and yet now I was more puzzled than ever.

I didn't need to ask what he had done. I had read the police interview. His crimes were clear.

"So you left," I said to Ryan, and he nodded, "and Dr. Daniels left . . ."

My hands started to shake. The connections weren't coming fast enough, yet I knew . . .

I knew . . .

"Dad?"

I stared at my father, seeing his heartache and grief with fresh, wide open eyes. It had been there all along, I just hadn't seen it.

I hadn't seen *him.*

"I loved her so much," he wiped his tears away. "I did everything I could to protect her, but it wasn't enough. I couldn't stop things from going too far. I wasn't there when she really needed me. And there are things I couldn't fix, no matter how hard I tried."

"What do you mean things went too far?" I whispered.

Dad took a shaky breath. "It's all my fault. She told me that's why it happened—"

"What did you do to her?" Ryan yelled. He dove toward my dad, shoving me out of the way to get to him. I fell to the side, watching in paralyzed horror as Ryan crashed into my dad, slamming him against the wall. Framed pictures fell and shattered to the floor. Ryan gripped my father by the front of his shirt, shaking him violently.

"What did you do to her?" he roared. This was the inconsolable rage of a heartbroken man.

My dad wasn't putting up any sort of fight. He seemed to curl into himself, muttering the same words over and over again.

"I'm sorry. I'm so, so sorry."

Ryan released him and staggered away. He looked at me, our alarm mirroring each other's.

Dad seemed so small. A shell of the man I thought he was.

"I loved your sister," he began and I wished I could block him out. I had been obsessed with finding out what happened to Jess. But now, faced with the blossoming truth, I was too terrified to hear it. A part of me wanted to go back to being the oblivious woman with a life full of unanswered questions. That would have been easier.

"She was everything to me," Dad continued. "But she was so very, very broken, Lindsey. In ways you can't even begin to understand."

20

BEN FADLEY

August 23, 1999

7:05 PM

I HADN'T HELD MY *daughter in a long time. I wanted to freeze this moment so it could last forever.*

I was scared of what waited for my girl out there. Of what would happen when the world found out.

I had failed her.

I hadn't protected her.

I couldn't explain to her why I did the things I did. How I loathed that part of me that desired things I shouldn't. That I loved her. That I loved her mother and sister, but they didn't fill the hole inside me.

I craved things that a well-respected man like me shouldn't.

I got off on the thrill that was lacking in every other part of my life.

I was a husband. I was a father. I was a businessman.

And it would never, ever be enough.

I hadn't wanted Jess to know about that ugly side of me. I never wanted her to see me for who I really was. But she had.

And in the process I had not only exposed myself, I had exposed a darkness in her that I never knew existed.

Jess pulled back, wiping furiously at her eyes as if the tears she had allowed to escape disgusted her.

"I'm surprised you're even here. Don't you have some young girl to screw?" She was being hateful. She never spoke to me like this. I was used to her smiles and her laughter. I didn't know what to do with this anger and hate. Yet, it was no more than I deserved.

In that instant, I realized she'd never let me forget. That we were stuck in an endless cycle that would go on and on forever. Her misdirected wrath would be our undoing.

"Who is it this time? Do I know her?" she demanded, pushing me away from her. "Tell me."

"There's no one, Jess. I promise."

She laughed. It was a far cry from the sweet giggle of her childhood. This was pain and misery. This was a woman who wanted to burn the world down.

"Like your promises mean anything."

"You have to stop this, sweetheart. This anger is consuming you." I tried to placate her, but that seemed to infuriate her more.

"I told you, I didn't want to do any of this. I didn't mean for it to happen," she cried.

I tried to reach for her again. "Shh, I know, darling. I know . . ."

She flung my hands away. "But they deserved it. If I didn't stop them, it would keep happening. More families would be ruined. More little girls would lose their fathers." Her lips began to tremble and my heart broke.

"You haven't lost me, Jess. I swear it."

"But I have!" she shrieked and I looked nervously over my shoulder at the kitchen door, hoping Cara hadn't heard her. "Because as much as you say you love us, you love them, too."

I recognized the signs of her losing control. And my little girl was dangerous when she got to that point.

"I know you didn't mean to hurt Tammy, or the others—"

Jess gripped her hair at her scalp. "They wouldn't listen, Dad. I tried to make them see reason. I thought I could talk to them. Show them what a broken family looked like. Explain how much it hurt. But they. Just. Wouldn't. Listen!"

This was the same story she told me every time. How she used her roommate's ID card and waited for her RA in the school's computer lab late at night. Jess knew Tammy went every evening before bed to check her email. My daughter explained that she coaxed Tammy outside behind the building and hit her over the head with a broken piece of pipe she picked up off the ground. It was pure luck that it stormed that night, washing away all traces of blood on the grass.

She claimed she didn't mean to do it. They'd argued but Tammy wouldn't listen. Jess had begged her to end her relationship with her teacher. She told her she was ruining someone's family.

"But she didn't care. So, I stopped her."

And then months later, she tracked Phoebe down at the library. She had asked her to talk outside. They argued, just as she and Tammy had. In the heat of that one, terrible moment, my daughter strangled her friend. Phoebe had said she was in love. She couldn't stop it. She didn't want to. That she planned to be with her lover. That she was convinced he would leave his family for her. Jess had cried and cried over Phoebe. That one had nearly destroyed her.

But then there was beautiful Meghan. Jess couldn't help herself. That one was entirely about me. If only I had been able to control myself, Meghan—and the others—might still be alive.

She was full of unrelenting anger that time. Before I could push the body overboard, Jess, in a rash decision, shoved something on the dead girl's finger.

I knew what it was. Jess broke my heart when she discarded the ring. She thought she was making a point. Letting me know what my actions had cost her. We both felt it. Our bond was now hanging by a thread.

"They wouldn't listen. This is their fault. I didn't want to, but I had no choice," she moaned sadly.

She took her anger out on the ones who deserved it least. Every single day since she killed those girls, I wished she had killed me instead.

"I know," I said softly, finally grabbing hold of my daughter again and pulling her close, rubbing her back like I had done when she was little.

She had called me each time to help her. Of course I helped her. I would always be there for her. It was as if she were in an altered state and it was only when the bodies were cooling on the ground at her feet that she would wake up in a panic.

I had wanted to go to the police.

My guilt and desire to protect my girl at all costs kept me quiet.

But this had to stop.

It had to stop now.

*   *   *

"She couldn't stop herself, so I had to step in. It's what a father should do."

There was a high-pitched ringing in my ears.

"No." Ryan's voice was far away. "You're lying."

"I wish I was." Dad looked devastated, yet relieved to finally share the truth. "I wish I could tell you something different." Dad looked shattered. He was broken into a hundred pieces.

"She k-killed them?" I finally asked, my voice barely above a whisper. *"All of them?"*

Dad let out a horrible sob as he grabbed me. "She was a good person, Lindsey. Don't think badly of her, *please.*"

My knees buckled and my father held onto me before I could collapse. I felt numb. Hollowed out. I was trembling all over.

How could this be the truth that I had been searching for all these years? My loving older sister, who had been missing for twenty-four years, was a killer.

And my father . . .

I pushed my dad away, his arms falling to his sides. I didn't want him near me. It felt wrong. *He* felt wrong. I stared at him, my eyes beseeching and then he continued. Though it was obvious now where this sordid story was going.

"I didn't want to," Dad moaned. "It was the last thing I wanted to do. But she gave me no choice."

Oh god . . .

Then the whole picture began to emerge.

*   *   *

Ben Fadley
April 23, 1999

I rubbed her back. I felt her bunch up my shirt in her unforgiving fists.

"This is all your fault, Daddy. It has always been your fault." Her words were horrible yet, in that moment, she sounded like my little girl again. When I was only her Daddy, the person she loved most.

And she was going to spend the rest of my life making me pay. She didn't even mean to do the things she did. I knew that.

Jess wasn't a wicked person with evil in her heart.

She was hurting. She was full of so much pain that she didn't know how to handle it other than to hurt others.

Those she felt were to blame for the mess her life had become.

She couldn't stand the thought of a family being torn apart. She blamed me. She blamed them. She blamed everyone but herself.

"Take it out on me," I implored her that first time after coming to the college late at night. I had parked my car in the library parking lot and found my daughter in shock, her skin white and her lips colorless, with a dead girl at her feet. I had bundled the body into the trunk of my car and driven us out to the place that had once been the site of so many wonderful memories together.

"Stop hurting these girls. You should be mad at me. Mat at that teacher." I was setting myself up for violence, I knew that. But I couldn't bear my child becoming a demon as a result of the pain I had inflicted.

"I am mad at you. At every man like you. But you're still my dad." Her voice had been tiny and fractured.

That was her only reason and in some awful way, I understood. Our love for each other had always been the best thing. Now it was the worst.

I helped her dispose of the bodies. She told me she had buried the first one, wrapped in the same blanket I had tenderly tucked around her when she was a baby. She couldn't remember where. The woods are large so I could never find the spot. I only hoped she had been smart about it. I couldn't imagine my diminutive daughter being able to carry a dead body on her own. But if there was one thing I had learned it was that I could never underestimate what she was capable of.

We had taken the paddleboat and gone out to the middle and tossed her other mistakes into the deep, deep water.

I paused, my eyes filling.

"This is all your fault," she whispered, no longer crying into my shirt.

"I know," I agreed.

She was a danger.

"I love you so much."

"I know, sweetheart."

She had to be stopped.

"I'm so sorry," my voice cracked. "I love you, Jess."

I wrapped my hands around her neck and squeezed.

She stared at me, eyes wide, mouth gaping.

In the end, I think she was glad. She could see how much it was destroying me. She liked that it hurt me. But she must have felt relief that it was going to be over.

It lasted a long time and my girl was strong. Taking the life of someone you love is the hardest thing you can ever do. And she fought.

But I had to protect her from herself. I had to protect Cara. And Lindsey. I had to protect every other woman that she saw as a threat.

Jess had become a liability to our family. She had become a danger to everyone. Especially to herself.

Eventually, it ended.

She stopped fighting.

Stopped clawing at me.

When it hit me what I had done, I started crying. I cradled her body, wishing she would wake up. Wishing I could take it all back.

This was all my fault.

More time went by and I could hear Lindsey yelling.

"Jessie!"

Then it turned to a scream.

In a panic, I put my baby girl's body in the trunk of the Mustang and went to check on my other daughter.

* * *

Lindsey:

"Where is she?" I asked, my voice taking on a strength I hadn't known I possessed. The ringing was subsiding. The realization finally settled into my gut.

Somehow, it all made sense. Perfect, horrible sense.

Everything from then and now, all combining into this one awful reality. Jess had killed all of those innocent women.

Because my dad had driven her to it.

And then he had killed her.

My father had murdered my sister.

"Where is she?" I asked again.

I watched as he shook his head, his face contorted in anguish. I glanced at Ryan. He was still staring blankly into space, his face ashen.

"I'm sorry," Dad whispered, his agony palpable.

I didn't care about his guilt, all that mattered was the truth.

* * *

Ben Fadley:

The police came. We filed a missing person's report.

All the while she waited for me in the garage.

That night after Lindsey and Cara were finally asleep, I slipped out of the house and hooked up the paddleboat to the back of the Mustang as I had done a hundred times before. Then I drove my little girl to the only spot I could take her.

I carefully bundled her up and prepared to put her in the boat. I stood there, on the shore, holding her like I had done a thousand times before. I rocked her, pressing her to my chest. The gleam of the water in the moonlight bore a sad witness to our tragedy.

"I'm so sorry," I cried, holding her one last time.

She was so beautiful. She could be sleeping.

A flash of lights at the shore startled me, I could see a car driving through the trees. The car parked, its music blaring.

In a frenzy to conceal her and retie the boat to the Mustang, I broke the right taillight with the metal hitch. I would never be able to bring myself to fix it.

And then, I made the long, terrible journey back home.

With my dead daughter.

Careful to be as quiet as possible, I lifted the garage door, turned off the engine and pushed the car and boat back inside.

Then, under the cover of that horrible night, I wrapped my sweet Jess in some plastic sheeting we had used when decorating. I secured it tightly with duct tape and then I put her in the bottom of the boat.

The same boat we used to take out on those still, murky waters.

And I kept her close.

Explaining the smell away and covering the stink of decay as best I could. Surprisingly, no one ever questioned it.

I always intended on taking her out to the lake, but eventually, I appreciated having her nearby. I could go out to the garage and talk to her like she was still there.

And in those quiet moments, I didn't feel her anger or her hatred.

Only her love.

* * *

Lindsey:

Dad led me out to the garage. He lifted the tarp, revealing the boat for the first time.

"She's in there." His voice cracked and he looked away as I carefully stepped aboard. I pulled back the old sheet that had covered her body for all these years.

I stared down at the bundle that was my sister, hoping that she hadn't suffered too much, in life or in death. Maybe I shouldn't feel any sympathy or kindness toward a woman who inflicted such atrocities. But this kind of love, like what

I felt for my sister, was black and sticky like tar—it would never go away, even if I scrubbed my skin raw.

"I tried to hide her as best I could. I didn't want anyone to know what she'd done. It was better for her to be missing than a monster," Dad rasped, his words strangled, yet strangely content.

I knew he truly believed he had made the right choice. He had protected her in the only way he could. And in doing so, he had been the father she deserved. The father he hadn't been brave enough to be when she was alive.

I glanced at Ryan, who had followed us out to the boat. His eyes met mine and I saw something there that looked like relief.

He finally knew what had happened to the woman he loved. Maybe he could move on. Now, knowing the truth about Jess, maybe he could forgive himself.

He gave me an imperceptible nod and slipped back into the kitchen, his phone pressed to his ear. I heard him talking to the dispatcher on the other end, giving our address, telling them what we found.

Dad stared at me, his expression filled with a wrenching adoration that wasn't meant for me.

"I've only ever wanted what was best for my girl. She's all that ever mattered," he rasped.

I carefully unwrapped my sister's body, forcing myself to look at the skeletal remains she had become. Her hands had been crossed over her chest. Some wisps of dark hair still clung to the intact skull. The bleached, white bones of her teeth created a ghastly smile. Even though the sockets were empty, I strangely felt her gaze on me. As if Jess were watching our reactions, enjoying the show.

Dad let out a strangled cry and climbed into the boat beside me, dropping to his knees. He gently, lovingly, touched the bones, an anguished wail ripping from somewhere deep inside him. Tears dripped down his cheeks.

"My sweet girl, I'm sorry I failed you," he whispered. He looked up at me, his eyes deadened with fresh grief. "Please, we have to keep her safe."

I didn't know what to say. I was paralyzed. Incapable of doing anything other than stare at my father as he wept over the naked bones of my long-dead sister. He rocked back and forth, whispering words for her alone. Words she couldn't hear, but he needed to say anyway. As if it would absolve him of his guilt and shame.

"I'm sorry, Jess. I'm so sorry, my beautiful girl."

I got out of the boat, leaving my father behind, cradling Jess's remains, sobbing uncontrollably for the daughter he had lost. A daughter who had become the stuff of nightmares.

A daughter he had stopped before she could hurt anyone else.

I knew then that I wanted no part of this twisted familial bond ever again.

"Lindsey . . . please . . ." he began.

I knew what he was going to ask. Everything inside me told me to reject it. To deny him this last comfort because he didn't deserve it.

And neither did she.

But for some reason—perhaps in a final act of painful, soul-crushing love—I found myself agreeing.

"No one will ever know. I promise."

He closed his eyes, his body caving beneath the weight of his hideous secrets as the sound of sirens wailed in the distance.

Ten Seconds to Vanish: The Unsolved Disappearance of Jessica Fadley

Episode 13

The Finale

Stella: Hi everyone. Welcome to . . . an epilogue of sorts, I guess. I'm your host Stella—

Rachel: And I'm Rachel.

Stella: And this is *Ten Seconds to Vanish: The Unsolved Disappearance of Jessica Fadley.*

Theme music plays

Stella: We ended this podcast three weeks ago, and a lot has happened since then. So much, in fact, that we had to go back and re-tape this final episode to keep up to date with all the news that's come out since calling it a wrap.

Rachel: Because guys, there's been an arrest in the case of the missing coeds of Southern State University. And it's not any of the suspects we were dancing around all season.

Stella: It's a bit frustrating. We researched so much and I swore it was the teacher!

Rachel: Well, my money was on the boyfriend. It was wild when we discovered he'd been involved with all four of the missing girls. Who saw that coming?

Stella: I know some of our listeners were convinced it was a nameless serial killer. That particular theory really picked up steam toward the end. If this were a book or a movie, it would make sense.

Rachel: Goes to show you, life is stranger than fiction. It's what keeps true crime podcast creators like us in business.

Stella: Very true. I do want to touch on one thing before we give you the big news. There's been quite a bit of criticism thrown our way about how we handled these cases. Saying we were making light of the disappearances and murders. I want to apologize to anyone who we may have offended. It was never our intention to minimize the deaths of these four women.

Rachel: Exactly. And it's actually made us do some soul searching. To really think about how we move forward with this podcast. We want to do some good, so that means acknowledging when we get things wrong.

Stella: Well said, Rach. We have an obligation to the victims, and their families, to be respectful. To remember that these are real people who experienced very real tragedy. This isn't about entertainment, but about giving them a voice.

Rachel: And that's what we're here to do, ya know?

Stella: Okay, back to the big break. So, Rach, you'll never guess who's now being charged with the murders of not only Jessica Fadley, but also Tammy Estep, Phoebe Baker, and Meghan Lambert.

Rachel: I know the answer, but I'll let you do the honors. Drumroll, please.

Stella: Benjamin Fadley! Lieutenant Jane Higgins held a news conference yesterday announcing they had arrested Jessica's father for all four murders. Turns out he confessed to every single one.

Rachel: And Jessica's remains were found in the house, actually in the garage in an old boat.

Stella: That's right, she had been there the whole time. I'd be surprised if that place wasn't haunted by a very unhappy Jessica.

Rachel: Definitely. I hope she's haunting the shit out of her crappy dad. What a psycho!

Stella: We're not too sure of the motive, but it seemed, like the pervy teacher, dear ol' Dad had a thing for the too young and very gorgeous. Maybe Jessica found out and he had to shut her up.

Rachel: God, I keep thinking about the poor sister. Can you imagine finding out your dad killed not only your sister, but a bunch of other girls, too?

Stella: I don't know, but from all accounts, Lindsey Fadley is the one that turned her dad in.

Rachel: Well, I hope she finds some kind of peace. She deserves it.

Stella: I heard that she's planning to move to New York to manage a posh hotel there. Sounds like the remaining Fadley girl is going to do just fine.

Rachel: And Jessica and Lindsey's mom? How did she take the news?

Stella: Cara Fadley hasn't issued a statement. All I know, from anonymous sources of course—

Rachel: Of course.

Stella: Is that Cara has filed for divorce—

Rachel: Obvs.

Stella: And she's selling the house and getting out of there. Can't say I blame her.

Rachel: I hope both she and Lindsey can move on.

Stella: As for our main suspect, the creepy professor.
  A little birdie told me—
Rachel: From more anonymous sources—
Stella: He had his retirement funds frozen by the
  university after the press got ahold of his name.
Rachel: And, we can say who he is now.
Stella: Yep, we can tell the world, or the thousands of
  you listening, that Dr. Clement Daniels preyed on
  his students.
Rachel: And his wife left him, too. Three cheers for
  wives kicking their skeevy husbands to the curb!
Stella: That's right. And Ryan McKay, aka the "hottie
  boyfriend," is actually an award-winning
  journalist with the *Chicago Courier*. He's written a
  three-part series on his search for Jessica, ending
  with the arrest of her father. Everyone is saying
  he could win a Pulitzer. And to think you thought
  he was guilty, Rach.
Rachel: I was so off the mark with that one. But it
  sounds like some good has come out of all this.
Stella: Well, that's it for *Ten Seconds to Vanish: The
  Now Solved Disappearance of Jessica Fadley*. But
  Rachel and I hope you join us next season as we
  dive into the cold case murder of Jenny Malone.
  A young woman who was found bludgeoned to
  death in a field six miles from her home in 1954.
Rachel: Oh no, that poor girl!
Stella: I know, right? Anyway, until next time, true
  crime babes, stay safe.

ACKNOWLEDGMENTS

Abbi:

This one goes out to the usual suspects (get it? It's a book about murder and . . . suspects . . . never mind). Ian and Gwyn, you've been with me on this writing journey from the start and are always my biggest cheerleaders and supporters. I'm sorry for all the watch lists I probably ended up on while writing this book—my search tab is a scary, scary place. Claire, my cowriter, my partner in crime (see, I did it again!), you push me to write when everything I put down feels like shit. You make me feel like I can, maybe, keep doing this. Though I think you're a tad bit biased. You're more than a friend, you're family, which unfortunately for you, means you're stuck with me. And to our beta readers Elizabeth and my girl Kristy—thank you for your amazing feedback. This book kicks ass because of you two.

Claire:

Every book is hard to write—especially when you're writing about murder! To get to do this with a friend is truly a gift I will never take for granted, so thank you, Abbi, for being such a great friend and writing partner and navigating the complicated world of murder and mayhem with me. I'm so glad that we got to do this together again. Thanks also to my wonderful family. You all give me so much encouragement, and it means the absolute world to me. Special thanks go to my eldest daughter, Becca. I love that you get as excited as me about all the little things. I love you endlessly.

And once more, with feeling, from both of us:

As always, a HUGE thank you to our amazing editor, Tara Gavin, for believing in us and our books. We're so grateful for all you do and can't wait to bring you many more stories. To the entire team at Crooked Lane Books, but especially Thai Fantuauzzi Perez, Rebecca Nelson, and Dulce Bortello, for your patience and willingness to work with us on our ideas. You never brush off our concerns and always strive to make our dream a reality.

There are always so many sets of eyes on a book before it goes to publication, from those first, half-deranged ideas, to the complete product. But we know (because we're readers ourselves) what grabs you is the cover. You feast first with your eyes, right? And what a cover it is! A massive thank you to Heather VenHuizen for this absolutely gorgeous design. We had so many grandiose ideas of what we wanted and you somehow took all of that and made something that quite literally took our breath away.

And last, but definitely the most important, thank you to all the amazing readers and bloggers for reading, reviewing, and sharing our books. We get to do what we love every single day because of each and every one of you. We write some dark, twisty stuff, and you embrace it each time. You just GET us. We hope you love this one as much as we do.